Praise For "Like I Used To Dance"

5 Stars!

Reviewed By Viga Boland for Readers' Favorite

The only way for me to begin my review of Like I Used to Dance by Barbara Frances is to say I loved it! For me to love a fiction book that is simply based on the ups and downs of a loving family in the late '50s in Texas is unusual. I truly didn't know what to expect when I began reading Like I Used to Dance. It's a long novel: would I be bored? Would I even finish it?

Well, Barbara Frances had me completely hooked in the first few pages and I couldn't read it fast enough. I was dying to know what would happen next to Grace and Bud and their three adult children, all raised as good Catholics. When one daughter becomes a nun, the younger daughter marries a mean, misogynistic drunk, and their son falls for a delightful Jewish girl, their peaceful life as farmers is more than a little upset. It becomes even more upset by the entry into their lives of Ceil, a wealthy, beautiful and generous woman with a troubled past she might never have survived if it weren't for the local black woman, May-May. Loved by everyone, May-May is feared by that rotten drunk husband who is hell-bent on killing her, and he nearly succeeds, but there's no way I'm going to be a spoiler here and tell you any more. You just have to read Like I Used to Dance and find out for yourself.

Barbara Frances offers liberal minded readers everything they crave: suspense, violence, evil, sex (never explicit) and tons of good. That timeless theme of good conquering evil propels the novel to satisfying conclusions, though some may question the likelihood of certain situations presented. But if I had to nail what most riveted me to this story, it would be the questions Barbara raises, through her characters, about being born, bred and raised into religions that we live by despite our questions and doubts. Grace, along with her two daughters, and thanks to Ceil, is troubled by the blind adherence to tenets drummed into us since we were infants. These three women ask themselves questions I asked myself as a child, and later as a teen. They, like me, find themselves being freed as they reach answers their religious upbringing would deem sinful. And in finding those answers, they find their real selves. And that self is a far more honest one of whom they can be proud.

Like I Used to Dance by Barbara Frances could almost be described as a "coming of age" book for the bulk of the characters in the story. And there are many of them. Too often for me, a large number of characters in a novel is a turn off. I hate struggling to remember who is who. But this doesn't happen under the skillful pen of Barbara Frances. She knows where she's going with this story, its events, its issues, and its characters, and we, the readers, enjoy every part of the journey. A 5-star book all the way, I highly recommend Like I Used to Dance and I look forward to reading Barbara Frances' next book. I hope she won't keep me waiting too long!

Like I Used To Dance

Barbara Frances

Positive Imaging, LLC
Austin, Texas

Published by
Positive Imaging, LLC
9016 Palace Parkway
Austin, Texas 78748
http://positive-imaging.com

Publisher's Note: This is a work of fiction. Names, characters, places, and incidents are a product of the author's imagination. Locales and public names are sometimes used for atmospheric purposes. Any resemblance to actual people, living or dead, or to businesses, companies, events, institutions, or locales is completely coincidental.

Cover Photo - **Canada Science and Technology Museum**

Cover Design - Margaret Roberts and Ernie Sharpe

Like I Used To Dance/ Barbara Frances

ISBN 9781944071707

For my mother

Deep gratitude to my husband, Bill Benitez, and my friends Margaret Roberts and Ernie Sharpe, for their guidance and support in bringing this book to the dance.

"Our kids, my, my, Gracie,
where did we go wrong?
One marries God,
another a Jew and
the last one the devil."

CHAPTER ONE

Grace heard the pickup roaring up the dirt lane. It skidded to a stop in the back yard before she could turn off the stove's burner. Chickens squawked and flapped their wings to avoid the wheels. *That could only be Billy Wayne.* Her stomach sank as she walked to the screen door. There he was, her son-in-law Billy Wayne Tarkin, getting out of the pickup and yelling, "Angie, Tessie, shut up!"

Grace flew out the door. *He has brought those babies with him.* Two little girls, still in pajamas with sleep-caked faces, cuddled together on the front seat.

"Oh, my sweet Angie and Tessie. Grandma has some warm kolaches and juice just for you."

"Grace, leave 'em there." Billy Wayne shooed her with his hand. "I don't have no time. Just come by to tell you that Regina's pukin' her guts out, so she can't go with ya'll all to that thing in San Antonio."

Grace hated his crudeness. *That "thing" as you call it is a blessing. Your wife's sister is becoming a nun today. But then what would you know of that?* Grace wished she had the nerve to speak her thoughts.

"Grandpa," Angie exclaimed. Bud was approaching from the barnyard with the look of disgust he generally reserved for his son-in-law. He didn't hold out his hand for a shake as he did with most other men. "Who's taking care of Regina?" he asked gruffly.

"Oh, she's alright," Billy Wayne answered. "She's just upchucking all over the place. With this one, she's payin' her dues alright." He hitched up the front of his pants. "I bet ya everything I got it's a boy and he's givin' her one hell of a time." His bark of a laugh snaked down Grace's spine.

"Well, who's going to take care of the girls?" Bud's voice had a hard edge. "You got to go to work, don't you?" Most people would have been alarmed. Bud rarely spoke with harshness, but Billy Wayne blew it off with a shrug of his shoulders. *I ain't afraid of you, old man,* he thought.

"Hell, they'll be okay," he answered defiantly. "Regina's just sick; she ain't dead. Besides, they ain't none of your concern."

Bud walked past Billy Wayne, yanked open the pickup door and said in a gentle voice, "Come on to Grandpa." He picked up Tessie. "Hush now, baby. Everything's going to be okay. "He handed her to Grace and then scooped up Angie and turned back to Billy Wayne. "Tell Regina to stay in bed all day and not to worry. We'll look after the girls." Without so much as a goodbye, he turned his back and followed Grace into the house.

Billy Wayne glared. "You sorry bastard," he muttered under his breath. "One of these days, I'm gonna…" He spat on a nearby chicken, hoisted himself into his rusty claptrap and rattled off.

Once inside, Grace began wiping the girls' faces with an old washcloth used for kitchen cleaning. Her intolerance for dirty faces didn't allow her to take the time to get a regular washcloth from the bathroom. "As soon as you eat breakfast, Grandma's going to get you in the bathtub."

She turned back to Bud. "All I have here are some worn-out play clothes. We'll have to stop by Regina's to get something nice for them. I want to check on her, anyways."

Bud nodded as he held a cup of orange juice for Tessie to drink. Grace knew he was hurting just like she was. *What kind of mess had their youngest gotten herself into? And how quickly a day can change.*

GRACE had started out her morning as usual with the reassuring warmth of a coffee cup between her palms. Unlike nature, her morning Folger's, always hot, always black, was something she could count on. The brief time she spent alone each morning, planning her day and enjoying the ordered beauty of kitchen or yard was a ritual that calmed and inspired her. But this morning when she looked out the kitchen window, she had grieved to see a back yard splotchy with grass patches and beds of flowers too wilted to hold up their heads. A couple of chickens were clawing through the concrete dirt looking for worms. Just yesterday she had watered, but the well was running low and Bud had warned her that if she kept that up there would be no water for what mattered most, the animals and humans.

But flowers matter too she had wanted to say, even though she knew beauty was an extra to him, like a new pair of socks when his old ones were still perfectly good. He'd save the good pair until she refused to darn holes on top of holes in the old ones. *I wonder if he ever gets a tightness in his heart when he sees the flowers giving up their colors.* Her soul needed beauty to keep on going, almost as much as her lungs needed air.

The morning was pleasantly warm, not at all like it would be in a couple of hours. The first of June and the summer furnace was already roaring full blast. A dark cloud bank had been forming to the southwest. *"Please dear God, let it rain,"* she prayed. *"The crops need it and so do we."* Grace protected herself in a shroud of worry. Trouble could never take her by surprise like it did when she was a child.

Bud would see her frown and say, "Oh, we'll be fine. Frettin' won't put money in the bank, so why suffer with it?" Sometimes he'd get concerned about the children and what they were doing, but that was about the extent of his worrying. His easy-going acceptance both sustained and irked Grace.

She looked towards the barns and saw Bud spreading hay for the cows. She laughed as he played dodge with a couple of the frisky calves, so energetic this time of the morning. God, he was such a good man, the only man she'd ever *known* in the Biblical sense. She was always aware that he loved her deeply, even though he didn't always understand her. "I like the mystery of you," he said one time as they were cuddling.

They married when Grace was eighteen and he was nineteen, had three children, two miscarriages and one stillborn. Both graduated from the Catholic parochial school, which went to the tenth grade. Grace had wanted to go on to the public high school and get a diploma but her dad had angrily snapped, "Goddammit, you want to end up in hell?" The prevalent belief was that the public school would drive a child right into Satan's pit.

Bud and Grace had a peaceful marriage, each with their defined roles. Communication was sparse and generally superficial. They would talk over meals or while riding in the car or waiting by the radio for the Amos 'n Andy or George Burns shows to begin. They discussed the crops, the cattle, the finances and sometimes the children and the neighbors, but that was about it. Wasn't that enough? They didn't seem to have the vocabulary or the nerve for sharing dreams, fears or longings. Grace would have liked more, but she was too unsure of herself to bring up what was going on in her mind or heart. She wouldn't even know how to explain herself. Sometimes she felt like one of those chickens scratching the hardened ground. Did other people ever want a more profound existence or were most people like Bud, content with the way things were?

Past the barns and across the pasture she could just make out Mayphelia hanging out a sheet on her clothesline. Every Saturday that woman got up at the crack of dawn to do her washing. By noon, she'd have everything folded and in its place. Then she'd put on her shoes and walk to town to get groceries. Mayphelia looked like a black matchstick bobbing against the white sheet, her orange turban, the phosphorus crown.

Grace was as close to Mayphelia as she could be, being white and all. Everyone agreed that there was no better baby birther in the county. After having the stillborn delivered by the drunken white Dr. Clarkson, Grace had insisted that Mayphelia deliver Regina, their last one, now twenty and pregnant with her third. There were rumors that Mayphelia also did other things, evil things, for women, besides birthing and helping them to keep from getting pregnant over and over.

Grace had been preparing all week for this day. She had brushed Bud's Sunday suit, starched and ironed his white shirt and shined his good shoes to a glow. Then, for herself, she had added a new collar and belt to last year's spring dress and redecorated her go-to-church hat with a new veil and flowers she had made with fabric that matched her dress. With some leftover grocery money, she had ordered new white gloves and a white patent leather purse from Montgomery Ward.

Finally, the day had arrived. This afternoon Angela, their oldest daughter, was going to become a Sister, a nun, at Sacred Heart Convent. Beautiful Angela with the thick auburn hair, the penetrating hazel eyes and the slightly olive skin, was giving her life to God. Grace's heart contracted at the thought. She felt such pride, yet she knew she shouldn't because *pride goeth before a fall.* Still, it was hard to remain humble when one of your children was chosen to follow Christ.

Bud, on the other hand, was not as pleased. "She's too pretty and…well, womanly, to be closed off like that," he had commented to Grace on one occasion, careful not to cloud her joy. Being the first-born, Angela held a special place in his heart. He knew she was "a cut above," as everyone said, and he didn't feel that the life of a nun was necessarily "a cut above."

He will come around to accepting, Grace told herself.

A SPLASH of water landed on Grace's face. "See, Grandma, I can already wash myself all over. Mama says so," Tessie announced.

"Yes, you're a big girl," Grace said, remembering that Tessie would be three in only a few months and Angie would be five the month after. She kept thinking of them as being younger.

"Grandma, Mama says I'm named after Aunt Angela," Angie said as she scooped up soap bubbles in the tub.

"That's right, darling."

"Me too, me too, me too," Tessie chanted, wanting what her big sister had.

Grace smiled. “Sweetheart, you’re named after St. Theresa, who was the Little Flower, just like you’re our little flower.”

“No, me Tessie,” she corrected her grandmother.

CHAPTER TWO

The 1949 Ford pulled into the visitors' parking lot. Bud found the closest spot to the convent's magnificent Gothic chapel where the ceremony would take place. Bud and Grace were never on time for anything; they were always early. Bud scrunched his neck to look up at the sky through the windshield. A good storm was brewing. "It looks like it's about to open up. We'd better go on in. There's a hill of steps to climb."

The girls slept soundly in the back seat, shiny clean and pretty as ripe peaches in the Easter outfits Grace had sewn two months ago. She always made their clothes a bit large so they could grow into them and was thrilled that for this occasion they fit perfectly.

She and Bud hurried up the steps with the girls in their arms. Angie woke up wide-eyed and happy for a new day. Looking over Bud's shoulder, she smiled and waved at Grace. On the other hand, Tessie was angry and letting them know.

"We're going to see Aunt Angela. Won't that be fun?" Grace tried to calm her.

"No, no, no!" Tessie wailed.

A soiled, frayed pouch stuffed with juice, cookies and toys swung from Bud's free shoulder. Grace sighed, embarrassed over the bag's condition. Regina didn't seem to be bothered by dirty or worn-out things. *Well, she's got so much other stuff to deal with,* Grace thought to herself.

Bud pushed against the heavy wooden doors. They swung open to the crinkled face of a smiling nun. "Welcome, welcome. Quickly come in." They crossed over the threshold into a spacious foyer just as the rain gushed down without the usual prelude of sprinkles. It was as if a dam from above had collapsed.

The Sister chuckled. "God must have been waiting for you to get inside before He blessed us with this ferocious baptism." Just then Tessie cried out and then spit up all over the front of Grace's dress.

"Oh, my, I bet you feel better now." The nun smiled at Tessie as if she were the most perfect child ever. Grace assessed her soiled bodice and shook her head. "Now what will I do?"

"I have just the thing. Follow me." The nun began leading them down a wide hallway, chattering "You're Angela's parents, correct? Wonderful woman. Will be an extraordinary nun." She stopped at a door marked Private. "Come here, little one." She took Tessie from Grace.

"Here's a washroom where you can clean your dress. Under the basin is some laundry soap. It's still a while before the ceremony, so you'll be fine." The nun pointed down the hall. "Your husband and babies will be just down in the family waiting room on the left past St. Joseph." Grace saw the statue and felt comforted. She had always admired St. Joseph. He had raised a child that wasn't his and had taught him to be a carpenter, yet he got so little recognition.

ANGELA allowed herself one last vanity as she gazed in the mirror. She looked like any regular bride: all in white, soft curls of thick hair peeking through a tulle veil. Soon all this rich amber would be chopped off, left in a weeping pile on the floor until Sister Verona swept it away into that place where perms and bows and sassy hats did not exist.

A moment of regret passed through Angela's mind. *Is this what I want?* For three years now, she had been preparing for this day. She reassured herself. *I'm just having a case of bride jitters.* Around the room her fellow postulants gazed in mirrors and adjusted hems, sleeves, bodices. There was no talking or giggling as with ordinary brides. All sixteen of them were still bound by the sacred silence they had been observing for the past ten days in preparation for this holy occasion. Today they would prostrate their bodies before the high altar and dedicate their lives to God and His service.

Suddenly James Riley popped into her mind. *Sweet James, would he love me with no hair?* She remembered the thrill of his hands mussing those curls and caressing her scalp. He was now married to Patsy, her best friend from high school. They already had a one year old. Regina had written that he was the cutest baby boy she'd ever laid eyes on. "But, you know," Regina continued in her large sideways scrawl, "James is not the same person he was. I bet Patsy's always going to live in your shadow. Serves her right for throwing herself on him as soon as you boarded the train." Angela relished her sister's loyalty even as she felt regret over James' heartbreak.

After high school Angela had planned to finish college and then get married. James was already working the family farm, but he was willing to wait. He ignored his father's badgering, "What does she need with a college education only to be a farmer's wife?" James wanted Angela to have whatever she wanted.

But after her freshman year she announced she was entering a convent. She could no longer ignore the feeling that she was being called to religious life. Poor James came over daily for a week. He would sit on the back porch, plead with her and even cried one time. That was the only time Bud really became upset with Angela. "I can't believe you're doing this to him. Where's your heart?"

"Daddy, I know you can't understand," she whispered.

Then two nights before she left, James came over one last time. They walked down to the west pasture and sat under the large oak. The horizon had just swallowed the sun, but insistent tendrils colored the landscape in soft oranges and golds. Being careful of his feelings, she tried to explain once again her desire to live a life fully devoted to God and to His work. "It's my destiny, James."

Through tears, he told her he could never love anyone as he loved her. His sadness and need tore at her heart. She took him in her arms and kissed him. He began kissing her face, her neck, her breasts. It seemed as if the ground beneath her began to sway back and forth. She was beneath him. He was pulling up her skirt, opening her blouse. His hands were going places they had never gone before. She was overpowered by wanting him, all of him. The heavy petting which they had engaged in since their junior year in high school was no longer enough.

For two people who had never done this before, they were surprisingly adept. There was no thinking, just an overwhelming need to do exactly what they were meant to do in that moment. They acted quickly but smoothly; it was classical music rather than ragtime. Soon they were undressed and took in each other's nakedness without embarrassment. As he moved on top, she accepted him completely while the treetops danced and the earth gave way beneath her.

How long it lasted, she didn't know. She woke up in total darkness, wrapped in his arms and legs. The moon highlighted blood on her skirt. How could that be? She hadn't felt any pain, only surges of pleasure that lapped at every cell in her body. Her little sister Regina, who was already pregnant a second time, had told her in explicit details how much it hurt.

James' hand was stroking her back. "I'll always love you. I hope I gave you a baby."

She lightly kissed his cheek, "You didn't." She said this with certainty, but how could she know?

There had been the dream. The night after she had her first period she dreamed that she was in a large house with many rooms. She went from one room to another looking for the children, but there were none. When she went outside, there were children who came to her. Then a voice told her she would never have children from her own body. She woke up believing this was a sign from God that she was supposed to be a nun and care for other people's children. She had recalled that dream the day she decided to request permission to enter the Congregation of the Sisters of the Sacred Heart.

Angela never confessed what had happened. No priest or mother superior or institution could ever convince her that what she and James had shared that evening in the glowing pasture under that almighty oak was a sin.

GRACE stepped out of the washroom painfully conscious of the wet spot over her right breast and heard rolling laughter coming from Andy, her middle child and only living son. She hurried down the hallway to the waiting room and smiled broadly upon seeing him. *He's already got big city written all over him,* she thought. The well tailored suit, crisp shirt with matching silk tie, shoes right off the rack were not farmer's attire. A woman was leaning on his arm and cooing at Tessie. This must be the girl he'd written about. She had short curled hair, peroxided, just like Grace had seen in Regina's movie magazines.

Grace covered the wet spot with her new white purse and approached her group. "Mom!" Never one for doing things halfway, Andy grabbed her in a big bear hug. Grace gasped for air. "For heaven's sake, Andy, we're in a convent." He let her go with a laugh and put his arm around the blonde's shoulder. "Mom, I want you to meet my girl."

"Hi, I'm Sheila." The smiling woman extended a hand with long, very red fingernails just like the girls in the magazines. As Grace shook her hand she thought, *it's as soft as a baby's bottom. I bet she doesn't scrub clothes or hoe any gardens.* Her red lips matched her nails.

"Andy's always bragging about you. I'm so glad to meet you." Sheila's genuine warmth immediately relaxed Grace. She seemed quite nice in spite of the peroxide and flaming reds.

A TINY bell sounded. Sister Verona softly announced, "Christ is calling." The brides lined up and followed the Sister through the twelve-foot doors into the hallway leading to the entrance of the cathedral where Mother Superior and the Council waited to escort them down the aisle.

The loud notes of a pipe organ brought the visitors to standing attention as a heavenly choir began singing *The Magnificat.* Grace and Bud joined the crowd in turning to watch the brides walk down the aisle. Each one held a lighted candle and a lily. Angela was at the end because she was the tallest. *Dear God, she is so beautiful.* Tears of happiness welled in Grace's eyes while tears of sadness stuck in Bud's throat.

The ceremony seemed to go on forever. Behind them the girls giggled as they took turns bouncing on Andy's knees. They loved their Uncle Andy. Well, who didn't? Handsome dark Andy with his laughing black eyes and self-assured swagger made everyone feel from the moment he met them that they were just about as perfect as ice tea on a hot day. *I wish he'd keep them a little quieter,* Grace fretted. *But I suppose laughter's better than crying.*

The brides filed out to the sacristy behind the altar and down a flight of stairs to the basement where other nuns awaited in curtained-off sections to cut off their hair and help them dress in the black robes of the congregation.

Rain was pounding the rooftop. Grace was overwhelmed that God was so abundantly blessing them with both rain and a nun in their family. Next to her Bud, deep in thought, picked at callouses on his hands. The rain couldn't wash away his unease over this ceremony. When he was a boy in Catholic school he thought the nuns were odd and often wondered if they really were women. He'd never understand his daughter doing this. But then, he didn't understand lots of things, like how Andy could turn his back on a nice farm for a furniture store in Houston. *What kind of work was helping rich women decorate their fancy houses?*

After the ceremony everyone crowded into the vestibule. It echoed with the excitement of joyous shouts and laughter as novices and families searched for and found one another. When Grace hugged Angela, who was now Sister Mary Grace, she said, "I've never seen you look happier or more radiant." After a hesitant pause, she added, "I had no idea you were taking my name. I'm so honored."

Sister Mary Grace kissed her cheek. "Come on, Mom, you know you've always been my hero."

Bud stood back and stared at her. Suddenly his daughter had thrown her arms around his neck in a tight hug. "What's wrong, Dad? Do I frighten you?"

Bud laughed and returned her hug. "Well, it's just I never thought I'd see the day when I hugged a nun."

Andy came up behind his sister and gently tugged her veil. "I've just got to see that bald head of yours." Grace wished she could swat him like she did when he was little.

"Just try it." Sister Mary Grace could take care of herself. "I may be a nun, but I can still throw a good wallop." *That sounds like the old Angela,* Bud thought. *Maybe she won't be that much different than she was before.*

Andy put his arms around her. "Come here, Big Sis. Stop with the blabber and let me hug you." He picked her up off the floor.

"Put me down," Sister Mary Grace cried out.

Grace looked around embarrassed and wished that her two oldest children had gotten just a fraction of her reserve, her shyness. Only ten and half months apart, they were closer than close, like twins who had shared the womb. They had always looked out and taken care of one another. They had to when Grace lost her way.

A reception in the convent's main dining hall followed immediately. Long tables loaded with chicken and ham, vegetables, salads, fruits and desserts were set up along one wall. Sister Mary Grace said that she and the other brides had been up until all hours preparing the food. "You should have seen us," she said with a giggle. "We baked chickens, kneaded dough and iced cakes without saying one word. We didn't even make eye-contact." She clasped a bow back into Angie's hair. "It's one of those mysteries as to how we did it."

THE drive home was quiet. The girls fell asleep as soon as Bud turned on the motor. Uncle Andy had chased them up and down the convent halls, once even going into a restricted area. "No, no, no. You're not allowed here," chided a very old nun shaking a boney finger at them. Grace suspected that the nuns were quite happy to see Sister Mary Grace's family make their departure.

It was still raining softly, the best kind that really gets down into the soil for a good soaking. Grace stretched out and rested her head back on the seat. Bud glanced over and wanted to put his hand on her leg but didn't. She wouldn't like it with the girls in the backseat, even though they were asleep.

It had been a marvelous day. A shadow briefly crossed over when Grace told Sister Mary Grace about Regina's severe morning sickness. "She bawled something awful because she couldn't make it."

"I'll write her a long letter tomorrow and tell her I could feel her here with me." Then Sister Mary Grace left for a moment. When she came back she was carrying her lily. "Tell her to press this in her prayer book and remember that I'm with her."

Suddenly the car skidded to the side and headed for the ditch. Bud pulled hard on the steering wheel and after a few twists got the tires back on the pavement. "These roads are slick. Too dry for too long."

He had almost let out a string of curse words when the car swerved but remembered his granddaughters in the back. He never wanted to set a bad example. *But they probably wouldn't notice since that dad of theirs can't open his mouth without letting out something foul. He's just white trash.* He frowned with these thoughts.

Ordinarily, Bud didn't take much to criticizing or name calling, but it was a fact that there were simple, country white folks like him and Grace and then there was white trash. The same thing was true with the colored people. Alex Williams along with his wife, Blanche, and their three sons owned a farm a mile down from Bud's place. They were Negro and as good and decent as anyone on the face of the earth, yet most whites put all coloreds together. He hated to think that there were people who would think of him and his family as being the same as Billy Wayne's.

Bud and Alex worked the fields together, slaughtered hogs and calves together, helped one another out. Blanche and Grace put up jars of vegetables and peaches every summer, taking turns at one another's houses. He'd trust Alex with more than he would any of Billy Wayne's bunch, and Bud didn't like it one bit that Alex couldn't go with him into Hattie's Diner for coffee whenever they were in town, yet Billy Wayne's dad was there every morning. It got to him so much that he stopped going to Hattie's himself, which wasn't that much of a hardship because Grace and Blanche could out-cook Hattie any day and their kitchens were much more comfortable than the noisy diner.

Alex was quiet like Bud. They usually talked about farming or politics, the campaigns between Eisenhower and Stevenson, and sometimes they'd talk about the people they knew, the colored folk and the white folk, those who were decent and honorable and those who weren't, no matter their color. Bud would have rather seen Regina marry Benjamin, Alex's youngest son, now away at college in the North, than that sorry Billy Wayne. But if that had happened, Benjamin would have been hung from a tree and Regina driven from the county. Bud shook his head and thought, *Sometimes there just ain't no way of figurin' out the way things are.*

CHAPTER THREE

Regina looked out the back door and down the road hoping to see some car lights. She wondered where everyone was. More than likely Billy Wayne was off getting drunk. She no longer asked where he'd been because he'd simply yell, "It's none of your damn business where I've been or where I'm going." Since her life was so much easier when he wasn't around, she looked forward to his time away.

After her parents and the girls had left that morning, she cried and heaved a solid hour. When she finally got herself to the kitchen to make some of the root tea Mayphelia had given her, she didn't much care whether she lived or died. She knew her mom and dad would take care of the girls, and they'd do a better job than she. At that thought, a big sob wracked her chest and came out in an anguished moan.

She was the black sheep in the family and had always been. Here Angela had become a nun that day and was doing holy, good things for people, and Andy was making money in Houston, an exciting place with big stores, lots of lights and nice places to eat. If only Angela had married James and stayed on the farm, then they'd have some little something in common. She dearly loved her big sister, but she was also painfully jealous of her at times, even though she couldn't admit that even to herself.

WHEN they all were little, Angela and Andy—both names starting with an A—would throw their report cards on the kitchen table showing the whole world their perfect A's. Regina would hide hers in a book and scramble about for as long as she could, pretending she couldn't find it until her mother loudly demanded, "Bring it to me. Now, Regina." Her mother would look at the B's and C's, mostly C's, and say in a way that made Regina want to crawl under the table, "Well, not everyone can make A's. As long as you're doing the best you can, that's all we want. "

Two things Regina was really good at were singing and dancing. She had won two talent contests. The first was at school. At the second, an older woman with long grey hair came up to her after she had won first place at the county fair. The woman wore a cowboy hat and boots, a flowered shirt and tight jeans. She had turquoise jewelry hanging from her ears and neck, around her wrists and most of her fingers. Never in Regina's twelve years had she seen anything like her.

"Honey, you're good. In fact, your voice is so good, you could be on the radio and Darlin', I could watch you dance all day."

Her family was standing all around, and they actually laughed. It was as if these comments were the most ridiculous things they'd ever heard. Regina surmised, *They don't believe in me. I'm a C.*

Regina had started dancing around the house when she was just a tot. Her mother never commented on how well she danced, only shouted, "Don't knock over the lamp." Regina had heard the saying, *"dance to the music"* but she felt the music dance her, like a puppeteer pulling her strings. When she saw a Shirley Temple movie, she was hooked. She began tapping and tapped everywhere, to the bus stop, to the barn, to the living room, to the kitchen. That Christmas Santa brought her a pair of tap shoes. She tapped, tapped, tapped until Grace couldn't stand it anymore and sent her out to the tractor shed. For Regina this was perfect. Since the tractors were in the field most of the time, the shed was her very own dance studio. Her taps echoed on the concrete floor and through the barnyard, making the dogs bark, the horses whinny and the hens stop laying.

Her dancing also led to her complete downfall. Billy Wayne wasn't much of anything else, but he was a great dancer. When those two got on the floor everyone stopped to watch them. Regina was the best, but Billy Wayne knew how to lead and gave her the opportunity to show off how good she was.

They'd dance till the hall closed its doors for the night. Then Billy Wayne would coax her once again into the bed of his pickup where he had a straw mattress with an old blanket thrown over it. They'd make out for a while, with her pushing his hands away from places they shouldn't be until she'd sit up and demand that he take her home.

Then one night it was different. He fought through her resistances and forced his hands where he wanted them. "You've been askin' for it all night long," he hissed in her ear. His hands were between her legs yanking her panties down. "This is what you get for egging me on as well as every other red-blooded man with all that butt swingin."

She kicked and tried to roll away and struck him in the jaw. A jarring slap across her face stunned her. He was so much stronger. He had pinned her down, "You're just making it hard on yourself for no good reason. I'm gonna get what I want."

Suddenly she felt a tremendous jab between her legs and then a ripping and pounding like darts hitting every organ in her abdomen. She almost passed out from the pain. She cried and yelled, but everyone had left. In the distance an owl screeched mournfully as if experiencing the invasion.

Everyone was in bed when he dropped her off. She walked past her parents' bedroom. "Regina, that you?"

"Yes, Mama."

"You're late. Past time to be in."

"I know. We had a flat. Go back to sleep, Mama."

She felt lower than dirt. She wanted to run in the room and throw herself on the bed between her mama and daddy like she did when she was a little girl. It would be all warm and they would put their arms around her and complain that her feet were cold as icicles, and then her daddy would tickle her with his morning stubble. She was too ashamed to tell anyone, even Angela, what had happened. She had to hide this.

When she was late, she ran to tell Billy Wayne. All he said was, "I knew I was a man." A week later they had a civil marriage by a justice of the peace in the next county. A week after that the curse came. She wanted to jump in the cow tank and drown herself.

Now she could kick herself for not leaving him then. Even a C person should have known better because by the next month she really was pregnant and stuck. Her mother insisted they get married the right way by a priest. They were living in sin the way it was. Grace bought her a soft powder blue suit with a large skirt because her tummy was already beginning to bulge. She couldn't wear white because she was not a virgin.

They couldn't get married inside the church either because Billy Wayne wasn't a Catholic, so with her mom and dad and her brother and sister standing by her side, she and Billy Wayne exchanged honest-to-God vows in the priest's living room. The priest's judgmental look prompted Regina to keep her head bowed during the entire ceremony. Billy Wayne's people weren't there because they wouldn't be caught dead at *any damn Papist thing.*

Regina dropped out of school. It was the beginning of her junior year. Sweet Angie came seven months later and then Tessie almost two years later, and now here she was going to be big bellied again. And God help her, she didn't want it. She sometimes wished she had seen Mayphelia in the very beginning before anyone knew. Maybe she could have helped her. What difference would it make? She was already damned.

While still in school, she had read a story about an ordinary family that had one really good child and one really evil child. Even then the story made her think of her and Angela. She didn't know where Andy fit in, probably somewhere in the middle. She knew one thing for sure, after this baby she was going to take Mayphelia's tonic to keep from having any more, no matter what the priest said.

She had learned about this drink from Sally, the beautician. Sally said she drank it every morning, secretly of course, and her youngest was now five. "Gerald keeps nagging me to go to the doctor to see what's wrong," she announced to everyone in the shop, while popping spearmint gum and rolling a customer's hair. "Men don't feel like men unless their women are loaded down with one kid hanging on the leg and another one cooking in the oven."

Sally had sent lots of women to Mayphelia, even quite a few Catholics. Sally was also indirectly responsible for Regina realizing that she had actually been raped. It was an article in *Real Confessions*, one of the magazines Sally kept in her shop that had educated her. She asked Sally if she could take it home so she could read it more thoroughly.

The true story was about a girl a lot like Regina, sixteen, nice and rather dumb. A boy had forced her to do it when she didn't want to. The girl confided to her favorite teacher, who explained that she wasn't responsible even though she was wearing shorts at the time. She didn't cause what had happened; she was a victim. After the second read-through, Regina threw the magazine across the room and pounded the empty space in the bed where Billy Wayne usually slept. "It wasn't my fault! It wasn't my fault!"

She felt a weight lift off her. She could have danced naked and it still wouldn't have been her fault. *He raped me. He's the criminal, not me.* Up to that point, she'd felt so guilty she didn't dare dance any more even when Billy Wayne had tried to get her to go with him. She had been afraid she would tempt other men like she had tempted Billy Wayne.

Suddenly rage consumed her. Their wedding picture sitting on the dresser mocked her. A nearby pair of scissors glinting in the lamplight lured her out of bed. She smashed the glass on the frame, tore out the picture and cut Billy Wayne to tiny shreds. Then she cut the shreds over and over until they sifted down like bitter ashes. She looked at her own picture. The frightened girl looking back at her seemed to ask, *"How could you do this to me?"*

If only her mom hadn't insisted that she get married again by a priest, she could still get out of this horrible mess. The Church said the justice's marriage wasn't a real marriage. If only she'd had the courage to leave as soon as she knew she wasn't pregnant. But now it was sealed. If she got divorced now she'd be excommunicated.

She had heard that rich Catholics could pay the Pope to annul their marriages no matter how long they'd been together. It wasn't called a divorce of course, but that's what it was. Even a C student understood that different words didn't change the nature of a thing. Yet she also knew that only people in the big cities got divorced. Country people, even Protestants, stayed married no matter what. Her Aunt Pauline said it best, "Once you make your bed, you got to lie in it." Regina was stuck and there was no way out. She gently rubbed her finger over her image, then placed it in the bottom drawer and shoved Billy Wayne's remains in the trash.

A BANGING on the back door interrupted the stream of memories. She jumped like a flicked grasshopper. "Regina, you awake?" Her mom and dad were at the door. She quickly grabbed the long-sleeved shirt on the chair and put it on even though it was hot as embers. She couldn't let them see the bruise on her arm where Billy Wayne had pinched her last night when she had refused to get him another beer.

"Coming." She ran to unlatch the screen door.

"Mommie! Mommie!"

Her girls pressed against the screen, leaving little indented squares over the tips of their noses. How could she have ever wished she had never met their dad? Yet it sickened her to think he was a part of them. She dropped to her knees and opened her arms and they flew into them. Grace smiled as she watched Regina hug and kiss every inch of their faces while they giggled uncontrollably. *Regina is so free with affection. I wish I had been more affectionate with my babies,* she thought and then remembered how she had fallen into the well of darkness. This awareness didn't alleviate the regret she felt.

Bud and Grace put several wrapped plates on the table. "Your sister, now Sister Mary Grace, did you know she was taking my name?" Regina shook her head.

"Well, she insisted that we bring you a sample of everything," Grace went on. "She made the strawberry cake for your dad, and he stuffed himself. But there's still some left for you." Grace began taking the covers off.

"I only had three pieces," Bud countered.

Regina was on the floor with the girls in her lap rocking them back and forth, back and forth. *Angela had taken her mother's name. Always the perfect daughter,* Regina thought.

"And here's the lily Sister Mary Grace carried down the aisle. She wants you to press it in your prayer book."

Regina looked at the lily and felt nothing but emptiness.

"The girls slept the whole way back," Grace said as she put the lily in a glass of water.

"Even when I almost hit the ditch," Bud added with a laugh.

Something snapped in Regina. She brushed the girls off her lap, stood up and faced her parents. "You let them sleep the whole time? How do you expect me to get them to bed now? I'll be up all night. You know how hard it is to get them down after long naps especially this late? Why can't you use your heads?" Her eyes were wild. She paced around the kitchen table like a caged animal looking for an escape route.

Grace and Bud backed away from the venom spraying the room. *She's beginning to act just like Billy Wayne,* Bud thought. "We'll take 'em home with us. Don't get yourself all worked up."

Regina fell into one of the chairs and started sobbing. Then the girls started crying. Grace was beside herself. She pushed a plate of food towards her. "Maybe if you eat something, you'll feel better."

Regina grabbed a dish cloth and blew her nose. "Mama, Daddy, I want to come home."

"Then get your stuff," Bud commanded.

"But isn't this your home now?" Grace said just above a whisper. *"You weren't a good mother. Just look at how this kid has turned out,"* her dad's accusing voice darted through her awareness.

Bud shot Grace a look. "Her home is where she wants it to be."

Silence overpowered sniffling girls and cicadas strumming their legs just outside the open windows. The unwound clock was stopped at three fifteen. Grace wished she had held Regina more as she gazed at this daughter with the pale drawn face partially buried in a dish towel, the bony body with the belly bump and the straggly, dull, light-brown hair. She could hold her now, but it would feel uncomfortable for both of them.

Regina took a chicken leg off one of the plates and bit into it. "Ya'll go on. Mama's right. Me and girls will be okay. I didn't mean to yell at you like that."

"You sure? At least we can take the girls." Bud's voice carried a pleading tone. Grace felt how much he cared. She couldn't have raised the children without him.

"Remember the last time. Tessie wouldn't go to sleep without me. Besides I need them close tonight," she pulled the girls up on her lap and began feeding them strawberry cake with her fingers.

CHAPTER FOUR

When Bud and Grace got in bed, he reached over and petted her arm, then began rubbing her stomach. Even though she was tired after all the day's ups and downs and didn't feel like it, she wasn't going to refuse. He asked so little of her. She cooked, cleaned, washed, mended, raised chickens and kept a garden, but she never did any field work like so many of the farmer's wives. He wouldn't hear of it, and she never set foot in the pasture, either, except for picnics. A few times since Andy had left she'd helped him birth calves.

After the two miscarriages early in their marriage, he put in a bathroom just for her, even though she told him that the outdoor toilet wasn't the cause. But later when she got pregnant and went full term, she conceded he may have been right. They were gifted with beautiful Angela. Now today, God had taken His gift back. She could imagine Sister Mary Grace sound asleep in her tiny cell holding her rosary, serene in slumber.

Bud was kissing her throat and breasts. She rather liked that. She often wondered why she couldn't get more out of this. She did in the beginning, but not since Peter. Some women her age, the coarse ones, would sometimes openly speak about their bed pleasures. One woman at the cake sale said it got rid of her worrying. She said the next day she could let the dishes go all day and not give a tinker's dam.

Grace returned Bud's kisses. She did love him. She just wished she could show it more. He was on top now, and she helped him get inside. These days, he took more time. She guessed it was from all the hard work and worry. Even though they hadn't spoken a word on the way home, she could tell by his sighs that he was sick about Regina and her life. He needed this.

As Bud entered and manipulated her body to fit his needs, her mind kept going over the past, the things she couldn't remember, just imagine. Out of loyalty to Bud, she'd force her awareness back to the bed and what she was participating in. Did Bud know she was merely going through the motions? Did he care? Having had no experience prior to Grace or since, did he simply accept their coupling as normal and think nothing else of it? She knew Bud didn't analyze life too closely, especially if it couldn't solve anything.

After several hard thrusts, Bud arched his back and moaned in pleasure. Grace moved her hips to give him even more. Then from somewhere in her came the words, "I love you, Bud." She could tell in the darkness that he'd opened his eyes and was looking at her. She had rarely said it first. Maybe she was learning how to be more loving. As Bud rolled off, he whispered, "You know I love you more than anything." He hardly finished the sentence before he was sound asleep.

Grace was glad because she could feel the tears start to come. She jumped up and went to the bathroom to clean up. As the water ran, so did her tears. Tears for her lost Regina and her lost Peter.

SHE held the baby in her arms. He couldn't be dead. He just couldn't. When anyone came to take him away, she screamed at them, told them he'd start breathing any time now. Bud's older sister, Pauline, took Angela and Andy outside to the pig pen to watch the baby pigs. They mustn't hear her craziness.

He was beautiful with dark brown hair and ten fingers and toes. He had strong limbs, fat cheeks, perfect boy parts and he had kicked up a storm while inside her. But now he wouldn't move; he wouldn't cry. As with the other babies, she had pushed and pushed and held onto to Bud's arm while he supported her back, but then the contractions stopped. What was wrong? She thought the baby was on its way out. They waited and waited. Finally drunken Dr. Clarkson gave her a pill and before long, hard rolling cramps started up again. Twenty minutes later, her second son was out. She fell back and looked up at Bud's face. Why wasn't he smiling? There was no cry.

She bolted upright in the bed. Her mother cautioned, "You should lie back down."

"Give me my baby, give me my baby." She was screeching like a hawk pouncing on its prey. "I said, give me my baby." With beating wings she threw off the covers and knocked Bud aside, grabbed her baby from her mother and settled down again. She cuddled him next to her breast. "He's the cutest one so far, Bud."

She looked up. Bud was crying. His mother had her arm over his shoulder. She'd never seen him cry before. But she didn't care about him or any of them. It was just her and her brand new baby. She sang to him and kissed his forehead. He was cold. "Get me some more baby blankets. He's freezing."

Bud leaned over her. "Gracie, let me have him for a moment. I want to hold him, too."

Reluctantly, she handed him over. "Do you still want to call him Peter?"

Bud let out a sob and handed the baby to his mother, who began to leave the room. Grace let out a long shrill scream which lasted until the doctor gave her something that put her under water. She was floating, waving back and forth, to and fro. She saw hazy forms looking down through the surface at her. Even though she couldn't speak, she could breathe. She looked through the shimmering ripples surrounding her. Was Peter down here with her? He had been swimming for nine months. She wasn't worried that he didn't know how.

For days, maybe weeks, the shots kept her under the water. When she finally resurfaced, she was gently told that Peter was buried in the garden next to her Queen Elizabeth roses. "You know he hadn't been baptized," Pauline told her. This meant he couldn't be placed in the family plot at the Catholic cemetery. Bud's father sat on the bed and took her hand, "Ground is just ground. Your rose garden is as holy a place as some patch where a priest sprinkled magic water over it."

The priest came to bless her but she stared at him vacantly. When he began to make the sign of the cross over her head, she raised her hand to ward it off. "I don't want your blessing. Go bless the devil." She leaned back on the pillow and closed her eyes. "Put your blessings in that holy cemetery. I'm finished with God."

After that, she entered into the desert of going through the motions of being alive while actually being dead. Her limbs moved, her lips spoke, but a great curtain had been drawn over her mind and her feelings. Bud would find her in the middle of the night running through the garden chasing Peter. "You see him? He's hiding behind that tree. He's the most active one of them all, wakes me up all the time to play. Bud, you go back to bed. You have to plow the south forty tomorrow. I can look after him."

Bud would pick her up and carry her back to bed, all the time terrified that she'd end up in the state hospital. He said nothing to anyone, not even his mother who had told him on several occasions, "I tell you honey, I think Grace has dropped her basket."

Sometime later, her mother asked her if she were pregnant again. Grace had no idea. She looked down at her stomach and saw that it was stretching out of her blouse, almost popping the buttons. How had that happened? She couldn't remember doing anything with Bud. Had she been visited by an angel? *Behold, the Handmaiden of the Lord, you are with child.* It's a miracle. No, it couldn't be. It was a curse, a punishment for letting them take Peter.

"Leave," she commanded her mother. "I'm cursed. You must get away from me."

When Bud realized she was pregnant, he cursed himself for doing that to her. He tried to take her to Dr. Clarkson, but Grace flatly refused. "You want this one never to cry? Babies got to cry." That's when Bud gave in and took her to Mayphelia.

MAYPHELIA had the powers; she knew things and her eyes could see things inside you. She could tell if your blood needed iron or if your spirit needed forgiveness. After the first visit to Mayphelia, Grace began to emerge from the desert. She was surprised to see how much Angela and Andy had grown. They looked healthy, but she didn't remember feeding them. They were clean, but when had she last bathed them? She wanted to tell herself that Bud, his mother or her mother had done everything, but she knew that wasn't true. She just didn't remember. God, what all had she not remembered? She had no idea how long she'd been pregnant. Bud said he figured it was about four months, and Mayphelia said it was four months on the fifth of the month.

Many people were afraid of Mayphelia and her powers. She was taller than most women and could look most men straight in the eye. She was midnight black, beanpole skinny with long legs and arms and eyes that, some said, could cut through steel. Mr. Carbon, the grocer, always laughed at the rumors. "That ole nigger wench has about as much power as my limp dick," he would say.

But then one day Mayphelia came into his store instead of walking over to the colored grocer's a mile out of town. She was there for a reason. Word was that Mr. Carbon put his right thumb on the far corner of the meat scale, where no one could see so he could overcharge the coloreds and some of the poor white folks.

As he weighted a pound of salt pork for Mayphelia, not daring to look her in the eye (he was more frightened of her than he let on), his thumb was in its usual spot. Suddenly the scale became as hot as a pot-bellied stove. Mr. Carbon jumped back and yelled, expecting to see his thumb seared. There was no sign of a burn. But the next morning when he picked up his cup of coffee at breakfast, his right hand began shaking so much he dumped the burning liquid right down his crotch, blistering and scalding his most tender parts.

After that, every time he so much as walked by the meat scale his right hand shook uncontrollably. He couldn't put his thumb on the surface without the dial dancing back and forth so much that even the most backward of the poor would notice. Plus there was something else. Every time he started to go up a cent or two on items that a colored was buying, he'd get something caught in his throat and would cough and cough. Nothing would stop it until a penny or two was taken off the regular price. He knew he'd been hexed.

He went to the doctor but Dr. Clarkson couldn't find anything wrong, not that Mr. Carbon put much stock in that red-blotched quack with the sour breath. So he went to his preacher at the Holy Ghost Baptist Church. When the preacher asked him why he thought she'd hex him, he said he didn't know. Now Preacher Jonathan was a cautious man. Mayphelia had cured him of chronic constipation, so he told Mr. Carbon that he probably needed to get things right with the Lord and not worry about Mayphelia.

Mr. Carbon went away swearing he'd never give another red dime to that Preacher Jonathan or his damn church. By now he'd gotten so scared of Mayphelia that every time she came into his store, which had become quite often, he'd tell his wife to tend to the customers while he went out back to smoke. Mrs. Carbon was glad to do it, grateful to Mayphelia for what she'd done to him. She was still angry over the case of clap he'd given her years ago, and she wished the hex had burned his whole thing off rather than just blistering it up good and proper.

Grace had gone to see Mayphelia every week during her pregnancy, and every week Mayphelia brought her back more and more to the land of awareness. When Grace's time came, Mayphelia's quiet, calm, shamanic presence guided her through the birth of Regina. But as soon as Regina came out, Grace turned her face towards the wall. "I don't want to see it," she said. The old phantoms came back and told her that this one was dead too, no matter how much she heard the little thing wail. Besides, it wasn't fair to Peter that this one cried. She didn't want it and she didn't want to see it.

Mayphelia's hands began going through her scalp, digging through her hair and into her head, prying deep into her skull. Grace felt the fingers pulling at the phantoms and saw them being cast down into a black churning pit. Then the hands went into her chest and began massaging her heart, going deeper and deeper until Grace felt a wall break and flake away into her bowels. She cried out as the walls came down. She fell back on her pillow, exhausted and released. Mayphelia placed beautiful Regina in her arms and Grace loved her.

GRACE dried the inside of her legs and looked in the mirror over the sink. Could Regina have known or felt that her mama wasn't aware of being pregnant with her? Could Regina remember in her infant brain that Grace had turned her face to the wall and didn't want to look at her? Is that why Regina's life was like this? Or was God punishing Grace for turning away from Him after Peter's death? She had started going back to Church as soon as Regina was born but maybe that was too late. The guilt was always lurking in a corner of her mind, even though sometimes from the pulpit she would hear that God was forgiving and merciful. But was that so? She also heard He damned people to hell. *I bet God holds grudges just like my dad did.* Grace turned off the water and hung up the wash cloth.

Back in the bedroom she sensed the old panic demon just beyond the open windows, impatient to enter her soul again. She hurried to the hall closet and dug out a large box. Upon opening it, she felt a calmness seeping into her pores. The demon was retreating. She sifted through the layers of her drawings, some in crayon, some in charcoal and some in pencil. These were what had kept her from falling completely over the edge. Now they held her onto this plane of existence.

There was the crayon print of Bud baling hay, one of three-year-old Regina walking down the lane towards the barn, one of Andy and Angela chasing butterflies. There were also the dark ones of monsters and caves and grabbing hands and dead babies. She stuffed the dark ones back down at the bottom of the pile and took out a pencil and pad and began sketching a grown Regina in her kitchen with the swollen belly. She wished with all her heart she could sketch Regina out of her hell. Her tears smudged some of the lines.

CHAPTER FIVE

Every little town had its town drunk, and it wasn't Dr. Clarkson or the owner of the cotton gin. Those were respectable men, men with money and more education than most. They could drink all day long and often did, but they weren't drunks because they weren't poor. The town drunk was the one who slept in ditches and went around in the afternoons looking for small jobs like cleaning out hen houses or rehinging screen doors for some housewife sick of waiting for her husband to do it. He worked to get just enough money to go to the still in the woods where Grady would sell him a pint or quart, depending on the day's earnings. This town's drunk had a family, a bent down wife and seven kids, two already dead from "not gettin' to the doctor on time," living in squalor in a three-room shack on the edge of town. Three or four times a week, he would stumble back to his bed where he'd attempt to father another. This town's drunk was Clem Sites. Everyone called him Clem because he never earned the right to be called Mr. Sites.

The night of the dance, Clem walked over to the hall and looked through the window. There was that pretty little Wolansky girl and that mean Tarkin boy dancing all over the place. Clem couldn't help but smile as he watched them, especially her. It was like she was some kind of bird, maybe a meadowlark, flying and flitting all over the room. He took the last swig of moonshine, shook the bottle to see if there was more, fell down and crawled under a bush before passing out. Hours later he was awakened by an awful sound. At first he thought his wife was having another baby. Then he thought it was a wounded dog. He pulled himself up, scratching his face on the branches of the thorny bush. Then he realized where he was and where the sound was coming from.

The Tarkin pickup was no more than ten feet away. He crept over on all fours and peeked over the edge. In the moonlight he saw what the noise was. The pretty little Wolansky girl was fighting, kicking and clawing at the Tarkin boy on top of her and crying out, "No, no, no, Jesus help me." He didn't stop. Clem wanted to do something, but he could barely stand and besides he was afraid of that Tarkin bunch. She was crying and crying. "I said shut up. You're gettin' just what you deserve," said the Tarkin boy.

Clem passed out again. He woke the next morning with ants chewing at the scratches on his face and tire tracks just inches from his head. Seeing those tracks jogged his memory back to the night before. He knew Mr. Wolansky. Bud, as everyone called him, had a nice big farm west of town and often gave Clem odd jobs but paid him only half of what he'd earned and then gave the rest to his wife. A lot of the farmers did that. Otherwise his family would have starved to death.

He liked Bud and wanted to go tell him what had happened, but would Bud believe him? No one believed a word he said. He was the town drunk. Sometimes he wished he could tell people that he knew more than anyone could imagine about the underbelly of this place. He knew which men snuck out at night and went down to colored-town to Viola's. He knew which women buried money in their vegetable gardens, so they didn't have to go begging their husbands. He knew which kids got beaten like dogs.

Clem wouldn't tell Bud because he was afraid. Billy Wayne's dad, Mr. Tarkin, had killed someone in the woods southeast of town. It was that pitiful Boudie, a man who had mush for brains. The sheriff said it looked like Boudie fell face-flat on a rock. Since Boudie was an idiot, everyone bought this story hook, line and sinker. His mama kept saying that Boudie had never had a falling spell in his life. But what else could it be? He was found out there in the middle of nowhere face down in a pool of blood. No one was around for miles.

But Clem was, and he knew that Boudie was out picking wildflowers when Mr. Tarkin came along and pulled down his pants and told Boudie to put his thing in his mouth and suck it. Boudie didn't understand what he was asking for, so he pulled down his pants too and started peeing, laughing the whole time. Mr. Tarkin must have thought he was laughing at him and got so mad he picked up a huge stone and smashed Boudie right on the nose and forehead. The thrust was so loud that Clem heard Boudie's skull crack all the way in the ditch where he was lying. Then old man Tarkin pulled up Boudie's pants, threw away his flowers, rolled him over, placed the stone under his forehead and left.

Clem had wanted to tell the sheriff about that but was afraid Mr.Tarkin or one of his bunch, would get even and kill him while he was passed out in a gully or on the side of the road. Clem shivered. There was too much bad all around him. That's why he drank.

CHAPTER SIX

The Fourth of July was a time of special celebration this year. The rains that had started the beginning of June continued to come every few days in soft afternoon showers. The crops were growing like wildfire and Grace's flower garden was bursting with colors and happiness. She and Blanche had been working round the clock to keep ahead with the canning from their vegetable gardens. Grace took a couple dozen jars over to Clem's family, a box load to Regina's and Mayphelia's and still her cellar shelves were full. Too much for just her and Bud, no matter how long the winter lasted.

That morning both Grace and Bud were in high spirits. What a difference some rains could make. During breakfast they shared their first letter, six pages long, from Sister Mary Grace. She was allowed to write home once a month and last Saturday marked the first month. Bud sadly commented that she was as happy as Regina was unhappy. He quietly added, "I guess being a nun isn't the worst thing a girl could do. She could have ended up marrying a no-good."

Grace stacked the dishes and told him that Regina seemed to be doing better since she had started seeing Mayphelia. She was looking healthier. Her hair was getting thicker and her eyes were brighter. Billy Wayne didn't know about these visits. "I shudder to think what he'd do if he found out," Grace said while filling the sink with soapy water.

REGINA had planned to go to her parents' for the Fourth, but on that morning Billy Wayne had demanded that she and girls go with him to his folks' get-together. He, his dad and brothers were going wild-pig hunting down at the creek bottom. Regina said, "But I don't want to go."

"You given' me lip again?" Just as he raised his hand to slap her, Andy knocked on the screen door. Seeing Billy Wayne's raised hand, Andy yanked the locked latch so hard it came out of the frame. Billy Wayne backed up, afraid of Andy. He wished he had a gun. He'd take care of this fancy big shot, get him when he least expected it. Andy had been the captain of the high-school football team and the homecoming king. He was handsome and smart and his dad owned one of the best farms around. Billy Wayne was eaten up with jealousy.

"You okay, Gennie?" Andy rushed in.

Billy Wayne lowered his hand and grinned at Andy, remembering that someday he'd be part owner of that farm and when that time came, he'd see to it that he got it all. It was even a sweeter deal now since the oldest girl had given up all worldly possessions. He examined the broken latch but maintained the possum grin.

"She's looking prettier every day, ain't she? I was about to give her a big hug." Billy Wayne raised his hand again, pulled Regina to him and tried to give her a kiss, but she turned her head out of reach. Her big brother always came to her rescue. Ever since she was a toddler, he could sense when she was in trouble. She had often heard how he had tackled her when she headed for the edge of Aunt Pauline's porch, three feet off the ground. *Where was he the night of the dance?*

The door opened and Sheila came in carrying a bag of surprises for the girls. "Hi, hi, hi." She looked like she'd just stepped out of a spring fashion magazine, in low-heeled mules, a flared skirt with a matching sleeveless blouse and long dangling earrings.

Billy Wayne didn't like her at all. He could tell she thought she was better than him. "What's all that?" he asked, pointing at the bag.

"Just a few things for the girls. Where are they?" She looked around the kitchen and into the living room.

"Well, it ain't their birthdays. I don't want them gettin' stuff all the time. They're rotten enough already, and we don't need people giving 'em things." Billy Wayne cleared his throat and puffed out his chest, daring any one to cross him.

Sheila's mouth dropped. She had never met anyone quite like this. "Sheila, take the bags back to the car," Andy gently commanded, keeping his eyes on Billy Wayne. "Don't worry, I'll fix the latch, but don't let me see or hear of you raising a hand to my sister."

"What are you talkin' about? I told you I was gonna hug her. If you're going to come in here accusin' me, you better just get the hell out right now," Billy Wayne barked.

Regina moved between them. "It's alright, Andy. He wasn't going to do anything. I'll get the girls and my things, so we can get on over to Mom and Dad's." She turned back to Billy Wayne and saw his fear, his anger, his weakness. "I'm real sorry you can't make it. If you finish the hunt before sunset, come on over."

Billy Wayne fumed, realizing he'd been outmaneuvered. What could he say or do with her big brother standing by? Andy was at least four inches taller and a good thirty pounds heavier. Billy Wayne was a pile of bones compared to him.

He watched her and the girls get into Andy's fancy car. His cousin had told him that Regina was seeing that black witch, and he knew it must be true because he could see the spell working on her. She wasn't nearly as skittish around him and she didn't seem to care if he came or went. She was getting like her mom, real stand-offish. The other night when he got mad at her, she told him to go on and hit her. "You want to kill your baby? It feels what I feel and it's probably already scared of you." He couldn't sleep all night long because her words kept worming around his liquored-up brain.

THE fireworks burst into thousands of stars over the backyard. Andy had brought a large box of these wonders. Bud shook his head over the foolish way his son spent money and wondered how he got to be that way. Everyone else was beside themselves with excitement and wonder, especially the girls, who had never seen such sights. Bud, meanwhile, worried that something might catch on fire even though a sudden rain had soaked everything that afternoon. It came suddenly just as the slow eaters were shoveling in the last spoonful of homemade peach ice-cream. Everyone ran inside carrying platters and casseroles of leftovers. Card tables were quickly set up in the kitchen and living room, and within minutes the sounds of dominos slapping the tables and words of thanksgiving for all the rain resounded through the rooms.

Bud's two sisters, Pauline and Ruby, their husbands and seven children were there. Grace's only sister, Violet, was there with her fifteen-year-old son, Carl, Jr. Her husband was off in an oil field working on a rig. Grace's four brothers all lived in West Texas, too far to come. Both her parents were dead. Grace's dad had died of liver disease when she was nineteen. Ten months after Regina was born, her mom got cancer and was gone in six months. Grace didn't miss them and felt guilty about that.

Bud had invited Alex and Blanche over but they said they had something going on at their church. He sensed they didn't like to come if other white people were going to be there, and the way things were he didn't really blame them. His sister Ruby and her husband were about as hateful around colored people as any two people he'd ever seen. They were both *Bible-quotin' morons* as far as Bud was concerned. They wouldn't have been invited except that Pauline had opened her big mouth, and then Ruby and her husband more or less invited themselves.

Towards evening the Hardgroves from the next farm with their four children and the Wallaces from six miles away dropped by for watermelon and the fireworks. Mayphelia also stopped by on her walk home from her church picnic. She didn't like cars and walked everywhere even when someone offered her a ride. Regina hugged her so long that Grace felt some jealousy. *Mayphelia has become Regina's real mom.* When Mayphelia broke away from Regina, she approached Grace, hugged her and whispered in her ear, "No one's takin' yo'r place." Grace pulled back and looked into those eyes that saw beyond. Mayphelia had heard her thought.

Regina and Sheila lay on a blanket giggling as they watched the sparkling night sky. They were becoming confidantes. Regina had desperately needed one ever since Angela had left, and she soon found it was easier to confide in Sheila than to her sister. Sheila wasn't as goody-

goody as Angela. She had made mistakes, too. She'd married at eighteen to get away from her parents but then got a divorce six months later. "He couldn't keep his hands off other women. Plus he was boring as hell."

Sheila had come home one day and found him in bed with the woman from next door. Later, he fled the country rather than go to prison for stealing five thousand dollars from his uncle's safe. "Oh, they don't make 'em more rotten than him."

Regina rolled her eyes. "You wanna bet?"

Sheila burst out laughing. "Let's have a contest to see which one was…is the worst."

The most amazing fact about Sheila was that she was Jewish. Regina had never met a Jew. The nuns had told her that they had killed Jesus, but Regina figured that was a long time ago and Sheila had nothing to do with it. Besides she liked Sheila better than anyone she had ever met. She was funny, loving, honest and generous. No wonder Andy was so crazy about her. She was a lot like him.

Sheila whispered in her ear that Andy said they couldn't do anything while they were at his mom's. "You're crazy to even think of that while we're here," I told him. Then you know what that brother of yours said? 'Don't worry, I'll sneak in and do my thing for you in the middle of the night, and if you don't scream no one will know.'"

They both giggled like a couple of wayward teenagers. Regina was amazed that someone could be so up front about doing it without being married. She couldn't imagine what her mom and, well, her dad, too, would do if Andy wasn't teasing and they actually did something. Oh, well, Andy could get away with anything; he always had.

MAYPHELIA walked down the dark lane towards her cabin. She knew the way so well that she had refused Bud's offer to give her a flashlight. "The moon, though it be a just a slice is enough for me," she told him.

She smiled and nodded her head as she thought about the good time Regina had had with Sheila. *That city gal be good medicine for her.* Regina now lived in a sacred place in Mayphelia's heart where only one other girl, also white, had lived. Long ago this girl, now a woman of forty-five, had fled to a city where she could be herself and not be afraid. "My sweet baby Cecelia, my sweet Cecelia," she softly chanted to the night.

Mayphelia regretted that she had never learned to read. When this girl ran off, Mayphelia sent word for her not to write. She didn't want anyone to read words written for her only. Every holiday, several packages would be at the post office for her. Inside those boxes were new worlds, all sorts of rare things like hairbrushes made for kinky hair, brightly colored scarves and blouses hand painted with birds and flowers, pottery dishes too beautiful to eat on, lavish pipes with sweet smelling tobaccos and delicious bundles of candies, nuts and dried fruits. Mayphelia had no idea what most of them were called.

Like Regina, this woman of long ago hadn't felt good about herself or who she was. They both had kind natures, sometimes too kind for a cruel world. But they were different, too. Regina was drawn to healing, quickly learning about stones and herbs and their powers. She had the knowing, too. Grace's intuition had been partially correct. Regina was Mayphelia's soul daughter.

Mayphelia began to hum a tune that her lover and partner, Radio Man, used to sing in the fields. He was given that name because he talked all the time, just like the men on the radio. "Oh that man, he always be tellin' a story, make ya laugh, and make ya think," she sang out to the darkness. At fifteen she went with him and loved him like a lap puppy for the thirty-nine years they were together.

Radio Man was beaten half to death back in Alabama because he'd stepped into a white women's beauty parlor, thinking he was going into the hardware store just next door. He looked up from the list he was reading when he heard some screams and knew he'd made a big mistake. When after three years he and Mayphelia were still childless, he blamed those Alabama crackers for kicking him so many times in his privates. "They's ruined me for makin' babies," he'd often say. Mayphelia, who had a seeing for others but not so much for herself, never knew for sure if he was right. Maybe their spirits didn't want to share with other beings the joy and happiness they had with each other. Just thinking of him could still quake her body and soul. She laughed out loud, raunchy and free.

About twenty feet from her cabin she stopped. Something was in the bushes. She heard the breaking grass and knew by the smell that it wasn't an animal. There was alcohol over pig smell and man smell. Standing perfectly still she focused on the spot where she knew he was hiding. A minute passed. Her eyes dared him to come out. The added smell of fear told her he wouldn't. In a low deep tone she warned, "Billy Wayne, you best leaves before I calls my wolf on you." She waited and then threw back her head and howled like a wolf. In the distance came a reply howl.

A shuffling, stumbling and running vibrated in the stillness. Mayphelia stood for several more minutes, not moving even an eyelid, until the sounds and the smells were completely gone. She saw the hunting knife covered in dried pig's blood, dropped in the sod. His evil was strong. Sweet Regina would have to have stronger powers and medicine against that no-count boy. She would need lots of wolf energy to keep her safe.

THAT damn wolf was right on his heels. Billy Wayne could feel its breathe on his back. He began to cry, then heard his dad's voice, *What kind of sissy boy are you?* He stifled the sob. It was close enough to bite him. Suddenly he stepped in a hole and pitched forward, twisting his ankle. When he looked around, there was nothing, just empty space and silence. He wrapped his arms around himself and shivered. That witch had set a ghost wolf up against him. His shirt and pants were soaked with terror sweat. He stood up and began running even though jabbing pain was sparking up and down his leg. He'd dropped his knife but he wasn't going back to find it now. Maybe another time.

He limped up to the back of Grace and Bud's house. He looked in the window of Regina's old bedroom. His wife had her hair up in big rollers and was getting her nails polished by Andy's whore, whatever her name was. To top it off Grace was sitting on the bed beside his two sleeping daughters, waving red painted fingers through the air, drying them. "By tomorrow night, after I've done scrubbing up all the pots and pans from today all this will be worn off," she commented.

"Go get you some kitchen gloves, Mama. They have 'em at the Five'n Dime. Remember you got me a pair when my hands were red and cracking open. Billy Wayne said it..."

She paused in mid-sentence and turned to look towards the window. Billy Wayne dropped to the ground before she saw him. Once again he was flooded in fear. What made her turn around to look out that window?

He belly-crawled over to the kitchen window and peeked in. Bud and Andy were sitting at the kitchen table drinking beer and looking over some papers. Bud was quoting figures. *They're plotting against me, figurin' out how to cheat me out of my share of the farm* ran through Billy Wayne's mind.

Bud leaned back in his chair and held up his bottle of beer. Billy Wayne didn't recognize the name. "Son, I'm going to have to agree with you. This is the best beer I've ever had. Even better than what your great-grandpa used to make."

"Yeah, it's my favorite. Just started coming to this country." Andy stood up and stretched.

"You know your great-grandad was well into his nineties and still making it?" Bud chuckled.

"Angela would've loved one of these." Andy took his empty bottle to the trash can. "I wonder if she can still drink beer. I really missed her today."

Billy Wayne crouched on the ground beneath the window but he could still hear every word. Bud and Andy made him sick with their nice ways. When he had told his dad he'd knocked up that youngest Wolansky girl, his dad had slapped him on the back and said, "Way to go, boy. A girl with property. You're turning out to be the best of the litter." That was the only compliment he could remember his dad ever giving him. Then he finished with, "Now don't be some damn knuckle-head. You get her to the justice before the sun sets."

What was he going to do now? He was so dirty that even he was ashamed to be seen by these people. His ankle was probably broken and his pickup was parked about a mile down the main road. If things had gone according to plans, he'd have killed Mayphelia and ransacked her shack for all the money he knew she'd been socking away all these years. He then could have gone back to his pick-up, fetched his wife and girls and gone home a rich man, and his wife would no longer be under any of her spells.

Now all he could do was crawl back to his truck, get back to town and wake up that sot of a doctor. Tomorrow he'd tell Regina that a wild pig had run him over and he couldn't come get her, not that she'd care. But that was the least of his problems. Mayphelia had called him by name. She knew it was him.

THE doctor told Billy Wayne it was broken. "From the X-ray, it looks like in three places. One thing for sure, you'll never be showing off on the dance floor again with your pretty wife or that Yokum girl from the Bottom."

Billy Wayne wanted to stomp him through the wood floor with his good foot. How in blazes did he know about Geraldine? After Tessie was born, Billy Wayne started sneaking off to see this girl in Gallester County. He would tell Regina he was going to some meetings, which was true about half the time. By this time in their marriage, Regina knew better than to question his comings and goings.

He'd met Geraldine when he was hauling moonshine for Grady. She was there getting liquor for her dad. She wasn't all that pretty, nothing like Regina, but she wasn't uppity either. After the second time he'd had his way with her, he told her she better not tell anybody about them or he'd beat her up good and proper. She understood what he meant because she had a pa a lot like that. The only dances they went to were clear across in the next county.

"Where in the hell did you hear such a lie?" Billy Wayne eased off the table. The heavy cast thumped the floor.

"Watch out and don't crack that thing. I'll have to charge you again." The doctor turned to wash his hands, tying up his bathrobe and rolling up his pajama sleeves.

Billy Wayne had never seen a man in pajamas. Regina had given him a pair right after they were married, and he told her he wouldn't be caught dead in them.

"I ast you a question." He raised his voice.

The doctor turned and grinned. "Oh, you know, boy, how things fly around in this little town. It's the damndest thing you've ever seen how everyone knows what everyone else is doing, no matter how tight you keep the shades drawn. I can't rightly tell you where I heard it, but I didn't put much stock in it, being you's married to such a fine gal."

Billy Wayne drove home in a fury. Rays from the rising sun were lighting up the road. Did Regina know? Is that why she refused him all the time telling him it wasn't good for the baby? Most men he knew had their way with their women up to the time they delivered.

When he came into the kitchen, he saw sacks and dishes from the day before stacked on the table and figured that Bud or Andy must have brought Regina and the girls home last night. Being as careful as he could, he looked in on his daughters and saw them sound asleep in brand new pajamas. Andy and Sheila must have given them those gifts anyway. "I need to straighten out Regina once and for all, going behind my back and taking things" he muttered through clamped teeth.

The fire had started burning in his belly. He wanted to be the one to give his daughters pretty clothes and nice things. His mother had taken charity from church ladies who'd come out to their house while he'd hide in the goat shed, ashamed and humiliated. This morning, however, the sleeping sweetness of those little faces doused the anger. He would not be like his daddy. He would straighten up and be the breadwinner.

He looked in on Regina. She was lying on her side, her newly curled hair flowing over to his pillow and her slightly extended belly showing through her gown. To think he could have gotten someone like her was hard to believe. He felt a twinge of shame about how he had gotten her. Her cries from the back of that pickup occasionally haunted him.

Suddenly he decided he was finished with Geraldine. Why would he throw all this away for a Bottom girl? He'd have to be as dumb as his dad always said he was. He crept back to the kitchen and made some coffee. Then he sat down and worried over how he was going to make money while his foot was banged up. He couldn't work the quarry half-crippled. The doctor said he'd be this way for a couple of months. There was always bootlegging with Grady, but he'd promised Regina he'd stop that. Outside, the neighbor's rooster crowed. Maybe God was punishing him for all his evil ways. Maybe he should go talk to that preacher over at Holy Ghost. A lot of people said he had a good ear.

"Daddy?"

He turned to see little Angie standing in the doorway holding a new little stuffed brown bear with a red tie.

"Daddy, where was you last night? I was scared." She twisted the hem of her pajama top.

"Come here, beautiful baby girl. I'm okay. Just hurt my foot a little. Come sit in my lap." Billy Wayne coaxed her.

Angie shook her head, "You smell, Daddy."

Billy Wayne laughed. If Regina had said that, a hornet's nest would have been kicked, but with his daughter he felt love. "Yes, I do. Tell you what. I'll go clean up jest for you and then I'll hold you. How about that?"

He hobbled off to get washed up. Angie dug into one of the sacks on the table and pulled out an oatmeal cookie, sat down on the floor, gave her bear a bite and then took a bite for herself.

CHAPTER SEVEN

Another class of people lived in these little communities, and they were the town folk. The town folk were the store owners, the banker, the gin owner, the doctor–those who didn't depend on the land, but depended on those who worked the land. If the crops failed, they suffered as much or more than the farmers. They lived in genteel houses on Pecan, Maple, and Oak streets that all had front parlors. They admired the farm owners but thought themselves a little higher up the ladder because they lived in town and had indoor toilets. On the other hand, the farmers generally thought *they* were a little better because they did an honest day's work tilling the soil and bringing food and cotton to everyone.

Each respected the other, knowing that their assets were more or less the same, but still they poked fun at one another when they were with their own. "Those town folk are so damn fat because they never get off their rears. Honestly, what kind of work is counting money or selling stuff. That don't even take brains."

"I swear those country folk carry an acre of land under their fingernails alone. Those Saturday night baths don't come often enough. And tight, they count every penny even though their land and all their machinery, not to mention their livestock, are worth a small fortune."

The town folk were mostly Protestants whose ancestors had migrated from Scotland and parts of Ireland, whereas the country folk were Catholics whose grandparents had come from Germany and Czechoslovakia. Many of their last names had been Americanized long ago to make them pronounceable to the English tongue.

Whether they lived in town or the country, everyone had one thing in common, and that was to take care of their elderly and sick loved-ones in their own homes. There were no such things as nursing or care facilities. In fact there weren't even that many hospitals around the area, the nearest one being twenty miles away.

At the end of Maple Street stood a two-story Victorian house that had seen better days. Contrary to the norm, it was inhabited by a Catholic undertaker and his wife. Mr. and Mrs. Dollard, a dour couple whose personalities matched their trade better than characters in a Dickens novel, had settled in, more or less, thirty years ago and never talked to anyone about anything except funeral arrangements. When the Protestant undertaker died three years after their coming, the Dollards were the only ones in town who could put you under, and eventually the Protestants began to use them rather than taking their deceased to the next town. The Dollards made no distinctions. They wore the same glum faces for the Protestant funerals as they did for the Catholic ones.

Their background was a mystery. No one knew for sure where they came from or much of anything about them, because outside of funerals they always stayed to themselves. Sometimes the neighbors would hear them screaming at one another, but other than that no one could tell you a thing about them. Some said they'd heard of a daughter who had jumped off a bridge, and others said that this daughter had run off with a colored man and was living up north, raising kids of every color. Some thought there was a connection between them and Mayphelia, who had moved here with Radio Man just a few months after they had arrived.

Ten years ago, Mr. Dollard had fallen down the basement steps, broken all his ribs and died of punctured lungs. Mrs. Dollard embalmed and dressed him and conducted his funeral, which was very small. No daughter came but Mayphelia showed up which really got people to speculating. Mrs. Dollard took over the business and did as good a job as her husband even though she wasn't licensed. They had never taken much care of their home, considering it prideful to show off one's wealth, and after Mr. Dollard died, Mrs. Dollard completely let the house go to seed. The paint was chipped and peeling; the roof was leaking in several places; the yard had become a jungle of vines and dead things.

THE morning after the July 4th celebrations Grace was in her easy chair sewing buttons on a new maternity top for Regina. She heard a knock on the front door. This alarmed her somewhat. Everyone usually came around to the back door and into the kitchen with its long table and homey comfort. She peeked through the glass on her front door. There stood Father Gilbert. *Oh no, what was going on now? They hadn't forgotten to tithe, had they?*

"Good afternoon, Father. Please come in."

Grace quickly raised the shades in her living room. She kept them drawn so the sun wouldn't fade the lovely fabric on her nice couch and chairs used maybe a half dozen times a year.

"Good to see you again, Mrs. Wolansky. I just dropped by for a moment. I'm on my way to see Mr. Vincent, who's dying." He smiled as he took out a handkerchief and wiped sweat dripping from his forehead.

"Here, let me get you a drink of cold water. Or how about some lemonade? I just made it." Grace wondered what she had to do with Mr. Vincent's dying.

Father Gilbert followed her to the kitchen. He'd been their parish priest for a little over two years, yet Grace had hardly said two words to him before now. He seemed like a nice man, not at all superior acting like the ones who had been there before him.

"That would be very nice. It's been quite a morning."

"I'd heard Mr. Vincent was in a bad way but then, I guess at ninety-four that's to be expected." As soon as she finished the sentence, she chided herself and thought *that probably wasn't the right thing to say at such a time.* She handed the glass to the priest, who gulped it down in one long drink.

"The reason I'm here is that Mr. Vincent's daughter went by to see Mrs. Dollard about the funeral arrangements. The doctor said her dad won't last through the night, and she wanted to take care of everything ahead of time. The funeral home was locked up without a light on, and so she went over to the Dollard house and knocked and knocked and finally looked through the window and saw Mrs. Dollard slumped over in her reading chair."

"Is she alive?" Grace was a bit startled even though she hardly knew Mrs. Dollard except through church. She had taken a pot roast over when Mr. Dollard died and sat with her for a while at the kitchen table, but they didn't talk.

"She's had a massive stroke, but she's still living. The doctor says she was probably sittin' in that chair since last night." The priest paused. "She once told me about a daughter living in California and after looking through her things, I found a piece of paper with a scribbled name and phone number stuck in her Bible. I called and the person I got knew the daughter and gave me her number. Her name is Cecelia Dollard.

Father Gilbert cleared his throat before continuing, "She didn't seem to care at all, but after a while said she'd take a plane and be here around nine tonight. I was wondering if you'd mind sitting with Mrs. Dollard until she gets here."

The priest set the glass on the table. "She has no friends, you know, and she once told me that you were such a kind person. She would probably be comfortable with you. She can't talk, but she does seem to be conscious."

Grace removed her apron. "Well, I guess I can go over until then. I'll have to go to the field to get Bud. He can drive me in."

GRACE stepped over a rotted board and on to one that creaked so loudly she feared it would crumble at any moment. She quickly hopped to the board closest to the front door and questioned whether she should just walk in. The thought hadn't left her head before the door opened.

"I thought you'd get here sooner," said Lavenia Stockly, the biggest busybody in town.

"Come on in. Everything you need to know is written on that tablet by the kitchen sink. I just gave her a dose of pain killer. She's one hateful ole lady."

Grace took a breath and was about to speak, but Lavenia kept going.

"But I guess that's to be expected from someone whose only daughter has to be practically bribed into coming to take care of her own mother. I guess Father told you all about it. I swear lately Mrs. Dollard has been in the church every time the doors have opened, but she's never so much as said 'hello' to me. If I weren't such a good Catholic, I wouldn't have come over here."

Lavenia grabbed her purse and was out the door and skipping over the decaying steps. Grace hadn't said a word. With a slight smile she realized that Lavenia would now, more than likely, go tell everyone how Grace Wolansky wouldn't even talk to her. *"You don't give anyone a chance to say anything,"* she retorted in her head.

Grace paused as she looked beyond the small foyer into the front room, the parlor. She'd never been in this part of the house. It was dark, dusty and dreary with not one picture on the walls. Heavy wood-framed furniture upholstered in browns and faded creams seemed to pull the room down into an abyss. A lonely floor lamp with a yellowed torn shade leaned over a reading chair. The black wooden floors were dull and scratched. The whole atmosphere was eerie and, yes, even evil. Grace hurried for the kitchen, which was brighter since all the shades on the tall windows were rolled up.

She had no sooner entered the kitchen than she heard a thumping on the ceiling above her. Mrs. Dollard was signaling for help. Along the wall at the base of the stairs Grace found a light switch. A dim gray lit up the stairwell. She took a deep breath and started up. With each step she climbed the thumping seemed to get more demanding. She wished she had asked Bud to come with her, but he had dropped her off saying he was going to get a haircut.

When Grace opened the door, she was horrified and wanted to flee. Rank smells made her gag. A skeletal figure lay on the high four-poster bed. A gurgling noise resembling a curse erupted through a slack jaw. A brown stained sheet covered the legs. The left hand held a cane which struck the floor with amazing strength. A long grotesque crucifix hung over the bed. The mouth of the figure on the cross was wide open, screaming in terror. Grace had to avert her eyes. A huge scratched-up chiffonier stood against a side wall. The rest of the room was bare.

"Hello, Mrs. Dollard. It's me, Grace Wolansky. I've come to look after you until your daughter gets here."

A dreadful wheezing inhalation of air followed by a hacked cough came from the bedded form. As Grace came closer, she saw that Mrs. Dollard had messed herself. The sheets, her gown and half her body were covered in a brownish tar. Grace put her hands over her nose and mouth. Mrs. Dollard turned her eyes on her. The stare was empty yet menacing. Grace audibly gasped before pulling herself away to raise all four windows, hoping the stench would drift to the outside.

Grace addressed the crucifix out loud. "Lavenia is such a good Catholic yet she couldn't even air out this room." Immediately contrite, she reminded herself of Lavenia's services. She kept the church spotless and put fresh flowers on the main altar for Sunday's services. She had been every priest's faithful housekeeper since Grace was a teenager. Some said she had provided more for some of Father Gilbert's predecessors than hot meals and a clean house. Grace wouldn't repeat the gossip but she often thought about it.

Grace was now feeling nauseous and knew she would have to get help. She couldn't clean up Mrs. Dollard by herself. "I'm going to make you comfortable, Mrs. Dollard, but I have to call someone. I can't do this by myself." Mrs. Dollard closed her eyes and seemed to relax.

Grace decided she would call Bud's sister Pauline, an expert with the sick and elderly. Pauline had nursed both her in-laws through long illnesses. Grace hadn't even taken care of her own mother in her last days, a duty that customarily went to the oldest daughter. Regina had been a baby at the time, and Bud didn't want her taking on anything else. She was still quite fragile both mentally and physically. Rather forcefully Bud persuaded her oldest brother and his wife to take on this duty. They grudgingly agreed, but from then on they resented Grace for shirking her responsibilities and would have nothing to do with her or her family. "Good riddance" was all Bud would say on the matter.

Grace had barely hung up the phone when Pauline and Mrs. Carbon appeared at the front door. Grace wanted to hug them both. Mrs. Carbon had been quilting with Pauline when Grace called and had offered to come along.

Somehow they got through the ordeal of bathing Mrs. Dollard with Pauline and Mrs. Carbon doing most of the work. One held Mrs. Dollard while the other washed. They managed to turn over the mattress and put on a couple of layers of bottom sheets. Then Mrs. Carbon did the practical thing and took a couple of sheets, cut them up, and made diapers for Mrs. Dollard. The old woman glared at them the whole time as if she wanted to send them straight to hell. "Just don't look at her and keep on doing what you're doing," Pauline whispered.

Once the job was done and the room was aired out and Mrs. Dollard had fallen into a deep sleep, Pauline took the soiled gown and sheets out to the burning can in the back yard and put a match to them. "I'm not washing that filth."

Grace went to the bathroom and scrubbed her arms and hands until they were red. She couldn't keep from shaking all over. There was evil in this house. She hurriedly finished up and sprang for the stairs without so much as a glance into Mrs. Dollard's room.

She had just finished making a pot of coffee for everyone when Bud returned. She heard his knock and ran to the front door. She wanted to fling into his arms, but held herself back.

"Why, Gracie, what's wrong?" Bud asked, worried.

"This place scares me and that old woman scares me." She tried to conceal a whimper. Bud put his arms around her and saw Mrs. Carbon watching them from the hallway.

"Grace, that wasn't an easy thing we did today," she said kindly. "I best be getting back to the store. Mr. Carbon doesn't know where I am." She laughed before adding, "He'll be terrified I left him."

Pauline came into the room and greeted her brother. "Why don't you two go on home? I can stay till the daughter gets here."

Grace was embarrassed. Bud's family had her labeled as weak and helpless, especially since she'd had the breakdown. Perhaps they were right. After all, she almost fell apart this afternoon. Grace took a deep breath. "Pauline, thank you for your help, but I promised Father Gilbert I'd stay."

Pauline gave her a sideways look and picked up her purse. "Well, now that Bud's here, I guess I can leave."

CHAPTER EIGHT

Cecelia Dollard blew into town on a dry gale. Bobbling like a bottle on a gurgling stream, the plane swayed and tilted before dropping onto the runway in San Antonio. Cecelia inhaled deeply as she marched down the stairs to the tarmac. Yes, it still smelled like Texas, and with that thought a knot the size of a grapefruit suddenly formed in her stomach. On the plane, she calculated that it had been thirty years and four months since she'd set foot on this soil.

In the terminal someone called "Cecelia." She hadn't used that name in ages. Everyone in California and other parts knew her as Ceil. It took her a moment to realize she was the one being summoned. The voice belonged to Nelda Hart, the woman who had once saved her life and was now waving her handkerchief and calling over the crowd. Nelda's hair had gone almost completely grey and her waist had gotten thicker since her visit to California fifteen years ago.

Ceil couldn't hold back the tears as she hugged Nelda. What a wonderful woman this was, already in her white nurse's uniform, ready for the job. Nelda hadn't hesitated a moment when Ceil called and asked if she would take care of her dying mother, but she did balk at the amount of money Ceil said she would pay her. "Wait till you get on the job," Ceil had warned. "Remember you don't know her. You might be begging for more in a few days."

There was rain to the west but no rain on Maple Street, just high winds. Ceil parked Nelda's car by the falling down mailbox, turned off the lights and looked up at the dilapidated house. She shook her head. Her father had money socked away in every cranny, yet they had lived like this. Mr. Dollard had always been tighter than the bark on a tree. She smiled to think how horrified her parents would have been had they known how extravagantly she lived. The only money her father had ever spent on her was to hire a private detective to find her when she ran away.

"Well, you ready to face the music?" Nelda asked softly, somewhat apprehensively. Ceil took hold of her hand for comfort, the hand that had reached out to her, a terrified fifteen-year-old huddling in the doorway of a warehouse on that early June morning.

CECELIA had hopped the freight train in the middle of the night with the intention of riding all the way to California, a place too far to be found. It stopped in San Antonio so that the car she was in could be loaded with baled cotton. When the door rolled open two men in dirty railroad clothes tried to grab her. "You good-for-nothin' little bitch, wait till we get hold of you."

She dodged one, then the other and leapt off. They chased after her a hundred yards or so. Her long legs soon left them far behind. Once she stopped to catch her breath, she didn't know what to do next. She was no more than a hundred miles from where she'd started, the place she refused to call home. She'd die before going back. Her only option was to wait and hop another train the following night. With only the nine dollars and thirty-seven cents she'd stolen from her mother's purse, she was aware she might starve to death before getting out of Texas.

The eastern horizon blushed in pink just as Nelda walked towards her apartment after the night shift at the hospital. Grieving over her husband's death due to influenza, she wasn't paying attention to the morning sky or the sidewalk around her. Cecelia was dozing in a darkened doorway. A heel jabbed into her left calf. Terrified that the men had found her, she jerked back her legs and hopped up, ready to run or defend herself. She saw a woman as tall as she, only older, staring back at her in confusion. Finally in a soft voice, the woman said,

"I'm sorry. Did I hurt you?" These words, spoken so kindly and with so much concern, cracked a shield within Cecelia. A long wailing cry that she could no longer muffle came out in breaking staccatos. A far-off train whistle mimicked the desperate sounds.

Nelda led her away, not saying anything, just holding an arm around the girl as she cried and cried. Once they got to the apartment, Nelda ran a tub of hot water and helped her undress, grimacing at the swollen red lashes on her back. She helped her into the tub and before leaving the bathroom said, "I'll put some clean clothes out on the bed. We're about the same size. I'll prepare some breakfast and after we eat, we'll talk if you want to."

Cecilia told her everything. The only other person who knew as much about her was Mayphelia. Cecelia hated that she hadn't gotten word to Mayphelia that she was running away. It would have been too dangerous. Even though Mayphelia would be drawn and quartered before giving out any information, Cecilia knew all too well the depths of her father's violence.

The two years that Cecilia lived with Nelda came as an answer to Nelda's prayers. She had deeply mourned both her husband's death and the child who had never come. Now a beautiful fifteen-year-old who could pass as her daughter had been given to her.

Cecilia soon got a job clerking at a general store and within three months became the owner's number-one assistant. She had a natural gift for business. With Nelda's help, she enrolled in math and business courses at an evening school. She became fascinated with the knowledge that one could make money with money. Years later, she used this knowledge to further increase her wealth.

CEIL breathed deeply and started for the door. A gust of wind howled from around the house and thrust her back a step. A male voice from the screen door warned, "You'd best come around back. You could fall through them boards and the porch light's not working."

Ceil and Nelda trudged through the weeds and high grass around to the back. "Can you believe this place?" Ceil asked. "They've hidden away more money in shoeboxes than most people have in a lifetime, and yet this yard hasn't been mowed in ages." As a twig slapped her face all the old angers snapped within her.

Bud held the back screen door open. "This way, ladies," he said. "These steps are more secure, but don't lean on that left railing." They squinted into a plain kitchen, brightly lit by a naked bulb on a long cord dangling from the high ceiling. It reminded Ceil of a lynching photo she had seen in a magazine. *How apropos,* she thought.

"Hello, I'm Cecelia Dollard, but I go by Ceil now, and this is my friend, Nelda Hart. She'll be taking care of Mother." The word, mother, as she said it, sounded hollow and fake. She swallowed several times and wanted to ask for water, but didn't.

Bud and Grace murmured "Hello" and "Nice to meet you," and fell silent. Both were shocked. Cecelia, Ceil Dollard, was nothing like the daughter they'd expected. This woman was beautiful with fine even features set off by a crown of thick blonde hair tied back with a yellow silk scarf that accented deep blue eyes. She was tall, at least five feet ten inches, and stood straight with assurance and authority. Surely she didn't belong to Mr. and Mrs. Dollard. They were short, dark people with heavy features, coarse black hair and black eyes. Grace noted her attire set her apart, too. She wore beige linen slacks with a tan silk blouse and leather sandals. Since the war, women had begun wearing slacks, but not around here, and silk was a fabric rarely seen or worn in these parts. Cotton was the overall norm. *She's really out of place,* Grace thought, *yet she seems so relaxed.*

Finally, Bud cleared his throat and said, "I'm Bud Wolansky and this is my wife, Grace."

Ceil smiled warmly, "So glad to meet you. You are a handsome couple."

Bud and Grace averted their eyes, somewhat embarrassed. No one had ever said such a thing to them. Even though Grace thought Bud was handsome and he would tell her she was pretty, neither of them considered their looks as worthy of comment. The parents of their generation never mentioned a comely appearance for fear of creating vanity and false pride. In fact, Grace's father thought it was his duty to point out flaws in both appearance and character and to withhold all praise. A lack of confidence was seen as humility, a virtue. Bud was the first person who ever gave Grace a compliment. "You're the prettiest girl in this here lunchroom." For the next several weeks, those words ran through her mind thousands of times.

Their refreshing lack of self-absorption made Ceil immediately like them. Sensing the discomfort, she quickly continued, "Thank you so much for coming. The priest assured me all would be fine until I arrived."

Overhead, a soft knocking began, and then became more and more demanding. "She must have awakened," Grace said just above a whisper. The woman before her both fascinated and intimidated her.

"I'll go up." Nelda picked up her bag and began to leave.

Ceil raised her hand, "No, I want to see her first."

Bud and Grace gathered up their things and started out the back door. Grace turned back to Ceil, "If you need us for anything, we live off Gatlon Road, the second farm on the left. It's about five miles from here."

Feeling panicked, Ceil blurted out, "Do you know of any place around here where I could stay?" Bud and Grace stared at her. There were four large bedrooms upstairs. Ceil continued, "I...I don't know if I can sleep here and well, I didn't see any travel courts coming in."

Grace and Bud couldn't speak. Who wouldn't want to stay in the home of her parents? But then Grace remembered how she never wanted to spend the night at her parents' home either. "Well," Grace hesitated and looked over at Bud. "We now have extra bedrooms since our children are grown. I've turned one into a sewing room, but we still have two others."

Bud spoke up, "But we have company coming." His tone implied disapproval.

Grace looked at him, surprised. *Why would he make up such a thing?*

"Of course I understand." Ceil nervously twisted on a loose strand of hair. Grace looked at her and saw beyond the sophisticated woman in the fine clothes. A young frightened girl now stood before her. What must have happened?

Ignoring Bud's inexplicable comment, she spoke up. "Our company won't be coming for a while. If you have time, come by tomorrow and I can show you the rooms. I think we will be able to help you out until you find something permanent."

The hammering overhead was drowning out the conversation. Bud edged Grace towards the door and after some "goodnights" they disappeared into the darkness.

Agitated, Ceil turned to Nelda, "Please make a pot of coffee. I'll go up."

Ceil trudged her way up the stairs and towards the thumping room. She swung the door open. It was pitch black. The spiders began crawling up her legs. In a panic she called out, "Where's the damn light?"

The noise stopped and a low shuttering intake of air came from the bed. Ceil fumbled along the wall until she found the switch. The ugliness of the room jolted her. The cane started tapping quickly, fiercely.

Ceil walked over and gently but firmly pulled it away from the old woman's grasp. "You won't be needing this. I'll get you a soft bell. It will do better." Mrs. Dollard's eyes turned to her daughter and a couple of tears threaded through the wrinkles of her cheeks.

"Hello, Mother. You didn't think I'd come, did you? Funny, I still call you Mother, and I still refer to him as Father. I hope you can understand what I'm going to say to you. I've brought a nurse who will take good care of you. I can't do it. I want to forgive you, but I'm not able to. Just so you know, I turned out to be a big success, Mother. I own my own company and make more money than you can dream of. I know that would be the only thing about me that you and Father would approve of."

Ceil eased down to the foot of the bed and laughed. "But in defiance of you and him, I have spent as much of it as I possibly can. There's not a hoarding bone in my body. But no matter how much I spend, more keeps coming in. Just the opposite of what you two tried to drill into my head."

The distorted face turned towards her, and Ceil saw recognition and the question.

"No, I've never married, nor had any children, but I've had several love relationships, the sort you condemn. Remember the attic when Father walked in on me and Gwen and like the saintly woman you were, you stood by while Father beat me. I still have a couple of scars on my back. You want to see?"

She stood up and began taking off her blouse. A crying moan came from the bed. Ceil leaned over and looked more closely. "What? You don't want to see the marks your mean spirit has left?"

Her expression changed as she looked closely at her mother. "I can't believe it, but I do feel sad for you, whereas I feel nothing but hatred for him. Someone told me how he died. I hope it was a push and not a fall that landed him at the bottom of those stairs."

The figure on the bed gasped several times.

"Don't worry. I won't say a word to anyone. He deserved it. I can't imagine him stumbling, no matter how old he was. I remember how careful, how precise he was about everything. But it doesn't matter how it happened.

The good thing is that he's gone. I couldn't come to his funeral because of the spiders."

Ceil left the room, running down the stairs trying to hold back the tears of rage and regret. She called for Nelda to go up and grabbed her purse. Once on the back porch, she lit up a cigarette, pulling the smoke deep within as far as it would go.

Mrs. Dollard thrashed the parts of her body that would still move. Her darkness was everywhere. *How did this child know what had happened?*

IT had been a stormy afternoon inside and outside their house. He had found and torn up the last picture of Cecelia that she had hidden. He took the pieces out to the burning can and then came back to work on a casket down in the basement. After he opened the door he stood on the small landing to turn on the light. As he was about to take his first step down, she suddenly appeared in the doorway and called his name. He turned to face her. "This is for Rachel," she yelled jabbing the end of a dust mop squarely in the middle of his chest and shoving with all her strength.

She stepped forward and watched him fall backwards down the steep steps, head bumping the stair treads and legs and arms reaching out as if to grab hold of something. He landed with a loud thump as his legs flew over his head in a somersault. She watched him lie perfectly still, but then she heard a moan. She turned off the light and walked back into the hallway shutting the door and locking it. She pushed a heavy chair from the living room and secured it under the door's handle.

Back in the kitchen she made a fresh pot of coffee. With a hot cup in hand she sat down in the living room and gazed out the bay window, relishing every pain-filled curse, every scream for help and every threatening cry. She sat there for the better part of three days, not three hours as with Jesus on the cross, but three days. Finally, all sounds had stopped. She grasped the railing and descended the stairs, praying he'd be dead and not in a coma or hiding in a corner *to do unto her*. She found him under the casket, all crumpled and stiff with the lining he'd been sewing wrapped around him.

She began to laugh. "I forgot. It does get awfully cold down here. My only regret is that I didn't have the courage to do this long ago."

CHAPTER NINE

Ceil hardly slept the entire night. All the unsettling memories rode with the haunting wind that shook the bay window and rattled every loose board in the house. She lay on the parlor divan which Nelda had made into a bed for her. When she screamed, "I can't go upstairs again," Nelda understood. Still sleep completely evaded her. She smoked one cigarette after another and realized that if she kept up at this pace, her last pack wouldn't last the night.

Nelda had moved into the room next to Mrs. Dollard, a meager space with a single iron bed and a surplus army table. Ceil recalled seeing a furniture store on the main highway into town. She'd have Nelda's room painted and buy some lovely furniture for her. She deserved the best.

Finally Ceil gave up on sleep and decided to go through some of the downstairs closets. After all, she'd have to be cleaning out everything once her mother died, getting it ready to sell. The doctor had said she wouldn't last a week.

The hallway closet was the first one tackled. She knew it was a smart choice once she turned the knob and found it locked. She remembered her mother hanging the key chain just inside a cabinet door over the stove. It was still there with dozens of keys. Her father had believed in locking everything, especially his heart. Once she got the door open, she knew she'd hit pay dirt.

On the floor she found a crate of elegant bone china that was postmarked from England. It was still packed in fine straw and had never been used. Her mother must have wanted nice things all along and had somehow socked away enough money to buy something beautiful. A foggy sadness began to penetrate her body.

Then in the corner of the top shelf she uncovered a shoe box with winter boots. Each boot was stuffed to capacity with cash for a total of nine thousand dollars. In a topcoat, she ripped out five thousand dollars sewn into the lining. She could still see him sitting at the sewing machine making linings for coffins. "I wonder if he could have accidently buried some of his money with one of those bodies?" Her voice echoed through the large room and the shadows laughed at such a ludicrous comment. He was much too careful for that.

She rummaged through another hall closet and the kitchen pantry and ended up with twenty-one thousand for the night. And she hadn't even started on the upstairs or the basement. She dumped all the cash on the kitchen table, made a pot of coffee and lit a cigarette.

As she stared at the stack of bills, she began giggling uncontrollably. The absurdity of this money and the lack of sleep were making her delirious. Not wanting to disturb those upstairs, she shoved all the bills into a paper bag and went outside to the car. She unlocked the trunk and dropped the sack inside. She giggled, "Father, here I am locking it away. Just like you'd want?" Daylight was breaking. She dropped into the back seat and slept the sleep of the dead.

BY early afternoon Ceil set out for the farm off Gatlon Road. She had awoken that morning after three hours of sleep with the worst crick in her neck she ever remembered having. When she went into the kitchen Nelda laughed at the way her head was bent. "I saw you out there all twisted up, but decided to just let you go. You want some toast and coffee? I'm cooking some runny, runny oatmeal for your mom. Ugh!"

"Just a minute." Ceil hurried to the next room and came back carrying the crate of china.

"What's that?" Nelda looked over her shoulder.

"This is what my mother eats off of until her last meal." She unpacked the elegant dishes and set them on the counter. She jerked open the cabinet doors and grabbed all the plates, bowls, cups, saucers. Every one was old and cracked or old and chipped or old and stained. "No one will ever eat off these filthy things again."

They made an awful sound as Ceil smashed them into the huge trash barrel just outside the back door. Nelda watched her and mumbled, "She has many more dirty dishes to smash before her soul can rest." Oatmeal boiled over onto the stove.

After toast and coffee, Ceil had gone to the furniture store and bought two cherry wood Duncan Phyfe bedroom suites with gold leaf leather inlays. She then picked an overstuffed wide recliner chair for Nelda. She ended with buying a half-dozen framed prints of flowers and pastoral scenes for the walls.

The owner, Mr. Needhim, had no idea who this woman was but was overjoyed by her spending spree. When she took cash from a paper bag stuffed with bills, he thought she might be part of some bank-robbing gang like Bonny and Clyde. After all, she was wearing pants just like those women criminals, but he didn't care if she'd robbed the bank in the next town. He was making more money in one day than he ordinarily made in a month or more, with the exception of December. After the crops were in, the farmers usually let go of some of their money for Christmas.

Mr. Needhim had almost dropped his loose-fitting false teeth when Ceil told him to deliver everything to the Dollard house. He mumbled, "That old falling down Victorian house on Maple Street?"

She flashed a smile. "So you do know where it is?" she paused, "Oh, and remove all the furniture in every single room. I'll be back to replace the rest."

He was dumbstruck. "But I don't take old stuff. Don't know what to do with it." Ceil reached back in the paper sack, took out a crisp fifty-dollar bill and said, "I'm sure you can figure out something."

CEIL drove slowly. The dirt road was full of ruts from the rains. Nelda's old Ford sent a shock wave through her with each bump. This was nothing like riding in her brand new 1951 Packard on the paved roads of Los Angeles. She slowed down to a crawl. In the distance, she saw a tall black figure pacing along as if late for prayer meeting. The figure was wearing the tropical green and yellow turban Ceil remembered buying. "Oh my god, is that Mayphelia?"

She stopped the car, jumped out and started waving her hands. "Mayphelia, Mayphelia," she screamed.

Mayphelia stopped dead in her tracks, put her hand over her eyes to block the sun and began to jump up and down. Then she broke into a hobbled run with outstretched arms, a bag of herbs and tonics flopping on her shoulder. "My baby, my baby, my baby."

Ceil was sobbing out loud and running as fast as she could. The women collided; Ceil slipped and in an instant both had fallen to the ground, holding each other, crying and laughing.

Finally, Mayphelia sat up and said, "Let me look at you, sweet baby. My, my, you's done got to be a beautiful woman, but then it was always pointin' in that direction." They began talking over each other, covering an abridged version of the last thirty years and making up for the lack of letters. There had only been the packages and two short phone messages delivered by the daughter of Mayphelia's cousin who had a phone and lived in a nearby town.

"I was on my way to see Grace and Bud Wolansky." Ceil opened the car's trunk and found an old towel. She began wiping the mud off her dear friend's arms and legs.

"Bud and Grace? They's my closest neighbors, not more than a fourth mile from me. I guess you knowed that we moved here right after you runned off."

Ceil hugged her again. "I wanted to get word to you, but I was afraid he might hurt you."

"Oh, baby, don't you worry none about that. We always talked from here." She put one hand over Ceil's heart and the other over hers.

"I remember when you first told me that. I've talked to you that way all these years." Ceil wiped her eyes on her shirt tail.

"And I always heared you, baby girl."

Ceil smiled. "So you moved near here?"

"Me and Radio Man was blessed by Mr. Bud with an acre in the woods just off his main pasture."

Ceil let out another sob. "I'm so sorry I didn't come to his funeral. I was too scared they'd find out and ..."

Mayphelia hugged her again. "Like I said, we knowed each other's feelings and that's what counts. He had the beautifulest funeral ever. I can't tell ya how I done broke down when ole man Jimmy, 'member the colored undertaker, told me that everything was taken care of by some person in Los Angeles. Of course, I knowed it was you. And the flowers, dear lord, no one's ever seen so many flowers at a funeral. "

Ceil walked towards the car. "Well, he was like my daddy, you know, the only kind man I knew growing up. I always wished he was my daddy." Opening the passenger door, Ceil went on, "Come on, get in. I'll take you where you're going."

Mayphelia balked. "As long as the Spirit moves these legs, I ain't gonna misuse that power by bein' idle and ridin' in a car." Ceil smiled. She was still the same stubborn lovable woman.

"You knows you can, anytime, baby," Mayphelia said as her eyes pierced into Ceil.

"What? What are you talking about?" Ceil gasped

"You's wantin' to stay with me. Can't be in that house. Come over after you sees Grace." Mayphelia began walking in her long strides. "I's got ta go now to see a white woman with a spiteful cancer. Today she be needin' hep to get on with her dyin.' Her spirit be more than ready."

Ceil watched her speed down the dirt road on her skinny legs with the healing bag flapping on her back. *And she still has those powers,* Ceil thought.

Ceil drove on down the lane towards Grace and Bud's place. She couldn't help but smile, realizing she'd been right about them. The attractive sprawling farm house and all the barns were well kept and orderly. Gardens with flowers surrounded the house. She had found kindred souls, people who honored beauty.

Grace had gotten up early that morning quite excited, a new and rather unfamiliar feeling for her. Ceil fascinated her more than anyone she could remember. There was something about this exotic woman that she immediately liked. And she didn't feel the least bit inferior around her, even though she knew Ceil's world was totally different from hers.

The night before, Bud had been dead set against having "some stranger coming into our home." He went on, "There's something wrong when a child doesn't want to stay in their own home to help with a dying mother."

"You don't know the whole story, Bud," she shot back defensively in an outburst which surprised her as much as it did him. Why was she being so protective? Until yesterday, she hadn't even been aware of Cecelia Dollard's existence. Yet she related on a deep level to the frightened child twisting that strand of hair.

Bud continued as he undressed, "I don't like the idea of renting out a room. Doesn't Mrs. Snow at the laundromat rent out rooms? We already got renters and you know how that's going." Bud got in bed and turned off the light.

"Bud," Grace said in her usual soft tone, "You know that's different. That's our daughter and her family, and she tries to pay when she can."

"Yeah, no thanks to that husband of hers." Bud reached over and kissed her and then turned his back to her. Soon she heard his deep breathing and knew he was sound asleep. She would give anything if she could go to sleep like that.

IT was true that Regina and Billy Wayne lived almost rent free in the Wolansky's Sunday house. Bud's grandfather built it long before there were cars. Back then, most of the farmers owned smaller houses in town. On Saturdays the families would come to town to trade, get groceries and store goods and then would spend the night so they could attend Sunday-morning services, thus the name Sunday house. Bud's parents moved there when they got too old for the farm and lived there until their deaths. They died within fourteen months of one another. Everyone knew that would happen. They were simply too close.

Regina and Billy Wayne moved in right after Bud's mother died and only a month after their marriage. Billy Wayne had rented a country shack and Regina's grandfather couldn't bear to see her living like that. She had always been his favorite.

When she was little he would sit through hours of her home dance recitals. After everyone else in the family had grown tired and left, he would still be there in a straight backed chair, clapping for every little routine she did. After his beloved wife died, he wanted Regina near him. She was a lot like her grandmother. He insisted they move in with him which thrilled Billy Wayne, who had never lived in such a fine home.

Regina adored her grandfather and took loving care of him as his health declined and Angie grew in her stomach. He promised he wouldn't leave until after he had held her baby, and kept his promise, living nine months after Angie was born. He had two other great-grandchildren from Pauline's son, but he felt an added affection for this tiny girl. He could soothe baby Angie better than anyone, even when she had colic. As soon as Angie was put in her great-grandfather's arms, she would snuggle up to him and go to sleep.

When Regina brought up the subject of paying rent, Billy Wayne would get angry, "What you talkin' about? He owes us money. Here you're cookin' for him, cleanin' up after him, takin' care of him." He paused long enough to catch his breath. "If it weren't for us, he'd be long dead. He should be paying us and not the other way around." Regina couldn't understand such cruelty. The way she had been raised, people took care of their loved ones without expecting anything in return.

When Bud and Grace inherited the little Sunday house they continued to let Regina and Billy Wayne live there, but with a condition. Bud believed that able- bodied people should pay their own way. The best way to build character in children was to make them responsible for their own lives. He took Billy Wayne aside and told him the rent would be due the first of every month. Billy Wayne agreed to the terms, then went home and yelled at Regina for nearly an hour about what a sorry, money-grubbing son-of-a-bitch her dad was. Every month Regina cut corners and scraped together what she could to give to her dad.

IN the living room Grace tied back the drapes and pulled up the shades. Everything got a thorough dusting even though it didn't need it. She gathered up three bouquets from the garden and placed them at welcoming spots in the living and dining rooms. Today, she would serve tea or coffee in the formal dining room, and they would sit in the front room.

Then Grace went to her room, put on a fresh dress, the latest one she had made, took care with her hair and even added a little make-up to her face, something she never did during the week. "Why am I getting so worked up over a stranger?" she asked the person in the mirror.

Grace was shocked when she saw Ceil get out of the car. She had mud on her slacks and blouse. Her hair was a mess, falling loosely over her shoulders. However, Grace admired how confidently she walked up to the door as if all were perfect. When Grace opened the door, Ceil smiled and said, "Yes, I know I look dreadful. On the road I ran into your neighbor, Mayphelia. I was going to look her up today and then, there she was."

Grace's confused look prompted Ceil to continue, "In the excitement, we slipped and fell onto the muddy road. Do you have a pump or someplace I can clean up before coming into your lovely home?"

Things were not going at all the way Grace had planned. They were supposed to enter the parlor and sit on the hardly-ever-used sofa or wingback chairs, admire the floral arrangements and sip coffee from the tiny cups and matching bread plates of her Sunday china using the lacy napkins she rarely used even with her family

"There's a wash basin and hydrant on the back porch. If you'll go around, I'll bring you some soap."

Ceil acted as if it were the most natural thing in the world to wash up on a back porch in the middle of summer on a farm in Texas. Grace brought her a washcloth, towel and bar of soap.

"If you'd feel okay, I can give you a robe and you can take those things off and I'll rinse them out. In this heat they will dry in no time," Grace offered.

"That would be the most practical thing, wouldn't it?" Ceil laughed.

Grace hurried to get the summer housecoat she had just washed. On her return, she was once again shocked. Ceil was standing next to the basin in black lace panties and matching bra. Grace turned her head and stood at arm's length to extend the robe to her, then quickly grabbed up the slacks and blouse and hurried into the kitchen. As she was running the water Ceil came in, "Oh no, I can do that. Please." Grace's robe was more than two inches above Ceil's knees. Yet this didn't seem to bother her either. Grace had never known anyone so at ease with herself.

Once the clothes were on the line, Grace picked up a pot of coffee and a plate of kolaches. "We can go to the dining room. "

Ceil said, "Oh, do you mind if we stay in here?" Ceil asked looking around. "It's such a warm, pretty room. I can sense the good times."

"I…I guess. I had just thought I'd show off my living and dining rooms. We hardly ever use them except on holidays. Everyone always ends up in here." Grace put the food down on the family table with its scratches and marks, mementos left by her three children.

Seeing her disappointment, Ceil changed her mind. "Oh, let's go fancy. After all, I'm dressed for something formal." Her laughter thrilled Grace. It was authentic and spontaneous.

Ceil walked from the dining room to the living room and looked around, noticing everything. "You have a talent, Grace. Like your kitchen, this is lovely. You're artistic." Grace felt her knees grow weak. No one, not once, had ever said such a wonderful thing to her. She realized she'd been longing for words like these all her life.

Ceil took a bite. "Oh my, these kolaches are wonderful. Is there anything you don't do well?" Grace tried not to giggle with glee.

She thought for a moment and blurted out, "Yes, sometimes I don't do living well."

As soon as the comment was out of her mouth, she was mortified. She had never said anything so silly, so revealing to anyone. Ceil's clear blue eyes seemed to look through her and into her soul and say, *I understand.* Grace wanted to weep, but instead she got up and adjusted one of the sofa pillows Andy had given her for Christmas.

Her nervous system was being strained. She suddenly felt she needed distance. She wanted Ceil to leave, to get away from her and her family. The ghost of impending danger was hiding in a corner. They continued to drink coffee in silence. Ceil cleared her throat. "I suppose my clothes are dry? Mayphelia is expecting me in a bit. I'll be staying with her."

"Of course," Grace tried to conceal her disappointment. She had imagined a very different sort of day. "How is it you know Mayphelia, if you don't mind telling me?"

Her tension was easing off. Grace offered and then refilled their cups. Ceil tapped the table with her clear well manicured nails. "Let's see. While growing up May-May was more of a mama to me than the woman dying on Maple Street. She began taking care of me from the time I was born. She worked for my parents and I stayed with her and Radio Man as much as I could when I was a child. That was before everyone moved here."

Grace was curious but didn't want to make Ceil uncomfortable. Intuiting her desire to know more, Ceil continued. "May-May and Radio Man protected me, you see. After my folks moved here, I lived in that house on Maple

Street only three weeks. I wasn't sure if or when May-May and Radio Man would move here." Unable to go on, she stopped abruptly and looked towards the window where a soft breeze was blowing into a crease of the drape, a stirring motion bringing up a tainted past.

Grace could tell Ceil didn't want to go on and squelched all the questions bubbling up in her mind. She picked up the coffee pot and headed for the kitchen. "I'll get your clothes," she said. Grace wanted her to stay, but knew that their time was up. She hoped she would see her again.

CHAPTER TEN

A week passed and then another, but Mrs. Dollard kept on living as if to spite the world. Ceil had had a hospital bed delivered to make Nelda's job easier. Then, on Grace's recommendation she'd hired Clem's oldest daughter, Lizzie, to come every day to clean the house, wash clothes, and do some of the cooking. She had hired several crews to refurbish the inside of the house, but they needed work and couldn't wait for Mrs. Dollard to die.

A roofing company from San Antonio with a crew of six had installed a new roof in the record time of one and a half days. Ceil had offered doubled wages to get the job done quickly; however, Mrs. Dollard didn't seem to be bothered by the constant hammering. Nelda, on the other hand, complained of a throbbing headache for two days.

Finally Nelda told Ceil, "I'm no longer a young woman with inexhaustible energy. I have to have some time off every now and then."

Ceil smoked one cigarette after another wondering what she would do. She could make and dole out money, and that was all. She didn't know how to give care and, furthermore, she didn't want to care for the woman upstairs. Even though Mayphelia, Radio Man and Nelda had shown her love and nurturing in her younger years, those instincts remained foreign to her.

When Margaret, her companion for over twenty years and her first true love, became ill with cancer, she could hardly bear to sit by her bedside. While Margaret's niece held and assisted her through the dying process, Ceil sat in the next room curled up in a ball on the lounger, frozen, unable to move. The guilt she felt afterwards almost drove her to suicide.

As a child she had always run to Mayphelia's for help. Now she did the same. "I can't take care of her, May-May. I just can't." Mayphelia knew about the spiders and the awful fears. Hadn't she sat up many nights and held her little white baby girl while she screamed in terror? Mayphelia understood that Ceil's spirit had journeyed through all the darkness she could handle in this lifetime. And so she agreed to help when Nelda needed time off even though she knew that Mrs. Dollard hated her intensely.

Ceil spent some nights at Mayphelia's and then some in Angela's old room. Grace insisted and Bud gave in. However, Ceil accepted only after Grace's fourth invitation. She sensed Bud's initial unease around her so she never stayed more than two nights at a time. Bud wouldn't admit it, but he was resentful. Ceil brought out a side of his wife he hardly knew. Grace became youthful and even jovial whenever this stranger came around and then would revert back to a serious, reserved person when alone with him. *"I've cared for and loved her all these years with all my heart, but I can't light up her face the way that outsider can,"* he told his cows as he untied the bale of hay they were waiting for. *"It's fun, though ,to see her all excited."*

Ceil was becoming the closest girlfriend Grace had ever had. She had never felt close to anyone, not school friends, neighbor friends or church friends. She was close to Bud but there were ideas and emotions she couldn't share with him, yet she wasn't all that concerned about it. Grace reasoned *that's just how it is between men and women, even married ones. Besides Bud and I share more than most of the couples I know.*

Before Ceil entered her life, she'd always thought that something might be wrong with her. Now she felt that perhaps she was like everyone else. Here was a woman friend with whom she could talk and share in greater detail than she thought possible. She was able to tell Ceil about Peter and her long dark night, a subject that haunted her so much she had kept the lid tightly clamped on it. However, with Ceil she'd lifted the cover off the pot and released the steam of guilt, hurt and sadness.

She had never spoken against her parents except to Bud, yet she told Ceil all about her alcoholic, abusive father and her weak, frightened mother. She told her about Regina and her nightmare life, and how she regretted that her granddaughters would also have to grow up like her with an alcoholic father. She talked about Andy and his freedom, and about Angela and her goodness. For the first time in her life, Grace had no secrets. In return, Ceil shared parts but not all of her life with Grace.

Most importantly they brought out the little girl in one another. Neither had been given much of a chance to play or to be carefree children. One day they spent several hours picking the last of the peaches, racing around to see who could get the most, tossing rotten peaches at each other, screaming and giggling. This letting-go and being silly for the sake of silliness was a new experience for each of them.

The basket of peaches sat on the table. Grace looked at them and decided she'd had enough canning for one season. "Let's make cobblers for everyone, Mayphelia, Nelda, Regina, Father Gilbert..."

"Stop!" Ceil interrupted. "You'll be making them alone. I barely know how to boil water."

"Well, there's no time like the present." Grace began getting out mixing bowls, flour, sugar and other ingredients. From across the table, she tossed an apron at Ceil and laughed as she watched this head of a corporation furrow her brow over the complications of bib and ties.

Ceil excused herself, "I prefer to keep any cooking skills I might have in the dark, in the closet."

Grace's mind flashed back to Sister Damien's scolding in third grade. Eight-year-old Grace was drawing a field full of flowers instead of doing her multiplication tables. *"You think doodling foolishness takes the place of arithmetic."* Sister took her drawing and threw it in the trash. *"Don't let me see such a waste of time again."* Since that time, Grace had more or less kept her drawings in the dark, the darkness at the back of her closet.

Over the years, Bud and the children had grown accustomed to times when she would close herself off in a room and "doodle" for hours, but she never showed them anything she did. Bud would tell the children to "let her be" when she went away like that. He knew her sketching had helped over the years to pull her out of the dark places, a little like his love of fishing had done for him.

Grace hurried from the room. "I've got something I want to show you." In the closet, she rifled through the box of drawings and sketches. Nervous and excited, she rushed back and spread out her favorite ones on the table.

Ceil glanced over them and then took her time as she studied each drawing, totally absorbed. Grace's heart beat faster. *What is she thinking?* Finally Ceil looked up and said softly, "Did you draw these?" Grace was tempted to shake her head *no.* It could be dangerous to reveal too much even to someone like Ceil. She fought an impulse to gather them up and put them back into the darkness. Sister Damien shouted, *"Put that nonsense away."*

"These are wonderful, Grace, simply wonderful. I've seen lots of art, been in many museums and galleries from New York to Paris to Madrid. These pieces touch my heart and soul as some of the greats have."

Ceil took her hand. "My friend, you are an artist." Grace felt weak and sank into the nearest chair.

AS the days passed, Ceil was learning to enjoy small-town living, something she never thought she could do. Before, smallness had always been too confining, too restrictive. But now with her parents more or less gone, she could enjoy the easygoing style. She loved to walk the pasture between Mayphelia's place and Grace's. May-May was teaching her how to "jest be easy." One night while they sat on May-May's porch, Mayphelia smoking her corncob pipe and Ceil her Camel, listening to the crickets and a distant owl, Ceil whispered, "I still see the spiders."

"I knows, child. I knows. You may sees them the rest of yo'r life, but you can take away that power they has over you. You gonna have to let go of dat hatred. Only then will the hurt stop." She blew out a long puff of smoke. "Make peace with yo'r granmaw. Yes, granmaw. It's time to stop calling 'em Mother and Father, even though they be poundin it in yo'r head so much you still calls 'em dat."

Ceil bit her lip. "I looked up my real father about ten years ago. He lives in the north tip of New York State. He had no idea I existed. He said that Father, I mean, Grandfather, reported him to the sheriff when he came back to get Mama. He was upset because my mama never wrote him."

"Lord, child, theys wouldn't let her out of the house for the longest, and then she was scared to death of yo'r granddaddy and rightfully so. I'm so glad you found 'im. He was the best looking white man I'd ever set eyes on. And he was crazy 'bout yo'r mama. She was as sweet as first corn. They love was good. You were begun in love, child."

Mayphelia leaned back in her rocker and closed her eyes in thought. "Makes me think of Radio Man. I misses him all the time and all 'is lovin'. I still gets all fluttery down there, just thinkin' of it." She threw back her head with an erotic moan.

Ceil laughed and shook her head. "Why, you're a dirty old woman, ain't ya? Stubborn and dirty."

Mayphelia poured them another glass of lemonade laced with her home brew. "You's right about dat."

Mayphelia stared across the pasture into the woods and remembered.

THE sobbing thirteen-year-old Cecelia bursting through the door and falling on the floor screaming, "How can parents hate their own child so much?"

Mayphelia had picked her up and decided then that this child needed to know the truth about her origins. She began, "Honey, they ain't yo'r parents. Yo'r real mama was adopted by them."

The young girl controlled her sobs to listen. She picked up the hem of her skirt, dried her eyes and blew her nose. She blurted out triumphantly, "I just knew in my heart they wasn't. I halfway remember some things. A young pretty lady with long blonde hair. Is that right?"

"That's right, baby. She had pretty hair like yours and it was long. I got a picture." Mayphelia opened her herb cabinet and from under some bags of medicines retrieved a small photo. "This was her last school picture."

The girl tentatively held it by the edges like it was a priceless treasure. Then she gently brushed the face with an index finger. "I look like her."

"The spittin' image," Mayphelia whispered.

"Can I have it?"

Mayphelia handed her the photo envelope, "I's been savin' it for years jest for you."

"What happened to her?"

Mayphelia sat down in her large stuffed chair and braced herself to tell the girl the whole ugly tale. "Come here and sits by me."

Cecelia nestled into Mayphelia's arms. "I was about twelve when I's started working for yo'r grandmaw and grandpaw. Everyone was afraid to work for 'em cause they had dat funeral home on the first floor and all the girls my age was afraid of spooks. But me, I didn't pay no attention to 'em cause I knowed even then I had the power over such stuff."

The tall gangly Cecelia nestled her head against May-May's bosom and stretched her legs across the little room. "Miz Dollard, yo'r grandmaw, never could get no baby in her tummy, so she goes to New York to a Catholic orphanage and adopted this little baby girl, yo'r real mama. She brought her home and right away, Mr. Dollard took a dislikin' to her cause she didn't look a thing like them. When he looked at her papers and saw she was Irish, he had a wall-eyed fit. But Miz Dollard refused to take yo'r mama back to New Yo'rk, sayin' that she was her baby no matter what. She baptize her with the name Rachel Cecelia. As the years went on, yo'r grandpaw let up some and began to treat her half-ways decent, but she suffered near as much as you. Now you's bein' there every day and lookin' so much like her is always remindin' him of what he did."

Mayphelia stroked the girl's back as she continued. "When yo'r mama was sixteen, a railroad crew came into town layin' out railroad ties puttin' in the railroad. They was young men, Irish mostly, from the north. One young man, tall, blond, handsome as anyone ever did see, named Timmy, was on that crew. Yo'r mama caught his eye while she was walkin' home from school. As soon as they eyes met, they was bit, and they came to sneakin' off and hidin' out in old barns and even an ole country church 'bout to fall down."

Mayphelia worried if she should go on. The thirteen year old who had already come into her womanhood was looking at her with such pitiful, wanting-to-know eyes. Mayphelia knew she had to tell the whole story. "After some weeks, the crew moved on to the next town and still yo'r mama and daddy did meet half ways, but before long, the towns were too far apart to run to or away from.

"Yo'r por little mama sort of lost her way then. She stopped going to school and the whippin's increased. Yo'r grandmaw tried to stop him, but then he'd turn on her too. Then one day when he grabbed yo'r mama's arm and yanked her out of the chair at the kitchen table, he saw her belly getting' big. He almost kilt her that night. I left out the back door runnin' across the field to get Radio Man. When we got back, yo'r grandmaw was holdin' a kitchen knife up to yo'r grandpaw's throat. Yo'r mama was in a heap on the floor. Radio Man and me took her home and nursed her back to health, and I knowed sure enough you was in there, and so I's started lovin' you then, cuppin' you in my hands while you was still a little fish in yo'r mama. One good thing was yo'r grandpaw was scared of Radio Man and never set foot near our place."

Not able to take any more, Cecelia jumped up and stomped the floor, "I'm gonna kill him, May-May. I swear to God, I'm gonna kill him."

"Hush, child, you ain't gonna do no such thing. He'll get his. Don't worry. It's already started. Watch how he always be lookin' around and fidgetin' – the demons are on 'im already. I bet he don't sleep more than an hour or so a night."

Cecelia puckered her lip, "Yeah, I've heard him hollering out at night. Did my mama die from a beating?"

Mayphelia took a deep breath and got up to get her clay goddess and the purple stone. "I wants you to holds this stone as I tells you the rest." Mayphelia pulled Cecelia back onto her lap and held the goddess over her heart.

"Yo'r mama pretty much stayed with us till you was born. I delivered you right on Radio Man's and mines bed. When you was born a light went on in yo'r mama. She held you for hours at a time, let you sleep right next to her, and kissed you all over all the time. But then with time she got to thinkin' about yo'r daddy, and she got restless and wanted to go lookin' for 'im. A friend done told her he'd come back lookin' fo her months before, but the sheriff run 'im off cause yo'r grandpaw told 'im to."

Mayphelia had to pause and take a deep breath. "Finally yo'r mama set up her mind to go find him. On that morning, she got up and put on two of everythin'– two pairs of underpants, underclothes and two dresses. She couldn't leave there with a bag of anything. She made me promise that I'd take care of you till she got back to git you. I knowed she'd be sneakin' off any minutes, but I didn't know exactly when. I figured it'd be that night. So in the afternoon, I was out on the back porch doin' the washin' and you was right under my feet playing with an old spoon and pot, just bangin' away.

"I was mighty nervous. I couldn't pay no attention to the clothes. Suddenly, I heared an awful ruckus upstairs, yo'r mama screamin' and yo'r grampaw yellin'. Then there was a breaking glass and a loud plop in the yard. Your grandmaw came runnin' out saying, 'He done it. God have mercy, he done it.'"

"I grabbed you up and headed around the house followin' yo'r grandmaw. As I passed dat corner, I froze dead and dropped to my knees as weak as a newborn kitten. There was yo'r mama layin' face up on a pile of stones brought over the day before to build a new wellhouse. She wasn't a movin' at all with blood all 'round her head. She gave up her spirit in a flash. I looks up and I sees your grandpaw standin' by the broken-out window in her room. He was hangin' on the curtain, blubbering, 'She just jumped, she just jumped.'"

"Now everybody know a person don't just goes and jumps through a closed-up window. I had done forgot that you had crawled out o' my arms when you went to screamin' and pointin.' What's yous was pointin' at was hundreds of spiders crawling up yo'r mama's legs. The fall had disturbed a ripe nest and they was crawlin' and crawlin.' I covered your face and ran all the way home. Radio Man rocked you all night long."

CEIL was shaking her shoulder. "Mayphelia, Mayphelia, What's wrong?" Mayphelia came back to the grown-up Cecelia sitting next to her, shaking her, and still seeing them goddamn spiders.

"God, you scared me. I thought you'd had a stroke," Ceil said.

Mayphelia laughed briefly. "No, honey. I was just off to a time when I told ya who ya was. It was a sad time. Now, bout yo'r daddy, do ya still sees him?" Mayphelia stretched out her tired back.

"He has a family up there and has asked me to come for Christmas several times, but I haven't. He writes every now and then and I write back. It's hard to go back." Ceil took off her blouse. "It's so damn hot out here and not a breath of air stirring. I'm going to get you some fans."

"Listen, child, make peace with yo'r grandmaw. It's what yo'r soul needs. She's not goin' till you do it. And stop thinkin' or sayin' theys yo'r mother and father."

Mayphelia paused and took a few puffs before going on, "She was weak, no question 'bout dat, but Lord knows she longed to do better and now the years and the rememberings has crippled her soul and her mind and her body. She be livin' in darkness and only you kin take her outta there."

"She never took up for me," Ceil muttered on the verge of tears.

Mayphelia nodded. "She be trying at first, but then she just got broke down."

CHAPTER ELEVEN

Billy Wayne had been working at the Dollard place for weeks now. After he had broken his ankle he tried to find work, but no one wanted him. Even Bud, his own father in-law, said he didn't have anything, then turned around and hired Clem's son, Donny, to help with the hay baling.

Then as luck would have it Regina got it in her head she had to go see her mother. Since she was about to start crying again and he wasn't working anyway, he agreed to take her and the girls out there. A tall good-looking blonde woman, wearing trousers, greeted them at the back door.

"Hello, I'm Ceil, and you must be Billy Wayne and Regina and these beauties are Angie and Tessie."

Billy Wayne was about to speak when Grace walked into the room. Regina began blabbing, "Oh Mama, Billy Wayne can't find work anywhere and we're just about out of everything."

Billy Wayne wanted to hit her for talking about their business, especially in front of this stranger they'd just met. He saw Grace glance at him with that dirt-on-my shoes look. Billy Wayne started for the door, "Regina, we'd best leave now. Come on. girls."

Angie ran to Grace. "I want to stay with Grandma."

Before Grace could respond, the woman spoke up, "Billy Wayne, do you think you could manage to clean up a yard and paint a house with that foot?"

Billy Wayne stopped abruptly and looked as if he didn't quite understand the question. "I sure can. Paintin' and yard work won't bother this ankle."

"Okay, be at the Dollard house at seven in the morning. You're hired."

Billy Wayne couldn't believe this turn-around with fortune. The smoldering anger vanished immediately. "Well, Regina, if you and the girls want to stay for a while, I can come back this afternoon." He walked with a jaunt in his good leg. "Oh, and thank you, ma'am. I'll be there at seven sharp."

The Dollard yard was so overgrown that it took him almost a week just to clear it out. Then he started planting bushes and trees and putting in flower beds. Ceil wanted him to repair and paint the outside of the house after that. She aimed to have if ready to sell as soon as possible after her grandmother died.

One day Ceil and Mayphelia were out working in the flower beds showing him where to plant the various bushes and flowers. "May-May, you know I don't have to sell this place. It can be yours, just say the word."

Billy Wayne almost dropped his shovel. *A colored living in a nice house like this? Whoever heard of such a thing?*

Mayphelia stood up straight and began to laugh. "Girl, you got a head on dem shoulders? I won't be lastin a day if I dares live up here in the middle of all these white folk. Besides it's too fancy for my tastes."

Billy Wayne breathed a sigh of relief. *I guess that ole gal ain't as ignorant as most of 'em. The Klan would have a field day if she decided to live here.*

Billy Wayne enjoyed working without a boss standing over him or warning him about coming in drunk or hung-over. Ceil offered him one price for the yard and then another for the house. Since he wasn't working by the hour, he could go as fast or as slow as he wanted. Plus he could go out to the shed whenever he felt like it and have a drink.

One morning he was filling a glass of water at the kitchen sink when Nelda pulled out four hundred dollars from an old dented kettle in the back of the cabinet. Ceil chuckled and said, "Finders keepers." Nelda objected but Ceil told her to consider it as part of her salary. Billy Wayne figured that ole man Dollard may have cubby-holed money outside the house, so he began making more frequent trips to the various sheds, digging around while sipping moonshine.

The only thing he really liked about Ceil was that she had lots of money. As a woman, she was way too bossy and sure of herself for his tastes. *Some man needs to take her down a peg or two.* Yet he had to admit that Ceil was more than fair, paying him a good wage, and he was determined to stay on her good side, be respectful and not tell her to go to hell when she issued orders. He reckoned if he toed the line he could have work for several months and by then his foot would be more than ready for the quarry.

Then one day Nelda told Ceil, "I don't like him coming into the house. He looks all around like he's sizing things up. Usually he smells of liquor, too." She finished folding the cup towel and faced Ceil with a single-minded look. "I don't trust him as far as I could throw him and I don't feel safe around him."

Ceil respected Nelda's intuition. "Okay, from now on, keep the doors locked."

She went outside and found Billy Wayne scraping the old paint off the house. "Billy Wayne, from now on Nelda will put a water cooler on the back porch for you, and I'd like for you to use the toilet at the filling station down the block. It's a job keeping everything inside clean and your shoes often track in dirt."

Billy Wayne knew that bitch Nelda had put her up to this. He'd seen her watching him like he was a bug under a glass. He couldn't even try to defend himself because the Ceil bitch who thought women were the same as men would probably fire him.

As soon as Ceil was back in the house, Billy Wayne went behind the shed and peed all over the wall. "You got another think comin' if you think I'm walkin' all that ways to relieve myself," he said out loud to the birds on the overhead branch. "I'll even shit back here if I feel like it."

A week later he was rummaging around inside the shed looking for clippers when he came across three hundred and eighty-two dollars stuffed into a dirty jar. That was more money than he'd ever seen at one time. He sang out, "She said 'Finders, keepers.'" He hopped in a circle on the dirt floor until a pain shot up his leg. "Damn, I'm gonna re-break this thing if I'm not careful."

He stuffed the money in his pocket. "And I ain't tellin' her about this, neither. Serves her right, agreein' that I'm too dirty to come in the house." He tore through the other jars and cans on the counter, then continued searching. Just as he grabbed fifty dollars hidden in an old tire he felt fire streaking up his arm. A scorpion had stung his thumb. He realized he'd been in the shed for well over an hour. "I can't blow this job now. I'll spend some time lookin' every day." Besides the shed, there was the garage with a storage room to its side, both crammed full of junk. Billy

Wayne figured he'd be a rich man before this job was finished.

He left an hour early that day and noticed the old busybody, Nelda, watching him from an upstairs window. He had to be careful around her. She had them creepy see through-you eyes like that black bitch. *She may see all this money in my pocket.* He quickly hobbled to his pickup and drove off in a cloud of dust.

His good mood took a slight turn when he got home and found Mayphelia in his kitchen cooking up some foul-smelling brew for his wife. Regina was probably faking it again. He was so tired of her being sick and looking like a half-dead calf. She had to spend two nights at her mama's just a few days ago because she couldn't get out of bed. It made him furious that she wasn't getting any bigger like she did with the other two. He knew this black witch was helping her kill his son. She'd hardly eat anything and when she did, she'd throw it all back up. The night before he had confronted her. "You're doin' your best to starve him to death, ain't you?" She just turned her back on him and didn't say a word.

But now he knew his luck had changed and so to hell with both of these women. His pockets were heavy and he wanted to get out and start spending his wealth. He walked past Mayphelia and Regina without so much as a hello.

His daughters were playing on the floor with new toys Andy's whore had sent. He got down on his knees. "Come here and let me give you girls a bear hug." Angie and Tessie shrank back. "Come on, now. Your daddy wants to love you." They slowly scooted towards him as if he were a stranger. As he put his arms around them, they slowly returned his embraces. *Damn that Regina, she's turnin' my girls against me.* Never did he consider they might be afraid of him because of the way he treated their mama.

He went down the hallway and into the bedroom. Thirty minutes later he came out all cleaned up, dressed in his good khakis and white shirt. He muttered, "I'll be home late tonight. Got a meetin' and some business." He slammed the back screen door behind him.

He had stopped catting around and had been a regular family man for several weeks now. But with Regina always being sick, always turning away from him and never looking at him, he needed to be with someone who appreciated him, so tonight he was off to Gallester County to see Geraldine. He was going to get some good whiskey, the store-bought kind, take Geraldine out to that nice diner over in Leary, and maybe take in a game of cards over at Jodi's. For the first time in a long time, he would have some fun. If he didn't get back till sometime tomorrow, then that's when he'd get back. Why would Ceil care as long as he got the job done? He'd work a good ten hours this coming Saturday.

CHAPTER TWELVE

Alone in the chapel Sister Mary Grace gazed up at the statue of Mary. She tried to pray but the words weren't coming. She was so homesick she could hardly breathe. She wanted to be with her mom cutting out cookies at the kitchen table, with her dad feeding calves at the barn, with Andy laughing and joking. But above all, she wanted to be with her little sister, helping her get through this pregnancy.

Regina's most recent letter shocked Sister Mary Grace to the core. Regina confessed to her what Billy Wayne had done. The rape was horrible but the worst part was that Regina had blamed herself all these years for what had happened. Sister Mary Grace cringed at the memories of her own judgments. She had been so embarrassed when Regina had to get married and had often felt superior to her. She had given Regina a good scolding for having "trash" magazines hidden under her mattress. "You're going to ruin your mind reading such stuff." What Sister Mary Grace had called a trash magazine had opened the window and let in the sunlight for her sister.

I guess God can speak through anything, she thought and then whispered to the smiling Mary, "My little sister couldn't tell me what had happened not only because she thought she was responsible but also because I always acted so holy, so righteous around her."

She paused, wondering if she really wanted this life, away from the world. She looked up at the statue. "Why do such terrible things happen to the innocent ones?"

AFTER Sunday-morning chores the novices received their weekly mail. As Sister Mary Grace read Regina's letter, she had begun to cry. The words cut through her heart. *"I don't know what I've done to deserve this life. All the music is gone out of my life and I can no longer dance."*

The superior, Sister Mary Clare, appeared beside her. "Is there a problem, Sister?

Sister Mary Grace swallowed the sadness. "I'm just homesick, I guess."

"This is your home now. If family letters upset you so much, then perhaps you should be denied getting them for the time being."

Her superior's words brought out the old Angela. "You cannot do that. Those letters belong to me." Sister Mary Clare was shocked to hear such a rebuff from one of her novices. "Is this how you're preparing yourself to take the vow of obedience?" she shot back.

Sister Mary Grace realized she had committed a serious transgression. She dropped her head, "I'm sorry, Sister. I will abide by what you decide."

But could she really *"abide by what you decide"* if Sister Mary Clare decided to keep letters from her? There was only so much blind obedience in her bones.

WHEN the bell rang for dinner, Sister Mary Grace slowly left the chapel and made her way towards the refectory. This was just a test, a test to see how strong she was. She would overcome this temptation and continue to dedicate her life to God. *Perhaps He had put that magazine in Regina's path so she could learn the truth.* Another thought quickly responded, *That's a small consolation.*

Suddenly, she saw James standing before her with his half grin and open arms waiting to take her back. She shook her head and the vision went away. James belonged to someone else now. What was happening to her? She wished she could go have a beer with her dad. That would clear up things.

Instead, she recommitted herself to God and prayed that these temptations be taken away, but as she entered the dining room she still carried the heaviness of longing for a life she had vowed to give up. She reached for the long rosary hanging by her side and held the crucifix over her heart. "God have mercy, Lord have mercy."

GRACE looked through her front window at the statue of Mary surrounded by the plumbago. "Thank you for blessing me with such a good daughter." With that she folded her letter to Sister Mary Grace. It was hard to get used to the new name, but part of giving up your life to God meant changing your name, similar to Grace's giving up her maiden name when she married Bud. At first she hadn't liked the change from Griffin to Wolansky. Wolansky seemed like a strange name to someone who wasn't Czech. Long ago, someone told her that Wolansky was more Polish than Czech. When she asked Bud about that, he replied, "I don't care one way or the other. It's just a name, and it's just a country."

Such comments from him often irritated her. Then she wondered why she was irritated. She too believed that it was the person and not the country or nationality that counted. But she could still hear her dad, "Well, what can you expect? He's a backward, turnip-eating Polack." Or,

"He's Czech. No wonder he can't figure out how to drive a tractor."

While growing up Grace had avoided her father as much as possible. He claimed to be English, with an attitude of superiority which didn't prevent him from being crude, mean and common. Her mother was German, "a Kraut-eating Kraut," as he'd often say. But as far as Grace knew, he never made fun of Bud. She was a nervous wreck the first time she brought him home to meet her parents; however, Bud was totally relaxed and totally himself. He had a confidence which her dad either respected or feared. A little of both, Grace suspected.

When her dad died she had no tears, only relief. She was glad her children would never know him. As the years passed she never stopped comparing Bud to him, and she never stopped realizing how lucky she was. Her sister hadn't fared as well. She married a man very much like their dad and now had become like their mother, frightened and sad.

She licked the stamp, flattened it on the envelope and decided to stroll to the mailbox. She'd have plenty of time to finish lunch for Bud and Donny once she got back. An apple pie was cooling on the rack and a pork loin was baking in the oven. This morning had been glorious with a sweet coolness as if autumn were whispering her approach, and here it was still the middle of summer. *What a blessing if autumn were impatient this year.*

She had awakened early that morning before Bud, and walked out on the back porch into the coolness. A bullfrog sat near her petunia patch. She spoke softly, "Did you come up from the tank and get lost or have you come just for me to make a picture of you?" She ran inside and grabbed her sketch pad and colored pencils.

Since Ceil's comments and praise, Grace no longer hid her art work. When Bud saw her drawings for the first time, he said, "These are good. I don't know much about art, but I do know what I like." He then put his hand around her shoulder. "I loved runnin' down hills when I was a boy. These sort of give me the same feeling. " When she found her voice, she whispered, "That's the most touching compliment I've ever gotten." She had wanted to run to the back of her closet and show him the ones she had drawn in her lost moments, the ones only Ceil had seen. But she wasn't ready to expose herself in such a way to anyone else, not even her husband.

She looked away from her frog. Bud was up and rustling around in the kitchen. She closed her pad and went inside. He was putting slices of bacon into a heating skillet. When he noticed her, he said, "Don't stop. I saw you out there, your face all lit up. I like that look on you."

An awful thought came to Grace. *Am I like my mother, sad looking? I want to look 'all lit up' during the ordinary times too.* True, she felt most alive when she was drawing, *doodling foolishness*. Designing a new maternity top, tending to her gardens or coming up with a new recipe for raisin muffins also made her feel alive, but nothing like transforming a blank sheet of paper into something else.

As she walked down the lane to the mailbox, she kept hearing Bud's words again and again, *your face all lit up.* What she'd been thinking about as the frog began to appear on her drawing tablet was Ceil. She could hear her steady, self-assured voice appraising the picture, telling her that the frog seemed to be breathing. *"That's how good you are."*

These past weeks Grace's whole world seemed to have been lit up. The sun was more brilliant, the rain sweeter, the roses more fragrant. Grace reasoned that the experience of having a close woman friend was changing her concept of everything and everyone around her. Ceil's life fascinated her beyond anything she'd ever imagined. Here was a woman, totally free, who did what she wanted when she wanted. She wasn't married and said she never wanted to get married. Grace had never heard any woman say that. In fact, besides nuns, the only woman she knew who never got married had devoted her life to taking care of sick parents. Ceil also said she had never wanted children. Grace couldn't imagine any woman feeling that way.

Ceil owned a huge cosmetics company in Los Angeles. Her partner, also a woman, started it years before Ceil came along. Ceil helped this woman develop and grow the company into a very successful corporation. The partner had died several years ago, leaving Ceil the sole owner. Grace was in awe of her accomplishments and could sit for hours listening to her fascinating stories.

Grace picked up a broken limb on the side of the lane and twirled it over her head like a baton. Once she got to the mailbox, she sent it flying across the road and onto the newly mowed wheat field. She kissed Angela's letter and placed it in the box. Far down the road she spotted the speck of a car coming along at a fast clip. As it sped closer, she could make out that it was shiny and silver. It looked brand new and Ceil was driving. She turned onto the lane to the house, stopped and rolled down the window.

"Hop in." Ceil called out.

"What in the world are you doing?" Grace grabbed the handle, overjoyed to see her again. She had been away in San Antonio for several days. Grace settled into the passenger seat and let out a big sigh. She had never sat in a car seat so soft.

"I decided I didn't want to keep on using Nelda's car," Ceil explained seeing Grace's apparent awe over the car. "She needs to go home more often." She went on to say that she had hired another nurse from San Antonio to work during Nelda's off time. "When this is over, I'm sending Nelda to Scotland for a couple of months. I remember when I was living with her she'd say, 'Someday, I'm going to Scotland to see where my grandparents came from.' The other day she told me she's never gotten there."

They came to a stop in front of the house. "I'm also hiring Lizzie seven days a week until school starts. In fact, she'll be living there too." She sighed in frustration. "Surely my grandmother will die before too much longer." Just weeks ago, such a statement would have shocked Grace, but now she realized that Ceil was just being honest. To hell with niceness, especially the pretend kind.

"Look behind you," Ceil commanded.

Grace turned to look in the back seat and let out a gasp. Laid out in neat stacks were art supplies that Grace had only dreamed about. There were boxes of water colors and oil paints, brushes of every size and shape, art pencils, canvases, a multicolored wooden box to hold all the supplies, and an easel, a strong, upright easel. The sorts of things a real artist would have.

"I figure an artist like you needs to have the proper tools of the trade. Under the boxes are some art books that I thought you might enjoy and might inspire you."

Grace was silent. How could she possibly accept such generosity? This was too much. Ceil had gone too far, and for the first time she became angry at her.

"Why do you think you need to give me all these supplies?" Grace's voice got louder. "I can get what I need myself."

Unable to absorb the reprimand, Ceil watched the family cat stretch itself under the giant oak. Grace continued, "You come here with all your money and know-how and take over. Bud said you were pushy and I think he's right, even though when he said it I took up for you."

Ceil swallowed and began in a low tone. "I am pushy. He's right. I wouldn't have survived if I hadn't been pushy. I ran away from home at fifteen. I hopped trains. I walked miles. I stayed in hobo camps. I lived in vacant buildings. I stole food, and I even sold my body a couple of times."

Grace couldn't believe what she had just heard. Ceil had been a prostitute? What kind of person had she become friends with? Grace started to speak, "I can't....

Ceil stopped her. "No, I want you to hear me out. I was a very lucky person. First there was Nelda who let me live with her for two years until my grandfather hired a detective. Then she bought me a ticket to Los Angeles but I got off in El Paso and sold the remaining ticket, afraid I would run out of my savings. I managed to walk and hitch-hike my way to Los Angeles where for weeks I wondered the streets doing what I had to do to get by. Then I met another woman, Margaret Gabrielle. I always called her my Angel Gabrielle. She had a small business and she took me in and gave me a life I never imagined. She taught me the business and made me her partner. I've been helped my entire life. Before Nelda there was Mayphelia, who kept me from jumping out a window like my mama had done. Now it's my turn to help. I like to give. Insulting you or lording over you was the last thing I would want to do to you."

Grace couldn't look up. Then she remembered the pork loin. "I've got Bud's dinner in the oven." She opened the door to get out. "Thank you very much for your thoughtfulness, but I can't accept such generosity."

Ceil turned on the car's motor. "They'll still be here if you change your mind."

Ceil quickly drove off while frustration roiled inside her like the clouds of dust billowing up from the rear tires. Had she been too forward? Could Grace tell how much she cared for her? Ceil hadn't had these kinds of feelings since Margaret. She'd had a few one-night stands. One with a waitress who was into roughness, which Ceil abhorred, and one with an aspiring actress who wanted to experience "all of life's spectrums." She knew what she was feeling for Grace could never be realized, and she didn't want to confuse or shock her.

Suddenly she stopped the car before turning onto the main road. She wanted Grace to know that she had moved into a rent house. She quickly scratched her new address and phone number on the back of a used envelope. The rental place was just down the street from the Dollard home. Now with new people coming in to care for her grandmother, she needed to be closer. Both Grace and Mayphelia lived too far out. Besides, Mayphelia's place lacked too many conveniences and she wasn't comfortable at Grace's because she sensed Bud's discomfort. Perhaps he knew what she was and was afraid for his wife. She dropped the envelope into the mailbox and drove off praying that she'd see Grace again.

CHAPTER THIRTEEN

The nightmare wasn't a dreamed nightmare. It had really happened. Regina tossed and clenched her teeth, aware even in her sleep that it was true. Yesterday she had been gathering up the clothes for washing. She could hear the wringer-washer churning away on the back porch and knew the suds were swirling around as the girls pretended to be mommies in the primitive play-cabin her dad had built for them. Something white had been stuffed in the back of the closet. *Who in the world had put a sheet back behind some shoe boxes? Had the girls made a bed for their cat, Trudy?*

She yanked the sheet out and something else, maybe a pillow case, fell onto the floor. She picked it up, then dropped it in horror. This couldn't be true. Billy Wayne had his faults. He could be mean and hateful, but he couldn't be part of something like this. Yet as the two eye holes and pointed top looked up at her, she knew it must be true.

Sheila had told her that the Ku Klux Klan was every bit as bad as the Nazis, except their main target was colored people. "But they go after Jews, too," she had said matter-of-factly.

Regina ran outside to the trash barrel and threw the hood and sheet in on top of a bramble bush she had hacked to death days ago. The kerosene can was almost empty. She shook out the last drop, cursed under her breath and shook it some more. Her hands trembled as she broke two matches before one ignited. She jumped back and watched the fiery tongues lick upwards and dance like some drunken ghost stumbling around. The smoke blurred her vision and choked her lungs.

She would have to tell her mom and dad about this. No more secrets. She would tell everything, absolutely everything. Then she saw the headpiece about to catch on fire and yanked it out. She had to show this to her parents. Back in her kitchen she had made the sign of the cross over the hood before stuffing it into a canister. Billy Wayne would never look there.

Suddenly Regina was fully awake gasping for air. Billy Wayne's side of the bed was empty, unwrinkled and unslept in. This was so common these days; however, she didn't mind. He constantly fussed about everything and had begun hitting her more frequently. He no longer seemed to fear that he might hurt the baby. Regina had told him that the shouting and meanness were also affecting the girls, especially Angie. "Well, they'd best grow up knowin' where their place is," he said and slammed shut a cabinet door so hard the dishes rattled.

Regina rubbed her hand over his side of the bed. *What if something happened to him?* She shook the thought away. He had once told her about being in danger because of some bootleggers. *"That ole man Jody wants to do me in. Says I stole off him."* A shiver made her pull up the covers.

The glowing statue of the Virgin Mary on her nightstand smiled at her. "Oh, dear Mother of God, please forgive me for such terrible thoughts. In the beginning he could be nice. That's still there somewhere. He can still be sweet with his daughters. Help me to remember that."

Yesterday while hiding the mask she heard a voice from within, *"You must leave him."*

But now this morning, the fear of going to hell was vying for control. *Divorce is a mortal sin,* she had learned in catechism class. She would be excommunicated, cast out from the Church. Even if it were best for her and her daughters, she didn't know if she had the courage to take such a big step.

Even her mother wouldn't oppose a divorce once she knew everything. Or would she? She could see her mother fretting over the family scandal, unable to face the shame. Then there would be gossip among the church members, the comparison of her with her saintly sister. Regina felt weak. Where would she find the strength? Yet she knew she must somehow.

If Sheila could leave a no-good, so could she. *I'd leave this very minute if I weren't so damn sick.* This affirmation created a comforting resolve within her. With these thoughts came another worry. She was already well into her sixth month and not getting any bigger, nor feeling any movements. *By this time, I should be feeling somersaults.*

Towards the end of the second month with Angie, she kept feeling this gurgling movement in her stomach. She had gone to Mayphelia afraid that something was wrong. "She just be swimmin' around, that's all. She be looking somethin' like a little fish right 'bout now, goin' through the stages of becomin' a person." At that time Regina let half the things Mayphelia said go in one ear and out the other. Now she realized that even though Mayphelia couldn't read or write, she knew more things than most people who had read the books.

In her sixth month with Angie, her mother had given her a manual about pregnancy that she had ordered from a housekeeping magazine. "I certainly wish I'd had something like this when I was carrying my children," Grace said as she handed her the package, wrapped in pink tissue paper with a beautifully crocheted angel on top. Her mother could always make everything beautiful, even a wrapped-up book. "I know now for sure she's a girl and I'm going to name her Angela," Regina told Grace.

Sure enough, beginning on page fifteen were pictures of the development of the fetus, and her little baby girl had looked somewhat like a fish in the beginning. As mother and daughter looked at the pictures, Grace commented, "All I had was what my mother and the older women told me."

Regina once again turned to look at the smiling, glowing statue of Mary. Something else gnawed at her mind. With her other pregnancies, Mayphelia referred to her fetuses as "she" almost from the beginning.

"Oh she be settled in today" or "She don't like last night's supper. Cut out eatin' garlic," Mayphelia would say as her hands moved over Regina's stomach. But with this one, she never referred to the baby as he or she. When Regina asked, Mayphelia turned her head, "I ain't sure jest yet."

As Regina sat up and began to get out of the bed, a pain jabbed through her abdomen. She held onto the bedpost as it subsided. What was going on? *"I think I need to have a bowel movement,"* she moaned.

On her way to the bathroom she peeked into the girls' room. They were curled up fast asleep with their cat, Trudy, nestled between them. Trudy opened her eyes, glanced over at her, then silently hopped off the bed and walked down the hallway. At the bathroom door, she stopped and waited for Regina. "You want to watch me go on the pot?" Suddenly, another crashing pain hit her.

She doubled over. Blood was trickling down her legs. "Oh my God, no." She grabbed a towel and put it between her legs and rushed to the phone as best she could. "Mama, get Mayphelia and come over quick. I'm bleeding."

Grace hung up and scribbled a note for Bud. He and Alex had left before sun-up to go look at a hay-bailer that a farmer in Gillett County was selling. She hadn't spoken to Ceil since the incident with the art supplies. She retrieved the envelope with Ceil's phone number from the junk drawer. When Ceil answered, Grace took a moment before speaking. "Ceil, I need your help. Regina is bleeding and Bud's already gone. Can you come get Mayphelia and me? I'll be at Mayphelia's."

Grace replaced the earpiece with a reprimand. *I didn't even apologize for the way I treated her the other day.* Grace's thoughts ran between prayers for Regina, *"Dear God, take care of my baby,"* and making amends to Ceil, *"You are a true friend."* She threw a dress over her nightgown and ran out the back door carrying her purse and a hair brush.

When the three women arrived, Regina was sitting on the blood-filled commode, white as a sheet, and clenching her teeth in pain. "I don't want to frighten the girls. Please take them away. They're still sleeping, thank God."

Trudy sat in the bathtub beside a bloody towel. Ceil backed away. "I'll take care of the girls." *All the blood was oozing around her mother's head. So much blood is death. The spiders were crawling up her legs and towards the blood. She couldn't do anything.*

Ceil steadied herself by holding onto the hallway walls as she went towards the girls' room. She couldn't help with Regina or her grandmother any more than she could help with her beloved Margaret. She was terrified of sickness, of death. *What if Regina dies? This couldn't happen to these little girls. Would they be treated the way she'd been? No one could take the place of their mama.*

She flung the door open with more force than she intended. Tessie's eyes popped open. "Cecie, Cecie." She held out her chubby little arms to embrace her. Tears clouded Ceil's eyes, *"She loves me. I am worthy of love."* Ceil took Tessie in her arms and held her tightly.

In the bathroom, Regina moaned in agony as she felt it pass out of her. She grabbed her mother's arm. "Oh God, I think it's come." She tried to raise herself up.

"Don't look, child." Mayphelia said. "We's got to get ya to yo'r bed now." She closed the lid before Regina could turn around. Grace got a couple of pads from the closet, put them between Regina's legs and held them in place while Mayphelia walked her down the hall to her bedroom. As they passed the girls' room Grace could hear Ceil singing softly. "Hush little baby, don't say a word, Mama's gonna buy you a mockingbird...." *I didn't know she had such a lovely voice.*

Mayphelia hurried back to the bathroom.

"Mama, what's happening?" Regina cried.

"There, there, you've just had a miscarriage. I had two before Angela was born. You'll be alright. There can be other babies."

Regina propped up on her elbows. "I'm not pregnant anymore?" Relief washed through every cell of her body, then fear. "Mama, did I do it? You know most of the time I didn't want to be pregnant."

"Oh dear girl, only God is in control of life and death and birth. You did nothing." Grace pulled off her gown and continued, "Rest while I get some water to clean you.

You'll feel better cleaned up and in a fresh gown. I'll change the sheets too."

She hurried towards the bathroom, then stopped. From the doorway, she saw Mayphelia taking what looked like a ball of bloody twine out of the commode. Grace shuddered. She could see the beginnings of a face, a misshapen face. Mayphelia wrapped up the ball in the towel. She rummaged under the sink and found a large brown paper bag, put the towel in it and started for the back door. "The sooner I bury this, the better."

In the car shed, Mayphelia found a shovel and a bag of lye. She carried everything to the back of the house. Under a wide shade tree, she dug a three foot hole and dropped the bundle into it. She covered it with lye granules before shoveling the dirt back over it. "With all that poison overpowerin' the blood smell, no varmints should be digging this up," she said. Then she extended her arms towards the sky and began chanting an ancient prayer in an unknown tongue.

By ten o'clock Regina was clean and resting comfortably in her bed with the girls and Trudy beside her. Angie was pretend-reading from a picture book. Grace was putting the finishing touches on the now-sparkling bathroom and Ceil was in the kitchen making tea.

Suddenly Billy Wayne yanked open the back door and staggered into the kitchen. The sight of Ceil caught him off guard and aggravated the pounding in his head. "I was jest on my way over there. You don't have to come and check on me. I always get the job done, don't I?"

About then Mayphelia followed him in from the back yard. He turned around and spat out, "What the hell's goin' on here anyway?" His fists clenched as he yelled, "Regina!"

"She just had a miscarriage," Grace said, walking in with a basket of blood-stained sheets and towels.

Once Billy Wayne's grasped this, he turned all his fury on Mayphelia. "You did this with all them nigger potions, making her sicker by the day." He put his finger up to her face. "You'll pay jest as sure as I stand here."

Ceil dropped the cup she was pouring. A she-warrior facing the enemy, she leapt between Billy Wayne and Mayphelia and thrust her finger within an inch of Billy Wayne's nose. "Don't you put your finger in her face!" she growled.

She was a head taller than he and overpowering. "You did this with all your meanness, the hitting, the running around, the stinginess. Have you shared with her any of the money you've stolen from me?"

The blood drained from Billy Wayne's face. *How did she know? Had she planted that money in the jar, the tire, on the rafter so she'd have an excuse to fire him?*

"You better have some proof if you're accusin' me of somethin,'" he spat out.

Ceil held him in her stare. "I won't file charges. Consider the thefts your last payment. Don't set foot on the Dollard place again."

Billy Wayne backed off a bit, and then smacked his lips with a smile. "I don't want your damn job, and this is my place so now you get your sorry ass out of my house."

He turned towards the hall. "Regina," he shouted, "where are the girls?" He began to walk towards the hall when Grace stepped in his way.

"Billy Wayne, this place belongs to Bud and me, and I'm telling you to leave now." She tried to control her shaking. Never had she spoken like this to anyone.

Billy Wayne grinned, "We're married. What's hers is mine, you crazy ..." He trailed off. A sharp pain drilled into the middle of his skull. He glanced over and saw Mayphelia's eyes piercing into his forehead. *She ain't got no power. It's just the hangover.*

He turned his fury on Grace. "Everyone knows how you went bonkers and are still bonkers. And let me tell you, your daughter is just like you, one crazy, helpless..."

Mayphelia put up her hand. Billy Wayne started mumbling, unable to form words.

"That's enough evil," she purred in a hoarse whisper "Now you best goes before I calls my wolf on ya." She smiled broadly showing nearly all of her chalk white teeth. Billy Wayne backed out the door. He was afraid of Mayphelia, no matter how hard he pretended not to be. He knew she walked in two worlds.

CHAPTER FOURTEEN

Ceil and Grace rode in silence. Mayphelia had insisted on staying with Regina, who was too exhausted and weak for the car ride back to Grace's. Although Grace worried that Billy Wayne might cause more trouble, Mayphelia reassured her. "He's plottin' but he won't come back today."

Ceil began gently, "Grace, why don't you know how to drive a car? You told me you drove your dad's tractor. I imagine that would be harder than a car."

Grace paused. "It's just not something women around here do, at least not the women my age."

"You know I could teach you," Ceil adjusted the rear view mirror, "if you'd like."

After a while Grace spoke. "Ceil, thank you so much for all your help today. You were really strong with Billy Wayne and I admire that. In fact, I seemed to get strength from you."

Ceil laughed, "I've been up against a lot worse than him."

Grace folded her hands in her lap. "I've always been timid, afraid to speak up. My dad was ... well, horrible, and I was scared to death to say anything around him. My baby brother called him Hitler, behind his back of course. When Bud and I got together, I couldn't believe that a man could be so nice. Even after we married he stayed that way, but I never could get used to talking freely."

"I guess we're similar in some ways in how we grew up," Ceil said. "But you've been protected by Bud so you haven't had to fight for survival. But me, a woman alone trying to find her way, well, let's just say I learned how to stand up to men at an early age."

There was a long silence before Grace began again, "I don't know what I'd do if I were in Regina's shoes."

"Hopefully, you'd divorce the son-of-a-bitch," Ceil barked.

"Divorce?" Grace sounded as if that were the first time she'd heard the word. "Oh, but we're Catholics and, besides, women around here, Protestants too, just don't do that."

"Well, maybe it's about time they do. Maybe it's time that women around here learn to drive cars, get divorces and speak up," Ceil said as she turned the car onto the lane to Grace's house. "Maybe it's time they think for themselves and learn to do what's best for them. Women give their power away to either a man or some religion and it's morally wrong."

The car stopped. Grace was deep in thought. Finally, she spoke, "Would you like to come in for some ice tea?"

"No, not today, my dear. Mayphelia's been hounding me to take care of some unfinished business." She sighed deeply. "Making peace with my grandmother."

"Well, I want to make peace with you, and accept your generous gift," Grace said. "I'm sorry I refused and said what I did." Grace fumbled with the door handle. "I felt embarrassed and like I would be taking advantage of you."

"Taking advantage?" Ceil laughed. "Grace, it's for myself that I give. Giving things, money, makes me happy.

I'm not capable of giving much of anything else and listen, my dear, you're not capable of taking advantage of me or anyone else. It's not in you."

Grace smiled. No one made her feel better about herself than Ceil. She pulled on the door handle.

"Your supplies are in the trunk. You can give me the first painting as payment and forget about them being a gift."

"Okay, it's a deal. Now come in for some tea. You can see your grandmother tomorrow."

Instead of having tea Grace and Ceil rearranged the sewing room, putting the machine and fabrics in one corner and then laying out all the paints, brushes and other supplies on the sewing table. They had a time putting the easel together. Once it was done, Grace set a canvas on it, stood back and admired her new toys. She couldn't wait to get started.

Ceil hugged Grace as usual when she was leaving. Then instead of letting go, Ceil held her closer and closer and kissed her on the mouth. Grace pulled away in shock. Bowing her head, Ceil apologized and ran out the front door. Grace slowly sat down, flushed. When Ceil's breasts had rubbed against hers, she'd felt a jolt of pleasure run through her whole body. She'd never experienced anything like it. Bud's kisses were tender and sweet but not as thrilling. No one besides Bud and her babies had ever kissed her lips. Maybe her reaction was just the delight of something new and different.

Grace had felt for some time now that she was becoming another person, a person possessed. She thought about Ceil all the time. She had hardly slept a wink since the day she thought she might have lost her friendship over some art supplies.

She heard Bud walk in the back door. "I'm in the sewing room," she called. When he saw all the art supplies and her expression, he asked, "What's all this? You okay? You look all red like you've been out in the hot sun."

She hurried to the kitchen. Bud looked over the table before turning to follow her. While opening the refrigerator and getting out vegetables, Grace began a breathless nervous explanation. "Regina had a miscarriage this morning. Ceil came and got me and Mayphelia. I left the note. See it there. We just got back, and Ceil gave me all those art supplies you saw."

She waited but he didn't say anything. "At first I refused them, but she insisted, saying I could pay her with my first painting and that seemed like a fair arrangement. "

"Regina had a miscarriage?" he asked, his voice rising. "Why didn't you bring her back here?"

"Mayphelia's with her. Regina was too worn out for a car ride." Grace put down the pitcher of tea and hugged him.

Bud returned her hug. "What's wrong, Gracie? You seem all edgy." He hugged her and buried his face in her hair. "Sometimes I swear it feels like you're goin' away. Not like before with Peter, but in another way, I can't explain."

Was it true? *Am I going away?* Her nerves were stretched as far as they could go without popping. She did feel like she was leaving the person she had always been. "Bud, I'm fine, just high strung from this morning. Regina had a horrible misshapen thing. She didn't see it, thanks to Mayphelia. I'm not going away like before ever again, Bud."

He hugged her tightly and she heard him catch his breath. Then he kissed her, and it felt good. What had happened earlier with Ceil was just something she'd never experienced before. That's all.

Bud sat down and filled his glass with tea. "Gracie, you know you could have gotten all those supplies yourself. I would have gotten 'em for you if I'd known. I didn't even know you liked to draw until some weeks ago." He sounded sad, betrayed.

Grace was at the stove. "Oh my dear, I didn't know I wanted those things until I saw them. I was content with pencils and crayons. When Ceil gave me all those paints and everything, she also gave me the idea I could go beyond what I have been doing."

Once again the feeling of uneasiness was lodging in Bud's stomach. He said quietly, "She always seems to be butting in. You give them back and the next time we go to San Antonio, I can…we can get that stuff."

Grace didn't respond. The only sound was the steak frying. After a while, Bud broke the silence. "As soon as I eat, I need to check on that sick calf, and then I'm going over to Regina's. I'll bring the girls back here so she can rest."

Grace placed a plate of food in front of Bud and sat down opposite him. "Bud, I'm not giving those things back to Ceil. It was a gift from my friend. I've never had a close girl or woman friend, even in school. I was always afraid to have a friend because they might want to come to my house and, well, you know how it was with my dad, never knowing how he'd act. Please don't ask me to give up the first gift I've ever received from a friend."

Bud couldn't look up from his plate. The food was difficult to swallow. One tasteless mouthful after another obstructed any talking. Finally the words were there.

"Alright then. From now on, just get what you need yourself."

As Bud walked down to the barn, he was torn between wanting Grace to be happy and fearing that she was being taken away from him. Her childhood had been so different from his. He and his sisters always had friends over; he still got together once a year for a fishing trip with his childhood buddies. Grace never had that. He had always been the only one in her life. She had looked to him for everything, and now she wasn't. The loss of her need for him hurt deeply.

Then the memory of his mother with her special friend, Vie, suddenly came up. He remembered those two sitting for hours talking, whispering and laughing like young girls. After their visits, his mom would always be more cheerful and happy, and his dad never minded. He wanted to be like his dad. *Why am I jealous? Yes it's jealousy.* Bud finally admitted to himself what he was feeling. *I'm afraid Ceil will take my place.* As he unlatched the stall door, his thoughts continued. *That's stupid. I'm selfish and possessive.*

CEIL looked at the half-empty bottle of Scotch sitting on the coffee table and then at all the worn-out, cheap furniture in the living room of her furnished rental house. She had thought she'd be here only a short time and could live with it, but her grandmother was so goddamn stubborn about dying. Plus, now Ceil didn't want to leave this crappy town.

"I'm transforming my grandparents' house into a dream mansion, a place that would be worthy of the beautiful Grace," she slurred her words out to the ceiling.

She got up to pour another drink. "Stop with the dreaming," she yelled. "It's not going to happen."

There was no more ice in the old cookpot that served as an ice bucket. She weaved towards the kitchen, then decided against it and plopped down once more on the couch. "Oh, if only my friends in L.A. were here. What a laugh they'd have seeing me make do with the likes of this."

After mixing a drop or two of water with a cup of Scotch, she gazed out the window as the sun dipped behind the house across the street. She'd been drinking all afternoon over a woman who didn't even know that monsters like her existed. She took a gulp of the drink, waved the glass in the air and spoke in measured cadence to the phantom Mayphelia sitting in a chair across from her.

"I know, I know, May-May, I'm not a monster. I'm just different. God made me this way. You always said that, but I never believed you because everyone else calls me and my kind abominations, sinners, freaks and, yes, even monsters. We have to hide all the time. It's easy to hide in a large city. Why, the goddamn KKK would lynch me if I lived here."

She began to cry. She put her glass down on the edge of the table. It shattered against the floor. Scotch ran around her feet but she didn't notice. The pain in her heart obliterated all awareness. She was in love with Grace, and she knew this love was hopeless. Her love could never be returned, not in the way she wanted. She had to get away from this town right now but knew she was too drunk to walk, much less drive. First thing in the morning, she promised herself, she'd get on a plane and get the hell out of there. Let her grandmother go to the devil with her dying. That was her last thought as she passed out on the couch.

CHAPTER FIFTEEN

The barn was stuffy and hot. Kerosene lanterns hanging from several of the rafters cast a shadowy light as far as the dilapidated pen that had once housed several pigs. Now a faint hog stench wafted up from the ground and off the boards. The barn had been abandoned after Mr. Katz's home had burned to the ground, killing his eighty-six-year-old mother. He moved his family to Houston, got a job and boasted to everyone he left behind, "It sure is nice to get a pay check every week instead of waiting a year for a harvest that might not clear enough to last till the next crop."

Unfortunately, he hadn't been able to get a buyer for his place so he rented it out to the Klan. The nearest neighbor was six miles away and the barn was far off the main road, an ideal location for a group that thrived on secrecy. Mr. Katz wasn't partial to the Klan, but after years of doing without he wasn't about to turn his back on making a little extra money.

Men straggled in straight from the fields in overalls and faded shirts wet from a day's sweat. Most wore oil soaked fedoras low over their foreheads as if they were afraid they'd be recognized. The air hung heavy with dashed dreams, failures and brewing angers. Huffing and wheezing, Mr. Carbon carried in the galvanized tub loaded with beer on ice and placed it on the ground. He always supplied beer for the meetings, more as a bribe than a gift. He was a wealthy man compared to these men but he needed them and their wives to shop at his grocery store. The men stepped forward. Their moods would be lightened but nothing could lift the heaviness of the breezeless night or the dense humidity, perfect for swarms of mosquitos.

One farmer bent with arthritis mumbled, "Damn, if I don't thank the Good Lord for all the rain, but seems like He could manage it without all these gauldern mosquitoes." He waved a misshapen hand in front of his face and swatted an insect to the ground. Laughter mingled with the popping of opening bottles.

The first gulps were the longest. Just as the cold liquid was settling raw nerves, Billy Wayne hurried in and broke the momentary peace. He bee-lined for the tub, took a half-empty bottle from his back pocket and poured beer in with the moonshine.

"Better go easy," Mr. Carbon said.

Billy Wayne turned on him, "I tell you, I got some action I want to git taken care of tanite, and I mean tanite."

The men shuffled about. Some chattered uneasily. They knew Billy Wayne and his moods. Old man Johnson spoke over the mumblings, "My bull got out the other day. I swear I'm gonna have to hog-tie that critter."

As the leader Mr. Carbon took charge. "Okay, then. Let's get started. The sheriff is suffering with his back so he won't be here and then Charlie and Harold are off fishing. Everyone grab a beer if you haven't already, and if you have, grab another." His roaring voice scared the pigeons in the rafters. Wings flapped as some flitted over to another sleeping beam.

The group headed to bales of hay scattered around. Some of the men pulled white sheets from wrinkled paper bags. Mr. Carbon put up his hand as a stop signal. "Gentlemen, due to the heat and humidity, I think we can pass over the formality of wearing our uniforms."

Billy Wayne shouted out, "Mine's disappeared, and it's all due to that nigger woman, Mayphelia. She kilt my unborn baby. It's time we burnt her out."

Many of the men squirmed as if adjusting their butts to the hay. Most knew that if they did anything to Mayphelia, they'd have all hell to pay from their wives. Mr. Carbon blanched. He wasn't about to go near Mayphelia. His hand still shook every time he went near his meat scale and his privates never had properly healed.

A farmer spoke up. "When my boy was so sick, throwin' up and runnin' out the other end, that doctor wan't helpin' at all. My wife threw a fit to get Mayphelia, and she done come over and fixed up some drink and then rubbed my boy's stomach and chest till it was orange-red. My boy went to sleep and woke up the next mornin', runnin' around and gettin' inta everything just as right as rain."

Another man chimed in, "And Billy Wayne, you know for the most part we leave the nigger women alone. It's them young bucks we got ta watch out for. The agee tators."

Mr. Carbon breathed a sigh of relief. The group thought more or less the same way he did, and that was to leave Mayphelia alone. Billy Wayne jumped up and began pacing around the men. He hissed, "You ain't nothin' but a bunch of sissies." His face was a blister red. "You ain't about cleanin' up this country of all the black scum. You jest about gettin' together and drinkin' damn beer."

He hawked loudly and spat on the dirt next to Mr. Carbon's shoes. Mr. Carbon stepped back a few inches. This little son-of-a-bitch frightened him almost as much as Mayphelia did.

Billy Wayne continued, yelling accusations, "We haven't kilt one nigger since I've been in this thing. I tell you what, you kin take your Klan and go to the devil. I'm finished." Several pigeons flew out of the barn. "I kin take care of things on my own, don't you worry." He threw his empty beer bottle at a nearby beam so forcefully that flying glass caused several men to duck. He grabbed another beer, saluted the group with a "Go to hell" and marched out. Shaking heads and sighs of relief followed his departure. *Those Tarkins were a mean bunch alright.*

Another person, crouched in a corner of the farthest stall, heard every word Billy Wayne said. Clem frequently came to these meetings, hid in the shadows and listened to all the bragging and lies that whirled off evil tongues. Because of Clem, young Nathan Drew got out of town before they could lynch him. They wanted to get Nathan because he helped one of the Klan's daughters get up after she had stumbled and fallen down some steps in front of the bank. Even though he was helping, he broke a major Southern rule–he didn't just look at a white woman, he touched one and in public, too.

Clem felt very uneasy in his gut about what had just happened. Maybe it was time to talk to Bud. But first he'd stay around till everyone left and see if he could find any leftover beer. These farmers weren't big drinkers when there was so much field work to do.

PAINFUL explosions vibrated through Ceil's head. After a moment or two, the knocking started again. Was she having a stroke? She never prayed, but suddenly "God, have mercy on me" escaped her lips. She rolled over onto the floor as the knocking began again, much softer now. Opening her eyes, she realized the noise was at the front door. She crawled up to standing and hobbled over.

"Yes, who is it?" she called, too broken to look through the window.

"It's me, sleepyhead," Grace called out.

Ceil opened the door to a smiling, bright-faced beauty. *Grace has blossomed since that first time I saw her, or is my love making me see her in a glow?*

"Hi, you gonna invite me in? Bud dropped me off at Regina's, but Pauline was over there and she likes to run the show, so I decided to walk over here to see you."

Grace walked into the living room. "Are you okay? You look sick." Grace began to fan herself with a flimsy little handkerchief. Ceil turned and walked to the kitchen. "I'll get some coffee started."

"Maybe you should let me get it. What's wrong?"

Then she noticed the nearly empty Scotch bottle and the dried-up liquor and broken glass on the floor. She recoiled, remembering the almost empty bottles and her dad snoring in his recliner or stretched out on the floor. Everyone had to tip-toe around all day and maybe the next and be extra careful not to upset him. After a few days he would be "well" again. But then after a short time he'd get "sick" all over again. That was how her mother described his condition to her and her siblings. Grace was a teenager before she learned that the content of those bottles was what made him sick.

"Grace, what are you doing here?" Ceil called out over running water.

Grace was caught off guard by this question. "I don't know. I just thought I would surprise you and take you up on your offer to teach me how to drive. Bud and I talked a long time last night. He's thinks it's a good idea. But I can come another time."

She turned to the door. Ceil said, "Please stay. I need to talk. I'll have some coffee and then we'll go for a drive."

Grace sat down on the edge of the couch and nervously twisted her handkerchief into rope. "First, I have something to ask you."

Ceil closed her eyes over the coffee pot and sighed deeply. *Here it comes,* she thought, *the big question. Are you a deviate, one of those*? Ceil didn't know what to tell her. Perhaps she should deny it and then go on with a friendship. After all, she would be going back to L.A. soon.

Quietly from across the room came the question. "Are you a drunkard? It's probably none of my business, it's just that the broken glass, the smell ..."

Ceil interrupted her with relief, "No, dear, I'm not a drunkard. Yes, I got drunk last night. I've done that a few times in my life."

"A few times," said as a statement rather than a question. "My dad did that about every ten days to two weeks. He'd just get to acting normal, then he'd start up again."

Ceil pulled up a chair and sat across from Grace. "Listen dear, I'm not an alcoholic. I let my confusion and frustration get the best of me last night. I wish my grandmother would hurry up with this dying process."

She rubbed her forehead as a pain shot through. "And I want to get back to L.A., but then I don't, because I'm starting to like it here. Lots of conflict and for some stupid reason I thought a bottle of Scotch could clear it up."

Grace was relieved. "When I get like that, not knowing what to do, I usually eat a chocolate cake." Grace laughed, remembering the time the children came home from school to find a half-eaten cake. She told them the truth, but they didn't believe her. "I know Aunt Pauline was here," Angela had stated with assertion.

She is so sweet, Ceil thought. "You ready for a cup of coffee?"

"No, I'm too hot from the walk over here. Can I open those windows?"

Ceil nodded her head and continued with an explanation, "Yesterday was a hard day for me. Seeing Regina and all that blood, and then knowing that I must go see my grandmother and try to make peace with her. Mayphelia says I have to for the sake of my soul, but I don't know if I can."

"I never made peace with my dad and sometimes I wish I had." Grace walked past Ceil and patted her shoulder. Ceil shrugged away and looked into her face, full of innocence. *Grace must think what happened was just a show of friendship between women, nothing more.*

"I painted all day yesterday after you left. I love oils. It's such a new experience. When Bud came in I had forgotten all about supper, but when he saw how happy I was he insisted on us going over to Lakey for hamburgers and fries."

Grace picked up a newspaper on the table and fanned herself. "We had the best time. I think I surprised him because I talked so much. I seem to be doing that a lot lately. We even talked about you. He said he was glad we're friends but that in the beginning he'd been a little jealous of you. Isn't that funny?"

Ceil realized Bud was probably more aware of her true nature than he was admitting to. She also realized theirs was a good marriage, and Bud was a good man. She wouldn't cause any problems. She would never come between them. She valued each of them too much.

SHEILA lay in the early morning light and watched her Adonis peacefully sleep. She still couldn't believe that she had found this simple adorable country boy, who took to the city like a kitten to a ball of yarn. He'd proposed to her on their third date. Aghast, she had said, "You don't even know me."

"Yeah, but I like you, and I'm pretty sure I can keep on liking you." That seemed to him to be enough of a basis upon which to build a marriage. Now after almost a year of being with him, she was convinced he had been right. She adored him. In fact she longed at that moment to lean over and kiss his beautiful face and then kiss him all over, but he needed his sleep.

He had started taking classes at night and working in the store during the day. Selling furniture and decorating houses were no longer enough. He wanted to design homes. His ideas were fresh. His first blueprint of a home featured an open area that flowed from living to dining to kitchen without dividing walls between. He'd been inspired by his mom's big kitchen. "It's really three rooms in one where we all gathered to do homework, eat, play cards, listen to the radio and entertain company. I'll always love that room," he said as he worked on the design.

Andy had not yet shared his ambition to become an architect with his family. "I'd rather not tell my dad, just yet," he'd told Sheila.

"For god's sake, why not?" she wanted to know. Gradually she pulled the story from him.

"After I had finished junior college, I told Dad I wasn't going to be a farmer and all hell broke loose. He refused to believe that I wasn't going to follow in his footsteps just as he had done and as his father had done and as had been done for generations. And I think he still feels like I'll grow tired of the city and come back."

When Andy left home for Houston, they'd had quite a falling out and Bud told him never to ask for a dime and Andy told him he'd starve to death before he would. Of course, the feud didn't last long; both were too goodnatured and loved one another too much for that. However, the result was that Bud never offered any help and Andy refused to ask for any. Sheila had experienced that stubbornness first hand, but that was the only flaw she had detected so far.

A little later, she brought up the idea of them living together in order to split expenses and relieve him of the financial stress. At first, Andy balked at the idea. "I'll take out some loans. Besides it's not respectable to shack up.

"How bourgeois," she said through giggles.

"Tell you what. I'll marry you instead."

She sat up. They were picnicking on a blanket in the park. "Andy, I'm not ready for that." He looked so forlorn she felt she would cry.

"Oh sweetheart, I didn't mean… yes, I want to marry you, but right now the thought of going through the ordeal of convincing my dad that I want to marry a Christian is more than I can deal with. Even though my first husband was Jewish and the worst piece of humanity around, my dad thought I should settle for him. His family was respectable. When I told my dad that I never loved my husband and that I got married just to get him and Mom off my back, he had a slight heart attack. Oh God, the guilt I felt."

Andy laughed, "Oh, yeah, the guilt. I think you Jews probably outdo the Catholics on that one."

"You kidding? We're the ones who created it, and to hear my dad, we should be damn proud of it." She poured some more ice water from the jug and poked him teasingly with her foot, "Besides, what do you know? You told me I was the first Jew you'd ever met."

"The first and the best." He grabbed her prodding leg and started crawling his fingers up her thigh and then stopped, noticing that nearby children were playing hide'n'seek. She loved him for being so respectful. He treated her better than anyone ever had. On her first visit with his family at the convent, she also noticed how respectful he was towards his mother. She knew he valued women and would do anything for his mother and his sisters.

Finally, after much persuasion, he agreed to move into her nicer apartment, but only after she took a solemn vow not to breathe one word to anyone in his family. Sheila did well financially. She was a top-notch hair stylist in one of the priciest salons in Houston. Almost every year, she went to New York or L.A. to learn from the best. She also had a small trust fund from a childless aunt. She hadn't yet told Andy about this money.

They took to living together like children take to playing in mud and quickly settled into a comfortable routine which left both of them feeling as if they'd been married for years and years.

Sheila thought about sprinkling water on his serenely still face. She could just imagine the wrestling match they'd have with him ending up tickling her until she wet the bed. He was so playful. She smiled recalling how he had joined in on the children's game of tag at the park, pretending he couldn't outrun those kids. People always ended up smiling when they were around Andy. She hoped one day her dad would smile around him.

Not able to wait any longer, she jumped up and headed for the bathroom to get the spray bottle. When she came back, he was gone. She stopped, startled, when suddenly he grabbed her from behind.

"You're not going to get away with it this time, you little vixen."

He began lifting her off the floor while she cried out and laughed. He dropped her on the bed and got the spray bottle away from her and squirted water over her face. She screamed. That's when the broom lady in the apartment above began banging their ceiling. They collapsed in laughter and began making slow, soft, Saturday-morning love.

CHAPTER SIXTEEN

In August, Mother Nature decided to take vengeance for June and July's mild, by Texas standards, temperatures. Now a furnace sun blistered men, plants and animals with triple digits day in and day out. The skies were cloudless, the air motionless and hot vapor waves belched up from the ground.

Ordinarily Grace would wade through these stifling days in a stupor, trying to keep busy so as not to think about the discomfort. She hated the heat and often thought she had been dropped in the wrong place at birth. *I belong up north,* often ran through her mind. This weather didn't suit her any more than the family she had been born into.

Windows and doors were always wide open for cross-ventilation and fans ran full speed in every room. Twice weekly the iceman delivered a huge block of ice that would be placed in a pan in front of the kitchen fan, a country air-conditioning system. Andy told her he had central air-conditioning in his apartment, and she wondered if such a marvel would ever make it to her home. Some people in town had gotten a new thing called a window unit but Bud believed it was unhealthy, especially for someone who worked outside all day. He said the sudden change in temperatures would make him sick.

However, this August was different for Grace. She went through the days full of energy. She had finished one oil painting and was thrilled to be half-finished with another. Despite the heat Grace was genuinely happy, enjoying the fun that had eluded her youth. As a little girl she learned not to trust those feelings of elation or being carefree, because chaos and sadness always rode on their heels. From early on she'd held back and didn't give herself over to happiness or joy, at least not completely. The letdown hurt too much.

She felt she had been released from a cage, and this sensation was invigorating. No longer did she have to suppress a desire to be openly creative with a talent she'd kept hidden since childhood. She began to feel powerful. Learning to drive was giving her a new sense of freedom, but above all, having a close friend was giving her a new sense of worth.

The first time Bud had taken time to notice Grace sitting alone in the school lunchroom, he was drawn to go sit down at the same table. He tried to get a conversation going, but she would hardly talk. He found her reticence attractive, having been raised with two sisters who never stopped talking long enough for him to say much of anything. She appealed to his nurturing, protective temperament. He felt strong and needed around her and he adored her sweetness.

As the years passed he saw that he, too, was more on the sober, serious side. In fact, Andy had often made him nervous because he didn't seem to take anything very seriously. Now Grace was beginning to be more like Andy and strangely enough, Bud began to feel that a weight was being lifted, a weight he didn't know he'd been carrying. Nonetheless, he wouldn't allow himself to attribute these changes to Ceil. I*t's probably on account of the woman changes taking place and her painting pictures,* he reasoned.

The day Grace showed her first oil painting was one of celebration. She had planned it for days. Only Bud and Ceil were coming. They were a safe audience. She wasn't ready to share with anyone else. Bud came in early with a box of chocolate covered cherries, her favorite candy. Then he got all cleaned up and wore the new shirt Andy had given him for Father's Day, even though his others were still perfectly good. His preparations thrilled her. She hugged and kissed him several times when he came out of the bathroom all spiffed-up.

Ceil had brought over a bottle of wine and some fancy cheeses. Grace felt like a celebrity. She asked Bud and Ceil to sit on the couch in the parlor. Slowly and carefully she furled the bed sheet from the easel revealing the newly dried canvas. It was a painting she had copied from an old black and white photo of the children.

Nine-year-old Andy stood on the creek bank with his little fishing pole while ten- year-old Angela held a wriggly worm for him. To the side and in the background five-year-old Regina looked on with awe at her older siblings.

There was a long moment of silence before Bud could catch his breath. "I've never felt anything like this. I'm… It touches my heart," he said and began to applaud. Ceil joined in. Grace couldn't remember such joy flooding over her, not even when her children were born. The wine was opened and for the first time in her life Grace got tipsy over the course of the evening. Sitting between Bud and Ceil, she hugged one and then the other like a child who had been away from its mom and dad for several days.

"Ceil, I know I promised you my first painting," she said, slurring her words, "but this one's for Bud. I hope you don't mind." Bud kissed her on the cheek. He felt like a prince.

Ceil paused with a serious expression on her face. "Well, I guess I'll have to take back all the brushes, canvases and stuff I got you." Laughter sailed through the open windows.

A few days later, Regina dropped by and stood for a long time silently taking in Grace's painting. Grace marveled at how pretty she was these days. She was regaining her health and an interest in her appearance. Finally, Regina said softly, "You paint like I used to dance."

Tears stung at the back of Grace's eyes. "You can still dance."

Regina shook her head, *never again,* she thought.

"You are looking so beautiful and happy these days, Regina. I know you're feeling better. That was a hard pregnancy."

Regina smiled. *Yes, I do feel better and look better. That's because Billy Wayne's hardly ever at home, and I'm getting more and more determined to get a divorce.* She longed to share these thoughts with her mother.

But she would wait. She first wanted to get her big sister's encouragement. She felt her dad would welcome a divorce but her mom would need Angela's approval. Her intuition told her that Sister Mary Grace would back her up even though she was a nun. A week ago, at Maypheli's insistence, Regina had written the Mother Superior asking for permission to visit Sister Mary Grace."Dat woman's got a heart that sees farther than a rule," Maypheli reassured her. Regina doubted her words knowing that the novices were kept isolated in prayer, meditation and study and were rarely allowed visitors.

BILLY WAYNE had come by the house only twice since she'd had the miscarriage. The first time was to see the girls and get some clothes. The second time was late at night after the girls had gone to sleep. He was drunk and remorseful.

"Regina baby, I'm going to change. All I want is you and the girls. I'm sorry."

Regina folded clothes in silence. He held out a wad of bills, "Here's some money. I'm back at the quarry, making a livin.'"

She got up holding a stack of towels. "Billy Wayne, I know about Geraldine. Did she kick you out? I'm not interested in being with you either."

"Why, you little bitch."

He came at her with clinched fists. She dodged as the blow came within inches of her face. She grabbed a kitchen chair and flung it at him with all of her one hundred and twenty pounds. He fell to the floor and looked up at her in disbelief.

"Mama, Mama." Suddenly both girls came running down the hall to the kitchen. They grabbed Regina's legs and peeked from the folds of her nightgown terrified of their dad.

Regina calmly said, "Everything's okay, girls. Hush now. Your daddy just stumbled," Regina calmly said.

Ashamed, Billy Wayne pulled himself up and hugged the girls who still clung to their mom. "Daddy jest fell. I'm okay, and I want to come back and be with you."

Regina wanted to pick up another chair but wouldn't, not in front of the girls. "You can come back to see your daughters tomorrow afternoon. It's too late now. They need to sleep." She tried to control the quiver in her voice.

Billy Wayne felt uneasy, a little like he did around Mayphelia.

"Kiss your daddy goodnight." Regina took the girls' hands and led them to their room and tucked them in with reassurances that everything was fine.

When she came back, Billy Wayne fixed his eyes on her. She tried to ignore the hate-filled stare. Finally he hissed, "That nigger woman's put a spell on you, and she's gonna pay. I mean it. She's gonna pay with her life." He stomped out the door dragging his bad leg.

Terrified Regina ran to call Ceil. When she took the earpiece off the hook Mrs. Lester who shared her party line, was telling someone how to cook collard greens. "I'm sorry to interrupt, Mrs. Lester, but I need to make a call right now. It's sort of an emergency."

The words were hardly out of her mouth when she regretted them. She knew Mrs. Lester might listen in and before morning everyone in the town would know that Billy Wayne had threatened to kill Mayphelia.

"Well, alright, dear." She hung up right away.

As Regina asked Bernadette, the operator, to connect to Ceil's number, she didn't hear the party-line click on. Maybe Mrs. Lester wouldn't listen after all. Regina remembered getting spanked when she was ten for listening in on a conversation. Hopefully Mrs. Lester had the same morals as her mother.

"Ceil, I think Billy Wayne is going to do something bad to Mayphelia." She repeated his threat.

Ceil hung up. Panic almost brought her to her knees as she fumbled to lock her front door. "Dear God, let her be safe."

Once in her car, she pushed the accelerator to the floor and took only ten minutes to get to Mayphelia's.

Her place seemed haunted, all black, dark and creepy quiet. As she opened the latchless screen door, Ceil swore, "Goddamnit, I'm going to have latches and locks put on her door and if she doesn't….."

Ceil screamed. A white phantom floated across the room towards her.

"Ceil, baby, be that you?"

"Damn it, May-May, you scared the crap out of me. That white gown…you looked like a ghost."

Mayphelia put her arms around her. "What's got you so scared? You gives me this gown. Remember?"

"Get your things, you have to come home with me. Billy Wayne has threatened to kill you."

"Oh, child, he ain't gonna do no killin'."

"Stop being so stubborn."

No amount of pleading or begging could get Mayphelia to go back with her. "Listen, baby, I don't see no stirrings. He won't hurt me none tonight. Now go on home, baby."

Ceil refused. "Okay then, you takes my bed," she said as she folded out the pallet for the floor. Ceil tossed all night on the squeaky bed springs amid spiders and flowing blood.

THE next afternoon Grace listened to Ceil's account of the night before. "Billy Wayne is dangerous," was Ceil's final sentence. Grace knew she was right. Her daughter and granddaughters weren't safe. She and Bud had begged Regina to move back home but she refused always saying, "Don't worry, Grandpa's watching out for me."

Grace rubbed her forehead. "I don't understand. This morning Regina never mentioned a thing about this. Of course she was so excited because she'd just gotten a letter saying she could visit her sister."

"That's wonderful," Ceil said. "She needs to get away and relax."

"Yes, I'm excited for her and I'm thrilled that we'll have the girls all to ourselves. I just pray Tessie will be alright without her mama for that long."

Grace rearranged a bouquet of flowers on the table. "But the most important thing is that they will all be completely safe during those days."

Ceil sighed, "I hope the same is true for May-May."

"Don't worry. We'll keep an eye out and check on her frequently."

While Bud was in town buying a train ticket for Regina, Grace freshened up her old room, getting it ready for the girls. As she was changing the sheets her anxiety over everyone's safety mounted. *Perhaps divorce is the best thing for my granddaughters, as well as Regina. What other way is there for them to get away from Billy Wayne and his cruelty? Anyway, who came up with stupid rules demanding that people live in misery?*

She stopped fluffing a pillow and stood staring across the room. *I'm having these thoughts and questions, and for the first time, I don't feel like I should go to confession. It's like dry skin is being peeled off my mind so that it can breathe.*

As a child, Grace had lost the belief that if she were good and prayed enough God would make things right. Her daddy remained as mean as ever no matter how many rosaries she said. Yet after Regina's birth she had gone to Church on all Sundays and holy days mainly because she was afraid not to. *Is a faith based on the fear of hell really a faith at all?* This thought sent another rush of freedom throughout her nervous system. But then the jailer appeared, weaker but still present. *How can you have such thoughts when you have a daughter who is a nun?*

CHAPTER SEVENTEEN

Grace was eager to get started on a portrait of Ceil. "I'll pay you with a portrait exposing your character and soul," she teased her friend. Since Grace would be tied up with her granddaughters the rest of the week, she persuaded Ceil to come for a sitting that afternoon. She had decided on a picturesque spot under the giant Cypress tree growing on a sloping bank where the creek poured over a ridge of stones. She had packed a picnic and thought about Bud's suggestion to take the camera. "You do real good work adding your imagination to a photograph. That way ya'll won't be in the hot sun."

CEIL had been plodding through the morning heat. Should she cancel her portrait appointment? She liked the idea of being with Grace for a whole afternoon but she also knew that a long visit would be painful. How could Grace be so oblivious to Ceil's desires? "Well for one thing, she's not a freak of nature like you," she said to the face in the bathroom mirror.

Over the past few days Ceil had called the airport several times to book a ticket back to Los Angeles, only to hang up before completing the reservation. She couldn't run away from the promise she'd made to Mayphelia.

"Child, you gotta make peace with yo'r grandmaw for yo'r sake as well as hers."

Mayphelia saw that headstrong little girl once again as Ceil set her jaw and remained silent. She then took her by the shoulders. "Listen, Ceil, she ain't gonna die till you make peace with her. It ain't right to make her suffer like that. Now you promise me."

Ceil wondered if Mayphelia knew the real reason for her procrastination. Once her grandmother was dead and buried she would have no excuse to stay here, yet she wasn't ready to leave Grace. She stopped putting on lipstick and once again spoke to the reflection. "You don't care how much that old woman's suffering, do you?"

As Ceil headed towards the kitchen to refill her coffee, she realized it wasn't just Grace. She now belonged to a regular family. There were two little girls who called her Cecie, and their mother who was as dear to her as she imagined a daughter would be. Andy made her laugh and Bud made her feel protected. A few days before when her car had stalled out, Bud got it started and then insisted on following her back to town. "Night's comin' on and it might do that again." Not since Radio Man had a man cared about her welfare like that.

With her morning coffee in hand she walked onto the front porch, where she prayed it would be cooler. Mrs. Carbon was out on her morning constitutional, carrying her parasol down low so the morning sun couldn't reach her thin skin.

"Mornin," Missus Ceil. How's your grandmaw doing? You've really fixed up her place. Don't look a thing like it did. Lordy, it's goin' to be the prettiest one around here. Well, I got to keep goin' fore this sun bakes me to the bone."

Ceil shook her head in wonder. *"I bet she thinks we just had a conversation even though I didn't say a word."* Though difficult to admit, she was beginning to like this god-forsaken place with its people who spoke to her about the weather and her grandparents' home. They treated her as if she were a member of the community, a person like them. Grace came to her mind, and she remembered she wasn't like them. She couldn't hide here like she could in Los Angeles. There she had a community of people like her who were more or less secure because of the anonymity of a large city.

"I would not be safe here," she said out loud.

She looked down the street. Mrs. Carbon was right. The Dollard place was returning to its former grandeur. Clem and his oldest son, Johnny, were painting the last section. She'd hired them on Bud's recommendation the same day she fired Billy Wayne. The second son, Donny, also worked on days when Bud didn't need him for farm work.

Clem was an excellent worker. Plus he and his boys were fast, hardly taking off time to eat lunch. As far as she could tell, Clem had never been drunk while on the job. It felt good to have him and his children on her payroll. When the first nurse quit at the end of two weeks, and the second after one week, Nelda said she thought Lizzie could do as good a job as anyone. That proved to be true.

Lizzie worked hard, never complained and took the initiative to solve problems. Ceil had already spoken with her lawyer about setting up college funds for her and her four siblings. They were all smart and deserved some breaks. She could never forget the breaks she had been given as a young runaway. Now it was her duty *to do unto others as had been done unto her.*

An enthralling fantasy popped into her mind. *I could sell my company and settle down here in the big house. I'd adopt both Grace's and Clem's families and put all the children through college or get them started in their own businesses. I'd get Mayphelia to live with me, so I could take care of her through her last years. Life would be so nice.* I *would be like a regular person.*

A fly landed on her arm. As she smacked it, reality returned. *Who the hell are you kidding with such nonsense?*

Ceil hesitated before giving Bernadette Grace's number. She knew Grace would be disappointed, and she hated the thought of upsetting her. "Hello, Grace… I can't come today… Yeah, I'm okay. It's just that I need to finish up that business with my grandmother. You know I told you what Mayphelia said to me… Nelda keeps telling me that she's just languishing. It's what I've got to do…. Yes, I'll be fine… Thank you, but no, I'll be fine by myself… Yes, maybe next week…. Working from a photograph is a great idea...Well that's good. You get started on that one then … Alright then. Bye."

Ceil felt such gratitude for Grace. Even though she had already packed the picnic, she was understanding and flexible. The name Grace described her perfectly.

Ceil walked into the tiny bedroom and looked through her wardrobe. She was going to have to buy more clothes if she stayed here much longer. She would also have to get a larger place. A four-room bungalow was okay for a short stay, but she missed her home in Bel Air with its spacious eleven rooms, four bathrooms and rolling lawns.

She wished her grandmother could have seen that home, and could now know how beautiful her own home was becoming. A lump came to Ceil's throat as she remembered the beautiful china dishes. Perhaps her grandmother had wanted nice things all along. Perhaps she had wanted to show her and her mother more love than she could.

The other day something Regina had said evoked a memory. "I have to hide the clothes and stuff you and Sheila give the girls because it makes Billy Wayne angry." She remembered her grandmother putting a new dress and shoes into her closet and telling her to be careful when she wore them, meaning *don't wear these around him.*

Ceil couldn't finish her coffee. Her stomach was jumping every which way and her hands shook as she selected a blouse. She resolved, "I'll get this done even if it kills me."

With weights on her feet she pulled herself up the stairs of the Dollard porch, now fully repaired and freshly painted. She knocked, reminding herself that she had to buy a doorbell, a nice chiming one. Lizzie opened the door. Ceil felt like an intruder. She had been in the house so few times since she had arrived. The improvements shocked her. Along with the remodeling, new paint and furniture, there was lightness throughout the rooms. Her grandfather's presence seemed to be gone.

Lizzie smiled self-consciously. She wanted to be like Ceil, but couldn't see that ever happening. Like Ceil she was tall but also gangly and awkward. She couldn't imagine Ceil had been the same at her age. Up to now Lizzie had been embarrassed by her height, mainly because all the popular girls were short. She could tell Ceil was comfortable and proud of her tallness.

"Nelda has gone to the grocery store, and Mrs. Dollard, your ah…"

"Grandmother," Ceil said, smiling warmly at her. Ceil studied her a moment. "You remind me of myself when I was your age. You keep working and learning the way you do, and you'll go far."

Lizzie, stunned by the compliment, couldn't find her tongue for several moments. "Oh..ah…,your grandmother is sleeping. She's had her bath. That always tires her out."

She hurried towards the kitchen. "I just made some fresh coffee. Nelda drinks coffee all day long. Would you like some? It won't be any trouble."

Several raps on the back door put a halt to her self-conscious prattling. When she opened the door her dad said, "Hey lovable Lizzie. I see Miz Ceil's car is here. Tell her I need to ask her something."

Ceil came up behind Lizzie. "Come on in, Clem."

"Oh, ma'm, I can't. My shoes is all dirty. You said you wanted us to tear down that old shed back there and put up a sittin' garden. Well, there's some boxes in there that you might want to look at, boxes with papers and stuff, before I throw it all out."

Ceil followed Clem through the back yard, now lush and vibrant. He yanked several times on the shed's warped door before it opened. The bottom dragged in the dirt and a couple of doves flew out. Inside were several lamps, a writing desk, two chairs and three bedposts. "As I told you before, Clem, any of these things that you can use, feel free to take them or sell them at the junk store and keep the money."

"Ma'm, I wasn't talkin' 'bout them chairs and stuff. I'm gonna take all that and thank you very much. No, back here, you see these three boxes. I opened one and saw it might be stuff you might need to see. There might be money in 'em like there was in that other box in the garage." Ceil was moved by his honesty as much as she was by Billy Wayne's lack of it.

"Okay, Clem, clean them off and then bring them in to the dining room table. It's too hot to go through them out here." She felt the sweat soaking through her blouse. How could she possibly fantasize about moving here? The sun would do her in quicker than the Ku Klux Klan.

The first box contained documents, birth certificates, her mother's adoption papers, deeds on several homes, bank statements going back to times before her mother was born. "They certainly didn't believe in throwing anything away, did they?" Ceil said out loud to herself.

She reread through her mother's adoption papers saying her name several times, Rachel Cecelia O'Connell on one line and Rachel Cecelia Dollard on the next. The picture Mayphelia had given Ceil was still with her all the time. She grabbed her purse and removed it from a small leather folder. "I'm sorry I had forgotten your name. I'm proud that I was named after you. You were just Mama when I looked at the picture."

"Do you need something, Miss?" Lizzie called from the kitchen.

Ceil realized she wasn't alone. She was so used to talking to herself that she often forgot when other people were around. "No, I'm fine. And don't call me Miss. I'm Ceil. On second thought, I would like an ice coffee," Ceil called back.

"Ice coffee? Well, okay. Do you want cream and sugar, ah… Ceil?"

Ceil leaned back and looked at the other two boxes. She didn't want to go through all this stuff. "Yes please, lots of sugar, three spoons, Lizzie."

Her eye went to the third box. Unlike the other two brown ones, it was a faded yellow with a store logo she didn't recognize. The other boxes were merely flapped closed, whereas this one was securely fastened down with loops and loops of tightly wound twine.

"Lizzie, bring me a pocket knife or scissors, please." Ceil shook the box and heard a rattling and a soft sound like "maaa." This definitely wasn't a box of papers. Lizzie carried in a coffee cup filled with ice and coffee in one hand and a large kitchen knife in the other.

"I don't know where there's a pocket knife or a scissors. Nelda changes things around. Will this do?"

Ceil smiled, "That will be fine, and Lizzie, the next time you bring me ice coffee you can put it in a glass just like you do ice tea. I had never heard of ice coffee either until I moved to California."

"I'd love to go there."

"You will someday." Ceil began slicing at the twine.

"How did you get there?" Lizzie asked, holding the box steady as Ceil cut through the lines.

"It's a long story. I ran away and hopped a freight train bound for California, but was forced off in San Antonio. Nelda took me in and I lived with her until I had to get away again. She got me a ticket but I sold the last half in El Paso afraid I'd need more than my savings once I got there. I then hopped another freight, walked some and once even got a ride with a trucker, but I never did that again."

Lizzie's eyes fill with admiration. "You are so brave. I could never do that."

Ceil inhaled deeply. "Oh yes, you could if things got bad enough and you had to save yourself."

The final string popped. Ceil opened the box and saw several packages wrapped in faded Christmas paper. A long-hidden memory began curling around her mind longing to unwind, needing to unwind. She handed the knife to Lizzie. "Take this back and leave me by myself for now."

With hands shaking Ceil took out the first gift. A note fell out. *To my beloved granddaughter,Cecilia. May she forgive me for all my trespasses.* Ceil dropped the note and leaned back in the chair. The memories wanted to come, but they were behind so many walls. She ripped off the shiny paper. A beautiful china tea set painted with posies sat before her. *Oh God, I can't let myself remember. I'll die.*

The second package was more elaborate, wrapped in shiny green paper with a big red bow and felt Poinsettias. As she pulled back the wrapping, all the walls began to crumble. Ceil fell back as the air was sucked from the cells in her body. There was her baby doll, the very one she had wanted. She was five and looking through a catalog. The house was quiet. She was sitting on the floor at her grandmother's feet. Her grandmother was reading the almanac. He was gone. They were peaceful, even happy.

Little Cecelia liked it when someone died and he wasn't there. She showed her grandmother the doll. Her grandmother smiled and said, "At Christmas, I promise. And what about that lovely tea set? That would be nice, too. Don't you think?"

Weeks passed and one night she woke up to loud arguing. She edged out of bed and went halfway down the stairs. Her grandmother sat at the table wrapping the baby doll. Her grandfather was yelling about bastards and damnation. Her grandmother was frightened. She put the gifts in the box and wound string around and around it. Her grandfather tried to take the box but she said, "I'll burn them tomorrow."

Swirling down the vortex of a whirlpool, Ceil felt the agony of all those years swallowing her up. Wounded animal sounds, deep and guttural, filled the room. The memories rode on swift winds to consciousness. Memories she'd shoved under the spiders and all the blood.

Her grandfather peering at her through the window as she was getting out of the bath tub. His walking past her bedroom late at night, turning the door handle. Her grandmother's screaming, "I swear I'll see you in hell before I let you near her." Her grandmother getting in bed with her, holding her, protecting her. Her grandmother carrying her over to Mayphelia's in the middle of the night. Her grandmother's blackened-blue eyes. Overhearing her grandmother's voice, hissing, "You pushed my Rachel out that window, but you'll have to kill me before you kill her daughter." Then a loud thud and her grandmother was on the floor. Her lip was bleeding. Running off to Mayphelia's. Mayphelia giving her another doll and some new clothes, saying, "Your grandmaw sent these over for you, but you gots ta keep 'em here."

Ceil fell to the floor weeping, "She tried. Oh God, she tired." She heard Mayphelia talking to her as a little girl, "Yo'r grandma's jest as scared as you. There's evil in this world and he's full of it."

Nelda was suddenly by her side cradling her. Ceil was falling down a well and, for the second time in her life, Nelda was there to keep her from hitting the bottom. Lizzie ran to the doorway and stopped, too frightened to go into the room.

"Should I get the doctor?"

"No. Call Grace and tell her to bring Mayphelia over here as soon as possible. Hurry up, then come back and help me get her upstairs." Mrs. Dollard's bell rang softly and stopped as if she were aware of someone else's needs.

For the next three days, Ceil let herself be taken care of. She had no choice. Every ounce of her body had been zapped of strength. She couldn't lift her head off the pillow. "The truth almost killed me," she whispered in Mayphelia's ear.

Mayphelia hummed softly, then said, "The spirit always know what a person can take and what's it can't take. You's stronger now than you ever was, but yo'r body needs time to heal all them buryin' places where you done put yo'r pain all these years."

Mayphelia opened the window and pulled back the curtain. The sunlight streamed in. "We's got ta herd all them demons to the light. Now rest easy, child, I won't leave yo'r side." She pulled the rocker next to Ceil's bed and sat there day and night while Ceil reclaimed her soul. Whenever she went to the bathroom, she made sure either Nelda or Grace were at her side. "She can't be alone. Too much aloneness as a child."

Grace drove over to Ceil's every morning even though she had failed her driver's test. Despite Ceil's instructions and Bud's prompting her to practice in the unplowed field next to the barn, she still failed.

"Well, you can take it again." Bud laughed when she told him. "I'll give you lessons this time. Ceil mustn't be much of a teacher."

She thought she detected a hint of triumph over Ceil's inability, but she was never completely sure how he felt because when Ceil collapsed, he encouraged her to help her friend. "You know first-hand what she's going though. I can manage the girls and I'll ask Blanche to help if I need it," he assured her.

However, when Grace got ready to leave on the third day, Tessie threw such a tantrum that Grace took them with her. This turned out to be a blessing. The girls' chatter and laughter, which Grace unsuccessfully tried to subdue, began to draw Ceil back to a world where children could be children with only make-believe monsters. She began to leave her own bleak childhood behind and enter theirs. She heard them scooting down the stairs on their rumps and then gleefully shouting as they raced back up to do it all over again.

Mrs. Dollard was also aware of their presence and the presence of her granddaughter next door. Now unable to open her eyes, nonetheless she could hear very well, even though she couldn't always assimilate or make sense of what she was hearing. However, she knew that children were playing in the house and sometimes outside her door. Could it be her little Rachel Cecelia or her dearest Cecelia?

Then there was the moment when the children's voices stopped and she felt the sun dip below her window sill and a hand take hold of hers. Then there were word sounds, but what did they mean? She tried to piece together the puzzles she was hearing. This was important; she needed to understand. Then she knew. It was Cecelia, the grown-up granddaughter, cradling her hand and sitting on the bed beside her. She wasn't angry anymore. She was soft and precious just like she was as a baby.

"Grandmother, I remember now. You tried to protect me, to take care of me, to give me toys and pretty things. I remember that he was as mean to you as he was to me. I remember you hated him as much as I did. I'm sorry I've treated you so badly all these years. I put your face as well as his on all the cruelty. I wish I had remembered sooner, before…before you had this stroke. I pray to God that you can understand what I'm saying."

Mrs. Dollard began to float towards the light. Peace was trying to surround her, but there was still some darkness that drove it away. The attic stairs ascended to the closed door. Cecelia and her brand new friend, Beverly, had run up there an hour or so ago. They had just moved here to this new town and already Cecelia had found a friend. She was happy for her especially since Mayphelia and Radio Man hadn't arrived yet.

She didn't want to bother the girls but she knew that he'd soon be home, and she didn't want something bad to happen again. Suddenly, he was there charging up the stairs like a rabid blood hound and flinging open the door. "Damn you to hell, you fiend spawned by Satan."

Slips, bras, panties being thrown about. Beverly flying down the stairs. Then the sounds of a belt hitting flesh, screams, cries, while she huddled in a corner unable to move. *"It's better to love a woman than a heartless man,"* stuck in her throat.

Mrs. Dollard finally got those words out the day he lay on the basement floor with one rib gouging his lung and another pressing near his heart. *"My life would have been so much better if I had lived it with a woman."* When he heard this a curse came to his lips, but all that came out was blood.

Two days after the beating Cecelia ran away and Mrs. Dollard never saw her again. Then she came to hate Mayphelia for saying she didn't know where her granddaughter was, even though it was the truth. One day Mayphelia did come over with an address, but Mrs. Dollard sighed and put it in her Bible. Too much time had passed. *Forgive me for hating that good woman.*

The circle of peace was almost completely around her. The anger, the hatred, the pain were fading into the light.

She had her granddaughter back and soon she'd be with her Rachel. She was sinking but before she left, she had to let her granddaughter know. Her tongue twisted, the words were there, waiting. "Love, love you." Ceil leaned in closer towards the labored whispering.

"Sorry, sorry, love, love you." The shattered glass of both their lives glued together in that instant.

Ceil said, "I forgive and I'm sorry too. I love you, Grandma, and always will." Mrs. Dollard lived two more days. Ceil never left her side and her grandmother knew she was there.

CHAPTER EIGHTEEN

Regina let out a deep sigh as the train pulled away. She waved to the girls and her mom and dad and watched them grow smaller and smaller until they were hidden by a warehouse on the outskirts of town. This was the first time she had been away from her daughters for any time longer than a half day. She relaxed back into the seat, happy to be going away, away from all her chores and responsibilities and even her girls. She wondered if her mother had ever done that. She couldn't remember her ever going anywhere without them. But she did remember times when her dad would give them their baths and do the cooking, while their mother stayed in her bedroom or walked out in the pasture. Once Regina peeked into her parents' bedroom and saw her mother scribbling in a large tablet. She knew now that she was drawing pictures, her way of getting away.

Grace had handed her a brown paper bag as she was getting on the train. "You may need a snack, especially since you were too excited to eat breakfast." She opened the bag and saw a tightly folded sheet of tablet paper next to the sandwich. Unfolding it, she recognized her dad's writing. A five dollar bill was taped to the bottom. *Gennie, you have a good time, you hear, like you did when you was a little girl. Don't worry about a thing. Your dad*

Regina smiled through tears. She felt so sorry that her girls wouldn't have a daddy like she had. *God, I could kick myself for remarrying by a priest. I hope Angela can help me figure out what to do.*

Here she was with two children and one miscarriage and yet didn't have a clue as to how it felt to be in love. She wanted to cry. In school, she had liked Billy Wayne but she never loved him. The thought of going through the rest of her life with him left her as dry as a parched skeleton. Could this really be God's will for her? What did that mean anyway, God's will? When she was little, she read about the lives of saints who were always doing God's will and getting killed.

From the very beginning she knew she wasn't cut out to be a saint, much less a martyr. Angela, on the other hand, had loved all those stories. Once when Angela kept going on about how much she admired the saints, Regina interrupted, "They make me mad for being so stupid, especially the ones who got killed."

Angela was horrified. "You'll have to go to confession for saying something like that."

Luckily the priest didn't give Regina any extra penance. He usually napped while the children made their confessions because they weren't all that interesting.

And now she was a martyr, sacrificing her happiness, her life, for a belief that didn't make any more sense to her than the saints' stories. Perhaps God was punishing her for what she had said about them. Mayphelia's words rang in her ears. *"God don't do no punishin.' We does that to ourselves,"* Then came Billy Wayne's," *Like it or not, you're stuck with me for life."*

He had come again a few nights before to see the girls. After tucking them in he announced that he was going to spend the night. "No Billy Wayne, you can't." She inched her way towards the ironing board where the warm iron rested. "I'm not healed yet and I'm still too weak."

Actually the opposite was true. She felt better than she had in years, but the thought of being in bed with him turned her stomach inside out. Besides, she still hadn't gotten Mayphelia's tonic to keep her from getting pregnant. One thing she knew for sure was that she didn't want any more children with Billy Wayne, no matter what the Church said.

He left in a huff, blaming Mayphelia and Ceil for interfering in their lives. "I'll get those bitches for turnin' you aginst me." When he couldn't get his way, he lashed out at whoever came to his mind. On too many occasions she had seen that chilling violence in his eyes and she never took his threats lightly. However, on that night, she decided not to call Ceil. She didn't want to get everyone stirred up again for no reason. Fortunately, the night passed without incident.

"Miss, your ticket please." The conductor brought her back to the present.

As she removed the ticket from her purse, she also pulled out her rosary. *Oh, I guess I'm supposed to pray now.* She began saying Hail Marys, but the words brought no comfort, no release from her problems. She put the rosary away and pulled out the egg sandwich. She wanted to stop thinking, stop trying to figure out everything and be a carefree girl again like her dad had told her to be.

Hints of gold, red and purple were sprinkled over the landscape. Her mom had said that this fall would be spectacular since there'd been so many earlier rains. She could tell her mom was excited about painting all the colors. Regina sadly wished she had some talent, one thing she could do besides taking care of children and a house. She glanced away from the window and caught the eye of a man sitting in a backward-facing seat several rows up. He put down his paper, smiled and winked. She quickly looked back out the window, feeling a warm blush come into her face. Self-consciously, she brought her right hand up to her collar and fiddled with the buttons.

She had been a silly teenager in high school the last time anyone had flirted with her and they were just boys. She glanced back and saw that the man was coming down the aisle towards her. He was youngish, early to mid twenties, dressed in khakis and a short-sleeved shirt. He stopped at her seat and leaned over.

"I'm sorry if I embarrassed you. You're just so pretty, I couldn't help myself."

"Well, I'm married," she stammered rather sternly holding out her left hand with the tiny sliver of gold on her ring finger, "and have two children." As soon as these words came out, she felt like a fool. The heat was rising in her face once again. *Damn, I wish I didn't blush so easily.*

The man was nice looking with clear hazel eyes and thick dark sandy hair combed nonchalantly to the side. He had a warm smile. Regina knew that he was the sort of man she could have been attracted to before she had ruined her life.

He smiled again, "Just my luck. While I was watching you look out that window, I imagined that you might go to a ball game with me tonight, that is if you're getting off in San Antonio." He smiled again. "So much for my imagination. I didn't mean to offend you. "

He began to walk away. Regina couldn't let this go. The spontaneous girl suddenly emerged. "Thank you for the compliment and for wanting to take me to a ball game. It means a lot," her voice began to break, "to me. I am going to San Antonio to see my sister."

He turned back, detecting her confusion. "You mind if I sit across the aisle from you?"

The seat next to Regina was empty, but he didn't ask to sit there. He was considerate. She felt so self-conscious she thought she was going to shatter into tiny pieces at any moment. She swallowed a few times and nodded. He sat down next to an elderly man, sleeping soundly with his cheek propped on the window.

Regina began, "I didn't mean to be rude."

He replied quickly, "I didn't either. I guess I was rather forward. My name's David."

"Glad to meet you. I'm Regina."

"I was really bored, reading the paper and trying to study, that is until I saw you. Gosh, there I go again being forward." He shook his head, a little disgusted.

"What are you studying?" she asked, curious.

"Oh, some electrical stuff. I'm working to get an electrician's license. I was just home for a family reunion."

"I'm going to see my sister. Oh, I already said that, didn't I? Are you hungry?" she asked, grabbing for the paper bag.

He laughed. He had a gentle laugh. "Sure."

They shared the oatmeal cookies and apple slices, along with bits and pieces of their lives. She more guarded than he. Regina told him about the girls, but not a thing about Billy Wayne.

He told her he was single, and that his sister had cerebral palsy and that one of his brothers was a farmer, like his dad, and his other brother was in the army, based in San Antonio. They got to see each other a lot. His home town was only thirty miles from hers. The two towns had played one another in some football playoffs.

Regina was enjoying talking with a man like this. He was interested in whatever she was saying, and he never once raised his voice, or cussed, or got agitated or angry.

When the train finally rolled into San Antonio she felt depressed, like a piece of paper being wadded up for the trash. As they exited the train together, he took her arm and helped her down the steps. She felt like a lady, a new sensation. "It's been nice talking with you and finding out about your family and life," she said softly.

Midway through the station, he turned and handed her a piece of paper with an address. "I know you're married, but still, I've really enjoyed your company. Here's my address, and if you ever feel like dropping me a line about Tessie or Angie or… anything… I'd love to hear more about them and you, too."

He gave her arm a little squeeze, turned and walked out of the station and her life. She wanted to run after him and beg him to take her away, but instead she entered the phone booth to call the convent for a car. Then she studied the address and stuffed it into a side pocket inside her purse.

CHAPTER NINETEEN

Regina sat on the straight-backed chair and looked up at the large picture of St. Thomas and tried to remember what the nuns had told her about him. Like her sister and brother, she had gone to the parochial school through eighth grade and then over to the public high school where a lot of saint stories faded from memory.

Wood wainscot polished to a mirror glow, a long couch and three chairs upholstered in a thick floral fabric that defied the severity of their austere frames fascinated Regina. This was a grand room, especially for a convent. A large globe stood between the two floor-to-ceiling windows, shuttered to keep out the hot noon sun. A wide overhead ceiling fan turned slowly but wasn't enough to move the heat.

She could feel the sweat coming through her bra or maybe it was some of the milk her breasts still occasionally produced since the miscarriage. She couldn't believe her body would continue to do this. She sometimes thought that if she hadn't messed up her life, she would have liked to have become a nurse. Nelda told her she still could, but she couldn't see how that would be possible. She hadn't even finished high school.

She heard footsteps coming towards the room. A nun walked past the doorway, looked in and said, "Peace be with you," and walked on. Regina hadn't seen her sister in over a year and she was nervous. She had never seen her as a Sister except for the picture her mother had taken.

Then Angela appeared in the doorway with arms outstretched, smiling radiantly. "My little sister, Gennie. Let me hug you."

Regina stood for a moment trying to take it all in. Was this really Angela? Angela's skin, usually a deep olive from her love of the outdoors, was now a chalky white. All the thick auburn hair forever poking out of every hat or scarf was now stuffed away under a bleached white cap with a white veil. The colorless form before her was so much thinner than the old Angela. What had happened to her sister?

Angela put her arms around her. They hugged a long time, both trying to hold back tears. Regina wished that everything could be like it had been. Her big sister helping her with her homework, letting her tag along to the movies, explaining to her about sanitary napkins and deodorant, chasing her out from behind the couch when James was there, fighting over a tube of lipstick.

How could they have ended up like this? Here she was, just twenty and already tied down for life, and Angela, beautiful Angela, everyone said so, stuck away like this, starving to death and fading away from a lack of sunshine.

"Let me show you your room." Angela picked up Regina's suitcase. "The cottage is being used by a visiting missionary, so you get to stay in a room just down the hall from my dormitory. A little like old times," Angela laughed merrily. "Well, come on. Don't lag behind," she commanded.

Regina obediently fell into step. Yes, this was her sister alright. Despite the outward transformation, she was still

Miss Boss. Regina's spirits immediately rose. For the next few days she could sit back and let Angela run the show.

They climbed several flights of stairs. *No wonder Angela was so thin*. On the third floor Angela said, "Here we are. This is where I sleep."

Regina looked into a large room with two rows of eight single beds precisely lined up, covered with plain white spreads, all made up with not a crease or wrinkle. A tiny wooden table stood beside each bed with a small wash basin with a water pitcher and towel. Regina was overcome. Her sister was preparing to take a vow of poverty, but she hadn't realized just what that meant until this moment. Three doors down the wide hallway, Angela ushered her into a tiny room with a narrow window viewing the belfry on the main chapel.

"This is your cell." Angela once again laughed. "That's what they're called." Regina couldn't understand her apparent happiness.

After she got settled in, Angela escorted her to the dining room where they snacked on cheese, strawberries and ice tea. Angela went over the schedule for the visit. Regina was going to be allowed to eat with her and the other novices at every meal. "Sister Mary Clare, my superior, is being so kind," Angela said, "but we can't talk at breakfast or dinner; however, we can talk at supper after a short spiritual reading." If Regina wanted to, she could get up at five and go to the chapel for prayers, meditation and Mass, or she could sleep late and join her for breakfast at seven. Afterwards she could assist Angela with her morning chores, which this week happened to be sweeping the stairs. Angela continued on with the directions. Finally Regina interrupted her, "Are we going to have any time just to be by ourselves?"

Angela beamed, "I was saving the best for last. I've been relieved of all afternoon duties for the next two days. After the noon meal and chores, we'll be free to do whatever until supper. During the mornings while it's still rather cool, you can stroll around the grounds. They are really beautiful. If you want, you can go downtown. The city bus stops right outside our gates."

At the evening meal Regina met the other novices. Like her sister, they were all joyful. The almost constant laughter made the experience so different from meals at her home, especially when Billy Wayne was there. Regina realized how much she missed being happy. Once again, that old resentment towards her sister began to rise. Angela, Sister Mary Grace, always did the right thing. Here she was living in a kind of prison, wearing hideous clothes, praying and studying all the time, yet she was beaming. There was peace here.

Later that night, unable to sleep, Regina prayed that somehow God would help her to attain the happiness Angela had. She had two precious little girls, lived in her grandparents' pretty little cottage, had a big bedroom, could wear what she chose, talk when she wanted, yet she was so unhappy.

Perhaps she should pray to forgive Billy Wayne and try to fall in love with him. With the thought of falling in love, David's image came to her mind. She immediately retrieved his note from her purse. He had a nice handwriting, small and rather cramped, a lot like her dad's. She read over the address and wondered if a city bus went by there.

She quickly put the note back, ashamed of herself. Here she was in a convent, with a chapel just down the hall and holy novices sleeping three doors down, and she was thinking about being with a man who wasn't her husband. With a shudder, she crawled back in the bed, turned off the light and prayed for sleep. A soft rap on her door bolted her upright. Angela was in her room, turning on the light and sitting on her bed. "I knew you wouldn't be asleep this early. Sister said I could come visit you for thirty minutes, provided I don't fall asleep during morning meditation."

Now this was her sister, in a cotton gown that showed curves which had noticeably diminished due to the weight loss, her hair cropped off but still full and shiny. Regina was relieved to see that her head wasn't shaved after all. The butch haircut similar to what the boys were wearing was really cute on her. She hadn't bothered to put on a robe, "because it's just too hot." The old Angela would have said "damn hot," but that was before she was Sister Mary Grace. Regina remembered her mom scolding Angela on several occasions for using bad language.

They held hands and just looked at each other for a moment. Angela said, "I can't tell you how much I've missed you."

Regina burst into tears. Then she was in her sister's arms and crying on her shoulder. This was the first time she had really cried since before the miscarriage, and now it was all coming out. She tried to stifle her sobs to keep from disturbing the sleeping sisters on the floor, but Angela kept saying, "It's okay. Let it out."

And out it came, barrels and barrels of tears. After a while, she was so worn out she could barely move. Angela laid her down in the bed, opened the window wider to let in more night air and kissed her on the cheek. "All God wants of us is to be happy." She turned out the light and left the room. Regina fell asleep immediately and slept as she had when she was a child.

She awoke late that first morning. The tower clock on the chapel showed 10:20. Before she could reprimand herself for sleeping away the day, she saw a note under her door.

So glad you're getting rest. Sister Rita said she would have some toast and coffee waiting for you in the kitchen which is just off the dining room. The bath is three doors down to your right. You should be able to have it all to yourself. See you at noon in the dining room. Hugs, SMG

The bathroom was large with three sinks along one wall and six doors leading into smaller cubicles; three contained commodes and three had bathtubs, all sparkling clean. Regina knew her mother would be thrilled by the immaculate cleanliness.

She took a long, leisurely bath. It had been a long time since she'd been able to sit and soak in the tub. *All God wants is for us to be happy* splashed through her mind much like the water cleaning her body. She dressed quickly and headed for the kitchen through the maze of halls and doors and more halls and doors.

After only two wrong turns she reached her destination. There she found Sister Rita, a short, plump woman who moved about quickly and laughed over everything. She fussed over Regina as if she were a queen. Even though the midday meal was less than an hour away, she insisted that Regina have a warm buttered bun with her coffee. Regina delighted in all the attention.

Sister Rita spoke nonstop as she bustled from the stove to adjust the heat to the counter to stir the cake dough to the refrigerator to take out a carton of eggs to the huge salad bowl to pour dressing, all in one seemingly giant motion. She asked Regina about Angie and Tessie by name and told her she was sorry about the miscarriage, but "God knows what's best."

In response to Regina's look of surprise, she explained that Sister Mary Grace often had kitchen duty. "She's the best worker of all the novices and I just wish I could have her every week, but the superiors think the new sisters need to rotate in order not to get attached." A slight smirk curled her lips, suggesting she didn't necessarily agree with this ruling. "Sister Mary Grace tells me everything," she said with a secretive laugh.

She put her finger to her mouth, "Shhh about that. They aren't supposed to talk while doing their chores. We get around that one by whispering." She giggled like a six-year-old. Regina had never met a nun quite like this, so down-to-earth, so human. All her teachers in grammar school had been more or less perfect, as far as she could remember, although Sister Alfreda, her fifth-grade teacher, was lots of fun, always making up learning games. Regina concluded that nuns were regular people, only in awful clothes, and perhaps Angela wasn't in such a bad place after all.

That afternoon Regina and Sister Mary Grace went to a piano room off the lower auditorium. It was cool down there and very quiet. Besides a piano and bench, the room contained two comfortable chairs. Sister Rita had given Regina a jar of cold lemonade and a bag of pecan cookies. With another one of her mischievous laughs, she told her to keep these goodies hidden from the others.

The sisters sat quietly for a few moments, so different yet so connected by filial love. Finally, Regina gave the latest news from home and ended with an account of Sheila and how close she felt to her. When Sister Mary Grace's turn came, she briefly explained her studies and life in the novitiate. Once again Regina saw that, unlike her, she was happy. Regina longed to be that way, too, and knew that to start being happy was to get rid of her secrets.

She began several times but stopped in midsentence out of shame and uncertainty. "You don't have to be afraid, Gennie," Sister Mary Grace said, as she offered her a cookie.

At first the words came out slowly and were difficult to say, but after a while the fear left and her tongue loosened and the darkness began pouring out much as the tears had gushed the night before. Regina retold Angela many of the things she had written in her letter, only in much greater detail. There was the rape, and the slaps, the hits, the punches, the kicks, the shouting, the name calling, the loss of confidence, the lack of money, the infidelity, the shame, the guilt, the fear, the constant fear - all the misery of these last four years and nine months.

She wanted to be free of Billy Wayne. "I don't care one bit about being kicked out of the Church," she said and then paused, startled she had let that slip out. But Sister Mary Grace's face didn't show any judgement or shock.

Regina went on, "The main thing is I don't want to hurt Mama. She'll be so worried because it's a mortal sin."

Regina blew her nose. The hand-embroidered handkerchief her mother had given her was soaking wet. "But the worst is that I can't see how I could make it on my own with two children. I don't even have a high-school diploma and I don't know how to do anything except clean house and change diapers."

Sister Mary Grace took a handkerchief from the folds of her skirt and handed it to Regina. Once again Regina blew her nose. "Billy Wayne doesn't give me enough now to buy groceries. If I didn't have Grandpa's house...., and if I get a divorce, he won't give me anything, I know." She looked out the window, "I can't let my girls live like this."

The lemonade was drunk and the cookies were eaten and the tower clock had chimed many quarter and half hours. Regina was spoken out. Sister Mary Grace hadn't said a word during the entire confession. For a moment she closed her eyes in prayer.

Finally she sighed deeply and began, "Regina, you must do what is best for you and your girls. This is your life and not Mom's or the Church's. You have suffered a great deal. Do you really think God wants you to suffer? I believe that God is bigger than any religion or man-made rules or doctrines. Turn everything over to Him and do what your heart tells you to do. I think God speaks to us through our hearts. Remember, He loves you more than anyone possibly can and He wants you to be happy."

Angela put the glasses on the tray. "Oh, and by the way, Mama will be fine. She's tougher than she lets on." She rose and adjusted her long skirt and the rosary hanging from it. "We need to start back. It's almost time for chapel and then supper. Tonight we're playing volleyball for recreation."

As they left the room, Sister Mary Grace turned back to Regina, "You know you can get your diploma by correspondence? Don't worry, Regina, you are very smart and talented, and you have lots of people who will help you get on your feet."

Regina floated down the wide hallway. Her sister had said that she was smart and talented. She knew her sister was saying what she really thought, not just being nice. *If Angela thinks I'm smart and talented, then I must be.* She entered the dining room.

That whole evening, Regina laughed almost continuously and enjoyed herself even more than she had on July 4th with Sheila. The novices were so full of life. Once the spiritual reading was finished the dining room erupted into conversation. Regina realized after a day of silence one has a lot to say.

Then later during the volleyball game with her veil tied back with a bright red ribbon, Sister Mary Grace became Angela. Her old competitive self was there, giving orders, spiking the ball, aggressively going after the serves. Yes, she was a winner, and now Regina was determined to become like her big sister. However, Sister Mary Grace had to slow down at times to catch her breath. Regina became a little worried. She never remembered her sister being winded.

The second morning Regina awoke early and joined Sister Mary Grace and the other novices in the morning meditation and prayers, attended Mass, ate with them and then helped her sister clean four flights of stairs on her knees, all without saying one word to anyone. The silence was broken only one time when Sister Mary Grace began panting out of breath. "Are you okay?" Regina whispered. Sister Mary Grace merely smiled and nodded yes.

In the afternoon they went on a long walk over the grounds and through various buildings. A substantial cloudburst had cooled everything off, making the trek enjoyable. The trees were still dripping.

The convent was connected to a college which the nuns owned and operated. Sister Mary Grace had already gotten her bachelor's degree and was now finishing a master's. They walked to the music building, where they sat quietly and took in the melodies of two violinists practicing a duet in an adjoining room.

Once the music stopped, they strolled over to the cemetery with simple white crosses all lined up in even rows. It reminded Regina of a picture of Arlington Cemetery. Sister Mary Grace pointed out the grave of their first grade teacher, Sister Frieda Rose. Regina could only remember that she had been very old and always called her Angela. They ended up in the arbor that contained the grotto of Our Lady of Lourdes. It was peaceful and shaded with water flowing softly from the fountain..

"You are really happy here, aren't you?" Regina asked. Her sister smiled and nodded.

"Do you ever miss James and that life?" Regina had to ask.

"Yes, I do, sometimes terribly. Remember, I am still a person under this habit. I'm going to tell you something very personal. James and I made love, my first and only time, a few days before I came here. Sometimes I miss those touches and kisses. Sometimes I feel sad when I realize I won't have a home and children like others." Sister Mary Grace took off her apron and wiped the rain from the iron bench. She sat down and motioned for Regina to sit beside her.

Regina was in shock. The perfect Angela had actually *done it.* Of course, she had known that they hugged and kissed because she had spied on them, but she never imagined anything more.

Sister Mary Grace laughed, "You're stunned. Well, I guess I would be too. You remember Mama often said, 'I swear, Angela, you do march to your own drummer, don't you?'"

"What made you decide to do this? I could never…"

Sister Mary Grace picked up the hem of her skirt, which had landed in a small puddle. She carefully wrung it out, deep in thought. "As you know, before you were born, Mama had a full-term baby that died. I don't know if anyone ever told you that Mama had a nervous breakdown afterwards. I had just turned five and Andy was four. Everyone pretended like everything was normal, but I knew it wasn't. Mama was gone. Both our Grandmas and Aunt Polly were there a lot, but still I took on a lot of responsibility. I took care of Andy all the time.

"That's when I began to pray. I found my own little place in the barn's hay loft. I would go there and talk to God. One day a bright light, I swear this happened, surrounded me and I knew it was God and that everything was going to be okay and that Mama was going to come back to us. Then you were born, and Mama came back. But then she gave you most of her attention, and once again I felt left out. I was very jealous of you. One time I even slapped you, not very hard, while you were sleeping in your crib. You started wailing and I crawled under Mom and Dad's bed.

"Mama picked you up and said, 'Oh, there, there, sweet Angie. I mean, Gennie.' In that moment, another flash came to me and I realized that Mama loved us all the same, just like God does. So then and there, under that bed along with the dust bunnies, I realized that I wanted to serve God and let everyone know of His love."

Impulsively Regina put her arms around her sister in a tight hug. "You are wonderful. I love you so much."

"I love you, too."

That night, Regina awoke when the tower clock chimed one o'clock. She put on her robe and slippers and went down to the chapel. Two other sisters were there praying. Regina sat in the pew for over an hour, not praying, just sitting and being in the stillness. The next afternoon she said good- bye to her sister and the others and got on the train, knowing for certain what she was going to do.

The day before, after they had finished cleaning the stairs and Angela had gone to her morning classes, Regina had gone back up to her room and taken out the paper with David's address. Angela had told her that the only phone in the convent was in the main office on the first floor just off the main foyer.

Regina had softly knocked on the door. A frowning Sister opened the door. "I'm Sister Mary Grace's sister, just visiting."

The Sister stared at her as if she had broken one of the Ten Commandments. Ordinarily Regina would have turned around and run down the hallway, but today she was full of courage. "I'm sorry to bother you, but I need to look up a phone number and was wondering if I could borrow a phone book?"

The Sister spoke with pursed lips, "Mother Superior and the Council are in a meeting. Wait here."

The door closed, then opened almost immediately and a book and pencil were thrust at her. "In case you need to write it down. I see you have paper," she said, referring to the crumpled wad in Regina's hand. "Leave it outside the door once you've finished."

Regina flipped through the book until she found David's name and address exactly as he had given them. With mounting excitement, she quickly scribbled down the phone number. She remembered seeing a phone booth no more than two blocks down the street from the convent gates and hurried to the foyer.

She pushed open the heavy door to a loud clap of thunder. Regina looked up and felt sprinkles hit her face. As she stepped back, a steady rain fell. *I'm being stopped from doing something very foolish.* She could hear Mayphelia. *"Da good Lord do always know what's best."*

CHAPTER TWENTY

The funeral was small. A cool front had blown in the night before, dropping the temperatures into the mid-seventies, which seemed cold after the blistering upper nineties. The gravesite was on the side of a small hill overlooking a pasture where cattle grazed. Mrs. Dollard had chosen her own plot right after burying her husband, purchasing one on the opposite far side of the cemetery.

The priest asked Ceil if a mistake had been made. Ceil replied with a smile, "Oh no, she knew what she was doing. One lifetime of hell has been enough for her."

After the service, a small group gathered at the Dollard house. There was Nelda, Mayphelia, Grace, Bud, Regina and the girls. Clem, his wife, Mable and their five children came in through the kitchen, but Ceil told them to come around to the front door and into the parlor where the town's merchants and businessmen were mingling. Father Gilbert, accompanied by Lavenia, showed up with the crucifix from the coffin. The priest handed it to Ceil. Slightly repulsed, Ceil blurted out, "I have no use for that."

Grace knew Lavenia would use this comment to poison anyone who cared to listen, so she quickly said, "I'll take it. She's not herself."

Just about everyone expressed amazement over the once-gloomy house. "This might just be the most beautiful home in this little Podunk town of ours," the banker announced to the group.

"Well, it's all because of Clem Sites and his sons Johnny and Donny. They're expert craftsmen and the hardest workers I've ever employed," Ceil said, hoping to drum up more employment for them. She wished she could add, *"Clem's never once come on the job drunk."* Clem and his sons had ducked their heads in embarrassment over being singled out for praise in a gathering such as this. Ceil also wanted to say, *"Hold your heads up. You're as good as anyone here."*

With Lizzie's help, Grace oversaw the food and made sure there were enough places for everyone to sit. She wanted to keep moving to avoid thinking about Ceil's departure to L.A., which was now imminent. After a few more finishing touches, the house would go on sale. The funeral parlor had been sold over six weeks ago to a young man just out of mortician school.

"You need any help, Mom?" Regina asked. She was holding Tessie, who kept her arms tightly wound around her mama's neck. Regina had hardly been able to put her down since getting off the train. Angie and Toby, Clem's eleven-year-old son, were playing with building blocks in the wide hallway leading to the back of the house. Regina sat down on the stairs and looked into Tessie's eyes, "You can go play with Angie and Toby. Mommy will be right here." She kissed her several times. As usual little Angie took charge. "Come on Tessie. You can build too."

From the moment Regina had stepped off the train, Grace could see that she was more rested and relaxed than she had been in a long, long time. During supper Regina said she had made up her mind about several things. There was something in her voice that kept Grace from asking about these decisions. Getting away and visiting with her sister had been the best medicine she could have had, and Grace didn't want to do anything to offset the remedy.

Earlier that morning, Regina had seen Billy Wayne watching her from the edge of the cemetery. She started going toward him. He looked directly at her and jumped back in his pickup and drove off. She had wanted to talk to him, but now it would have to wait.

The gathering was thinning out. Ceil stood at the front door thanking each person for coming. Grace urged Lizzie to go with her family. "Everyone's leaving and Bud and I can manage the rest of the work. You've been doing so much around here."

"Thank you, Mrs. Wolansky." Lizzie took off the apron and left. Grace watched her do a skipping run to her dad's car. She was still a girl but had worked like a woman these past weeks.

Besides Bud and Grace, Nelda was the last to leave. She saw to it that all the medications and sickroom paraphernalia had been cleared out and had made arrangements to have the hospital bed picked up the next day. As she was saying her goodbyes, Ceil handed her an envelope with a round-trip ticket to Scotland and a wad of cash. Grace knew the whole town probably heard Nelda's screams of joy. After walking Nelda out to her car, Ceil came in and started up the stairs. "I am exhausted. Lock up for me, will you?"

Bud and Grace continued cleaning and putting things back where they belonged. When Bud came in from taking the trash to the burning barrel, he put his arm around Grace's shoulder. "We need to get back. The animals gotta be fed."

Grace looked around at the remaining dirty dishes. She hated to leave. "Why don't you go? When Ceil awakens, I'll get her to drive me home." He nodded and pulled her to him for a long kiss.

She watched the car drive away, deep in thought. Bud was becoming more affectionate every day, or was it that she was becoming more accessible? She recalled the day Ceil had said, *"It's time you came out of the dark ages and got behind the wheel of a car."* Then as a sort of added incentive, she added, *"The more independent you become, the more you'll free up Bud."*

Perhaps this new independence was making them appreciate one another more. She picked up a rag and looked around at the newly renovated kitchen. "Whoever buys this place is going to get a treasure," she said to the new stove as she began wiping.

Grace dried the last dish and put it away. During the course of the clean-up, a heavy cloud had begun to descend over her. *Ceil will soon be leaving. Will I still feel free and joyful, like a new person whom Bud wants to kiss for a long time? Will I continue painting and learning?* Grace was terrified she would go back to being the way she had been. Could she survive without the prodding, pushing, praise, encouragement, and friendship Ceil had been giving her?

Ceil had lined up a gallery in San Antonio to host an art show for her in November. Grace would have never had the audacity to get something like that done for herself. In fact she had wanted to retreat behind a wall when Ceil showed the art manager two of her paintings. "Just look at these," Ceil had said. "The public deserves to be seeing her work." Grace still got a little embarrassed when she remembered how Ceil had persisted, "I'll take care of all the advertising." Once the deal was finalized, Grace became excited over the prospect of getting paid for her paintings. She realized she might be able to help pay off the new tractor Bud had gotten the previous spring. And when she thought about helping Regina with extra money, she was thrilled beyond words.

The last dish was dried and put away and every chair was back in place, yet Ceil hadn't come down. She had been asleep for over two hours. Grace decided she'd best wake her up. The sun would soon be down.

The tea tray was elegant with china, a newly bloomed chrysanthemum in a crystal stem and finger sandwiches Mrs. Carbon had brought over. Grace carefully maneuvered up the stairs, tapped lightly on the door and entered.

The blinds were drawn but Grace could see that Ceil was sleeping soundly. She looked beautiful in her lacy pink nightgown, her blond hair haloing her peaceful, wonderfully featured oval face with the high cheekbones. Grace carefully put the tray on the bedside table, then sat on the edge of the bed and began to gently rub Ceil's arm.

"It's time to wake up, sleepyhead."

Ceil opened her eyes and smiled to see Grace there beside her. "Oh, my darling Grace, I feel a tremendous weight has been lifted from me. Perhaps I'll just sleep for a week or so," Ceil reached over and caressed Grace's cheek as she spoke.

"That's probably the best thing you can do for yourself. But first would you like some tea and a sandwich?" Grace began to pour the tea. Her hands shook.

Ceil noticed. "I'm going to miss you too, Grace, terribly. I'll come back from time to time and then you and Bud can come to see me."

Grace bit her lip, trying to suppress the tears. She needed her friend to be closer than California in order to sustain her new life.

Ceil sat up and put her arms around Grace. "It's going to be fine, my dear."

Grace put down the tea pitcher and grabbed Ceil in a warm desperate embrace. Ceil began kissing her on the cheek and then moved to her neck. Grace sighed and gave herself over to the warmth and tenderness of Ceil's lips, which were on her mouth and then her neck again.

She felt her dress being unbuttoned and removed. The tenderness, the softness continued as she was pulled down on the bed. Slip, bra, panties were removed. Grace surrendered completely to the pleasures and allowed her body to feel what it had never felt to this extent. Fingers were probing her depths. A tongue hungrily tasted every part of her body. The pleasure was beyond anything Grace had ever experienced. The waves rose and subsided, over and over until they came crashing through the walls of her body. She screamed out, then became limp and without form.

Some time later she was awakened by a ringing phone in the distance. Ceil had her arms and legs wound around her. It was dark outside. *"That must be Bud. Oh my God, what happened?"* Quickly putting on her underclothes, she bolted out of the room and down the stairs.

"Gracie, you all okay?" Bud's kind voice indicted her on the spot.

"Oh, yes, we're …fine." She wound the cord around her finger. "Ceil slept all afternoon and then I fell asleep… on the couch… waiting for her to wake up." Grace was lying to Bud. Had she ever done that before? She had avoided the truth, but never lied outright to him. Now she'd opened that door and another betrayal came between them.

"You want me to come get you?"

"Well, yes, maybe that would be best. Ceil is awfully tired. Have you eaten? I'll prepare a dish with all this leftover food." Clem and Mayphelia had taken several platters, but the refrigerator was still full.

"Can you come now?" Grace finished and inhaled loudly.

"I'll be right over. You sure you're okay? You sound kinda funny."

"I'm just not used to an afternoon nap, that's all." Another lie. The gap was widening.

When Grace reentered the bedroom, Ceil was sitting up in bed, totally naked. It had really happened. As Grace had run for the phone, she thought, *It was just a dream, nothing more.* But now she knew she couldn't lie to herself. *Dear God, what kind of person am I?* She grabbed her dress and shoes and turned to go to the bathroom.

"Do you hate me now?" Ceil asked, a slight catch in her voice.

Grace turned towards her. "You didn't force me. Somewhere in me was that longing. It's my sin, my disgrace. I don't know who I am any more. For the first time, I want to go back to the way it was before you came."

Ceil slid down in the bed and pulled the covers over her. "You're not the same as me, Grace. You never will be." She turned away and closed her eyes. "Goodbye, my love."

Grace didn't say a word on the way home. Fortunately Bud was in a talking mood. He told her about the letter they'd just gotten from Andy. He and Sheila were coming in a couple of weeks. "He wants to talk to us about something. Reckon what that could be. I hope he's not planning on marrying just yet. He needs to get ahead a little more."

He didn't seem to notice that Grace was staring straight ahead, not responding. He continued, "I'm gonna sell a couple of those steers. Beef prices are way up now. Besides the hay is getting low." He then told her about helping Alex dig out a deeper cow tank. "I told him there's no telling when we'll get enough rain to fill it up, even though the hot days are gonna get fewer and fewer." He reached over and patted her knee, bringing her back from selfrecriminating thoughts. She took his hand and squeezed it tightly.

In the kitchen Bud ate the food Grace had brought while she soaked in a hot tub. *If only this were baptism water that could wash away my sin,* she thought. *I need to be cleansed now and not when I was a tiny baby. I must undo to Bud what I've done to him.*

She dried off and put rose water lotion all over her body. She wanted to give Bud as much pleasure as she had received. She put on a gown of soft cotton, freshly laundered, and got in bed and waited for him. When he came, she made love to him as she had never before, initiating and participating fully. After a while she realized she was feeling pleasures she had never experienced with him or with Ceil. She gave herself over more completely. Bud had never once been unfaithful to Grace, but that night he felt like he was with another woman.

Once Grace heard Bud's deep steady breathing, she wrapped a blanket around herself and went outside to sit on Peter's bench. Across the field, she could see a light on at Mayphelia's and wondered if she were up brewing some of her medicines. Grace felt a deep warmth and peace come over her. *Ceil has given me yet another freedom, the freedom to enjoy my body.*

In the distance an owl began to hoot, reprimanding her. Suddenly the good feelings were replaced by crippling guilt, remorse, and shame. *I have committed the worst sin and I enjoyed it. I'm not worthy of the good life I have with Bud. My God, what would Sister Mary Grace think if she knew? Or Andy and Regina?*

Then a new thought emerged. *It never happened. I imagined the whole thing just like I did before, when Peter died and I would see him running out here. I dreamed the ecstasy, the release from some unknown bondage.* She dropped to her knees over Peter's grave. She had to face what she had done. Prayers fell from her lips and vaporized in the still night air, going nowhere, bringing no solace. She saw Mayphelia's light go out as did her hope of ever regaining grace, despite her name.

CHAPTER TWENTY-ONE

Billy Wayne had left the cemetery in a rage. That morning when he awakened and looked over at Geraldine, he had become terrified that this would be his life. He knew she would look a lot like his mother in a few years, haggard and coarse. He looked around the trailer and knew that this would be the extent of his future unless he changed his ways. A gift from heaven had dropped into his lap the day Regina told him she was pregnant. He never dreamed he'd marry into in a family of landowners. To him, Bud and Grace were rich people.

Geraldine stirred. She was not pretty or refined like Regina, but she was pliant and agreeable and she looked up to him. She didn't care if he didn't wipe his feet before coming into the house. She didn't ask him to chew with his mouth closed and she never turned away from him in the middle of the night. But she could never give him a farm or prestige, and those were more important than anything. Regina was his ticket to rise above his station in life, but first he'd have to throw away the bottle, get a decent job and be good to his wife.

Blowing the opportunity to better himself would prove that his dad was right about him. *"You always was as dumb as a bedpost."* He wasn't going to be dumb any more. Besides, he loved his girls. He wanted to be with them and watch them grow up to be like Regina, not white trash like any kids he and Geraldine would have.

By the time he got to the cemetery he was full of remorse and resolve. This time when he talked to her, he would be sober and from now on things would be different. He would vow to stop drinking and seeing Geraldine. He would start going to church and give her all the money he made.

As soon as he stepped out of his pickup, he saw her. She looked so very pretty, but he could sense a disturbing change in her. She held her head a little higher than before, like maybe she thought more of herself than before. His girls stood on either side of her, looking like they'd just stepped out of a catalog. They wore brand new clothes, clothes that he hadn't bought for them. How many times had he yelled at Regina not to take any charity? Here she was openly disobeying him again. He knew she was determined to turn his girls against him, just like the rest of that damn family. "I'll straighten her out once and for all," he muttered.

The anger was suddenly back in full force. Everything about the scene awakened the sleeping furies that clawed at his insides. Bud, Grace, Ceil, that old nigger baby killer, the others, all acting so high and mighty. Regina turned and looked directly into his eyes. Her usual expressions of fear and apprehension were gone. She dared to look at him like she felt sorry for him, like he was some wounded animal that needed help. He had to get out of there before his demons stormed out and raised all the dead lying in the ground. As he sped away, he grabbed the jar of moonshine under the seat and took a long, soothing gulp. Immediately he felt calmer, stronger and powerful. *I'll smear that pity off your face for good. I'll show them all.*

LATE that night while Billy Wayne continued to drink, Ceil paced throughout her large empty house, miserable. She scolded herself for letting her desires and passions get the best of her. She prayed she had not done irrevocable harm to Grace. Tomorrow she would put the house on the market and fly back to Los Angeles. Emotionally distraught and worn out, she lay down on the couch directly across from the picture window and fell asleep.

THAT night while Andy studied and Sheila drank a glass of wine and scrubbed the kitchen sink, Sister Mary Grace lay on her cot and worked to catch her breath. It was getting harder and harder to breathe. Was God testing her? She poured a glass of water from a pitcher on her nightstand. Feeling dizzy, she quickly lay back down without taking a sip. Her lips moved in silent prayers.

THAT night while Mayphelia sat on her back porch staring into the night at a possum digging in her potato bed, Billy Wayne walked around and around the outside of the house where his wife and daughters lay sleeping. Mayphelia drew in a lungful of smoke from her pipe and suddenly jumped up. The tobacco was soothing but it didn't drive away the fearful vision that kept coming to her.

BOTH the front and back doors were closed and locked. *Damn, Regina.* He couldn't force his way in without waking the girls. He walked around to the window of their bedroom and dug into his pockets for his knife. In this heat, the windows would be open. He'd cut the screen and crawl in. He swore under his breath as his finger poked through the hole in his pocket. The knife must have fallen out somewhere.

MAYPHELIA snuffed out her pipe and grabbed her shoes. She had to get over there. She needed to hurry. It was close to five miles. Maybe she should wake up Bud and Grace.

EVEN though the window was high off the ground, Billy Wayne figured he could get in without making a sound, but he had to find something to cut the screen. He smiled. Tonight she would pay for looking at him like she did. She'd never look again at anyone. Then he'd go get that black devil. As he stumbled over to the shed looking for a cutting tool, he bent over a couple of times. His guts were rolling over and tying into knots. He'd been drinking rot-gut liquor since leaving the cemetery that morning.

MAYPHELIA started running but soon realized her body couldn't go the full way like that. She'd have to get Bud and Grace. She headed across the pasture to their house. There was nothing stirring, not even their cats. She rapped gently on the back door. Nothing stirred, so once again, a little harder this time. Then she heard Grace, "Bud, wake up. There's a knocking coming from somewhere."

"It's me, Mayphelia. Somethin's wrong."

Bud and Grace appeared at the door pulling on clothes. "I jest knows something's not right with Regina. It's Billy Wayne. I sees 'im with a knife." Within a couple of minutes, all three were in Bud's truck.

THE damn door to the shed was locked. To hell with it, he'd go get Mayphelia first. His sotted brain now switched to her as the cause of all his problems. Then, of course, there was also Grace and Bud but he knew, even in his inebriated state, that he couldn't get even with everyone.

He headed down the road and up the country lane where he had parked his pickup.

BUD saw no movement nor heard any sounds as he carefully stepped up on the porch. He had told the women to stay put. He turned on his flashlight and shone it up and down the porch. Everything was secure and in order. He began to walk around the house, somewhat disgusted with Mayphelia and her visions.

He was afraid not to believe her yet sometimes he felt she was a bit touched. Then his light shone on Billy Wayne's shoe prints below Regina's window. There was no mistaking the slight drag of the right foot, a result of cutting the cast off two weeks before the doctor said it was healed. Bud's light glinted off something on the ground. It was the pocket knife he and Grace had given Billy Wayne the previous Christmas. He'd been so proud of it, claiming he'd never had such a good knife. Mayphelia was right. Bud quickly examined the screen on Regina's window. What if he were too late?

Bud heard something behind him. He turned, ready to defend himself.

"He done gone," Mayphelia whispered with a deep sigh of relief.

Bud's muscles relaxed. "He was here though. Here's his knife and see all the foot prints."

"Daddy, is that you?" Regina's terrified voice shot through the darkness behind the screen.

"Yes, Gennie. Sorry I woke you up."

"What are doing out there?" A lamp was switched on and Regina looked out the window. "Mayphelia, that you, too? What's going on?"

Grace walked up, "Everything's okay, honey. Mayphelia had a vision."

"Billy Wayne's been here. Unlock the door so we can come in." Bud started around the house.

BILLY Wayne sped fifty yards past the Dollard place before slamming on the brakes and backing up to the front yard. A dim light was on in the front room. Before taking care of the black bitch, he'd make this white bitch regret ever firing him. He picked up one of the stones bordering the sidewalk. *After I laid up every one of these goddamn rocks, she did that to me.* With all his might he hurled the stone through the plate glass window. It shattered with a resounding, frightening crash. He ran to his pickup and drove away so fast he almost lost control, laying skid marks all across the road.

The stone sailed over Ceil's head, smashed into the bookshelf and dropped with a cracking thud. Shards of glass covered Ceil. She remained very still and felt blood ooze from several cuts. It took some time to gather her thoughts and remember where she was. As in a dream she heard squealing tires and a motor backfiring.

Remaining remarkably calm, she carefully picked the pieces of glass from her right leg, hip and arm. She went to the bathroom and applied iodine to the cuts and as she looked at the bathroom mirror she felt grateful. It could have been so much worse. Luckily she had been sleeping on her side with her face towards the back of the couch.

When she called the sheriff, he was mad as hell. "You gettin' me up at one-thirty in the morning over a broken window. I'll be there sometime after eight in the morning." Ceil hung up. *It was time to get* back *to a civilized place where there were law enforcement people who cared about people who had a stone almost the size of a boulder thrown into their house in the middle of the night.*

Billy Wayne had blacked out for a few seconds. He jerked back to consciousness just as his pickup ran over the shoulder and headed towards a ditch. He hit the brakes and steered back onto the road, mowing down bushes and tall grass. A deer ran in front and missed being slaughtered by an inch. Billy Wayne swore loudly at the creature, "You son-of-a-bitch." *I could have been killed just like my dad's oldest brother,* he thought remembering his uncle with a buck's horn driven right through his throat. All the sheriff could say was, "He musta been goin' awful damn fast."

His night of terror was coming to an end. Mayphelia would have to wait to get hers. He had to get back to Geraldine before he blacked out for good. He turned the pickup around and headed back in the direction he'd come from. Besides he was actually afraid to go to Mayphelia's by himself. He needed backup, someone who could shoot that wolf in case she sicked it on him again. But he couldn't count on the Klan. They were worthless. Geraldine had a couple of cousins who might help him.

"I DON'T want you staying here by yourself with these girls." Bud was angrier than he'd been in a long time. "Who knows what he was up to, here at this time of the night."

"They was mighty dark, his thoughts, they was," Mayphelia said as she sipped on the coffee Grace had poured for her. They all sat around the table. Regina was visibly shaken. "I'm going tomorrow to file for a divorce. I've put it off long enough."

Grace nervously scraped crumbs from the night before into her hand. "Maybe you should consider an annulment."

"An annulment can take up to two years. I've already looked into it. I want out now." Regina pushed back on her chair.

"But still…" Grace began when Bud interrupted her.

"For God's sake, Grace, our daughter's life is more important than some church's laws."

Grace was startled. Bud rarely, if ever, spoke to her like that. She lowered her head feeling responsible. *Have I brought this on? Punish me, not my daughter,* she prayed. A reply came back immediately. *Bud is right and you know it.*

Mayphelia patted Regina's shoulder. "Honey, it be time to tell 'em." Regina looked at her, terrified.

"Tell them what?" Grace asked.

Regina sat frozen. She was still too embarrassed to talk about it to her parents. "You tell 'em, May-May. I can't."

"Billy Wayne raped Regina." Mayphelia paused for this to sink in.

Bud felt weak. "I suspected as much."

Now that it was out, Regina had the courage to go on. "It happened after the dance at the Veterans' Hall. I was too ashamed to tell anyone. He said I'd brought it on myself." She paused.

"Another thing I want you to know. He belongs to the Klan." She walked over to a cabinet and pulled out the white hood from the canister. She threw it on the table. "I burned up the white sheet he wears."

Bud sank down in a chair. Grace recoiled from it. "My God, I knew he had a bad streak, but this is terrible."

"That settles it. Get your stuff together, Regina," Bud said as he got up. "You and the girls are coming home with us."

BELIEVING that light repels evil, Ceil turned on every lamp and ceiling fixture in the house before going downstairs to the basement. She felt a chill, sensing her grandfather's malevolence. Tomorrow she would have Johnny clear out everything down here and panel the walls and tile the floor. Then she would get Mayphelia to cast out any evil that was still present.

Now, however, she was grateful that the old man's gun closet was still standing. She found the bolt cutter, snipped the padlock, took out a twelve-gauge and loaded it. A few years back she had taken up skeet shooting and had won a couple of medals. She could handle a gun just fine.

Going back up the stairs, she felt certain she could kill Billy Wayne. She knew it was him from the sound of his dilapidated pickup. She sat down in a yellow wicker rocker on the front porch, laid the gun across her lap, lit a cigarette and said, "Okay, you sorry piece of trash, come on back. I'm ready for you." Distorting glints of light coming through what was left of the plate glass window surrounded her. From the street, it was a frightening eerie sight.

And just as she knew they would, the headlights did come back. She stepped down a couple of stairs onto the sidewalk, lifted the gun to her shoulder and cocked it.

Billy Wayne kept blinking his eyes, trying to stay awake. When he noticed the Dollard place he grinned, "It's all lit up like a fuckin' Christmas tree." He laughed out loud. "I guess I woke that bitch up."

Then he saw the huge gun pointing directly at his head. "That bitch!" He couldn't stop or take cover; he had no choice but to drive past her and the twelve-gauge. He gunned the motor and zoomed past. In the rear-view mirror he saw her aiming at the back of his head. He ducked down. The steering wheel whipped around and smacked his jaw. When he managed to sit back up and glance through the rear-view again, he saw her put the gun down and laugh. His pants were soggy. He had messed all over himself.

CHAPTER TWENTY-TWO

Around three o'clock the next afternoon, Sheriff Clive drove out to the grove of saplings on the edge of a large wooded area where Billy Wayne's trailer was parked. The trailer had been a trade for three crates of stolen liquor and an old clock he'd found in a shed behind the Dollard house. Billy Wayne figured that Ceil didn't know it existed. The guy trading the trailer acted like the thing was as precious as gold because it was in a fancy carved wooden box that had three chimes. He didn't care that it wasn't even running.

The car bounced over the deep ruts, exacerbating Clive's arthritic back. It had not been a good morning. When he had gotten to Ceil's at nine forty-five, she was red-faced with anger. "You call this some time after eight, I suppose?" She glared at him, pointed to a chair that wasn't strewn with glass and motioned for him to sit down, then escaped behind the swinging kitchen door.

He could hear her talking on the phone with her hot shot lawyer in Los Angeles about last night's attack and asking him if she had grounds to file charges. Even though she lowered her voice, he heard her say, "The country moron they call a sheriff doesn't know or care one thing about the law."

He got up to leave thinking *it will be a cold day in hell before I give that big city bitch the time of day.* He then noticed the twelve-gauge shot gun propped up with books on the dining room table, shoved up against the broken window. The barrel was aimed at the street. He decided it might be best to stay put.

Soon Bud Wolansky's truck stopped at the fence. Bud was stomping up the walk, not looking at all happy. *What was going on? All this over one goddamn window?* Bud walked in without so much as a knock. Clive remembered someone telling him that Bud's wife and this Dollard woman were thick as thieves.

For the next hour, he sat and listened to Billy Wayne this and Billy Wayne that. Then Bud insisted that he go over to his Sunday house and look at the footprints. He was right about the right foot dragging, but that didn't prove anything. The pocket knife could have been there for days. In the end, however, Clive had decided that he'd better do something, so here he was in the middle of nowhere with pains continuously shooting from his butt up to his neck.

To tell the truth, Clive was a little afraid of both Bud and that Dollard woman. She wasn't like a regular woman who kept her mouth shut and showed respect towards menfolk, and Bud was liked in the community. Elections would be coming up in a couple of years and a man like Bud could ruin his chances of staying in office.

He pounded on the door for the fourth time, each time with more force. Finally, it jerked open halfway and Geraldine poked her head around the frame. "What ya want?" she yelled and then saw who it was. "Oh sorry, Sherroff, we ain't got up yet."

"My god, girl, it's 2:30 in the afternoon."

She was clinging to a filthy sheet that almost covered her pudgy naked form. Her hair was in a matted stack on top of her head and her face looked swollen, but he couldn't tell if that was from sleep or from being hit. According to Bud, Billy Wayne often hit Regina. Bud had acted like that was as low as a man could get, but Clive knew that sometimes women had to be put in their place. Yet Clive had seen Bud's daughter around and she seemed like such a sweet meek little thing that he couldn't help but feel some disgust for Billy Wayne, who had no business being out here with this lowlife gal.

"I need to talk to Billy Wayne. Go on and get him up."

"He in trouble?"

"Why else would I be out here?"

"He's been sick. Didn't get to bed till four or five this mornin."

Clive was getting impatient. "Are you gonna git 'im or do I have to go in there and drag 'im out?"

Geraldine was scared Billy Wayne had killed someone. He was always talking about getting even and doing someone in. In fact, one time he'd even said he was going to make Clive pay for something. When Billy Wayne had come in this morning, smelling to high heaven, she figured he'd seen his wife because he had his way with her over and over, sometimes really rough and mean and sometimes needy and sad. He was that way every time he saw Regina. It was like he couldn't get enough, and she didn't care if he was thinking of his wife; she loved the attention.

Billy Wayne stood in the doorway buttoning up his pants and squinting from the darkness. Clive had to step back and turn his head away. The putrid smell was overwhelming.

"For heaven's sake, don't you believe in taking a bath once in a while?"

"You got business with me or not?" Billy Wayne was petulant and irritable. Clive gave him a long, hard look. He looked even worse than Geraldine if that were possible. Nausea from the stench began to make the ground beneath his feet swell and wave. He removed a handkerchief from his back pocket and put it over his nose and backed up several steps towards the trees.

"Let's go over here where there's fresh air. You're in a heap of trouble."

As soon as Clive started talking, Billy Wayne interrupted, "I was here all night. Go ask Geraldine."

Clive turned away, disgusted. "Well, that Dollard woman saw you."

"She tried to kill me. Pointed a shotgun right at my head."

"You just said you were here all night. Did she come out here with that gun?"

Billy Wayne kicked at a stump and swore under his breath. He couldn't believe how stupid he was. It was the liquor. It was drowning his brain in piss. He remained silent from then on listening to Clive tell him that Ceil and Bud both were talking of filing charges against him. He detailed the footprints showing a dragging right foot, the knife, the broken window.

"That Dollard woman said she was filing charges for stolen money and a stolen antique clock as well as the broken window." Billy Wayne blanched. "The clock? There's no way…." He drifted off remembering that he had stolen that in the middle of the night. Billy Wayne felt spooked.

Clive went on to tell him, "Bud's getting court orders to where you can't so much as step on any of Bud's property or near Regina or your daughters without going to jail."

"They can't prove nothing," Billy Wayne yelled.

"She saw you, Billy Wayne."

"You can't go to jail for drivin' past a house. But you can go to jail for trying to kill someone which is what that bitch did to me."

Clive moved farther away. Billy Wayne smelled like an over-used outhouse. "Regina wants to meet you this afternoon at 5:30 at Hattie's to talk. Go in now and get cleaned up, and I'll drive you over there. Bud made me promise I'd keep an eye on you while ya'll talked."

Billy Wayne stood there trying to figure out if he was going to do what this man said or just take off running through the woods. As fat as Clive was he could never catch him. Besides, he crinkled up his face with every step like he was seriously constipated.

As if reading his thoughts, Clive said, "You'd best do as I ask you. As a member of the brotherhood, I'm going to give you some advice. After this meeting, I think you should leave these parts. Make yourself scarce. They can't do nothin' if they don't know where to find you. I know you don't want to end up like your older brother. He won't be seeing the outside world for another twenty years."

Billy Wayne slumped, defeated, and headed for the trailer.

REGINA had gotten a back booth next to the kitchen. The diner was small and quite full at this time of day. Many of the shops in town were mom-and-pop operations and many of the husband and wife owners ate supper here after closing up for the day.

Regina was glad for the crowd because the more people, the less likely Billy Wayne would create a scene. She took a sip of Coke. Even though her life was in a state of turmoil, she felt relieved. There were no more secrets. She had made a decision and was moving forward. Tomorrow she was going to a lawyer. She was taking steps towards regaining her happiness, and it felt good.

Just as Billy Wayne was parking his pickup in front of Hattie's the sheriff's car pulled in beside him. Bud sat on a bench across the street outside the dry goods store.

Billy Wayne walked in and looked around several times before spotting her. Slowly he sauntered towards the booth. He seemed to be having trouble pulling his right foot along. He scooted into the seat. Regina caught her breath as she looked at him at close range. For so long now she had been turning away or looking in another direction whenever he was around. She hadn't noticed his gradual deterioration. She didn't want to, but she felt compassion for this person across from her.

He had been a good-looking boy, really cute with his blonde crewcut hair and deep blue eyes. He had been energetic and full of pranks. The naive teenage Regina had loved going down the school halls beside him. Now a drawn, pre-maturely aged and somewhat emaciated man sat across from her. Sad, dull eyes looked out from an unhealthy, blotchy face. His hair was dirty. His attempt at a smile revealed yellowed teeth. His hands shook as he cleared his throat.

The change in the way he looks had been so sudden, she thought. *Or had it been?* Shortly after Tessie was born the physical abuse began and that's when she started ducking her head, averting her eyes, afraid of him.

"How are the girls? I haven't seen 'em in a while, but I want to. Maybe tomorrow?"

Regina twisted in her seat and began. "Please listen and don't interrupt until I've finished. I've planned out what I need to say." She paused to gather her courage. "I'm filing for a divorce."

"You can't get no divorce 'cause of your religion. You've said so yourself." His raised voice turned a few heads in their direction.

"I've never loved you and you've never loved me. In the beginning I tried to, maybe we both did. You've forced yourself on me too many times. It's wrong."

Billy Wayne took a deep breath and shrugged. "A man has a right to his own wife."

The anger rose in Regina. "That first time I wasn't your wife."

The sheriff entered the café and sat by the door. Billy Wayne could barely control his rage. He was being watched like some mad dog. Regina remained on course. "Just look at what's become of you. You're killing yourself drinking all the time. It makes you crazy and mad at everyone. You're the girls' father and for their sake I want you to do something with your life. I don't want to keep them from you, but I will as long as you're drinking and living the way you are."

Billy Wayne had dropped his head until it was almost resting on the table. A few greasy strands of his uncut hair fell forward. Finally, he looked up, his bloodshot eyes filled with more hatred than Regina had ever seen. For a moment she sensed a demon was sitting across from her. "I will never sign any goddamn divorce papers." He hissed a putrid smell.

Billy Wayne was out the door and gone before Clive or Bud could get up. The road before him was fuzzy and moved up and down. He knew he needed help. His sight was coming and going. Dr. Clarkson was locking up his office as the pickup crashed into his newly painted sign.

Billy Wayne got out, staggered to the first step and fell over. His entire body began shaking uncontrollably. The doctor tried to hold him down to keep his head from banging on the concrete step.

An ambulance rushed him the fifteen miles to the closest hospital. By now, Billy Wayne had lapsed into a coma from acute alcohol poisoning. The hospital doctor felt his chances of recovery were minimal. If he did recover, there would probably be brain damage.

"It's that damn homemade hooch these backwoods people drink. It seems like all those stills could be destroyed by now," the doctor said, thoroughly disgusted.

CHAPTER TWENTY-THREE

From her kitchen window, Grace watched Andy and Sheila play hide-and-go-seek with Angie and Tessie. Andy put Tessie behind the wheel barrow and then ran to find a place for himself, but before he could get settled, she was toddling after him, calling "Undy, Undy," her combination word for Uncle Andy. Angie had corrected her hundreds of times, but it did no good, so now she was also beginning to call him that.

"Nine, ten. Ready or not, here I come," Angie yelled from her post at the clothesline. She opened her eyes and there Tessie stood in full view. Angie shouted, "You are supposed to hide. That's the game. Tessie, can't you learn one little thing?" Tessie turned and giggled at her sister. *Peas from the same pod,* Grace thought.

Grace recalled her Angela trying to teach Regina how to tie her shoe laces in this very kitchen. Regina would untie the lace and say, "Show me again." Then she'd giggle. Finally Angela stomped out of the room shouting, "You don't want to learn."

Andy and Sheila had arrived the night before, lifting the energy and spirits of the whole farm. Her fun-loving, happy son lived in a special place in Grace's heart and she was grateful that he had found someone as wonderful as Sheila. They were like a couple of kids, always picking on one another, hugging and laughing.

Over Bud's protests they came in bearing gifts, as usual. Grace knew this was mainly Sheila's doing. She was a generous soul, like Ceil. There were clothes, books and puzzles for the girls, a lovely dress for Regina and a larger coffee pot for Bud and Grace. "What are we going to do with the old one? It still works fine," Bud complained, then caught Grace's sharp look and followed it with, "But it will be nice when we have company and need to make more than four cups."

After supper Andy moved the table to a side wall, turned on the radio and began dancing with the girls. Before long he pulled Regina out of her chair, ignoring her protests. Finally, Regina let go of her self-imposed penance and began dancing like she had years ago. The girls jumped up and down, giggling and hugging one another. They had never seen their mother dance. Grace's eyes teared up. In that instant she came to a decision: she would not discourage Regina from doing what she had to do to be free again. Grace would no longer believe in a God who wanted people to suffer and be miserable.

Later that night after the girls were asleep, Grace was delighted that everyone gathered in the seldom-used living room. It was the first time that Andy and Sheila had seen her paintings. Several of her works adorned the walls, and now Andy and Sheila were showering praises. "If you're interested in selling any of these, I know I could find a gallery in Houston that would show them," Sheila said.

"She's going to have a showing in San Antonio in late November," Bud announced proudly. "She's been painting practically day and night." It was true. Once the urge to draw and paint was brought out from the closet, Grace couldn't find enough hours in the day to create. Her strict regimen of keeping everything neat, clean and on time had loosened up considerably. The washing would be put off a day or so. The floors suddenly didn't need cleaning as often and the speck of dust on the shelf didn't catch her attention. Bud's meals were sometimes late and sometimes over or under-cooked. Bud didn't mind. He was happy that she was happy and he wasn't bothered so much anymore that Ceil's influence was mainly responsible. Sometimes the old jealousy would start to come up, but he'd squelch it with *everybody's got to have a special friend besides their mate.*

"Mom, you're going to have to get a tray for events such as this." Regina entered balancing a bottle of wine and five glasses atop one of Grace's cookie sheets. "This is the first time I've ever bought wine, so I hope it's good." She set the sheet down and began pouring. "Dad, the owner remembered me coming in with you and didn't ask for my ID, thank God."

Regina had spent most of the previous morning at the lawyer's office. It wasn't that Regina had that much business to conduct since there was no community property to negotiate. But her lawyer, Mr. Davenport, had been her granddad's close friend and wanted an update on the whole family. Since he was retired, she had called him to get a recommendation, but he had insisted on drafting the papers free of charge to help out *the granddaughter of a fine man and good friend.* Regina took this as a sign that her grandfather was indeed looking out for her.

She left his office feeling so good and hopeful about her future that she wanted to kick up her heels and do something special. She thought of the crumpled paper with David's phone number snuggled in the special pocket of her purse. She could still feel his hand on her arm as she was getting off the train. She looked around for a phone booth. *Stop it, Regina. You're not divorced yet. Go buy beer to celebrate.* Then she remembered that Andy and Sheila were coming. *Sheila is too sophisticated for beer. I'll get wine instead.*

Ordinarily wine was served only at Christmas, and that was the brew Uncle Louie had made the previous year. Occasionally it was nice and smooth but most times it was sour and heavy. As far as Regina knew, this was the first store-bought wine that had ever been in her parent's house. After a few sips, everyone complimented her on her choice.

Nestled in a corner of the couch and feeling relaxed, Regina began telling her family about the lawyer's visit. "I'm getting a divorce for sure and I'm going to use the money grandfather left me to finish high school and then go to beauty school."

"No, you let that money be. I can help you. There's calves that are ready for selling," Bud said sternly.

"That's my money, Dad. I want to do this on my own. Ya'll have already done more for me than you've ever done for Andy or Angela."

"Regina, no one's keeping score," Grace said.

"Well, I am," Andy popped up.

Sheila poked him in the ribs. "You don't keep up with anything," she teased.

Absorbed in what she was going to say, Regina went on, "Me and the girls are moving back to the Sunday house tomorrow. Billy Wayne's still in a coma and he may be that way for a long time." She felt a little ashamed. Billy Wayne had been in the hospital for over two weeks, and she hadn't once gone to see him. "He can't do anything."

After this news settled in, Andy pulled Sheila closer to him. "Well, now that everything's settled with Regina, I have some news and I'd better get it out before I get cold feet. This marvelous woman has agreed to marry me. I present your future daughter-sister-in-law."

"Good grief, you didn't actually agree to this, did you, Sheila?" Regina shouted and then she put her arms around both of them in a threesome hug.

"Wait, wait, wait, there's more to it," Sheila looked at Andy for support. She wanted to get this out before any celebrating started. She took a deep breath, a sip of wine and spat out, "I'm Jewish and I'm divorced."

Silence. Grace and Bud didn't move an eyelash. Their children were taking them into foreign lands. Their past experiences had not prepared them for these territories. Their baby had seen a lawyer about a divorce. Their son was going to marry a Jewish divorced woman. They knew only one woman in their town who had been divorced and she had long since moved away. And there had never been a Jew living in their town as far as they knew. Now they would have one in their family.

Relief flooded through Regina. *Finally, no more secrets. My life is in the open and so is Andy's.* She had recently read an article on astrology that said the planets were now in some kind of perfect alignment bringing in harmony and integrity. Regina believed in this, especially since Mayphelia always said everything was guided by the stars.

Finally Bud cleared his throat. "Well, the only Jew I ever knew was the owner of a feed store over in Reedville, and he was a mighty fine man, honest as the day is long."

Andy felt a lump in his throat. His dad was accepting Sheila. All the past bickering and difficulties melted away.

He knew he would never again have anything but the highest regard for his father.

Sheila had armed herself for a conflict, for objections, for a scene. The preparations had been useless. She sat limp on the couch fighting back the tears.

Grace's calm demeanor masked a mind that was straining to go towards the darkness, that murky cellar she had begun to think was forever sealed. The fears and selfrecriminations were bubbling up again. Her good God had disappeared and the harsh, judgmental one was back. *It was my fault. One child getting divorced and another marrying ...I really like Sheila...I neglected Andy during the breakdown. There is my terrible sin. A just God makes people pay for their sins.*

Everyone waited for Grace to say something, anything, but she was twisting the cloth belt around her waist. Bud knew this state and wanted to cover for her. "Well, with marriage, some of us are lucky the first time around," he said softly

He took Grace's hand away from the fidgeting and held it. "But if we're not lucky the first time, I don't see any sense in living with a mistake. All I can say is I think Andy is as lucky as his ole man was." Grace looked up at him and knew that the good God was back. He was in her husband. Once again, she turned away from the judgmental one.

Sheila couldn't contain herself. "You are so kind," she cried. Andy put his arm around her. "There, there, I told you it wouldn't be so bad, didn't I?"

Grace drank the last of her wine and smiled at Sheila. "Dear Sheila, I know you'll be as happy and loved as much as I've been with Andy's dad and our family is fortunate to have you." Her voice shook.

She quickly got up and headed for the kitchen. "I made some lemon cake today. It will taste good now." Standing by herself over the counter, she cut the cake with determined thrusts. Her mind wouldn't stay away from the old sickness. *It was adultery, only a different kind. I committed adultery. And everyone will be punished.* She slapped the knife down and shook her head. "Stop it, stop it," she said out loud. "I won't listen."

CHAPTER TWENTY-FOUR

After the broken-window incident, Ceil knew that she'd have to stay put a little longer. A phone conversation with the vice president of her company assured her everything was running smoothly and that she could take as much time as she needed in Texas. Ceil realized she was more or less superfluous as far as her business was concerned, thanks to the competent and loyal people she had hired. She felt really good about that and wished she could feel as good about what had happened upstairs in her bedroom.

Only Mayphelia could help her. As she began to turn down the dirt lane, she looked over at Grace's house. Even though her desire was to see Grace, her hands kept turning the steering wheel onto the other lane. Mayphelia was crouched in her garden picking mustard greens for supper. Ceil quietly walked up behind her bent-over form. Without turning, Mayphelia said, "You ain't gonna scare me. I heared yo'r car. Besides, I know yo'r smell."

"What don't you know, May-May?"

"I ain't exactly sure when I'm gonna die, but I knows it will be a spring day when all the new green is out and little critters is being born, and I'll be in my garden. And I knows I shouldn't be tellin' you 'cause now you's gonna try to take me somewheres every spring."

"Have you seen your death, really?"

"As plain as day. I'll be digging new potatoes. But it don't look exactly like it do now. Somethin' 'll be changed."

"What do you see about me?'

"Right now, I sees you scared and you wants me to come stay with you. That boy is dangerous, but he ain't gonna bother you no more.'"

"Please, May-May. I've hardly slept at all. The last few nights, I've stayed at a travel lodge. I can't be alone at night. I'm afraid he'll come in the middle of the night like my grandfather used to do. I'll bring you back early every morning." She looked towards Bud and Grace's. "And I'm sad, really sad."

Mayphelia stood up, straightened and stretched her back. The sack of mustard greens was full. She shook it down and tied a knot to close it. Mayphelia looked directly into Ceil's eyes. "Ya know, honey, it can't be the way you wants it. Ya'll two will be close friends forever. I sees that. She'll always love you, but she can't love the way you wants, and you knows it. Nature didn't shape her exactly the same way it did you."

"But it did happen. Maybe she is like me."

Mayphelia started for her house. "Come on, if I'm gonna stay with you, I needs some things. I'll cook up these for us tonight. Put 'em in the car."

Half way to the house, Mayphelia stopped and turned back to her. "She give you a family, and you gives her freedom. Don't mess that up 'cause you be wanting mor.'"

As they were driving down the lane, Mayphelia said, "Dear Lord, I'm getting' used to this car ridin.' Done more since you come than in my whole life."

Seeing Bud in his yard, she commanded, "Bud loves my mustard greens. Drive by over there and tell 'em to come to supper tonight. We can git some pork ribs and have a feast."

Ceil shook her head. "She won't want to see me."

"It weren't nothin' but having some pleasure. Now yo can't hide from one another forever, so do likes I tell ya."

When the car stopped, Mayphelia held the bag of greens outside the window. "Fresh mustard greens. Ya'll come over ta Ceil's and hep us with 'em." Bud didn't hesitate in accepting the invitation.

The meal went well. Ceil was glad Regina and the girls had also come, a welcome diversion. They had just moved back to the Sunday house and Regina was grateful to get a break from the unpacking. The girls wanted to sit next to Cecie which made Ceil feel very special. Grace was friendly but distant. Every time Ceil made eye contact with her, she quickly averted her eyes.

She have to do some powerful unbelievin' 'fore she can be alright in her head about what happened, Mayphelia thought. She considered having a talk with Grace, but she never gave advice without being asked. Maybe this was different.

THE nurse at the front desk gave Regina a frigid disapproving look. *It's about time you show up*, she thought and then said, "He's in 214 just down that hall." Regina dragged her feet along the sanitized tile floor, with grey-black lines. *If only those lines were ropes that would tie me up before I reach the door,* she wished. Her mother had called that morning and told her she needed to go see Billy Wayne, no matter how hard it was. "It's just the decent thing to do, Regina."

Breathing deeply, she swung the door open and felt relief and some joy upon seeing that Billy Wayne was no longer the derelict in the restaurant. His face had filled out and had a healthy color. His clean hair, golden in the sunlight, had been nicely trimmed. With eyes half-open in a coma state, his chest moved in and out in cadence with loud exhales.

Geraldine looked up from a movie magazine and scooted out of the chair, as if to leave the room.

"Please don't leave. I'm staying for only a moment." Regina motioned for her to sit back down. "I'm Regina and I suppose you're Geraldine."

"I done seen your piture, so I knowed who ya are," Geraldine flopped back down.

"How's he doing?"

"The same. The doctors, they don't talk much, said he could be like this all his life."

"I'm sure he'll recover. He's young and strong."

Regina continued to stand just inside the door, unable to move closer to the bed. Even as incapacitated and helpless as he was, she didn't want to be too near him. Finally she leaned in and talked in the direction of his ear. "Billy Wayne, the girls are fine, and they want you to get well so you can play with them again."

Geraldine's puzzled look evoked an explanation.

"I've heard that even though people are in a coma they can hear, so it's good to say encouraging things to them."

"Oh, okay."

Regina walked around the bed and stood close to Geraldine and whispered, "It's so good of you to look after him like you've done. I'm really glad he has you." Regina gently patted her arm.

Geraldine swallowed. She had never met a nicer person. Regina continued whispering, "I've filed for a divorce, so perhaps when he's well again, you'll be able to get married."

That was too much for Geraldine. She dug in her purse for the handkerchief, wadded and stiff from the drafts of dried tears.

AS Regina passed Ceil's house on the way back she saw that Clem and Johnny were working on the plate-glass window. She shuddered to think about that night and whispered a prayer that Billy Wayne would be reformed after he got well.

She hoped everything would soon be back to normal yet normal would never be what it had been. Even if Billy Wayne was rehabilitated, she was still getting a divorce. Then Ceil would be leaving, creating a huge gap in all their lives, especially her mother's. *I guess things will never be like they were before, but then they never really are.* Regina laughed, "I wonder who started that saying. There's no such thing as *going back to the way it was."*

FIFTEEN days later, Billy Wayne woke up. "My girls want to see me and I want to play with them. Call Regina to bring them over," he ordered Geraldine, who had been napping.

Geraldine snapped to attention, stunned he had come out of the coma looking and acting as if he'd only been asleep for a short time. She attributed this miracle to Regina and hurriedly left the room to tell the doctor. Moments later she was back, "The doctor says he's comin' but you can't see your girls right now."

When the doctor came in, Billy Wayne told him he needed to see his daughters. "I'm afraid not today," the doctor began. "We need to do some tests this afternoon. Remember, you've been very sick."

Billy Wayne settled down and seemed at peace. He was agreeable, even friendly and spoke kindly to Geraldine and the nurses. But as the day wore on he became more and more agitated.

"Geraldine, I got a bottle under the seat of my truck. Go get it now. If I can't see my girls, then I'm gonna drink."

"They won't let me bring no liquor in here, you know that." Geraldine backed away, seeing the fury come to his eyes.

"You sorry whore. You do as I tell you."

He picked up the bed pan and slung it at her. The loud clang brought in two nurses who tried to hold him down as he fought to get up. Another nurse entered with a hypodermic and injected him. He fell back limp and unmoving.

Two days later the doctor called Regina and told her that Billy Wayne needed to be admitted to the county hospital for alcohol treatment. "Could you come in and sign some papers tomorrow morning?"

When she arrived two doctors and several nurses were conferring just outside Billy Wayne's room. Geraldine was crying, standing apart from them. Thinking the worst, Regina hurried to them. It was the worst, but not what Regina had thought. Billy Wayne had escaped that morning.

Before visiting hours, Mr. Tarkin had entered the hospital, told the receptionist he had to be at work soon and demanded to see his son right then. Ten minutes later, he thanked her on his way out. Soon after, a nurse on her morning rounds discovered Billy Wayne's empty room with a cutout window screen. Geraldine didn't know a thing about it. She had gone home for the night and neither Billy Wayne nor his dad had said anything to her.

Regina panicked. *I have to get back home.* She raced out of the hospital and jumped into Ceil's car. *He'll go directly to his daughters.* Ceil and Mayphelia were taking care of Angie and Tessie. *He has threatened to kill both of them. Dear God, why did I move back to town?"* Her thoughts raced as she sped down the street.

Clive spotted Ceil's car going over the speed limit. With delight, he took out after her. Oh, how he would love giving that Ceil Dollard a huge ticket. But the car went right past the Dollard house, turned on a smaller street and pulled up into old man Wolansky's place. *What was going on?*

Clive pulled up behind the car just as Regina jumped out and ran to him. "Thank God you saw me. Billy Wayne ran away from the hospital, and I'm afraid he might be inside with the girls."

Clive rushed to the door with Regina on his heels. He yanked it open and stepped in. All seemed to be in order. Ceil was sitting on the floor coloring a poster with the girls, and Mayphelia was shelling pecans at the kitchen table. Regina grabbed her girls in a big hug and carried them off to their room.

"Come on, my darlings, we've got to pack, because we're going back to Grandma and Grandpa's."

The girls didn't object. They began gathering up toys while Regina threw clothes in a suitcase. "Grandpa said I can help him drive the tractor the next time I come," Angie shouted.

Regina tried to smile, "That's nice, baby." She stifled a sob. *"Will I ever have peace again?"*

Clem was replacing a rotting board on the front porch. He heard everything. His spirit sank in self-loathing. He was a coward. He knew he would never stop drinking until he reported what had happened to both Regina and Boudie. Sheriff Clive was right there, but he was Klan and Klan protected one another, even for murder. He didn't want to get killed. What could he do with these awful secrets?

CHAPTER TWENTY-FIVE

The days were getting shorter. Crisp chilly mornings warmed into perfect Indian summer days. Bud spent them in the fields gathering the crops with several hired hands. This time of year he especially missed the fast moving Radio Man, who entertained the other hands with one interesting, funny story after another. The other workers raced to keep up with him so as not to miss a single word. Bud could always count on him to get the cotton picked in record time.

Bud still laughed out loud remembering some of those tales. If times had been different, he was sure that Radio Man could have been on the radio. Bud also thought about his generosity, how he gave a good portion of his earnings to the colored children for books and school supplies and how after Bud had increased his wages poor families would find boxes of food on their porches. The day Bud gave him and Mayphelia that acre of land was a close second to the happiness he had felt on his wedding day and the births of his children.

The first frost ushered in the annual ritual of hogkilling. This was a celebratory time, especially if like this year the crops were good. The neighbors would gather at each other's farms to help with the killing and dressing.

This year Bud had decided to slaughter two hogs. He wanted to share with Mayphelia and Clem's family.

Grace fussed good naturedly, "You missed your calling. You should have been a missionary."

He laughed that easy laugh of his and said, "Well maybe I am one." Sparks of love and appreciation prompted her to drop the brush and palette and give him a tender hug and kiss. She recalled the time she had asked about Mayphelia's and Radio Man's delinquent rental payments, and how, with hesitancy, he told her he'd given them that land. Then he asked her not to mention the gift to anyone, not even his dad.

At an early hour on killing day the men gathered in the barn and closely followed a humane ritual. First the hog to be slaughtered was separated from the others in the outside pen and driven into a narrow stall inside the barn. A trough full of food scraps was waiting. Once the animal became content and absorbed in eating, the executioner would aim a rifle and fire directly into the skull. Immediately someone would slip a rope behind the hind legs and another person would hoist him up by a pulley while the throat was being slit. The blood flowed into buckets stacked nearby. These three actions, the shooting, hoisting and slitting, had to be swift and well-orchestrated to insure no suffering and thus good-tasting meat. There was no terrified pig squealing. After the blood was drained, the limp body, still warm, was lowered into a cauldron of boiling water for a second or two to guarantee an easy skinning.

The colored families would come to take the blood, head, feet and intestines, from which they'd make blood and head sausage, pickled feet and chitlins. They often shared these specialties as payments, but Grace would accept only a couple of pickled feet for Bud. She was revolted by the rest.

Once the men skinned and butchered the carcass, it was up to the women to preserve the bounty. They salted down some cuts, put some in the smoke house for curing and lately had begun wrapping a good portion for freezing. Since the mid-forties when electricity had been wired into the farm houses, most country people now had freezers sitting out on their back porches or in their car sheds. By mid- afternoon the women had also prepared a meal of roasted pork ribs and fried pig skins served along with the last of the gatherings from the gardens. As the western sky glowed with the autumn setting sun, everyone headed home, tired and full.

This year Grace couldn't get as enthused as usual about the tradition. In just a few weeks she would make her public debut as an artist and was focused on completing several paintings. Meanwhile, she was also helping with Angie and Tessie so Regina would have time to work on the correspondence courses. Bud came in one day and found her making a peanut butter sandwich while holding a paint brush between her teeth. "Where's the camera?" he asked laughing. "That's what a real artist looks like."

On the day of the killing Grace had more help than she could shake a stick at. Ceil and Mayphelia showed up at the crack of dawn before the four other farmers' wives arrived. This was Ceil's first experience with any kind of slaughter and she insisted on going with Bud to witness the gory process. "I want to show you I'm not a squeamish city gal," she said, pulling overalls over her cotton slacks.

Rather than being horrified, Ceil was relieved to see how much care was taken to avoid fear and pain for the animal. "He'll die with no fear in his veins. Fear can ruin good meat," Bud explained to her as he lifted the rifle. In a flash it was over and the blood pulsed out with each beat of the slowing heart.

Since her mom had so much help, Regina asked if she could leave for a study session at the school library. She had begun taking courses while Billy Wayne was in the hospital, but now that she was back with her parents, she was progressing rapidly due to having help with the girls. She had made up her mind to finish as quickly as possible, and so she worked nonstop every day, cramming and taking exams. The studies seemed surprisingly easier than they had been five years ago. "My brain must have stretched with my belly during the pregnancies," she joked with her mom.

Only the math section was causing her problems. The librarian, Miss Foley, who had always liked Regina, arranged for the high school algebra teacher, Joseph Hensley, to tutor her during his free period. Joseph had graduated with Angela, but neither he nor Regina remembered one another. However, it became obvious very quickly that he remembered Angela with great fondness.

He began each tutoring session by asking Regina how her sister was doing. Finally, she told him that Angela was in a convent. Then one day he invited her to coffee after the class, but she declined by telling him she was married. But the real reason was on a scrap of paper in her purse. Before going to sleep each night, she would study David's handwriting and remember the touch of his hand on her arm in the train ststion. She went to sleep dreaming of his easy way and calm manner.

Regina had to use all her will power to stay focused on her studies. There were other distractions besides the scrap of paper in her purse and the tutor who considered her an Angela substitute. There was the constant fear that Billy Wayne wouldn't give her a divorce. She desperately wanted to be rid of him and back in her grandfather's house. Although he had not been seen or heard from in weeks, her parents wouldn't hear of her moving back to town. "It's not safe for you, Regina," her mother said, while her dad admonished, "Those girls have been jostled back and forth too much. You let them be." Regina wondered if it ever would be safe. *He could still hurt me even if we're divorced.*

Bud had told her the only way he'd agree to her moving back was if he bought her a gun and gave her shooting lessons. Grace became upset when she heard that. "You know good and well I've never allowed a gun in this house and I never will. You think I'd let my daughter have a gun in her house with my granddaughters living there?"

Bud immediately backed down. Since the day they got married, his shotgun and the box of ammunition had to be kept hidden on the rafters of the barn.

GRACE was ten years old. She and her mother were sitting in her aunt's kitchen. A loud pop came from outside. Grace jumped up and looked out the screen door. A tiny trail of smoke was coming up from the cellar. Someone hadn't shut the cellar door. Her aunt screamed. Her mother commanded Grace to stay where she was. They ran to the cellar. There was loud crying and wailing. Grace became so terrified she peed all over her aunt's clean kitchen floor. But no one seemed to notice the pee when they came back–her aunt barely able to walk, leaning on her mother.

Over the next few days little Grace heard people talking. "He shot himself in the head. Stuck the barrel in his mouth and pulled the trigger with his toe." She liked her

Uncle Arthur. He was so much nicer than her daddy. Her daddy wasn't sad at all. All he said was, "That baby brother of mine always was as crazy as a bat."

A few days later she came home from school and found her mother hammering her dad's gun into a pile of twisted, flattened metal, muttering, "This illness runs in the family."

From then on Grace was terrified of guns, even though she often wished her dad would do as his brother had done. Several times while she was in the black pit of her breakdown, she had heard her mother's words, *This illness runs in the family.*

CEIL had begun dropping by Grace's most mornings after taking Mayphelia home. Even though Clem had installed security locks on all the windows and doors, she still didn't want to stay alone at night. Mayphelia didn't mind the sleepovers; however, she insisted on being at her house as soon as the sun peeked over the horizon. She didn't like the "city." The noise of an occasional car going by disturbed her and she wouldn't wear shoes unless it was cold or she had to walk a distance. Late one evening she was sitting barefoot on Ceil's front porch and Lavenia walked by. She stopped and said, "Girl, where's your shoes? We're civilized around here."

Mayphelia glared at her. "I don't see no girl round here. Is bein' unpolite part of bein' civilized?" About that time Ceil came out of the house and planted herself behind Mayphelia. Lavenia decided to move on. She had sense enough to know she'd better not say anything else. But she didn't care. She now had at least a day's worth of new gossip to keep her charged. *You know that Ceil Dollard just lets that Negra woman of hers do and say whatever she pleases. I think she's even got her livin'with her.*

Grace saw the Packard pull up to Mayphelia's. She quickly put on a fresh pot of coffee and darted about slicing homemade bread and sweeping the kitchen. Even though she still felt a little strange around Ceil, she was very grateful to have her help with the girls while Regina studied and she painted.

Bud finished his second cup of coffee, looked out the window and said, "Here comes Ceil tearin' up the road. And Mayphelia's still in the car."

"Something must have happened," Grace said as she ran to the bedrooms to check on Regina and the girls, all sound asleep.

When she got back to the kitchen, Ceil was already there. "It's awful. You won't believe."

Mayphelia went over to the coffee pot. "Looks like Billy Wayne is come back," she said quietly as she took a cup from the cabinet.

Ceil pointed at Mayphelia. "There's blood smeared all over her house. Mayphelia says it's hog blood. I'm sick. God, I'm beside myself."

Grace put her arm around her. Ceil clutched her in a tight embrace. Grace didn't pull away, knowing that the sight of any blood was her biggest fear. That and the spiders.

"I's wanted to stay and clean it up, but she dragged me back to the car. I didn't mean for her to be seeing dat." Mayphelia sat down at the table.

"You think it was Billy Wayne?" Bud asked.

"Oh, it was him. I feels his presence as soon as we drove up, and I made the mistake of tellin' Ceil so she got outta the car too. He be back." Mayphelia spoke without a hint of fear.

Ceil cried out, "He wrote on the side of her house, 'after the pigs, then the niggers.'"

"Shhhh, you'll wake the girls," Grace said as she turned to Bud. "We need to call the sheriff." Ceil broke away from Grace and sat down right next to Mayphelia.

Bud burst out, "Hell, he won't do nothin.' He's Klan, too." Grace watched as Bud's body became ram-rod straight with anger. She understood this pose. She'd seen it a lot lately if Billy Wayne's name was mentioned. She prayed he'd stay in control if he did see Billy Wayne. Years ago, a farm hand got a taste of Bud's retribution after he had roughly shoved nine-year-old Andy down for not holding a tote sack just right. Bud appeared out of nowhere. After a few minutes the farm hand limped to his pickup with a bloody face.

"Bud, Klan or not, you need to tell the sheriff." Grace picked up a towel and began wiping the table.

Bud seemed to ignore her. "Come on Mayphelia, I'll help you clean up. How the hell did he get that blood? Wonder if he was hiding out around here that day."

Mayphelia studied the floor. "There's hog killin' going on 'round the whole county."

She sighed deeply. "Appreciate it, but I has to clean it up myself. That don't mean I won't refuse a ride over ta my place. Jest let me finish off this coffee."

"Naw, naw, go on with your coffee and help yourself to a sweet roll. I've changed my mind. I'm going over to get the sheriff. Grace is right. I want him to see it before you do any cleaning." He gave Grace a quick kiss and was out the door.

Clive was cleaning his finger nails with a pocket knife when Bud entered the small office and gave his report. Clive put down his knife and looked up at him. "There ain't been no report of Billy Wayne even being back in these parts. I saw his mama yesterday and all she talked about was her rheumatism."

Without another word Bud turned and walked out. That sorry-no-good wasn't interested in seeing blood smeared on a colored person's house. When Bud got back home he removed his rifle from the barn and put it on top of the kitchen cabinet, with the box of shells next to it. "I don't want to hear a word, Gracie. It stays here for now." Grace nodded.

He handed Mayphelia a large cow bell. "If you see or hear anything, you ring this as loud as you can and I'll be there in no time."

THE next days passed without incident so Ceil and Grace left as planned to prepare for the art show in San Antonio. It turned out that another beginning artist, Guillermo Tobias, also being featured, was showing twice as many painting as Grace which was unsettling. Thank goodness Ceil had convinced her to frame some of her earlier water colors, crayons, and pencil sketches. Her five oils would have been a meager showing besides all of Guillermo's.

"What's this?" Ceil exclaimed when they entered the gallery. Guillermo had placed all his works at the very front, leaving only the far back walls open for Grace. She continued, "You're going to have to move some of these to the back so that my artist can also display at the front."

Guillermo shook his head. "I was the first to arrive so I get first choice."

"We'll see about that." Ceil marched out, found a phone booth and called the gallery owner. By the afternoon Grace has some spaces towards the front.

They left the gallery exhausted. "If Bud had been here we'd have been finished hours ago," Grace complained.

Ceil cheerfully countered, "But we got it done, didn't we?"

Bud had refused to leave Regina, the girls and Mayphelia alone overnight because of the threat of Billy Wayne being in the area. He would drive over the next day for the show. Besides, Regina was stressed with last-minute cramming as her final exam dates were fast approaching. She needed both Bud and Mayphelia there to help keep the girls out of her hair.

When they got to the hotel, Grace began to feel uneasy; she and Ceil would be in the same room. Bud had said he couldn't see the point in paying for two rooms since he wasn't going, and Grace feared it might raise suspicions if she insisted. *I would rather die than have Bud know,* she told herself yet knowing that someday she would have to tell him. A day didn't go by that she didn't think about what had happened. The worst part was that she couldn't exorcise the memories of the pleasure she had experienced no matter how many Hail Marys she said.

Ceil heard Grace's sigh and saw her look of relief as soon as they entered the room. It had two beds. She smiled and said, "Don't worry, Grace. Once again, I promise I won't bother you."

GRACE remembered the same promise made on the day of the blood smearing, Mayphelia had worked all day scouring her home until it was spotless. Then she insisted on spending the night there because she had to do a ritual cleansing similar to what she'd just done to Ceil's basement. She'd smudge it with burning herbs and special grasses and chant ancient prayers.

"This spirit cleansin' has to get done," she said while putting various charms and power pieces around her neck and arms." Billy Wayne ain't coming back for a while. He knowed I wadn't here."

Once again Ceil was twisting a strand of hair around her finger. "I can't be alone. Grace, please stay with me just one night. Billy Wayne has it in for me too."

Grace hesitated before Bud spoke up, "Grace, don't worry, I can manage the girls and supper. You go on."

Ceil wanted them to sleep in the living room so they'd wake-up if Billy Wayne walked up on the porch or tried to open the door. She folded the couch down into a bed. "Here, you sleep on the couch and I'll put a pallet here on the floor. I want to sleep on the floor so I'll hear if it creaks."

Grace felt sorry for her and was glad to be there even though her presence didn't seem to have a calming effect. She cringed as Ceil took her granddad's shotgun and put it next to her. "I swear I'll shoot that son-of-a-bitch this time."

"Ceil, you'll have to put the gun away, on the table or in the corner. I can't relax with it so close to us."

Ceil immediately moved it to a chair by the door.

She is always considerate of me was Grace's last thought as her head touched the pillow. The whole day had exhausted her beyond anything she had ever experienced. First of all, she had tried to soothe Ceil's fears as best she could. The self-assured, competent, independent Ceil had been replaced by someone Grace hardly recognized. Yet Grace knew that a childhood experience can cripple one in certain ways for life. Ceil kept saying over and over, "You can't imagine all the blood." Half the time, Grace didn't know if she were talking about Mayphelia's cabin or her mother's body.

On top of dealing with Ceil, Grace was worried Regina would find out that Billy Wayne was back. Now would be an especially bad time for her to find out, what with the stress of studying for finals.

Some time during the night, Grace awoke, realizing that Ceil's arms were wrapped around her. She sprang up, "What are you doing? We can't, not any more, Ceil."

Ceil whimpered. "I know. I know. I dreamed my grandfather was after me."

Grace felt ashamed. She could be harsh, unsympathetic. She began to rub Ceil's back. "My darling, I'm sorry. I'm here for you. I just don't want anything else."

Ceil looked up at her. "Can't we just cuddle together? I promise that will be all."

Grace lay down and opened her arms to Ceil. She snuggled into the embrace and immediately fell asleep. Grace knew she was holding a motherless child and was grateful that she could give comfort and security to her friend who had given so much to her. The least Grace could do in return was to keep the blood and the evil grandfather away from her this one night.

CEIL plopped down on her bed. "Hadn't you better get going?"

Coming out of her reverie, Grace hurried to the bathroom to freshen up. The tiredness and anxiety evaporated. She was going to get to see her oldest daughter. Sister Mary Clare had given permission for a one-hour visit at six o'clock. The permission came after four letters requesting, begging for a visit.

An hour later, Ceil pulled up into the convent's parking lot. "I'll wait here in the car."

"You can come in. I'd love for you to meet Angela."

"I thought she was now Sister Mary Grace?" Ceil continued, "You only have one hour and you haven't seen her in months. Go on. I brought a good book and I can walk the grounds if I get antsy."

Grace waited in the huge reception room, hardly containing her eagerness to see her daughter.

"Mama." Grace looked at a stranger calling her Mama, but then she recognized those hazel eyes. "Angela, my dearest."

She hugged her and quickly pulled back, alarmed. "Why you're nothing but skin and bones. What's happened? And you are so pale. What's wrong?"

Angela gave a feeble laugh. "Oh, it's nothing. I've had a sort of cold that I can't seem to shed and I haven't had much of an appetite" Then with a big smile, she said, "Don't worry, Mama. I'm fine. I just don't get out in the sun like I did on the farm."

Angela led her to the couch where they sat down. Grace noticed her daughter's deep breathing, tired eyes and lethargic movements.

"I'm so proud of you becoming a painter, Mom. Well, you've always been an artist. I remember sneaking into your closet and looking at some of the pictures you'd drawn."

Grace was startled by this. "You did what?"

Angela put her hand over her mother's. "I never said anything because I knew you wanted to keep that part of yourself a secret. Forgive me. I can't wait to hear how the show goes. I hope you become famous and rich. Listen to me. A nun probably shouldn't talk like that." Only a feeble laugh followed.

Grace remembered that not long ago Angela could shake the walls with her laughter and vitality. Did becoming a nun suck the life out of you? Grace was beginning to feel that old fear, that fear of helplessness, that fear of knowing a child of yours was leaving this life. *Oh, God, not another Peter.*

"Angela, I want you to see a doctor. Has your superior said anything about taking you to a doctor?"

Angela looked down at her hands as if she were embarrassed. "Religious life is hard. One has to be strong and endure the rigors…"

"Stop, Angela. That's just stupid talk." Grace got up. "I need to talk to your superior, Sister, what's her name, Mary Clare?"

"Mother, please don't say anything. She was so kind to let me see you. Most novices hardly get any family visitation and I've already gotten two. I think she let me see you because I have been sick."

"So it's been more than a cold? Have you seen a doctor?"

Slowly Angela shook her head.

"Okay, then get Sister Mary Clare for me. I mean it, Angela."

On the verge of tears, Angela left. Grace was fuming. She could just imagine how Bud would be reacting if he were here. With a flash of insight she realized that in the past she could shut herself off from these strong emotions because Bud was always there to react for her.

Sister Mary Clare entered, a corpulent woman with a round, no-nonsense face. *It doesn't look like she's going with-*

out a meal, Grace thought; however, she forced herself to remain calm and kind.

"I'm sorry to bother you, Sister, but I think my daughter is ill and I would like for her to see a doctor. Her father and I will be happy to take care of the bills."

Sister Mary Clare looked at Angela, "Sister, do you think you need to see a doctor?"

Angela remained silent. Sister Mary Clare continued firmly, "Child, you have to let me know. You are responsible for your own well-being. So do you wish to say anything?"

Slowly, Angela nodded her head and almost whispered, "Yes, please, I would like to see a doctor."

"Very well, then, we'll see about it tomorrow."

Sister Mary Clare turned to Grace. "Don't worry, Mrs. Wolansky. God will take care of her."

With that she defied her large size by gliding from the room. Grace's face was flushed with anger. *Well, God wasn't taking care of her until I showed up.*

Grace wondered what had happened to the daughter who was always more than able to express her will and concerns.

Angela hugged her mom. "I've kept thinking it would go away. Sister is right. I have to look after my own well being. It's not her fault, so please don't blame her."

Grace pulled back and looked at her daughter's sunken face. "I'm not blaming anyone. I'm just glad I came."

Once Grace was assured that Angela was going to see a doctor, she relaxed and talked about Andy and Sheila and their wedding plans for the following June. "It will be here before we know it."

Grace paused, wondering if she should tell her that they were talking about having two ceremonies, one Jewish and one Catholic. Grace herself was still trying to come to terms with this arrangement. Would it be too great a leap for her nun-daughter?

"Yes," Angela said, "Andy wrote and told me that he had applied for a dispensation from the bishop so that they could have a Jewish and a Catholic ceremony. I wrote him back and told him that if he couldn't get one, he should just have both ceremonies and not tell anyone." Angela laughed.

Grace felt some joy. Her daughter was still in there, despite all the discipline and expectations of self-sacrifice. The spirited, independent-thinking girl, who marched to the tune of her own drummer, may have been subdued but she hadn't left.

CHAPTER TWENTY-SIX

Surprisingly, Grace's early sketches were selling better than her paintings. Of course, they weren't marked as high, but still she was amazed that the works she had done in the middle of a breakdown were appealing to this many people. Perhaps it was because they were so truthful.

Bud smiled broadly as he watched Grace move through the groups of people discussing her paintings and drawings. She seemed so confident and looked beautiful, a real knockout in fact. He loved her dress.

Ceil had taken her shopping and more or less ordered her to buy a particular dress that cost three times more than Grace had ever spent on one. And then she managed to get her to buy a particularly fetching pair of high heels. "To be successful, you have to look successful," Ceil kept telling her.

Grace's money canister in the kitchen was down to fifteen cents. She had been saving to get a new wheelbarrow for her yard work, but instead now she had a dress and a pair of shoes that were too good to wear anywhere besides an art show. *Oh well, that's how it goes,* she thought as she handed over her hard-saved funds. Ceil would have been delighted to buy these things for her, but remembering Grace's reaction to the art supplies thought it best not to offer.

That morning Grace and Ceil had awakened in the same bed in each other's arms. Ceil untangled herself and said, "I'll be going back to L.A. as soon as the show is over."

That would be best for both of us Grace thought as she sat up and threw on her nightgown. Her beloved Bud would be here in a few hours. Yet she didn't feel regret over last night's pleasure that released the pain and fear.

Yesterday evening as they were driving back to the hotel, Grace had been beside herself with worry. "I know it's bad, Ceil. She looks terrible."

Ceil took her hand. "My dear, don't make problems for yourself. Wait to see what the doctor says. A common cold that isn't properly treated can really bring someone down."

Grace pulled away. "Keep your hands on the wheel. It's dangerous. The driver's manual said so."

Once in the hotel room, Ceil continued trying to comfort Grace. "I'm calling room service. After a good meal with some wine, you'll feel better. Worrying isn't going to make Angela well."

The food arrived, but Grace sat and stared at it. Finally Ceil had had enough. "Grace, snap out of it. You are coming out as an artist tomorrow. Think of that and celebrate that. Sometimes I feel like you enjoy suffering. Now eat."

Grace looked up at her, startled. "Do you really think that?" she asked. "That I enjoy suffering?"

Ceil emptied her wine glass, "I don't know. Sometimes, maybe."

Grace took a bite of the Chateaubriand. Any other time, this steak would have been delicious, but tonight it kept sticking in her throat. The wine helped wash it down. After a while she had eaten half the food on her plate and consumed two glasses of wine. She felt like she was on a boat in a choppy sea.

"I've got to get ready for bed," she said as she headed for the bathroom.

She held onto the wash basin and looked in the bathroom mirror. *Oh God, it's happening again. I'm going to lose another child.* The dark shadows were enveloping her. With a whimpering cry, she fell to the floor.

The bathroom door swung open. Bud was picking her up, no, it was Ceil. "My darling, my darling?" It was Ceil's voice.

Now Grace was in bed and Ceil was holding her. Grace began sobbing. "If she dies, I won't be able to go on. Somehow I got through losing one child, but I won't make it through another."

Ceil caressed her back, "It won't happen again."

"Oh please, just make the pain go away," Grace sobbed.

Ceil began kissing her cheek. Grace responded and pulled her mouth to hers. Once again Grace was tumbling into the sweetness and gentleness of this woman, or was it Bud? Suddenly she had a flash, a remembrance of the night Regina had been conceived. She had said to Bud, "Make the pain go away. Make the pain go away." And he was holding her, caressing her, kissing her. Yes, it was the same. Bud, Ceil, were they the same person?

Grace felt the crashing of pleasure and release and then the solitude of deep, deep sleep. She awoke but didn't open her eyes. She felt Ceil's breast resting on hers and recalled feeling Bud's penis resting on her leg. It was all good, wasn't it? It was the same, wasn't it? Just showing love for another human being. She shook her head because the demon of judgment was standing at the foot of the bed.

She opened her eyes. It was morning and Ceil was saying, "I'm going back to L.A. as soon as the show is over."

"Wait till after Thanksgiving," Grace whispered.

ON the way home, Grace put her arm around Bud's shoulder and leaned over and kissed his cheek several times. She felt so happy, so free, so much more loving. Being with Ceil seemed to be a tonic that awakened her to all of life's pleasures.

On top of that, she had two hundred and ten dollars in her purse, a new experience for her. Granted, she had sold eggs, butter and canned goods when funds were short, but those ventures were connected to Bud and her life on the farm. This money came from her alone, from her own hands and soul. Grace found it hard to believe all except one of her paintings and four sketches had sold.

Plus, she had been contracted to do a painting of an old barn for an elderly man. As she looked at the faded yellow picture, he told her it was where he had learned to milk a cow at age seven. A woman then asked her if she would come to her home and paint a portrait of her cat. Grace accepted the requests, adding, "I won't be able to finish until after Christmas." Many others asked for her phone number.

Grace lowered the car window. "Bud, I want you to put this money on the tractor. How much do we still owe on it?"

Bud leaned back, "Oh no, no, no. That money's yours. You open your own checking account at the bank and put it there. I want you to be independent like them women in the cities. Independent. Like Ceil."

"Why, that's silly. We've always had a joint account and your hard work has put it all there. I won't hear of it."

Bud laughed, "Okay, but from now on, don't ask me if it's okay every time you want to buy something. Just do it. I'm not gonna play daddy anymore."

Grace looked out the window. What a dear man he was. She hated to tell him what she knew she must. "Bud, there's something you have to know. I put it off till after the show." She fiddled with the clasp on her purse before she could say, "Angela's sick. She looks awful and I more or less ordered her superior to get her to the doctor."

Bud slowed the car down and looked in the rear-view mirror. "I'm gonna turn around and go back."

"No, Bud, listen. She saw a doctor this morning and had some tests done. Sister Mary Clare sent word to the hotel that she'd call us as soon as the results come back. There's nothing we can do now but wait."

Bud resumed the speed. Grace went on, "I was so worried last night, like I might have a breakdown like I did with Peter, but ...ah, I jumped to the worst conclusions, you know how I do."

"Grace, Peter's death was hard on me, too." His voice was hardly audible.

Grace watched the fence posts speeding past. *Dear Jesus, I've been so self-centered and immature all these years. What pain he must have gone through losing a son and then me, too.*

She turned towards him and put a hand on his leg. "Forgive me for never once considering the pain and suffering you were going through."

Bud allowed himself to feel the helplessness he had covered up all those years ago.

In the distance, Grace watched a flock of geese heading south and thought. *I will never fall apart again. I will continue to fly like those geese, no matter what.*

CHAPTER TWENTY-SEVEN

The day after Thanksgiving dawned early for everyone when Tessie started looking for gifts from Santa around five a.m. Over turkey and dressing the previous day, Sheila had said that Santa would be in Houston stores the next day. Tessie's little ears received a different message, and now she was distraught because Santa had not come. The only one not awakened by her wails was her sister.

Bud took down the big calendar from the kitchen wall. "See we're on this day and then here is when Santa comes. That's how many days? Let's count them."

"No, I don't want to. Santa's supposed to come now," she cried, more angry than sad.

"Tessie, how can Santa come when we're not ready for him? We don't have a tree up or any decorations. Grandma hasn't made any Christmas cookies. He loves Grandma's cookies. And we don't have any hot chocolate for him."

Wide-eyed, she listened and accepted her Grandpa's reasoning. Once convinced, she settled down on his lap and went back to sleep.

Regina lifted her sleeping daughter into her arms. "Oh Tessie, you are a mess, my sweet mess. Your mother should have known better than to stay up half the night playing forty-two. I'm going back to sleep too." She headed towards the bedrooms.

Andy twisted on his small cot. *Between this cramped room and my niece's yowling, it's impossible to get rest.* As soon as he had moved out, his furniture had been shoved to one side of the room and his mom's sewing station was moved in from her bedroom. "What's wrong with Angela's or Regina's room?" he had teased his mom. Now since his last visit the room had also became an artist's garret and, adding insult to injury, she had given his bed to Clem and replaced it with a small day cot. Now he really gave her a hard time. "Next time, you'll have me sleeping out in the barn."

"You can see I needed more room for the easel and canvases and paints. Besides your room has the best lighting."

"You've never forgiven me for smashing your rose trellis, have you?" He was referring to the time he came home with a few too many beers under his belt and had run over the roses swerving to avoid hitting a deer. At the time, his mom had been so mad he chose to keep quiet and not slur out the truth about some deer.

As he snuggled down under the covers he longed for Sheila's soft, sweet-smelling body crushed next to his, but under this roof Sheila had to bed down with Regina and for now he must settle for the smell of paint, a wobbly cot, and a sewing machine rubbing up against his scalp. "Maybe I could bribe Regina into switching places with me. This cot is more her size and it can't be comfortable sleeping with a woman," he muttered to an almost blank canvas." He dozed off thinking, *But after Billy Wayne, maybe not.*

Grace knew she couldn't go back to sleep. Ceil was leaving that afternoon for Los Angeles. Grace was driving her to the station. "I'm taking the train back to give myself time to reflect and prepare for a very different life," Ceil had answered when asked why she wasn't flying. Even though the ride to the depot was short, Grace was glad to have some time alone with her. She could no longer deny that she had loved her in a way that went beyond mere friendship.

For some reason the fear of damnation over committing an unnatural act didn't sully her feelings for Ceil. However, there was the unsettling fear of what Bud would do if he found out. But then why should he? Her infidelity had opened her heart to loving him more than she ever had and tomorrow Ceil would be hundreds of miles away. The thought *there's no need to tell him. It would be sinful to hurt him like that* eased her conscience somewhat.

She was relieved when everyone left the kitchen. She pulled up the bottom of her apron to absorb the tears that wouldn't stay inside any longer. What would she do without her friend's laughter, wisdom, and encouragement? *Her leaving is for the best.* This self-directed advice didn't help, just as Ceil's decision to keep her car and the Dollard house didn't help. "I will be coming back for regular visits and plan to stay for several weeks. For sure from Thanksgiving to Christmas."

The Thanksgiving celebration had been storybook perfect. The formal dining room was decorated with orange and yellow chrysanthemums mingled with twigs of fall leaves. The table was laid with Grace's best china, a mixed set from both her mother-in-law and Bud's great-aunt. Everyone dressed in their Sunday best. Andy and Sheila had provided wine and a pumpkin pie made by a chef in Houston. The day before Ceil had a turkey delivered. Before the eating began, Angie recited the Pledge of Allegiance and Tessie sang a made-up song with a country melody. At everyone's request Mayphelia was persuaded to give the blessing. "Lord, we is so blessed. Just look at all this wonderful food, these good people, here together in love. We knowed it's yo'r doin' and we're much obliged. Amen."

When Mayphelia arrived with her legendary buttermilk pie, Ceil noticed her hair was cotton white. Usually the snowy crown was concealed under a knitted cap or one of the colorful turbans Ceil had given her. Then when Ceil took her hand, now withered, she realized with a catch in her heart that her May-May might not be around much longer.

Perhaps I should rethink moving permanently to Texas. The people seated around the table had come to be her family. Phone calls, letters, or money gifts would not be enough. She wanted to be with them.

"I'm not going to run off like I did last time," she had told Mayphelia.

"Listen, ya do what ya wants, but I don't need no one to be fussin' over me."

Everything was in order. She had given Clem fulltime employment as the overseer of her property to keep everything up and running and Lizzie was hired to keep the house clean. She loaned her car to Grace. "Promise me you'll drive it often so it won't get rusty." For once, Grace hadn't objected. "I promise."

Grace's head throbbed. Angela's medical tests should be in today. Sister Mary Clare had called a day ago to say she'd let them know as soon as she was notified. Sister Mary Grace had been confined to bed in the infirmary with "Sister Rita hovering over her like an old mother hen," Sister Mary Clare said jovially. This news eased some of Grace's worry especially after Regina had told her that Sister Rita was very loving and particularly fond of Sister Mary Grace.

Regina entered the kitchen fully dressed. "I'm tired to the bone, but I can't sleep." She took her coffee cup and sat down on a stool at the counter next to the window, keeping her eyes glued on the widening rim of golden yellow in the east. Grace knew she was worried about her test scores. Since Monday she had run to the mail box every morning only to find nothing there for her. Grace wished she could ease this daughter's worries. She had not been dealt the same cards as Angela and Andy. She could hear Bud's dad say, *"Life blesses some with full houses and others with only a pair of deuces."*

Regina was anxious, not only about her test scores but also her future. The beauty school in San Antonio was out of the question. No money had come from Billy Wayne in weeks and even though she was using her grandfather's inheritance only when she absolutely had to, she knew her dad was right about it not lasting forever. Above all she was tense about the divorce. Billy Wayne had disappeared. His mother had told her that she hadn't seen "hide o hair of im," but Regina didn't believe her. Her dad had checked on the trailer. "It looks like it's been deserted except for a bunch of rats, the smaller kind, you know?" he said with disgust.

By nine o'clock Regina was on her third cup of coffee when she shot up, tore out the door and began running down the lane. The mail man's car stopped at their box. By the time she got there Mr. Dooly was holding a large envelope out for her. "I know you've been waitin' on this."

She grabbed it, mumbling incoherently, not noticing him drive off. The letter was heavy in her hand. What if she didn't pass? Would she be able to face her family? Would she be able to work and support herself and the girls? She couldn't open it now.

She turned and saw Angie racing towards her. Tessie trailed behind. *I must have slammed the back door. They depend on me. I have to face whatever comes.* She tore open the envelope and read the through the pages. The girls wrapped their arms around her as she sunk to her knees.

"Your mama's a high-school graduate," she shouted. They didn't understand the importance of this moment yet they enthusiastically hugged her.

Andy sat at the table in a sleep daze when Regina stormed in and slapped the certificate down under his nose. "See, you didn't think I could do it, did you?"

He read the report with exaggerated slowness while Regina fidgeted. When he finished, the hand holding the coffee cup began to shake over the papers. "There…there's got to..to..to be some mistake," he stammered. Regina screamed and snatched the reports up.

"What's going on?" Grace rushed in carrying a load of laundry.

"Look, Mama. I did it."

Once again Grace couldn't keep the tears from coming. *This must be my crying day,* she thought as she hugged Regina. Andy was hugging her too. "Little sis, you just keep on doing things to spite me, you hear? I'm very proud of you." These words made Regina feel as if she had finally arrived. She was as capable as her brother and her sister. Their compliments meant more to her than anything her parents could say.

Having heard the joyous news from the bedroom, Sheila ran in. "This calls for a celebration. What do you say we all go into town and do some Christmas shopping?" The girls could hardly contain their excitement. Tessie sang, "Santa Claus is coming, Santa Claus is coming."

Regina had already run out the back door towards the barn waving her certificate. "Daddy, look, I even passed the math."

ONCE everyone had left for the holiday shopping spree, the house sank into peacefulness. For days it had been overcome with nonstop activity and noise. Grace hung up the dish towel and headed for the bathroom, determined to relax in a tub of hot water before taking Ceil to the station. She lay back on the inflatable pillow Sheila had given her and promptly fell asleep.

Minutes later she heard ringing from somewhere. It was the phone. She quickly wrapped up into her robe and smiled. Maybe Ceil had decided to stay until after Christmas. "Hello…Oh, yes. Hello, Sister Mary Clare."

Sister Mary Clare's voice was solemn. As Grace listened she gripped the receiver tighter and tighter. The veins on her clenched hand stood out. Suddenly she crumpled down to the floor. A mournful cry echoed through the stillness.

The receiver dangled from the cord.

REGINA looked in a store window at several mannequins in winter coats and wished she lived someplace where she could wear a winter coat more than two or three times a year. Here a coat could last for years unless the moths got to it, yet every year Farley's managed to sell some. The girls were taking turns skipping on the sidewalk. "Step on a crack and break your mama's back," Angie kept telling Tessie, who would then hop onto the next crack.

"Well, at last, I've found you."

Regina caught her breath at the sound of this voice. She turned, hardly believing that David was standing in front of her. "What are you…? " The words stuck in her throat.

David laughed. "After yesterday's Thanksgiving dinner, I decided to drive over here and just walk the streets, hoping that you'd be shopping. And here you are?"

Regina was speechless. She'd dreamed of a reunion ever since they'd parted at the train station. She fumbled in her purse and took out the wadded paper he had given her. "I've carried this around ever since."

Angie tugged at her skirt. "Mama, who's this man?"

Regina caught Tessie in mid-skip and positioned both girls in front of her. "Girls, this is David, a nice man I met on the train. David, this is Angie, and this is Tessie."

David held out his hand for a shake, "Hello there, you're just as pretty as your mama."

Both girls looked up at him in suspicious wide-eyed wonder with arms planted firmly at their sides. Finally, David withdrew his hand and said, "Well, how about an ice cream?"

This broke the spell, at least for Tessie. Anyone who offered ice cream was okay with her. Angie was still cautious. David continued, "I saw a little diner just across from the square. I bet they have ice cream." He winked at Angie, who scowled back.

He bent his elbow for Regina to take. Regina looked around nervously. Where were Andy and Sheila? There were lots of people in town today. What if someone saw her with another man? She wished Andy and Sheila would appear.

David saw her look of apprehension. "I just want to buy you a cup of coffee and ice creams for your girls. Don't worry."

"I'm not divorced yet," Regina mumbled in his ear.

"Come on, Mama." Tessie pulled on her skirt.

David paused to look directly at her. "So you are getting a divorce? I knew you weren't happy."

They walked on in silence as Tessie ran ahead. Angie stayed close to her mother. *How could he tell I was unhappy? Is it possible for someone to know another so well after such a brief meeting?*

As they entered the diner, Regina looked around at all the tables. There was gossipy Lavenia, the moral standard for the whole parish, sitting with her daughter. Regina wanted to crawl under a table. "This isn't such a good idea." Regina tugged at David's arm.

David whispered, "Don't worry. Just tell them I'm your brother."

"Everyone knows my brother. We grew up in this town. Everyone knows everyone."

Regina moved into the booth next to the girls, with David and his lovable smile across from her. She was happy to see him again, but she was also afraid of what people would think and say. Everyone in this diner knew Billy Wayne, too. How many would run to tell him? How many in here knew exactly where he was? Lavenia looked over and broadly smiled, exposing a row of horse teeth. Regina pulled her sweater tighter around her.

With a mischievous wrinkle of his brow, David said, "I got it. Tell them I'm going to be your second husband." Regina was taken aback. Was he teasing? "That will keep their tongues going till way past Christmas." He laughed out loud. Lavenia turned in her chair to look.

He had the same playful qualities as Andy. Blushing, she replied a little harshly, "Yes, that would be a great scandal to chew on for a while."

The waitress approached. "I want lipstick ice cream." Tessie said. Angie poked her and said in a grown-up voice, "She means strawberry, and I would like a chocolate, thank you very much." David couldn't keep from grinning. He already loved these girls as well as their mama.

"Also a couple of coffees," David flashed a boyish grin at the young high-school girl, who swooned back to the kitchen. Regina realized that she was really proud to be seen with this man, which was a new and good feeling.

"Hello there, Regina." Regina looked up. This couldn't be happening. There stood Joseph Hensley. "Have you gotten your scores yet?"

Regina's face turned redder. She didn't want David to know she hadn't graduated from high school, at least not yet. She nodded her head and then ignored him by turning to the girls and tucking napkins under their chins.

"How were your math scores?" He wouldn't take the hint.

God, she wanted out of here and fast. Fortunately, before she could answer she spotted Andy and Sheila just across the street. "Just a moment, there's my brother." She bolted out from the booth.

"I was just saying I wanted some coffee and pie," Andy said.

"Listen, there's someone here. I met him on the train." Regina whispered.

"You are kidding me?" Sheila blurted out in disbelief. Night before last in the wee hours of the morning Regina had told her all about this man on the train, how she could still feel his hand squeezing her arm and how she prayed every night they'd meet again. Fighting to stay awake, Sheila had thought *fat chance.*

By the time they got back to the booth Joseph had left and David was making an animal out of a couple of straws while the girls intently watched. Regina introduced everyone and then stood back.

Andy looked him over and remarked, "You look like one of our family. Are we related?"

Regina wanted to clobber him. He could be such an ass. "God, I hope not," David remarked with a jolly laugh.

Andy scooted into the seat beside the girls, forcing Regina to sit beside David. Then Sheila pushed Regina over so she could sit down. Regina was now thigh to thigh with David. She could feel the heat coming from him. Suddenly, her panties were moist. She knew she was going to burst into flames at any moment. This was the worst afternoon she'd ever been through.

In her early-morning-awakening dreams, she had always been seated on a park bench under a lush weeping willow. It was misty and the leaves on the branches almost kissed her cheeks. No one else was around, no children, no relatives, no townspeople. She would look up and see David walking towards her. He would sit down and they would look out towards the sunrise. Then he would lean over and gently kiss her on the lips. Generally the kiss would bring her to a fully awakened state with embarrassment over her silliness.

Someone was calling her, "Mama, I have to go to the potty." Tessie held up her arms for a pickup. Sheila jumped up and said, "Come on, baby. I'll take you." Regina immediately moved to the far edge of the bench.

GRACE slowly pulled herself up and leaned against the wall. Her head ached in the worst way. Rubbing her forehead, she kept repeating, "I knew something serious was wrong. I knew it. Dear God, tuberculosis." Sister Mary Clare had said it several times. Grace looked up and grabbed the phone receiver, "Hello, Sister, I'm sorry, I dropped the …" The phone was dead. She looked up at the ceiling and called out, "Why punish her for my sins?"

What had Sister Mary Clare said? "Sister Mary Grace is being taken to a sanitarium. The novitiate is being quarantined." Grace hung up the receiver and tightened the robe around her. She leaned against the wall and loudly vowed to the four walls. "I will not go into the darkness this time. I will be strong. I will be strong for Angela, for Bud, for my whole family."

Grace began recalling the conversation. Angela's recovery would take time and after the sanitarium stay, she would have to come home until she was completely well. *I'm going to have my oldest daughter back with me again.* Grace couldn't help but feel some happiness with that thought. *Maybe God isn't punishing me after all.* She inhaled, knowing that her thinking had moved to another room, a room much more open and airy.

The honking car outside startled her. *Oh goodness, Ceil is here.* Grace ran to the bedroom and threw on some clothes, grabbed a brush and headed out the door. She couldn't do anything for Angela this minute. "What happened to you?" Ceil asked as Grace crawled in. "I fell asleep in the bath tub." She couldn't talk about Angela, not yet.

Grace saw a small bag on the back seat. "Is that all you're taking?"

"That's it. I gave Lizzie all the clothes I brought with me. I have almost a warehouse of clothes in California."

Grace shook her head. "I just can't get used to the way you rich people live."

Ceil was thinking of something else and didn't respond. "My heart is almost breaking. Clem told me last night that Mable has uterine cancer and may not last until spring. God, I'm so glad I got them that home."

Grace remembered the day Ceil had dropped by in tears. "I just took Lizzie home. Did you know they live in a three room shack?" Ceil bit her lip. "I could tell she was mortified to have me see where she lived." Then in the next breath, "I'm going to do something about that."

Twelve days later, Clem and his family moved into a seven-room ranch house, two streets over from Ceil's. "I'm doing this for myself," she explained to Clem. "With the likes of Billy Wayne being around, I'm afraid. Now you can easily check on me morning, noon, and night."

Taking Clem's pride into consideration, Ceil charged him a pittance for rent each month, then when she promoted him to overseer, she gave him a raise that more than covered the house payment.

"I went by to tell them all goodbye. Clem's voice shook so much he could hardly speak while Lizzie cried like a baby. Mable and the four other children mumbled their goodbyes through tears. It was very emotional making me so weak I didn't know if I'd make it to my car."

"You now have another family that will forever draw you back to this place," Grace said softly.

Ceil held back tears and reached for a cigarette.

Grace added, "You've changed a great number of lives for the better," Grace added.

Ceil nodded, "And a great number of lives have changed me." She recalled Mayphelia's words as she held her tightly in a good-bye hug. *The daggers of hate once stabbin' yo'r soul have been melted down. Now they's become vessels of kindness.*

Ceil and Grace didn't speak as the car sped along even though Grace had so much she wanted to say. Finally breaking the silence, Ceil said, "I'm thinking of selling my business. It doesn't interest me anymore. With the inheritance and all I've acquired, I can live out several lifetimes in luxury."

Grace wasn't listening. "Ceil, I don't understand how it's possible to love both you and Bud in the same way," Grace sighed.

"You mean sexually?" Ceil took a long drag on the cigarette. "You know years ago, I had a male lover for several months. In the beginning I was attracted to him that way and even though we loved one another and wanted to be like ordinary people, the relationship quickly faded because he preferred men and I preferred women."

She paused, searching for the words. "Your sexual attraction for me will soon fade because you're made for Bud and you know it. We'll always be close, but just as friends and not lovers. My going away will give each of us time to come to terms with these realities."

Grace saw the depot ahead. "I'm going to miss you terribly." She inhaled a sob.

Ceil clutched the steering wheel as if it were a life support. "There's nothing I'd rather do now than take you back with me. But that can't be and we both know it."

Grace turned in her seat and caught a fleeting glimpse of someone who looked like Regina with a good-looking man in an airman's leather jacket opening a car door for her. Then a building obscured the view. Grace shook her head; her eyes were playing tricks.

The train was pulling into the station. In turmoil Grace blurted out, "I guess God is punishing me through Angela."

Confused, Ceil faced her. Before she could ask, Grace blurted out in one breath about the phone call. Looking down at the steering wheel, Ceil shook her head. "What an awful God you believe in, Grace. I'm really saddened that you think what happened between us merits punishment. You can't let go of your old ways of thinking, can you? Will you ever be free from all that poison?"

A rapier blade sliced through Grace's heart. She bowed her head. "I want to be. I want to be free. I don't want to go back to the old thinking, but it's so hard for me and now with you leaving I'm afraid…"

"Grace, you're strong. You don't need me. Once I'm gone, you'll realize that. You can never go back, not completely anyway, to where you were."

When Ceil reached back for her travel case, Grace took her in her arms and hugged her tightly. "Thank you. You helped me save myself," Grace whispered. She paused before going on. "Perhaps I'm being given a second chance. After Peter died, I fell apart and wasn't there for Angela. Now I have a chance to be."

Ceil smiled. "Grace, I love you."

Ceil began to get out of the car, but Grace pulled her back and kissed her on the lips. Ceil gave in at first and then pulled away. "Grace, we can't have it both ways."

She got out of the car, walked to the train, boarded it and never once looked back.

Grace was dry-eyed and calm. "She's absolutely right," she whispered.

BY the time Andy had finished his coffee and pie, he and David were old-time buddies. Sheila and Regina sat by quietly as the two of them talked about everything from horses to electrical appliances. They even bantered about who would pay the check. David finally won out.

Out on the sidewalk Andy picked up Tessie and said, "Regina, why don't you bring David out to the house? Girls, you can ride home with us if you promise not to look in any of the packages on the back seat."

The girls were delighted. The game was on! They would do everything they could to peek into those packages with Undy reaching back and tickling them as soon as they tried

Regina felt both gratitude and anger towards her brother. She liked the idea of having some alone time with David, but she was angry that he thought he could make arrangements for her. Since Angela had become a Sister, he had taken over the job of bossing her around.

Then just as David was holding the car door for her, Ceil's car passed and she saw her mother looking out at her. Regina stopped. She had disappointed her parents too many times; she wasn't going to scandalize them now by bringing a man home while she was still married to another.

Stepping back from the car she called, "Hey Andy, wait for me."

She turned back to David. "I can't spend time with you until I'm divorced and I don't know when that will be. My husband's disappeared and no one seems to know where he is. Besides, he's said he won't sign divorce papers. It's all a big mess and I don't know when it will be over."

The look of let-down and disappointment on David's face melted her heart. She didn't want to hurt this considerate man who had walked the streets today looking for her. "I'm really very sorry. When it's over I'll get in touch, and if you're still interested then we can see each other."

She turned to walk towards Andy and the others. David grabbed her by the arm and turned her around. "I'll be waiting. I don't even know your last name?"

"Tarkin, but I'll be a Wolansky again as soon as I'm free. Goodbye. And thanks so much for remembering me. I've thought of you so often." Regina walked away.

CHAPTER TWENTY-EIGHT

Regina looked around Angela's old room, now cluttered with the girls' dolls, books, stuffed animals and dress-up clothes. In a few weeks Angela would be living here again. Regina dreaded packing up but she was not going to risk exposing her girls to tuberculosis despite the doctor's assurance that Angela would not come home until the danger of transmission was past. Both Regina and her mother had already been tested since both had had contact with Angela while she was contagious. Both tests turned out negative. "Thank you, Lord," Regina said while the doctor was still talking.

Plus Angela would need lots of peace and quiet in the beginning, something not possible with Angie and Tessie in the same house. Bud reluctantly agreed to the move only after hiring Clem's son, Johnny, to keep a close eye on the place. He gave Johnny his old shotgun and then agreed to Johnny's request to move into the storage shed behind the house. "I think I should be close by during the night time, too," he told Bud.

Regina was a little confused by all the precautions. As far as she knew, Billy Wayne had not been around since his escape from the hospital. No one ever told her about the blood smearing incident. Still, when she recalled the night Billy Wayne had tried to break into her bedroom she was grateful that Johnny would be close by.

She picked up a teddy bear and said, "I would like to cuddle next to David just like Tessie cuddles next to you." *What a yummy thought.* She dropped the bear in a cardboard box on the bed. *All these feelings–happiness to be back in my own home; terrified that Billy Wayne might come back; worrying about Angela's health; longing to be with David.* She looked in the mirror over the dresser. "As usual, you're a mess," she said.

Her parents had left early that morning to visit Angela. A half-hour later Mayphelia dropped in using the excuse of giving them some of her newly dug turnips.

That morning, Mayphelia had awakened with a strong sense of danger around Regina but had received no clear vision. All she knew for sure was that she needed to look out for her and the girls. Stepping into the kitchen she said, "Why don't ya'll come to my place since yo'r mama and daddy is gone? Da young 'uns can hep me make some pecan brittle."

The girls were excited. "Can we, Mama? Can we, please?" Angie ran to get the new apron her grandmother had just made for her. Regina liked the idea of being alone for a while. "I need to stay here and pack, but if you're up for it, the girls can go."

Mayphelia frowned, then looked at the girls, "Okay I gonna let you hep me, but nobody kin know how I makes that candy."

Mayphelia was known all over the county for her chocolate covered pecan brittle. It was true no one knew her secret and she slammed her mouth shut if anyone asked. Some said her witchery made it so flavorful.

"Now ya got to promise me for life." The girls nodded. "Here, you takes hold one of my pinkie fingers, give me three deep breaths and say, 'I promise, May-May.'" Solemnly the girls made the vow.

As they were leaving, she turned back to Regina. "Now you makes sure all da doors be locked."

"May-May, you seem nervous. What's wrong?" Regina asked.

"I wants you all safe, that's all."

Once they were gone, Regina opened a drawer and began packing pajamas and underwear. For over a month now since Mr. Carbon had been sick, she had been working part time at the grocery store. In the quiet, her mind began to fly in all directions. *I have to find permanent work but who will take care of the girls? Mom can't when Angela comes home. Mayphelia wouldn't want to.* On several occasions Mayphelia had said, "God knowed what he was a doing when he didn't give me no kids. I ain't cut out for it. Jest a few hours atta time be all I can take."

Regina recalled the ride home from town. The girls had fallen asleep, "Little sis," Andy said, "I can tell he's crazy about you, and I can tell he'll treat you the way you should be treated."

"Yes, he's a winner," Sheila added.

Regina walked on air that entire evening in spite of the devastating news of Angela's illness. *Maybe good things are coming my way after all, she* thought, along with *Oh dear God cure my sweet sister.*

Thankfully the girls seemed to have forgotten about David and said nothing to her mom or dad. As would be expected, Angela's illness had dominated the conversations. Bud called both Sister Mary Clare and the doctors at the sanitarium to find out exactly what was going on. Every one of them had taken turns crying during the course of the evening.

Regina pulled out a half-eaten cookie from under the girl's panties. Sugar ants ran over her hand. She swatted them. "Those girls," she yelled. She dropped the panties and headed for her room. "I have David's number. I'm going to call him. Put myself out of this misery."

The phone rang before she got to her purse. She jumped. *It must be David. He's reading my mind.* She couldn't keep the excitement out of her voice. "Hello!"

"I want ta git my girls." Her knees weakened at the harsh voice on the other end of the line.

"Billy Wayne, where have you been?"

"None of your damn business, you whore. I heard about the day after Thanksgiving and how you was parading around town with some strange man. The whole world could see you was makin' a fool of me."

Regina held the phone and said nothing. Her voice was gone. Sheila's words, *You don't have to take it,* kept spinning through her mind.

Billy Wayne shouted, "So I'm coming. My girls ain't stayin' with a whore."

Regina hung up on him. A moment later the phone rang again. She ignored it. Her hands shook so much she could hardly pull on her coat or tie her headscarf. She headed out the back door, locked it and began walking at a fast pace, but as her terror mounted she broke into a sprinter's run towards Mayphelia's.

DRAPPED in white gowns and masks, Bud and Grace walked down the immaculate corridor. This was the first time since Angela's confinement they had been allowed to visit. Upon entering the room they were forced to pause while their eyes adjusted to the dim lighting. The sounds from various machines were frightening. *I bet hell feels this way*. Bud thought.

A loud sob tore through his throat as he recognized the frail, shrunken form lying under an oxygen tent. Grace put an arm over his shoulder. "She'll be okay, darling; she'll be okay." Fortunately Angela continued to sleep.

They sat down next to the bed, their eyes glued on their daughter. "I should have never let her go off to that place," Bud whispered as he took out a handkerchief to wipe his eyes.

Grace took his hand. "Bud, the convent had nothing to do with it. Besides, you know how headstrong she is. She would have gone even if you had locked her in her room."

Bud nodded with a slight smile. "I guess you're right about that. She was a high-spirited one alright and ..." He couldn't go on.

"Well, one good thing to remember is that she'll be with us during her recovery. Let's enjoy every moment of that."

"Yeah, you're right." Bud took a deep breath.

Sitting on the bedside table, Grace noticed the statue of an angel that looked vaguely familiar. "Bud, is that the angel we gave Angela on her First Communion?"

Bud picked it up. "I don't remember."

Now a sob caught in Grace's throat. It was the same angel. "Bud, I can still see our precious little girl in her white dress and veil walking down the aisle, so beautiful, so devout."

Bud put the angel down and looked over at Angela. "I wish I could hold her for just a moment. She is so tiny and all in white like on her Communion Day."

A nurse walked in and leaned over them. "You can stay a few more minutes and then come back this afternoon for a while. We need to bathe her. There's a cafeteria on the ground floor where you can have lunch while you wait."

"Why can't we stay longer?" Grace demanded. "We've driven over two hours and have to go back this evening."

The nurse spoke kindly. "Ordinarily those are the rules for someone as sick as your daughter. But I'll try to reach the doctor and see if he'll extend your time."

Grace thought back to earlier that morning when Bud had refused to take Ceil's car. She had been annoyed at the time because the faster car would have allowed them more visiting time. Now it looked like that wouldn't have mattered anyway. If only Angela would awaken to see that they were there.

"Mama."

Grace barely heard the breathy whisper. Had her wish been granted? Angela's eyes flickered open, then shut and then opened. "Angela, baby?" Grace softly cried out.

She and Bud crowded closer to the side of the bed. Grace reached under the oxygen tent and sheet, took her daughter's hand and squeezed it several times.

"We've come to rob you," Bud joked. "But these masks don't fool a smart girl like you, do they?"

"I'm so glad …." Angela struggled to speak as her eyes filled with tears.

"Shhh, shhh, baby. We're glad to see you too," Grace spoke calmly.

Bud bent closer to her. "You don't worry about a thing now. We're here."

The door opened and the nurse returned. "The doctor will be coming by this afternoon. Now I have to get on with the bath."

"We'll be back after we eat. Don't go anywhere," Bud said and tapped the tent.

When Grace and Bud returned from the cafeteria, Dr. Meyers was waiting for them in the hallway. After the usual exchanges he began, "Your daughter will probably be here for three more weeks. As you know, she came in with quite an advanced stage, but she is responding very well to the medications. She's got a lot of fight. It's remarkable that she was able to keep up with the rigors of convent life being as sick as she was."

Bud shook his head in disgust. *Couldn't those nuns in charge see she was wasting away?*

Grace's mind was going in another direction. *Making a good impression has always been something I've stressed to my children. Was Angela trying to impress her superiors by working while she was sick?*

This daughter had been her pride and joy. Around the church people, Grace could hold up her head in spite of Regina's disgrace. Grace clutched her purse to her bosom. "Can I stay here with her?" she asked. "I can get a hotel room and be here every day." There was still some money from her paintings tucked away in her purse. Bud had insisted she not deposit all of it.

The doctor thought for a moment. "Angela really needs to do nothing but sleep at this point. I suggest you go on home today, but perhaps in a week or so it would be helpful for you to be here with her. I'll let you know when."

Grace was disappointed. She wanted to sit by her child's bed and watch her every breath, willing her back to good health. Donning the gowns and masks again, they reentered the sick room. Angela was flushed. She was panting with shallow, rapid breaths. The nurse reassured them that she was not worse, merely worn out from the bath and eating.

Angela opened her eyes. "Tell me about everyone." She whispered. She closed her eyes.

Grace and Bud pulled chairs up close to her bed. They told her about the harvest, the cattle, the new refrigerator, and on and on ending with the Thanksgiving and Christmas holidays. "Angie got a new doll for Christmas dressed in a bright red evening gown," Grace laughed, "and then she named it Sister Mary Grace."

Angela smiled and whispered, "Bright red, I like that."

"Then Tessie got mad," Bud began, "when Santa ate all the cookies. She cried, 'He should learn to share like Mama says.'"

Angela began laughing. Suddenly the laughter became a coughing spasm. In a panic Bud reached under the tent, picked her up to sitting and patted her back, but it continued.

Grace rushed over to the door. "We need a nurse," she shouted. "She can't stop coughing."

Several nurses ran into the room. Bud and Grace couldn't see what they were doing, but eventually Angela's breathing became steady and even. Before leaving, one of the nurses said, "She needs to rest now."

Bud and Grace approached the bed. Grace kissed her gloved hand and touched Angela's cheek. Bud leaned over, "We'll be back in a few days, sweet pea. Now that the crops are in, I don't have a thing to do."

Angela whispered, "Daddy, stop fibbing."

With that Angela blew them an air kiss and fell asleep.

CHAPTER TWENTY-NINE

It was one of those retribution mornings. Clem was grateful for the cold air as he stumbled along the lane to work. The bone chill was subduing the bees he felt stinging throughout his body.

Last night he had done it again, gone on a bender that left him shaking, hung-over and ashamed. True, those nights weren't nearly as often as they had been before when he didn't have steady work.

Since Clem had started working for Ceil he was there every morning, no matter how bad his head throbbed or his stomach roiled. A couple of times he'd been so sick he could hardly walk, but he accepted the pain as penance. The nuns who had beat the fire out of him as a schoolboy would be proud to see he had learned that he must suffer for his wrongdoings. However, Clem knew he would feel greater torment if he disappointed Ceil. He was devoted to her.

The memory of the night he was too drunk to help the Wolansky girl gnawed at him a great deal. That, along with reliving the day Mr.Tarkin had smashed Boudie's skull, woke him at night and wracked him with self-loathing. It didn't matter how much time had passed, those incidents seemed like they had just happened. Once he had come close to telling Ceil these dark secrets. If he could unburden himself to just one person, maybe he wouldn't turn to the bottle for comfort. *Who am I kidding? I was a drunk before those things happened?* "And I'm a coward who deserves to be hung by the Klan," he muttered aloud.

This particular morning, Clem felt compelled to go check on the Wolansky Sunday house before going to the Dollard place. Since Regina and the girls had been living at the farm, he had been keeping an eye on it. That was the least he could do. Time after time Bud had given him and his boys work at more than a fair wage, and Grace had always shared her garden crops and baked goods with them.

As he approached the Wolansky place he stopped and came to sudden sobriety. Billy Wayne's truck was lodged up against the front porch as if he had intended to drive right through the house and then had had a last minute change of heart.

Billy Wayne was slamming his body against the front door. *Thank God for the new locks.* Billy Wayne rubbed his shoulder and cussed, then pulled out a long hunting knife and headed towards the window.

Clem hollered out, "Hey you, get away from there."

Startled, Billy Wayne turned around. He snickered through brownish yellow teeth when he saw who it was. "What you doin' up at this here hour, you worthless ole sot? Trying to find yo'r way back to that shack where yo'r wife's spittin' out another one like some stray cat?"

He raised the knife up like a spear ready for a throw and charged towards Clem. Clem ran towards the shed. If he got there, he could grab a shovel or hoe to defend himself. His legs felt like rubber. He could hear the demon gaining on him and imagined the knife plunging into his back. Then he heard a loud curse.

He glanced back. Billy Wayne was sitting on the ground, his foot tangled in a fence wire Bud had put up last spring for Angie's and Tessie's Easter chicks. "God-damnit, I should'a ripped this damn thing down like I threatened to," he shouted. "Those girls didn't need no son-of-a-bitching chicks to look after."

Clem now had enough time to get inside the shed. His lungs were close to busting. He slammed the door shut, grabbed an ax and watched through a slit in the boards. Billy Wayne stood up and looked around like he didn't quite know where he was. Without a word, he turned and went back to his truck. It backfired a couple of times before speeding off. Clem doubled over to keep from passing out.

REGINA burst through Mayphelia's door in near hysterics. The girls stood on chairs at the cabinet next to Mayphelia, dropping pecans into a large bowl. All three turned to face her. To hide her terror from the girls she turned to face the wood stove and held her hands over the top, willing the fire to give her strength.

"Mama, what's wrong?" Angie asked.

"Oh, I just ran over here and now I'm out of breath. The wind was blowing so hard my eyes got stung." Regina took a handkerchief out of her pocket and blew her nose.

Mayphelia put the bowl aside and lifted the girls down from the chairs. "Babies, this be needin' to sit for a while, so while that be workin' I wants ya'll to set down over there by the door and play with them straw dolls. Here's some popcorn. You let yo'r mama and me talk."

Mayphelia's home was one big room with a loft. A large wood stove used for warmth and cooking separated the living and kitchen areas. In the summer it was covered with an oilcloth and used as a table while Mayphelia cooked outside on a fire pit Radio Man had built. After Radio Man died, Mayphelia moved their bed downstairs from the loft leaving little room for the two easy chairs, end table and curio cabinet stuffed with herbs and potions. Still it was comfortable, a snuggly and inviting home.

Mayphelia pulled Regina over to what had been Radio Man's chair. "Tell me. He be back, huh?"

Regina nodded as she sat down. She stopped panting and began to breathe normally.

"Someone told him I was with a man, you know the one I told you about…now he's coming for his girls. Said I was a whore." Her whole body began to shake.

"There, there, baby." Mayphelia took out a small bottle from her curio cabinet. She mixed the clear liquid with warm water. "Here, drink this."

Regina felt the liquid enter her stomach and seep into the nerves of her body. Mayphelia stood over her and began pressing her fingers into Regina's scalp at different spots. Within a few minutes, the fear left and with it, the shaking. Mayphelia kept glancing out the window.

She stopped the massage and spoke softly, "He's just pulled up to yo'r folks' house. Now you're gonna take yo'r girls and go down the little cow path till ya gits to the circle of hay stacks, remember?"

Regina nodded. Mayphelia whispered in her ear, "You keep the girls in there till I comes for ya. Y'all gonna be safe. Be calm now for yo'r babies."

Then Mayphelia walked over to the girls. "Listen, ya'll gotta do somethin' else for May-May. Go with yo'r mama now and see if you can find that pea hen along the trail. If she's not there. Wait in the hay fort till she comes. You gotta be awful quiet for her to come, now. Here's some feed for her."

She handed Angie a little brown paper sack. "Careful so's not to spill it."

As soon as they were out the door, Mayphelia hurriedly removed a dark brown bottle from the very back of her cabinet. She took several big swallows. Then she doused a rag in a can of yellow ointment, smeared it over her face and tied it around her neck. A loud pounding shook the door.

She tore off her head scarf and picked up the old dirty blanket covering the floor by her bed. After wrapping herself in it, she slowly cracked the door open just enough for Billy Wayne to see her yellow-gray face surrounded by white hair spiking out in all directions.

"I come for my family," he barked at her.

"They all goes somewheres today to see a sick relative."

"You lyin' bitch. How could Regina answer the damn phone if she was gone like you say? I know she's out here somewhere."

The wind picked up the foul odor of the ointment. Billy Wayne backed up to the edge of the porch waving a hand in front of his nose. "God, you niggers smell awful."

"I jest knows they's was all goin', that's all."

"What's Ceil's car doin' there?"

"You's best ast her."

She could see Billy Wayne's fist clenching and unclenching and decided she'd better act now before he struck her.

"I's been awfully sick with the consumptin." As she finished, she began coughing and spitting up a vile brown liquid in Billy Wayne's direction. Some splattered his face and the front of his flannel shirt.

"Goddamn you, you crazy good-for-nothin' black bitch."

"I's sorry. You best goes now. I fear it's a contagion. I ain't suppose to be 'round no body."

Billy Wayne wanted to smash in her face but was afraid she might spit more disease on him. He yanked his shirt off and wiped his face with it. He coughed and spit several times on the ground. Before getting in the pickup, he threw the shirt on the ground and put on a jacket from the front seat.

Mayphelia watched him and chuckled. "His mind gonna make 'im sick but he'll blame me." She forced herself to puke up the rest of the vile potion she had drunk.

As Regina and the girls huddled quietly at the back of the partially enclosed circle of hay stacks, a peahen stepped lightly through the opening. Soon the cock strutted in regally with its beautiful plumage fanned out. Tessie clapped her little hands while Angie gazed in wonder. Regina felt tears sliding down her cheek. *They deserve better than Billy Wayne.*

Regina began to rock back and forth on the hay bale. Her nerves were coming unwound again. *Where was Mayphelia? What if he's hurt her?* Regina was afraid she was going to lose her mind. She couldn't take the constant fear and worry. Mayphelia's concoctions helped but she couldn't live on them the rest of her life. Last spring in a drunken rage Billy Wayne had said he'd sooner see his girls dead than have them grow up with her and her goddamn family. Then in the next moment he had said, "Know what? I'll jest kill you and then I'll have 'em all to myself. I am their daddy."

BILLY WAYNE could hardly swallow. His throat seemed to be closing up. Every time he went near that black demon something bad happened to him. He knew he was going to have to take care of her, not just talk about it. But for now all he wanted was to get back to Geraldine.

Then it came to him that Regina had to be somewhere at Bud's. He had just called her there. He turned the pick-up around and headed back. Once again he banged on the door. He yanked the handle but it was locked. He went around and looked in every window. "Regina, you whore, you'd best come out and face the music. I'll find you sooner or later. Tessie, Angie, it's your daddy."

The house seemed to be deserted. He knew his girls would make some noise if they heard him, unless they'd been turned all the way against him. "That's what that sorry family has done. I know it," he shouted to the wind.

He glanced over towards the barns and sheds. *Hell, they could be hiding anywhere.* As he walked towards the main barn he heard a truck coming down the lane. It was Alex Williams riding high in a brand new pickup. Billy Wayne shook his head in disbelief. "If that don't beat all. One of them owning a new truck like that. Daddy always says, 'The coloreds gonna take over the country if we don't stop 'em now.'"

Alex got out of his truck. "Howdy, Mister Tarkin. How you doin'?"

"What're you doin' here?" Billy Wayne asked sarcastically.

"Mr. Bud asked me to feed his stock while he's gone out of town."

"Did everyone go with him?"

"I suppose they did, alright. It seems Mr. Bud said somethin' about some of 'em leavin' out for Houston." Alex knew it was best to lie or say as little as possible to this white man. Bud had told him all about his son-in-law. "Now I's best get to work."

Alex walked right past him and on towards the barn. Billy Wayne wished he had the nerve to attack him, but he knew this man could tie him up like a dish rag. Alex was square and solid, powerful.

The thought that his girls were with that son-of-a-bitch Andy fired-up every resentment his body held. "Goddammit, I can't take this no more. I got to do some…"

He couldn't finish. He grabbed his throat and gasped for air. He was about to collapse when his lungs suddenly filled up again. Terrified, he ran to his pickup. As he sped away he vowed between panting breaths, "Prison and the chair ain't gonna stop me no more."

That night Geraldine had to take Billy Wayne to the hospital where he stayed for two weeks. The doctor said one of his lungs had collapsed, "from smoking and chewing too much tobacco." Billy Wayne insisted Mayphelia had spit something on him that ruined his lung. "She said it was the consumptin." The doctor walked out of the room shaking his head in disgust.

WHEN Mayphelia returned to the hay circle, she called out, "Ya'll ready to finish that brittle?" She looked at Regina, "Ya'll best stays with me till yo'r folks gits home."

Regina was grateful to be able to sit by the warm stove and listen to May-May and the girls sing gospel songs. While the brittle was cooling on the porch, Mayphelia told the girls to go out and wait for the "feas," Tessie's name for the peacock and peahen. "'Fore sunset, they be comin' up to scratch in the yard."

"No, they have to stay close by." Regina loudly commanded. Mayphelia paused, understanding her anxiety. "Yo'r mama's rite. Ya'll stays on dis porch. They won't come if you goes down to the yard, you hear?" Mayphelia propped the door wide open despite the cold air coming in so that Regina could watch them.

"Ease yo'r mind, baby, he ain't comin' back." Mayphelia pulled her chair next to the stove, took out her pipe and began to fill the bulb. "You be needin' more of them drops. You's shiverin' again."

Regina sipped of the rest of the potion left in the cup. The potion, the fire's crackling, Mayphelia's pipe puffing and the girls' happy voices surrounded Regina in a soft veil of safety.

Then the veil lifted and she began to chatter like a wound-up clock. "I'm doomed and besides, even if Billy Wayne gives me a divorce, I won't ever be safe, but what's worse is I won't be able to be with David or any man no matter how much I love him because I can't stand the thought of, you know, doing that. I don't like it at all. Never have liked it. I dream of kissing and cuddling with David, but that's all. He would want more, but I couldn't do it."

She paused and looked at Mayphelia. "God, those drops are making me talk like a magpie and I don't even know what that is. I remember it's some bird in a nursery rhyme, I think."

Caught in the middle of a deep inhale with smoke trapped in her nose and throat, Mayphelia choked with laughter. Outside, the peacock and peahen had come up and glided about, pecking in the dirt. Regina looked out. "Oh dear, Angela is growing so fast these days. I'm going to have to get her a new coat."

Regina turned back to Mayphelia, "You okay, May May? Were you laughin'?"

"Yes, honey, I was. Them drops do make a tongue loosen up, but that's what you be needin'. Yo'r insides can't hold no mo."

Mayphelia took another long inhale and waited for the smoke to trail through the cabin. "Listen, child, you is full of pleasure places and with the right man you ain't got nothin' to worry 'bout. What Billy Wayne done to ya in da back of dat pickup wound you bad, but yo can heal. I be hurt that way when I be only twelve by a neighbor man and fo years I couldn't be thinking of a man in that way neither, but then Radio Man comes into my life and he heals me and gives me back my woman side. Don't fret, child, this young David just might be yo'r Radio Man. 'Member in da Bible a David kilt a giant. I bet this one can slay that giant of loathin' 'n coldness in you."

CHAPTER THIRTY

Grace and Bud drove down a tree-lined street in Houston's River Oaks. Bud looked around at the stately mansions and said, "You sure this is the right place?" Grace looked once again at the map and directions Andy had given her. "According to this, their house is down on the left."

It was still March but the trees were already showing off their fresh green foliage. Bud and Grace both loved spring with the planting, the birthing of calves and pigs and the hatching of chicks. It was a time of renewal: new plants, new life and new hopes.

"I'm sure glad you talked me into taking Ceil's car. We may not have been allowed to come to this part of town in our ole buggy," Bud laughed and looked over at Grace's worried face.

"I had no idea her folks were this rich. Sheila seems just like us. Do you think I'm dressed okay?" she asked as she inspected and adjusted her art-show dress, grateful for Ceil's insistence on getting such a nice one.

"You're as pretty as a field of daffodils. Now smile. This is going to be fine and don't worry, your best friend is probably richer than them and that never bothered you, and you know Andy or Sheila wouldn't want us to be uncomfortable. And remember, if the good Lord's willin' we'll be sharing grandkids with these folks."

"This is it," Grace said, pointing to a house. "My God, how many rooms do you suppose that has?"

"More than you'd want to clean," Bud laughed again. "Our kids, my, my, Gracie, where did we go wrong? One marries God, another a Jew and the last one the devil."

Grace couldn't keep from laughing with him. A year ago such a comment would have seemed sacrilegious to her. *But I've changed, am changing,* she thought with a smile, *and life is much easier.*

"Hopefully, our baby will soon be free," Bud said, as they walked up the steps to a wide porch with more furniture than Grace had in her living room. She wondered exactly what had transpired between Bud and Billy Wayne a few days after Billy Wayne had been dismissed from the hospital.

BILLY WAYNE had come out to the farm on Valentine's Day. Bud told him he didn't want him going near the Sunday house, "I've hired Johnny to make sure you don't. You're welcome to see your girls at our house." Billy Wayne didn't like this arrangement but he missed his daughters and decided not to make a fuss.

During his visit Regina stayed with Angela in her room while Grace worked on a painting in the sewing room with the door wide open. One time, Grace saw Billy Wayne go out on the porch and take a swig from a flask tucked in his back pocket.

Grace went down the hall and told Regina. "I better get Daddy. He's going to get mean if he's drinking." Regina left for the tractor shed.

Minutes later Bud came in. In a friendly tone he asked Billy Wayne if he'd like to see his new mower. Having grown tired of the girls' constant chatter, requests and questions, Billy Wayne jumped at the invitation. He and Bud stayed in the tractor shed for quite some time. When they came back, Billy Wayne asked Regina if she'd come out on the porch, because he had something to tell her. Bud nodded to her that it was okay.

Regina stood near the door and watched Billy Wayne pace back and forth with a smirk on his face. "Listen, I been thinkin' that we need to jest go on and git that divorce. The girls is all I care about and I'll still see them."

Regina grabbed the door knob for support. She could hardly believe her ears. "I really do appreciate it" was all she could say.

As soon as he left, Regina excitedly told everyone. Bud nodded and said, "Well, that's good." He wasn't about to tell her or her mother that he had promised to give Billy Wayne four hundred dollars once a divorce was final. Nevertheless, Grace knew something had transpired.

BUD knocked before noticing the button for a door bell. Before he could push it, the door opened to the smiling face of a young girl dressed in a maid's black and white uniform. "You must be the Wolanskys. Please come in." She spoke with a strong Eastern European accent.

The others were already seated in a white and silver parlor. The only colors came from fresh flowers, wall paintings and the dark wood of a baby grand piano in one corner. Tall windows extended from the floor to the ceiling; the room was open, airy, cloudlike.

Sheila and Andy greeted them with warm enthusiastic hugs. "You look great, Grace," Sheila said as she led them to her parents. "Mom, Dad, I want to introduce you to Mr. and Mrs. Wolansky."

Bud extended his hand, "Just call us Grace and Bud, please. We don't go much for formal stuff."

Sheila's mom took his hand, "We don't either. We're Ruthie and Jacob."

The afternoon glided along with amazing smoothness and even camaraderie. The Wolanskys and Blumbergers had a lot in common in addition to the soon-to-be union of their children. Both families had suffered great losses under Hitler's mania. All of Ruthie's family except for her younger sister had been killed as a result of a Nazi round up of Jewish families in their neighborhood.

She and her sister had been walking home when a Catholic couple rescued them from being captured. The couple had heard of a Jewish round-up taking place on the next street. Upon seeing the teenage girls, they stopped their car and begged them to get off the sidewalk and onto the floor of the back seat. They spread a blanket over them and sped away. For fourteen months, Ruthie and her sister lived with them at their apartment, never once going outside. Finally the couple was able to get them to America. With tears in her eyes, Ruthie said, "I shall always have the highest regard for Catholics and your religion." Grace's heart swelled with gratitude.

Bud then told the story of how three of his cousins and uncle were executed by a German firing squad. Grace remembered how Bud's mother reacted when she learned that Grace's mother was German. She had glared at Bud, "What are you thinking to bring a German girl into my home?"

Both his dad and Bud had to intercede for Grace. However, gradually his mother's hatred for all Germans subsided as she came to know Grace. After a few years, she loved Grace as she did her other daughters. And Grace, who could hardly produce a tear at her own mother's death, wept for days when she died.

As they chatted they drank tea and snacked on sandwiches and all sorts of pastries. At one point, Jacob took Bud out to his garden, where Bud gave him lots of good advice about increasing its productivity. Meanwhile, when Ruthie found out that Grace was a painter, she took her around their entire home, showing her paintings from all over the world.

The talk eventually got around to the fall wedding. Jacob very quietly announced that they would be having an engagement party at their club in June. Then he looked squarely at Bud and Grace, and said, "I know your religion means a lot to you, just as ours does, and it will be fine with us if they get married by a priest and then a rabbi."

Sheila popped up, "Don't we have a say in this? Andy and I don't think we want to get married in either religion and, as far as a party at the Jewish country club, well, I just refuse to have that. I did all that the first time and look how that turned out."

Both parents sighed. Ruthie shook her head in disappointment. "Ach vey. Don't make a problem." Bud worked to suppress a grin. He really liked his future daughter-in-law. She would keep Andy in line for sure.

Grace asked, "Are you all talking about a justice of the peace wedding?" Bud gently patted Grace's knee. Andy remained silent.

Bud cleared his throat, "Well, I'm a practicing Catholic, not as practicing as some, but still I go along with it for the most part. But I think everyone should do what they're most comfortable with. Like you, Jacob and Ruthie, we tried to raise our kids to be independent and, well, when you do that, you take a big chance that they'll think different from you."

There was dead silence in the room. The Polish girl entered with coffee refills. All heads shook. No one wanted coffee. Andy patted Sheila's knee, a habit he had picked up from his dad, the calming pat.

Bud broke the ice again. "Gracie, you remember how we got married?"

Grace blushed. Their children had never heard this story. Andy sat forward. He knew so little about his parents. Up to this point, he'd never thought much about their early lives.

"Gracie, you want to tell them?" Bud asked.

Grace fiddled with her purse strap. "Well, my dad was an unkind man, no, that's not right, he was a mean man, but I don't want to talk about that. Anyway, we ran off in the middle of the night. The older brother of Bud's best friend had just become a priest, and he married us in a run-down mission church in south San Antonio. Father Jerome was his name.

"At the time, he said the Bishop probably wouldn't approve of what he did, but he was headed for South Africa to do missionary work where he knew he'd have to bend the rules, so he needed to get used to it. He was a priest of a different cut. Several years later he was killed in a car accident, and my dad said it was God's punishment because he'd married us."

Grace stopped abruptly, suddenly aware that she had said more than she had all afternoon. Had she revealed too much?

"Gracie, you left out the best part," Bud said with a huge grin. "We had our reception at a honkey-tonk with a room full of strangers, more fun than relatives. We ate hamburgers and danced to the best country 'n western band you've ever heard."

Everyone was entertained. Grace was so glad he'd added a light note. Why had she ended a good story with her dad's harsh judgment? Andy impulsively piped up, "And just look at ya. You're still married, good and solid and still hittin' the honkey-tonks."

Grace looked at the two men she loved most in this world. They were much more alike than she had ever realized. Over the years, the two had argued and were at odds many times. Bud pushed Andy to farm and he resisted. All the old tensions were fading, although Bud still fretted over what would happen to his beloved farm. It had been in his family for nearly a hundred years.

However, the tension between Sheila and her parents was not decreasing. As far as they were concerned, the only right thing Sheila had done in years was to find Andy. Even though he wasn't a Jew, they knew he was a good man who came from a good family. Ruthie reasoned, *why should I mind? None of this would be happening if it hadn't been for a Catholic couple who saved me from certain death.*

ON their way home, Andy and Sheila had their first argument. Sheila was fuming about her parents planning everything without once consulting her. Andy made the mistake of saying, "Don't be so hard on them. I thought it was pretty nice that they suggested we have the two ceremonies, thinking of my family, too."

His words came as gust of wind fanning a low flame into a roaring fire. "Thinking of 'my' family! What about thinking about you and me and what we would like?"

"What's wrong with pleasing both our parents, especially since it doesn't matter that much one way or the other to either of us? What's the harm in that?"

"I guess you want them running your life the way they've tried to run mine all these years. I can't believe you don't understand that by now with all the things I've told you," Sheila spat out.

"You're being a little unreasonable."

"Stop the car, I'm getting out. I can't be around you."

"Don't be stupid. We're in the middle of a highway."

"Oh, so I'm unreasonable and stupid, too."

With that Andy started laughing, and he couldn't stop. He reached over and pulled Sheila next to him. "Yes, you're my stupid, unreasonable love who I will do anything for. Tell me, do you want me to tell our parents to go to hell and that we're getting married in a nudist colony by a Buddhist monk? For you, I'll do it." Sheila couldn't help herself. She started laughing too.

By the time they got to their apartment, they could hardly get to the bedroom fast enough. They were in such a heat that Sheila almost forgot, "God, Andy put on a raincoat. It's the fertile time of the month for me. I can't get married in the nude with a big fat belly."

Andy swore and then rushed to the bathroom. Afterwards, nestled in Andy's strong arms, Sheila whispered in his ear. "I guess the priest and rabbi will be okay, but absolutely no country club crap."

"Sounds like a fair compromise. I hate country club crap myself." He began to kiss her. "I think I'm going to have to put on another raincoat."

CHAPTER THIRTY-ONE

Angela was grateful to be back in her childhood room. She remembered the doctor's words. "If you had gone without treatment much longer, you would not have survived. You are a fortunate young woman."

This close brush with mortality occupied a great deal of her waking thoughts. *Thank God Mama came when she did and took over. Once again she's given me life.* She felt foolish when she examined her motives for the senseless suffering and useless sacrifice. *Had I wanted others to look up to me as a martyr, a saint?*

The words, *she continued to make selfless sacrifices and do her chores even when she was at death's door,* could one day have been written in a biography about Saint Angela or Saint Sister Mary Grace. She had to laugh at the vanity.

It was peaceful being back on the farm, waking up to the mooing cows and the crowing roosters. She didn't really miss the convent and this bothered her somewhat. Hearing her mother stirring around in the kitchen and the occasional bits of conversation between her mom and dad were more comforting than the chiming chapel bells.

"You know, I think that I'll rotate those crops in the west field this spring."

"Sally Mechna's baby is due any day now."

Though she was still very weak, she did manage to sit on the porch on warm days and watch the beginnings of life emerge in her mother's flower beds. She prayed and meditated. *Has God given me a message through this illness? Is religious life for me?* Over the last three years, she had had strong doubts, but Sister Mary Clare had told her that was normal. "The devil will make you question your decision."

Now she wasn't so sure the devil could put anything in her mind. She knew if she left religious life her mother would fret about what she had done to bring about her daughter's change of heart.

Her mother's self admonishments ran through her mind. *"Well, I was in such a deep depression when you were a little girl, and now you want to leave and…*

I should have taken up for Andy when your dad was being hard on him. Now he's marrying a non-Catholic, even worse, a non-Christian.

I was always too easy with Regina to make up for the way I was with you and Andy, and now look how her life's turned out."

But did her mother still think like this? She was different, more confident, relaxed and less constricted. After their return from meeting Sheila's parents, she had overheard her mom tell her dad, "They have just the one child who does exactly as she wants. What if they had three like us?" Then she actually laughed. Angela doubted she had heard correctly.

Regina and the girls came over about twice a week. Although Angela loved her nieces dearly, she was usually glad when they left. Tessie had learned that by screaming like a banshee she could often push her older sister into giving her what she wanted. These vociferous sessions could go on for several minutes. Regina would usually put Tessie in the room down the hall, but still the wails penetrated into Angela's room. On those occasions, Angela would recall the peace and quiet of the convent. During one of these outbursts Regina came into Angela's room and sat on the edge of her bed almost in tears, "Do you think she's going to end up being like Billy Wayne?"

Angela smiled and said, "No, she'll end up being Tessie. You're a wonderful mom." Once again a compliment from Angela lifted Regina's spirit. When the screaming stopped, Regina went to the room and took Tessie in her arms. "I love you so much and so does your sister and she wants you to be happy. I know you want to make her happy too." Tessie kissed her mother's cheek leaving a residue of tears and snot. She ran to the hall and called, "Angie, you can have the ball and go first." Regina thought. *Sometimes kindness seems to work better than scolding.*

WITH money on the table Billy Wayne was more than ready to sign the divorce papers. But then the visitation clause was explained to him. It stated that as long as he was drinking, he would not be allowed to be alone with his daughters or have them ride in a car with him. Mr. Davenport tried to come up with a supervised visitation plan that would be agreeable, because he figured that eventually Billy Wayne's greed would triumph over his desire to have his daughters all alone. But Billy Wayne balked. "If I'm gonna sign somethin' like that, I'll have to have more money from that bastard."

A week passed with no signing and then another and then another. Not knowing the reason for the delay, Regina assumed Billy Wayne was off in a drunken coma. When she said something to her dad about it, Bud told her about the money offer. "After he found out about the visitation clause, he wants more," Bud admitted, somewhat embarrassed.

"You're paying him to divorce me?" Regina couldn't hide the anger.

"It's the only way, Regina," Bud said. "Once he starts to thinkin,' he'll end up favoring the money instead of his daughters."

"Ya'll don't know him like I do. He has nothing to lose. He'll either get more money or I won't get a divorce." Regina walked out on the front porch to get some fresh air.

Weeks before Regina had already decided she was not going to sit around any longer waiting for something to happen. She wanted to get on with her life. So without telling her mom or dad, she took some more of her grandfather's money and enrolled in a beauty school that had just opened in the next town. Three days a week she had classes and on the other two she worked as a shampoo girl and receptionist at the local beauty shop. On top of that, Mrs. Carbon was still occasionally calling her to help out at the store on weekends.

Ledia, her best friend from childhood, had agreed to look after Angie and Tessie. Ledia had a two-month-old baby and didn't want to go back to work, but needed extra money. The girls were delighted by the new baby. After the first week Angie asked, "Mama, can you have another baby for me and Tessie? We know how to take care of a baby."

Regina shook her head. "I have to work now. Maybe someday." She thought of David. *What would it be like to have a baby with a man like that?*

AS GRACE read Ceil's letter, she was filled with sadness and some jealousy. Ceil wasn't coming back until June because she was dealing with selling her business and then going to Hawaii to visit a friend. Who was this friend? Would Ceil replace her with someone else? *You can't have it both ways.*

Grace's heart was often in turmoil. She wanted to be with Ceil even though she felt a consuming love for Bud. The guilt over her unfaithfulness was forever on the back burner, sometimes barely a simmer and then sometimes a rolling boil. She would decide to tell him and then would think, *Why should I hurt him just because I can't live with my guilt?* At these times she would retreat to her flower garden and Peter's grave. She'd sit on the little wrought-iron bench contemplating how to best resolve her wrongdoing.

During one of these times, Angela had come out on the front porch. She saw her mother but didn't say anything. The sun was still too weak to penetrate the morning's chill, so she huddled on the lounger in an igloo of blankets and marveled at the power of this unknown brother. Her mother turned to him far more than to any of her living children. She wondered what he would have been like. Would he have wanted to stay on the farm and follow in her dad's footsteps, or would he have taken off on his own venture like Andy? *"Thou art Peter, and upon this Rock I will build my Church."* Perhaps he would have been the priest in the family.

"I can't fill your shoes, Peter." Suddenly Angela was seared by a blazing insight. As a child she knew that part of her decision to become a nun had been her desire to make her mother happy. True, she was devoted and felt close to God, but the kernel of her desire to serve God was to ease her mother's sadness over Peter. She had come to measure her actions by the yardstick of her mother's happiness. *This will make Mama so happy. She'll be so pleased.*

She was startled by a voice within. *"Let your mother find her happiness and you find yours."*

Grace rose from the bench and walked towards the front porch. She smiled when she saw Angela. "Oh, I didn't know you were out here. Are you warm enough? You're looking more and more like your old self every day." She bent and kissed her on the forehead.

"Mama, I can't make up for Peter's death any longer."

Grace stepped back and looked at her, bewildered. "Angela, what in the world are you talking about?"

As if she were in a trance, Angela spoke in a monotone. "I can't go back, Mama. I don't want to be a nun. I still want to serve God, but not like that. I was doing it so you could be happy. You were sad all the time. I wanted to make you happy." Angela fumbled with the blankets. "I'm sorry. I don't know what I'm saying." She stood up. This uncensored, impulsive revelation stunned her as much as it did her mother.

Angela walked as fast as she could to her room, to privacy, to isolation. A tightly wound ball of string within her began to unravel. Panting from the exertion, she fell into the bed. *"I've always felt like I was supposed to make everyone happy. When Mama was sick, I protected Andy and let him have his way. I picked up all the toys when Mama didn't see them everywhere because I didn't want Daddy to have to when he was already tired from the fields. After Regina was born and Mama got well, I kept on taking care and no one took care of me."*

She pulled the covers up to her neck and let all that sadness from her childhood wash over her. She didn't cry. The catharsis came in the recognition.

Grace knew that her breakdown had affected everyone in her family, but she had never faced it as she now did.

Feeling weak herself, she went inside and softly knocked on Angela's door. "May I come in?" She was alarmed by Angela's flushed face just above the covers. "Oh God, do you have a fever? The doctor said we must watch for that." She put her hand on Angela's forehead.

Angela spoke in a raspy whisper. "Mama, there's nothing physically wrong. It's my soul that's burning. I hated Peter for taking you away from us. And even now you go to him more than to any of us."

Grace gently put her hand over Angela's mouth. "Shhh, shhh, my dearest. I know. I understand." She sat on the bed and cradled Angela in her arms and hummed a soothing tune. She kissed her forehead from time to time. Angela dropped off into a deep sleep. Grace sat on the bed holding her oldest baby for a long time.

Carefully she laid Angela's head on the pillow and tucked her in. In a dreamlike state she went to the sewing room and put a fresh canvas on the easel. She opened several paints and began drawing broad, dramatic strokes. She was cut in half and all the shadows were falling into the paints and being cast out by the brushes, her magic wands. She worked at a fast pace, racing to get all the wraiths out, once and for all. Her painter's smock hung on the rack; the entire front of her dress was splattered in colors from the past.

Angela ran a high temperature for two days. From the beginning she refused to go to the hospital. "Let me be," she said. "I'm burning up resentments."

She had always considered herself an independent person, but that had been an illusion. This realization brought on bitterness as well as sorrow. She wasn't different. Like everyone else she had been bound by the chains of conformity. *Becoming a nun is what devout Catholic girls do.*

In the midst of the fever, a power began tossing her thoughts and emotions in one direction and then another, paralyzing her with despair, drowning her in sorrow and scorching her with guilt. She dreamed, not knowing which were waking dreams and which were sleeping ones. There were people–her mother, her dad, her sister–looking down at her, guiding her to the bathroom and holding out spoons of food, but she didn't know if they were any more real than the dark beings floating by her bed coaxing her to stop living altogether. She had entered the dark night of the soul, the realm where there was nothing to believe. The slate was blank, wiped clean. Suddenly her mother's spirit was sitting beside her saying, "I know this place. I once visited it. Just don't stay here."

As her mother drifted away, a light started to emerge. "No, I won't stay here. I'm not perfect and I don't have to be. All I have to do is love." With that a surge of new life-energy entered her body.

The following morning, she awoke to rain pounding on her bedside window. She imagined taking off all her clothes and dancing naked in the downpour, feeling the drops moisturizing her skin, the wetness lubricating her bones and the flow revitalizing her heart. She was light and spacious. She knew she had been healed.

She got up and went to the back screen door. Her dad sat on the porch holding Tessie on one knee and Angie on the other. *That's what I want, she* thought. *I want a husband who someday will be sitting on our back porch with a grandchild on each knee. I want my mama's life. I still want to serve…what or who? I don't know, but I want to serve.*

Angela could see her dad was pleased about the rain. A farmer depended more on the weather for his livelihood than anyone on the planet. She remembered he always got a bit riled when someone referred to rain as "bad weather." She knew that from this day on rain would always be a reminder of her resurrection.

"Nancy is getting wet." Angie pointed at the grazing horse.

"Don't worry; she'll go under the shed once she's had enough," her grandpa explained.

Angela opened the screen door. Her dad smiled. "Angela, you up? Now go easy and take your..."

Angie's enthusiasm interrupted him. "Auntie A, you're up. We've been very quiet today, like Mama said to," Angie wrapped her arms around Angela's knees. "We tiptoed everywhere." Angela smiled at her caring niece.

"Ledia's baby got sick last night, so Regina brought them over this morning," Bud explained.

"Daddy, the fever is gone."

Bud slid Tessie off his lap and got up to hug her. "I knew you'd get through like you kept saying the whole time." He hugged her like she was a fragile baby.

"I remember you on that basketball court. You've always been a fighter," he said softly, then hurriedly went on, "Listen, there's soup on the stove. Your mama's at church helping with collecting things for the Yanzy family. Their house burned to the ground last night, from lightning."

He started for the kitchen, then turned back. "I bet she checked on you a dozen times this morning. I had to more or less push her out the door. Come on, I'll warm up your mama's cure-all chicken soup."

After soup and a short playtime with her nieces, Angela returned to the quiet of her room, got out her stationery and began composing letters to the bishop and Sister Mary Clare. There was no need to delay informing them of her decision. They would be the first to know. She would wait a while to tell her family.

Carefully she constructed her sentences, explaining that her illness had left her in a condition too weakened for the rigors of religious life. Even though the doctors were optimistic that she would make a complete recovery, she decided she'd tell white lies rather than explain the real reasons. She didn't want to hear about devils' temptations, selfishness or vanity. This illness had transformed her, not into a rebel, but into her true self. She felt more invigorated and stimulated than she had in years.

She read over the letter and then tore it up and began again. This time she wrote that she no longer had the desire to be a nun and would not be coming back and gave no explanations or excuses. She thanked the Sisters and the convent for the three wonderful years of religious training and pledged to make donations every year to help with their ministry. She closed by saying that she would always relish and benefit from her experiences in the religious life.

Once she sealed the envelope she jumped up, wanting to go someplace, drive into town, eat a hamburger at Hattie's. She wondered if she'd still know how to drive a car. Unfortunately, her mom had Ceil's car and the family car had been loaned to Regina for as long as she was attending beauty school. Disappointed, Angela realized she wouldn't get out in this weather in her dad's pickup. However, there was nothing stopping her from getting out of the nightgown and into regular clothes. She would take a long bath and get all dressed up.

Going to the closet she prayed her mother hadn't given away all her clothes. She stopped and looked in the floor length mirror, something else she hadn't done in a long time. As a Sister, she was to look in a mirror only to see if her veil and coif were straight. Now she almost jumped at what she saw. Her uneven hair spiked out on all sides, straight and wild. Her face was sunken and her body was incredibly thin. She couldn't believe no one had said anything about how bad she looked. Even Andy had said nothing. Back when she was twelve he had called her Bony Maroni until their dad threatened him with complete grounding, "school and home and that's it."

Three skirts and several blouses hung in the closet limp and unused. She pulled off the gown and looked at her protruding ribs. Though she still had some hip bumps, the skirt fell over them and down to the floor. Even her full breasts were shrunken and the blouse, like the skirt, was at least two sizes too big.

She pulled the gown back on and dropped on the bed exhausted and remembered her fellow novices and the Sisters at the convent. She would miss them. They had been her family. With many she had taken on the well-rehearsed role of older sister. Closing her eyes, she said a prayer of thanksgiving that none of them had contracted the disease. *I must have been singled out for this illness and I'll take it as God's way of telling me I wasn't where I belonged.* With that she drifted off. She dreamed of swimming downstream in a wide river with the sun warming her body.

CHAPTER THIRTY-TWO

David slowly walked Janie to the door. She turned, waiting for a good-night kiss. He hesitated, knowing her expectation. "Thank you for a very nice evening." He turned and walked to his car. Janie stood bewildered; their third date and still no kiss. During dinner he hadn't said more than a few sentences. Even though he was handsome and very polite, she made up her mind not to go out with him again.

But she didn't have to worry about that. David hurried back to his apartment, opened a beer and sat down on the couch to read Regina's letter once again. He had read through it so many times since this afternoon he practically had it memorized. He was very sorry to read that her husband had had a change of heart about the divorce, which had been scheduled for this month. *"This disappointment is making me think of you all the time. I hope you'll still be interested in getting to know me if I ever get out of this."*

Was she kidding? Still interested? He had hardly thought of anything except her and her two beautiful daughters. "You're a damn fool falling for someone who has two children," was his older brother's encouraging comment.

The last paragraph troubled him a little. It said that she wanted to tell him everything and *"if after you know the whole story, you still want to see me, I would like that."* The whole story? He stretched out. He didn't really give a damn what the whole story was. He had never in his life been so miserable and so happy at the same time. He was aware that his behavior bordered on the crazy. After all, he'd only been with her twice and both times had been rather short, yet he could not get her out of his mind.

While riding on the bus to morning classes he'd think he saw her walking on the sidewalk. When he went on dates, he'd spend the whole evening thinking of her while he ate, talked and even danced with another woman. As a little boy he had heard his great-grandmother tell about people in the old country using spells or witchery to get their way. Even though he knew these stories were the ramblings of an old woman, he now felt as though he'd been bewitched or put under a spell. He reread her PS: *"You are really a handsome man and my brother likes you a lot."* He smiled from ear to ear and finished off his beer. *To hell with it; I don't care if I am under some spell.*

He fell asleep and heard conjuring coming from his clothes closet, and soon he was drifting into a land of foggy mists where old crones were telling him not to be afraid that fairy wings were growing out of his shoulders. Then he was flying over stars and around moons. He was looking for something but couldn't find it. He kept flying until his mind closed down into the dark slumber of no dreams.

LATER that night, Mayphelia awoke from a dreamless sleep and sat up in bed. Someone was outside her cabin door. She smelled gasoline fumes and heard a splashing sound. She counted two sets of footsteps leaving the porch. She pulled the covers around her as torch light reflected off her window pane. A fire ball was flying towards the cabin. Flames erupted into a roar, engulfing the dried wood of the porch and outside wall. Mayphelia felt weak. She had not foreseen this at all. She had seen herself dying in her garden, never in an inferno. She shook herself into action. There was no back door for escape.

She remembered Radio Man had cut a small escape door in the loft "jest in case a fire happens sometime." She scrambled up the ladder. *Help me, Baby, help me.* Mayphelia could feel her dear man's presence. The smoke was quickly rising to the loft. She crawled over to the small door leading to the outside. After years of never being opened, it was sealed with tree sap and bird shit. Sitting on the floor and supporting herself with her arms, she leaned back on her hips and kicked the door with both feet as hard as she could. It opened only to a wide crack. A tree limb had grown across it over the years. The room below her was quickly going up in flames. She could feel the heat coming up through the boards. Smoke smothered her.

Mayphelia pushed her face and nose through the opening to take in a gulp of fresh air. Somehow she had to squeeze through this narrow space. If she could get her head through, she thought she could manage to get the rest of her body out. Willing her skull to collapse, she pushed and strained, scraping the skin off the sides of her scalp and face and slicing one of her ears. Finally her head sprung from the crack like a chick's from its shell. Then she had the sensation that the rest of her body was being pushed out from the other side. She came to after a short blackout to discover that she was free of the loft and crawling along one of the limbs. She looked down through the foliage and saw Billy Wayne and his dad Mr. Tarkin, silhouetted in the firelight. They were passing a bottle back and forth, taking long swigs and coughing with laughter.

She would have to try to get down. The tree would probably catch on fire once the roof went up in flames despite the good rain they'd gotten as few days ago. It was too far to jump. Every one of her rickety bones would break. For now, she lay stretched out flat on her stomach on the farthest branch, wondering how *in the name of Jesus* she had maneuvered over that far. Last night she had decided to put on her black nightgown instead of the white one. *"You was the one tellin' me ta do that, wasn't you, Baby? They'd see the white up here."*

Sadly, she watched as her beloved home gave way to the fire. It had been the first home she and Radio Man could call theirs. They had put up the porch, built the loft, repaired the roof, put in new windows and sanded the floors to a lustrous shine. They had been so happy there. Now the fire was eating it all up.

"She's burnt toast by now, that's for sure." Mr. Tarkin's loud voice was as clear as a bell.

Billy Wayne laughed. "Yeah, she won't be interferin' in my life no more," he yelled over the popping flames. "Turnin' my wife agin me. Killin' my baby. Tellin' Bud not to give me what's rightfully mine." Billy Wayne abruptly stopped his tirade seeing a light at Bud and Grace's. "Son-of-a-bitch."

Through the smoke Mayphelia saw Billy Wayne and his dad running, staggering towards the main road where their pickup was parked. Then she saw Bud and Grace's kitchen light in the distance. She could barely make out the back door opening and two people running off the porch. Just as Bud's headlights came on, Billy Wayne and his dad pulled away with their lights off.

"Now ain't you glad I parked this far off?" Billy Wayne said between deep breaths. "All that fussin' and I saved yor ass."

The fire was licking at the branches just over the loft. Mayphelia felt dizzy. The smoke was wrapping around her. She held on tight. She didn't want to fall. As she went in and out of consciousness, she thought of Billy Wayne's words, *"Tellin' Bud not to give me what's rightfully mine."*

BILLY WAYNE had driven up into the yard. She and Bud were sacking up corn and barley seeds in the barn. Bud walked outside. She heard the conversation.

"That lawyer says I can't see my own daughters unless someone's with me." Billy Wayne kicked some dirt in Bud's direction.

"That's right. For now we think that's best for the girls."

"Well, if that's so then I think I'm gonna have to have more money." Billy Wayne puffed out his chest like he'd just won a medal for bravery.

Bud tried to speak calmly. "Listen, we don't want to keep your girls from you. If you really love 'em, you won't want to take a chance of hurting 'em." Billy Wayne cursed and kicked the tire on his pickup.

Bud continued, "You get awful mean when you're drunk, and you've already driven off the road and into things more times than you can count. If your girls had been with you, they could have been hurt. Go get yourself cleaned up, stop drinking and then we can talk about being by yourself with them. Otherwise it stays like it's written."

"Well, you hear me good, old man. I ain't gonna let no one tell me how to do with my girls unless I get more money, you understand?" Billy Wayne took a couple of steps towards him.

Bud eyed the ax leaning on the fence. He had a strong urge to plant it in Billy Wayne's skull but he knew that wouldn't solve anything. To regain control of himself he turned and walked back into the barn. "That sack by the door is full of watermelon seeds. Take some of them too," he said to Mayphelia, his voice shaking with anger.

Mayphelia could see that Billy Wayne was trying to listen. She shook her head, "No, I's got more of them seeds myself than I can plant. Give 'em to Mr. Alex."

Bud took a few deep breaths and then went back outside. "Billy Wayne, I'm not givin' you more money and you're not getting one red dime from me until them papers are signed."

Billy Wayne backed up and pointed at Mayphelia, who had stepped outside. "You let that nigger tell you what to do and you obey her like some whipped dog and if you think you're better, listen, I done seen your wife and that Dollard bitch. They was hugging like no women should be, and I…."

Before he could finish, Mayphelia's eyes drilled into his chest. His heart skipped a beat as he backed away.

"Oh, you'll be sorry. Believe me, you won't get a chance to look back on this."

NOW spread out on a branch with the flames getting nearer, Mayphelia understood that he had been speaking directly to her. *He thinks I shakes my head telling Mr. Bud to not give 'im money. Money,* a *root of evil.* With those thoughts, she passed out with her arms tightly wrapped around the tree limb.

BILLY WAYNE and his dad sped down the road, drinking and jovially cursing everything in sight. As they passed Ceil's home, Billy Wayne's foot hit the brake. "I'm gonna blaze that bitch's house up too. We still got enough kerosene."

"We've done enough for one night. Save it for the next time we need some fun. Now git me home, goddamnit." Mr. Tarkin swung at his son, but missed.

"Okay, okay. Don't start hittin' on me or I'll kick your sorry ass out of this truck and you kin jest find your own way home." He stepped on the gas and sped off.

A couple of miles out of town he turned off onto a dirt road, weaving the truck from one side of the road to the other before getting it under control. He and his dad continued to pass the bottle. A possum ran across the road and was smashed under the right wheel. "That's what I'm gonna do to Regina's old man."

"Well, bide your time, son. You'll get your chance," his dad reassured him.

They raced on in silence as Billy Wayne plotted out that scenario. The night was totally black except for some distant stars and a sliver of moon. The headlights illuminated no more than a hundred feet in front. Suddenly the large figure of a man loomed in front of the truck. Billy Wayne swerved to the side, losing complete control. His last thought was *I'll be damned.That's Radio Man.*

The pickup rolled over several times before being stopped by a barbed-wire fence. Both Billy Wayne and his dad were thrown over the fence into the stubble pasture. The headlights cast an eerie glow on the two bodies.

EARLIER Angela had awakened feeling dread, as though something bad were about to happen. She decided to go to Peter's bench in the rose garden and say a rosary. Though she was full of doubt about religion, she still felt close to the mother of Jesus. On the second decade, *Hail Mary, full of grace,* something like a fireball flew through her peripheral vision. She turned towards the grove where Mayphelia lived and saw what looked like a fire on her front porch. She walked as fast as her breath would allow. She flipped on the kitchen light and called out.

"Mom, Dad! Mayphelia's house is on fire!"

Her dad ran in and looked out the back door. "Gracie, we got to go now." He turned to Angela, "Call Alex to come."

By the time Bud and Grace got there the house was ablaze. Running up as close to the cabin as the flames would allow, they yelled and yelled, "Mayphelia, Mayphelia." Bud knew he could not go inside without killing himself. Grace began to cry. "My God, my God, how did this happen?"

Bud picked up an empty gas can in the yard. "This was deliberate."

Grace sank to her knees. "Dear God, no. Dear God, no."

"I'll be damned if I sit by this time and let it go. He's killed someone, and I'll get justice, Klan or no Klan."

"Shhh," Grace waved her hand. "I hear something."

A faint, "I is here, I is here," rode on the waves of wind and fire. Bud ran to the tree and looked up. "Grace, get the flashlight."

Grace cried out in relief when she saw Mayphelia's arms and legs wound around the tree's outermost limb. *How in the world did she get all the way over there?* Grace made the sign of the cross. The flames were beginning to lap at the tree, but Mayphelia was still safe.

Bud pulled his truck under the tree but it wasn't tall enough for him to reach her. He needed a stepladder. Fortunately Alex and Blanche came roaring up just then.

Studying the distance to the branch, Alex said, "I got a couple of tool boxes."

Within a few seconds, he and Bud stacked the boxes on Bud's pickup bed and stood on them. Still they weren't close enough to reach Mayphelia.

"Mayphelia, you're gonna have to let go. We'll catch you," Bud coaxed. She didn't move.

"Come on now, just drop off. We're close enough to catch ya for sure," Alex repeated a few times.

Finally she unwound her arms and legs and rolled over and fell into the men's arms. They gently lifted her down and laid her on a pallet of tote sacks laid out by Grace and Blanche. The women stayed in the back of the pickup holding Mayphelia while Bud tried to avoid every bump on the drive back home.

CHAPTER THIRTY-THREE

After midnight Clem got up unable to sleep. All the regrets of his life haunted him. His dear Mable had died three weeks earlier. Her dying wish was for him to give up the bottle. At the time all he could muster was a feeble promise that he would try. He was afraid to make a vow he knew deep down he couldn't keep.

Except for the last seven months of her life, his wife had lived in a shack because of his drinking. All the clothes she ever had were handouts from the church. He had been a lousy husband in both life and death. He couldn't even pay for her funeral. Once again Ceil had come to the rescue. "I'm really sorry I can't come to the service. Please let me help you out with the costs," she had begged. And being the bum he'd always been, he let her pay for the whole thing, easing his conscience by fooling himself into believing he was doing her a favor.

Clem paced the floor. He hadn't had a drink since Mable died, but he knew tonight he was going to have to or else go mad. Putting on heavy boots for the three-to four-mile walk, he left the house. He remembered seeing one of the local bootleggers bury some bottles next to a stack of railroad ties left over from the days when the railroad came through town. Carrying a shovel and flashlight, he set out cutting through neighbors' yards in a straight route to the liquor.

Once he had gone some distance, he crawled over the barbed-wire fence. If he remembered correctly the buried liquor was no more than a few yards away. In the distance headlights from a pickup danced from left to right and back again. He ran towards the railroad ties praying no bootleggers were coming. The lights were still a ways off so he hurriedly began to dig in the area. He heard a clink almost immediately and quickly retrieved a bottle. As he took his first swallow he saw that the lights were almost at the spot where he had crossed over. In a panic he covered the hole, picked up his shovel and hid behind a tree off to the side. A strange, strangled scream caused him to turn. Two bodies were flying over the fence as the pickup jumped off the road, rolled and tangled into the wires, screeching and scratching to a stop.

He waited a few minutes before mustering the courage to come out from hiding. Bootleggers often carried guns, but neither of these men seemed likely to be able to shoot anyone. He made his way to the first body, which had been thrown the farthest. He gasped as his light shone on the face of Mr. Tarkin. His eyes blinked and then held Clem in a menacing stare. His lips moved in silent cursing commands. The rest of his body was paralyzed.

Clem searched the ground nearby. Soon he returned with the perfect round rock. Mr.Tarkin's eyes watched in terror as Clem straddled him and held the rock over his head. "This is for Boudie. Something I should have done a long time ago." Mr. Tarkin opened his mouth in a silent scream. The stone crushed his nose and forehead. Clem then turned the body over with the rock placed beneath his face and extended his arms over his head in exactly the same way Mr. Tarkin had left Boudie's body.

The second person began to moan. Clem headed towards him. The lights on the pickup were just a low dim by now. When Clem turned on his flashlight, it took him a while to recognize Billy Wayne. He had a huge gash across his forehead, showing cracked and crumbled bone. If he didn't know better, Clem would have sworn that someone had hit him with an ax. "I'm just going to let you lie here and die a slow death. This is your payback for what you did to that sweet Regina. I pray to God you can hear what I'm saying." He kicked Billy Wayne in the groin as hard as he could. Billy Wayne cried out, gasped for air and drew his legs upward like a dying spider.

Clem turned to leave. He felt the bottle in his pocket. As if holding a hand grenade he torpedoed it over the bodies and started for home. He felt better than he had in years. He never took another drink. In the years ahead, he endured the torments of wanting a drink but did not take one. It was his penance for his crimes in the field on that night of reckoning.

NO one knew if the new doctor practicing just outside of town would come. Dr. Clarkson refused to treat a colored person, which Bud said, "is just as well since he's killed half the people in the white cemetery." Dr. Fenden was not from the South and didn't quite understand the racial divide. He readily came to the house and treated Mayphelia with the same care he would have given anyone. After doing what he could for her lungs and breathing, he sewed her ear back in place, dressed the head wounds and body scrapes. Before leaving, he told Grace that if she weren't better in the morning they should take her to the hospital.

Grace called Ceil as soon as the doctor was gone. As soon as Ceil heard Grace's "hello," she blurted out, "What's wrong?" Upon hearing what had happened, she could not control her crying. "I'm catching the first plane out."

Early the next morning Grace and Angela left for San Antonio to pick up Ceil. Blanche was staying with Mayphelia and as word had gotten out during the night, several other women from the colored church showed up to help. As the day wore on white women, mainly poor ones whom Mayphelia had helped with a delivery or with keeping the babies from coming every year, looked in on her. She had treated their children for the croup or worms and other maladies without charging a penny, except maybe a few eggs or some canned goods, and they were grateful.

Everyone knew that if Mayphelia could tell them what to do for her, which herbs or plants to use, she would get better much faster, but she continued to sleep. The doctor, who had come back that morning, said rest was the best thing. He no longer felt she needed a hospital but said he would check on her again in the afternoon.

Grace was skittish about driving in a big city and so Angela gladly took the wheel of Ceil's luxurious car. She still found it hard to believe that her mother had a driver's license. So much had changed since she'd left. Angela was also feeling good about her changes. She had gained ten pounds, and Regina had styled her hair into a cute bob. She was ready to step out into the world and let people see her. Sister Mary Clare had responded to her letter telling her to reconsider her decision once she was fully recovered. *"As soon as you are well, I'm sure you'll have a change of heart."*

Angela discarded the letter and made no reply. Her mind was made up and there was no need to discuss it further. While she was feverish, she had a vague recollection of her mother's words softly whispered in her ear, *"You do what will make you happy and never again worry about me."* She knew those words, real or imagined, were partly responsible for her recovery.

When Angela saw her mother and Ceil embrace at the airport, she knew they had a special friendship. A light seemed to click on in both women. She and Ceil had flown into each other's arms like the young couples in newsreels after the war.

Once Angela had fully recovered from the fever, Grace showed her the painting she had had been working on. It was an abstract of six ethereal figures dancing around what looked like a lump of coal from which was emerging another figure, fluid and transparent. The painting was powerful, touching Angela so deeply she had to sit down in her mother's sewing chair. "What does it mean?"

Grace laughed. "Whatever it means to you." Angela looked disappointed.

"Well, I identify with the lump of coal," Grace began, "who's trying to ascend from her original state. And the figures around me are those beings who have assisted me in rising from the coal. I call it the 'Sacred Seven.'"

Grace stood behind Angela and rested a hand on her shoulder, "Mayphelia always says seven is magic. It's certainly been for me."

"Who are the six?" Angela had to know.

"Your daddy, you three kids, Mayphelia, and the last is Ceil. You'll get to meet her someday."

After a long pause, Grace whispered, "I painted it for you."

AROUND noon Judd Ford was creeping along in his pick-up checking the fences. A couple of his cows had been found walking along the far end of the road, and he had to find where they had gotten out. Suddenly he saw the problem. About a fourth of a mile to the right, an over-turned pickup looked like it had tried to take a shortcut through his pasture. A short distance away he saw two clumps of three to four vultures tearing at something. "Good God, no," he stepped on the gas. As he hopped out of his truck, he shouted, "Shoo, shoo, you damn no-good things."

His worst fears were confirmed when he got near. Two bodies were mutilated something terrible. He bent over, catching his breath, knowing he couldn't get any closer without losing the bowl of chili he'd just eaten. How the hell was he going to keep the birds away and get help at the same time? The black fiends were perched on the limbs of several trees, waiting for him to leave. Maybe he could pull the bodies onto the back of his pickup, but he knew he wasn't strong enough for that. He was still getting over his last heart attack.

He saw the discarded bottle and then took a closer look at the pickup. "Yeah, it's Billy Wayne, all right," he said with a shake of his head. "Tain't no surprise."

As luck would have it, he spotted his son-in-law coming from the opposite direction on his tractor. Judd waited until he got closer, then began waving his arms and calling. As soon as Judd turned to face the road, two of the birds made a beeline for the bodies.

His son-in-law always carried a shotgun and when he saw what was going on he dropped two of the harpies before they could spring from the limbs. He couldn't look at the bodies either, but he had a good time shooting vultures while Judd raced into town.

Once Sheriff Clive and the new undertaker arrived, it was almost five o'clock. The sheriff had been tied up going over the ruins at Mayphelia's. Bud showed him the footprints, once again a dragging right foot, and the gas can and told him he was sure it was Billy Wayne. The sheriff tended to agree, but he wasn't going to let Bud know that. Now as he looked down on what remained of Billy Wayne's body, he was glad the drinking had taken care of the problem of questioning him. He was afraid of that whole Tarkin bunch.

It was easier to identify Mr. Tarkin because he had landed on his stomach with his head face-flat on a rock. The vultures could only get to his back. The sheriff was stunned. He remembered that Boudie's body was positioned in exactly the same way. Suddenly he shuttered all over feeling spooked by some evil spirit.

Ole Charlie had told Boudie's mama that he had seen Mr. Tarkin walking with Boudie in that field that very afternoon. When Boudie's mama reported this to the sheriff, Clive simply said, "You can't believe what that crazy nigger says. Why, he can't see no further than you can spit." A few months later Charlie died. Then not long after that, Boudie's mama. Clive shrugged his shoulders with a loud exhale and thought *ole man Tarkin and his no-account boy are all facin' their judgment now without me having to lift a finger.* However, that reasoning didn't ease the festering in his intestines. These and other wrongdoings were developing into a non-treatable cancer that would take his life by the year's end.

REGINA had put the girls in the bathtub and was cleaning up the kitchen dishes. David's letter sat on the counter. She could hardly refrain from opening it, but she wasn't going to until the girls were asleep and she was snuggled in her own bed with a nice glass of lemonade. A tingle went up her spine as she thought of the wonderful things he may have written. She looked on the postmark and realized he had mailed it the same day she had sent one to him.

As she was putting the last glass in the cabinet, the phone rang. At first she couldn't make out who was calling. Between the sobs, slobbering and mumblings, she finally realized it was Geraldine, and after several repetitions, she was able to decipher, "Billy Wayne's dead. He's been kilt." Regina's heart sank. She leaned up against the counter and caught her breath, almost afraid to ask, "Who killed him?"

"He did it hisself. Drove off the road, drunk. Kilt his daddy too."

"Oh my God, my God. When did it happen?"

"They think some time last night. Maybe after midnight. They was seen goin' through town real late." Geraldine went on to say she didn't know much more, but that she'd call later.

As Regina hung up the phone, she sat down at the kitchen table. She could hear the girls laughing and splashing water. She was going to have to tell them. But she didn't think she could do it alone. She picked up the phone and called home, grateful her dad answered. "Daddy, Billy Wayne's dead." She told him what she knew and ended with, "Can you come over and be with me when I tell the girls?"

As Bud drove to Regina's, he thought about what Mayphelia had just said. He knew there was far more in this world than he could begin to understand, yet he often wondered about Mayphelia and her undeniable powers. Before leaving, he had gone into the bedroom where everyone was keeping vigil, sitting in a semicircle around Mayphelia. Ceil was on the bed holding her hand. Bud spoke softly to Grace, "I have to go to Regina's. Billy Wayne's been killed." Suddenly from a deep coma-like sleep, Mayphelia opened her eyes, raised up on her elbows and said in a gravelly whisper, "I knewed my man would take care of 'im." She closed her eyes and continued, "They's wanted to kill me, but my Radio Man hept me git out."

When he got to Regina's, he found the girls squeaky clean wearing the new pajamas Undy and Aunt Sheila had sent weeks ago. Regina had made a point of hiding them when they arrived because Billy Wayne had told her he was coming over, and she didn't want to launch him into one of his tirades.

That visit had been the last time he and the girls had seen one another. He brought each of them little sacks of candy and balloons. While Johnny worked on her flower bed in the front yard, providing a measure of safety, Billy Wayne stood on the porch and told her he'd sign all the papers if she'd let him see the girls for a little while. Even though she didn't believe him, she thought her girls deserved to be with their father. Angie had been asking about him. She could smell liquor on his breath but he didn't seem to be angry. Now she was thankful she had allowed him this time with his daughters.

She hoped the new pajamas might lighten the blow of what they were about to hear. Excitedly, they had opened the fancy sack. Angie immediately became serious and asked apprehensively, "Will it be okay with Daddy?"

Regina remembered her mother's warning, *"Be careful what you say even when you think they're not listening, especially with Angie. She's just like Angela. Listening and looking out for everyone's feelings."*

"It will be okay, darling. See how they fit. Do you like the color?" Regina bit her lip. This was going to be so hard. Where was her dad? She had just started reading the fourth page of Cinderella when she heard his pickup stop out front. She closed the book, "Grandpa's come to see us." With that both girls jumped up and ran to the door. "Grandpa, Grandpa!"

After some milk and cookies, they settled back in the living room. Regina asked them to sit on her lap. Praying for the right words, she began, "Girls, I have something very sad to tell you." Both of them became still, waiting for her to continue. "Your daddy and Paw Paw were in a very bad accident last night, and they died. Your daddy isn't here anymore."

After a long silence, Angie said, "They're like Clem's Mabel?"

"Yes, darling, like Clem's Mabel."

Angie slipped from her mother's lap and fairly stomped across the room. "He was drinking that stuff that makes him crazy?" Stunned, Regina was unable to say anything, amazed at how much this little girl knew. Bud tried to pick her up, but she started screaming and kicking. "I want to see my daddy. I want to see my daddy."

Tessie didn't fully understand what was going on, but when she saw her sister's reaction she also became upset. Soon both were sobbing. Bud simply held them close to his chest, saying, "He loved you both very much, and he'll keep on loving you all the time."

Regina sat on the floor beside them and began to caress their arms and legs. She knew that Angie was feeling real grief for her daddy, and that Tessie was feeling for her sister. Her heart was also about to burst, but she was not going to let them see her break down. They were going through enough without being concerned about her.

After a while Tessie fell off to sleep. While Bud got up to take her to bed, Angie lay on the floor whimpering and rubbing her eyes over and over until they were red and puffy. Regina sat limp on the couch.

"Angie, sweetheart, you want to come up here with Mama?"

"No, I want my daddy."

Regina thought about all the times she had wished that something like this would happen, that Billy Wayne would just disappear, even die. She shook her head, trying to dispel those awful memories. One time, she had vividly imagined him driving off the road and into a huge ditch filled with water. How could she have had such cruel and heartless wishes?

When Bud came back into the room, he asked, "Angie, you want to come home with Grandpa, see Grandma and Auntie A? She sat up and sadly nodded her head. Bud picked her up, telling Regina, "I'll bring her back in the morning."

Regina went into her girls' bedroom and lay down beside Tessie. Her sweet little face was nestled next to the stuffed rabbit Billy Wayne had given her last Easter. Regina looked into her face glowing softly in the night light and realized how much she resembled her daddy.

Billy Wayne had been good-looking and funny but always at someone else's expense. Regina realized that the arrogance covered feelings of inferiority. Even then she knew that he was embarrassed about his folks and his brother's imprisonment. Many of the "better" kids wouldn't have anything to do with him; however, the girls who liked to flirt with danger flocked to him. And he had his way with many of them. Regina heard the rumors, yet she had thought he would be different with her.

He started walking Regina to her classes and sitting with her in the cafeteria. She was a sophomore and he a senior. Some of the older girls gave her dirty looks that frightened her. Their first dates were to high-school sock hops, where they dazzled everyone with their dancing. He never kissed her until sometime later at the drive-in, but he backed off as soon as she pushed him away with a "no." However, he drove her home so fast she was frightened. If only she had been a little older, she knew she would have never gone with him again. But then she wouldn't have this sweet little cherub on the pillow next to hers.

A week or so later he asked her to the Saturday night dance out at the Veterans Hall, and even though her mom and dad had told her they didn't want her going with him, she had said okay.

"I forgive you; I forgive you; I forgive you." She turned over and wept into her pillow. She cried for herself, her barely sixteen-year-old self who was pregnant and terrified, her little girls who thankfully would be spared growing up with an alcoholic dad, and she wept most of all for Billy Wayne. He was doomed from the start. How could someone coming from a shithole like his ever pull himself up to a better life? Last, she wept for Geraldine and her sad, sad life.

Amidst the tears and heartache and the forgiveness, she drifted off to a deep, deep slumber, the most restful sleep she'd had in her own home in five years. David's letter lay on the kitchen counter, unopened, forgotten.

SOMEWHERE in the distance, a phone was ringing. She wanted the noise to stop. . When she finally woke up, it took her a while to realize that she was in the girls' room, still in yesterday's clothes with Tessie next to her and the sunlight streaming in. Yesterday's tragedy came back to her. She stumbled to the kitchen.

"Hello."

"Regina, are you okay?" Her mother's voice was full of more concern than Regina wanted.

"I'm okay, Mom. How's Angie?"

"She's still sound asleep. She slept with us last night and never once stirred. Your daddy said she was out before he got a mile down the road."

Regina looked at the clock. She was supposed to be at work in forty-five minutes.

"Mom, I've got to go. Tessie's still asleep. Oh god, I'm going to be late for work."

"My goodness, Regina, your husband just died. They'll let you off."

Regina realized this was true. She needed to be with the girls, and there was the funeral to plan. Panic began to set in. Would his family want her to take part in anything? Should he and his dad be buried together?

Grace's voice brought her back to the kitchen. "I can come over as soon as the doctor leaves."

Regina became alarmed. "What doctor?"

"Your dad didn't tell you?"

Regina sank down into a kitchen chair as she was told that Billy Wayne and his dad had tried to kill Mayphelia the same night they drove to their deaths. "May-May will live, but she's going to have a rough time. Her lungs took in a lot of smoke and she skinned both sides of her scalp, face and body, trying to get out through an opening not much bigger than a two by four."

"Oh, my God," Regina began to cry. "I was feeling so sad and sorry for him, and now I'm hating him again."

Grace paused. "I know. I feel both ways, too."

"Mom, I can't talk anymore. I feel like I'm going to throw-up."

"Oh, listen." There was a short pause. "Angela just said she's coming over and will bring Angie."

"Okay."

She had just hung up when it rang again. This time it was Andy telling her he would be there shortly after noon. In a daze she listened and thanked him. As she hung up the phone she saw David's letter. A rush of elation came over her. She would no longer have to be afraid that Billy Wayne wouldn't give her a divorce. She no longer had to worry about her or her girls' safely. Just months ago, Angie had told her, "Daddy almost knocked down Paw Paw's shed he was driving so funny."

"My God, it's over. I'm free. We're safe."

She dropped David's letter in the junk drawer and closed it. It wouldn't be right to read it today. It took almost a week for it to be right. In that time, there had been conflict. When Bud offered to help with the funeral expenses, Mrs. Tarkin took the money and then said, "That gal of yours is the cause of all this. What she done to my boy is worse than murder. I hope to never see her agin."

Nevertheless, Regina went to the funeral along with her mom, dad, and Angela. They sat on the very last pew of the little country Holy Roller Christ Church. The caskets were closed because of the damage done to the bodies. Regina was thankful for that. No matter how strong her hatred for him had been, she didn't want to see him dead. Geraldine sat up front with Billy Wayne's family and cried during the entire service.

Ceil had taken the girls to the zoo in San Antonio. Over hot dogs and sodas, Angie said to Tessie, "You know Daddy won't be coming again, so Mommy won't be crying."

"I know," Tessie answered. "Can we go see the elephants again?"

Tessie had gotten up late the morning after her dad's death, wanting to know where Angie was. When she found out that Undy was coming, she spent the entire morning looking out the window for his car. She never asked about her dad. Angie was sad for a few days but she too, quickly seemed to put him away. Over the last two years they had been forced to let him go. Often many weeks, even months, passed without their seeing him. Their uncle and grandfather had been in their lives more often and always in a more positive way. *They will be fine,* Regina prayed.

The day after the funeral Mrs. Tarkin, sixteen-year-old Arnold, her youngest son, and Geraldine all picked up and left town. If anyone knew where they had gone they weren't telling. Regina knew that Mrs. Tarkin hated her but was nevertheless surprised that the girls' grandmother would leave town without so much as a good-bye.

Two days later, Regina and Angela helped move Mayphelia over to Ceil's and into Mrs. Dollard's old bedroom. Regina wept when she saw Mayphelia. She hardly recognized her. "I'm so sorry, May-May. I'm so sorry."

Mayphelia lightly patted her hand and said in a hoarse whisper, "Jest keep forgiven', Honey. Don't carry no hatred."

Regina hugged her frail body, careful not to break her.

That evening Regina got the girls to bed early. Tomorrow they would all be back on their regular schedules. After a hot bath, Regina went to the kitchen and prepared a cup of steaming tea using some of Mayphelia's herbs for sleeping. She opened the junk drawer and felt a thrill. It was still there.

Back in her bedroom, she carefully folded back the covers, fluffed up the pillows and got into bed. She wondered if this were how brides felt on their wedding night. She never had a wedding night. Billy Wayne had stayed up drinking with his dad and uncles and passed out on the porch.

With care, she opened the letter. As she read, she snuggled down farther into the bed. He told her he would wait as long as it took for her to get a divorce because she was worth the wait. He told her she was the sweetest and prettiest woman he'd ever been with. He told her how much he liked her little girls. Then he told her some things about himself: how long it would be before he got his electrician's certification; how he planned to work and save and eventually get his own business; how he really liked San Antonio and would like to live there. Being a growing city, it would be good for his business. Then he closed by saying that he thought of her every day and almost every moment except when he was studying. He told her he still wanted to take her to a baseball game.

Regina folded the letter and put it under the statue of Mary and said a prayer. She turned out the light and pulled the covers up to her chin. The feeling was delicious. No man had ever said these things to her. Her grandpa would always tell her she was pretty and sweet, but this was different.

CHAPTER THIRTY-FOUR

Angela looked down at the scrambled eggs on her breakfast plate and knew this was the day. Taking a deep breath, she said softly, "Mom, Dad, I'm not going back to the convent. I realize that life is not for me."

Bud glanced at Grace, anticipating disappointment. Instead he saw that she was relaxed with a hint of a smile. "Angela, all we…I want, is for you to do what you want with your life."

Bud quickly added, "That's right. That's all we want." Grace took a sip of coffee and said, "You've always thought things through and I know you've given a lot of thought to this."

Angela's face reflected her surprise. She had not expected it to be so easy. All she could manage was a mumbled, "Thank you."

She heard the big clock ticking. "And I've already gotten a job teaching at the public high school. Mrs. Farley finally retired. It seems God is still looking out for me."

Bud was amazed. "When did this happen?"

"I got the call the day of the funeral just as we were leaving. I had to pinch myself all during the service to keep from smiling. I was so happy."

Suddenly very hungry, she put a forkful of egg in her mouth . Everything was going so smoothly. She inhaled the rest of the eggs and sausage and then got up to clean the table. At the sink, Grace came up beside her. "From now on, you just look out for yourself," she said.

Bud grabbed his straw hat. "Well, I'd better get to the plowin." He hurried out the door after giving Grace and Angela each a peck on the cheek. On his way to crank up the tractor, he wanted to skip, wave his arms and shout in joy and relief. Joy over Angela's decision and relief for Regina and his granddaughters. Angela's choice and Billy Wayne's untimely death left him feeling happier than he had been in years. "Dear Lord, give Billy Wayne peace," he said out loud.

Then Billy Wayne's words came back. "*...your wife and that Dollard bitch hugging like no two women should.*" A cloud began to brace up against the joy. He jerked open the shed door. *Here I'm lettin' the words of a mean, ignorant dead man bother me.* He slammed shut the lid on the troubling thought and began talking to the tractor. "I hope you're up to a good day's work. We got acres to cover."

GRACE debated whether to walk into Ceil's home. She knew Ceil wouldn't find it impolite but Grace's upbringing forced her to remain on the back porch until someone opened the door. "Oh hi, Mrs. Wolansky, come on in," Sarah, Clem's middle daughter, held the door opened. "Ceil is upstairs helping Lizzie with Mayphelia."

"You look real nice in them pants, Mrs. Wolansky." Sarah complimented Grace on her new slacks. Grace smiled and said, "Well, even though more and more women are starting to wear them, I'm still not comfortable. They just don't feel right."

LAST week she, Angela and Regina had delivered one of her paintings to an elderly dentist practicing in downtown

San Antonio. Weeks earlier his wife, who was also his receptionist, had sent Grace a picture of their only child as a boy at age five, attempting to get a drink from a public fountain. He stood on an apple crate and laughed as the water sprayed above his head. That little boy grew up to be killed in World War II. Grace put all the love she felt for her own children, especially Peter, into the painting. She cried while saying prayers of thanksgiving that her Andy had been too young to go off to fight.

In the office's reception room, the dentist and his wife eagerly stood by as she and Angela removed the brown paper and leaned the painting against the wall. Grace turned to look at the parents. They stood next to each other holding hands as tears filled their eyes.

That's all the payment I need, Grace thought. *God has blessed me with this gift so I can give people enduring remembrances.* She opened her purse and handed the mother her newly ironed handkerchief.

Finally the dentist spoke just above a whisper. "You've brought him back to life in a way no photograph could."

With that, Regina broke down and wrapped her arms around the elderly couple. "I'm so sorry, so sorry. He looks like a saint in Mom's painting and I know that's what he is now."

Grace tried to refuse, but they insisted on giving her ten more dollars than the agreed-upon fee. "Please, don't say no. We want you to have it." The mother said. Grace nodded. She understood.

Feeling prosperous and being near so many large stores, she told the girls she wanted to buy each of them a new outfit. After they made their selections, they insisted that she buy herself a pair slacks.

When they left the store and started for home Angela made a wrong turn. "Angela, you needed to go on St. Mary's," Grace instructed.

Regina giggled with excitement. "Mom, we want to stop at this restaurant I've read about. Supposed to be very good. Reward yourself. You won't have to cook once we get home."

Grace shook her head. "Your dad's been repairing fences all day. The least I can do is have his supper on the table when he comes in."

"Oh, I told Dad this morning to go to Hattie's for supper since we'd probably be late," Angela said. She and Regina exchanged knowing smiles.

Grace was angry. "Your dad doesn't like Hattie's."

They drove in silence the rest of the way to the restaurant. As soon as the car stopped, Regina was out and quickly ushered her mom towards the door. Once inside, a good-looking young man sitting near the back got up and began walking straight towards them. Regina almost skipped over to him and gave him a slight embrace.

"Mom, I'd like to introduce you to David. And Angela. This is David," Regina announced in a somewhat higher pitched tone.

David held out his hand to Grace. "I've heard so much about you. It's really nice to meet you."

Grace didn't know what to think. *What was going on? It hadn't been six weeks since Billy Wayne died.* She looked at Angela, the former nun, who acted as if there were no improprieties going on. They sat down and ordered, chit chatting as if nothing unusual were going on.

Grace remained in the dark during the entire dinner. No explanations were given as to how the two had met or how long they had known one another. Grace didn't dare to ask any questions for fear of losing her patience with Regina and making a scene in front of this young man who, Grace had to admit, was very nice and polite.

On the way home Regina related the whole story: their meeting on the train, his searching and finding her the day after Thanksgiving, then two letters before Billy Wayne was killed, and since then, more letters and phone calls. She ended by saying this was the first time they had seen each other since the brief time at Thanksgiving, but she intended to see more of him. "I've waited mainly for the girls' sake," Regina concluded. Grace felt somewhat better.

Angela said, "Regina, he is so thoughtful."

Regina beamed. "So Mom, what do you think?"

Grace sighed. "A restaurant you read about? I wish I could still send you to your room for fibbing."

"Mom, come on. I did read about it in David's letter. I wasn't fibbing."

Grace couldn't keep from smiling. "Well, I look forward to getting to know him better."

Regina and Angela gave each other wide-eyed looks, and Angela thought *Mom is full of surprises these days.*

CEIL crept up behind Grace as she stood in front of the window gazing at the new fountain. "You want a cup of coffee?"

Grace jumped. "For pity's sake, don't sneak up like that."

Ceil laughed. "Off in another world, daydreamer?" Ceil opened the refrigerator. "I think I'll have a Dr. Pepper instead. You want one?"

Grace nodded. "Sounds wonderful. How's Maypheelia?"

"She's ready to go back home, keeps forgetting that it's no longer there, and when I explain I'm having another one built, she emphatically informs me it had better be just like the old one or she won't like it. When I told her I was putting in running water and a bathroom I thought she would have a fit. 'I can't do no businez inside where's I live,'" Ceil said, then groaned.

Grace got a glass from the cabinet. She didn't like drinking from a bottle. "Is her breathing getting any better?"

"Some. The doctor says she's making great progress even though one of her lungs was badly damaged. He seems to think she'll be able to be on her own again. I sure hope Billy Wayne is suffering for what he did."

"He suffered his whole life. I hope he's at peace," Grace said.

"Oh Grace, you're too damn nice on everyone. Everyone except yourself." Ceil headed towards the living room. "Come on, let's sit on the comfy chairs in the living room."

Propping her feet on the coffee table, Ceil leaned back and closed her eyes. "There's no excuse for cruelty and, frankly, I feel like there are some things that are unforgiveable."

Grace watched Sarah walk up the stairs dusting the bannister. *She's the same age Regina was when she had Angie. So young. Perhaps some things are unforgivable.*

"Grace, I'm worried about Mayphelia's mind," Ceil interrupted Grace's stream of thoughts. "Yesterday, she asked me to mix some herbs for a tonic she needed. When I brought it to her, she became angry and said I was trying to force her to go to sleep. I left and when I came back she said she was so blessed to have such a good daughter. She calls me daughter all the time." Ceil's voice cracked as she said the last words.

"Well, you are a daughter to her. Have been your whole life. I'm sure with time she'll get her right mind back."

Grace put a coaster under her glass and nervously began chattering. "Can you believe school will be starting next week? Fall is almost here." Grace gazed outside the bay window but saw nothing. Her thoughts were all over the place today. "The wedding, or should I say weddings, will be here before we know it. What a mess! Bud says they should pick one religion or the other and be done with it."

Ceil laughed, "Oh, I love that Bud. I feel the same way."

Grace stopped and looked at her a long time. Then she looked upstairs to make sure Sarah was not in earshot. "Bud knows, I can tell. There always something in his voice and I sometimes catch him looking at me, studying me."

Ceil stretched out on the sofa. "That's just your well cultivated Catholic guilt playing with your mind again. How could he know anything?" She yawned. "God, I'm so tired. I feel like I could sleep for a week."

"How much longer will you be staying?"

"Until the weddings are over and Mayphelia no longer needs me. This is the first time I've been able to care for a sick person, and Grace, I have you to thank for that.."

"It's good to know that I've helped you, too."

"We've been good for one another. You've also helped me find myself, a gentle self that I didn't know. You've given me a family. I now have my own clan." Ceil sighed and took a sip of her drink. "Nevertheless, once Mayphelia's in her house and on her feet, I'll be going back to Hawaii."

Grace looked startled. "Hawaii?"

Ceil realized that in the chaos of the last weeks, she hadn't told Grace about the changes in her life. "I've sold my L.A. home along with the business, and I've purchased a lovely hacienda on a cliff overlooking the ocean on Maui. I can't wait for you and Bud to see it."

Grace felt like a pillow was being held over her face. She struggled to catch her breath. "That's so far away. It's still all so hard for me. I'm like a child who wants it all."

Ceil sat next to her. "Grace, you do have it all."

Ceil leaned over to hug her, but Grace pulled away. "No, don't. Why did you decide to move so far away? I've never even been to California."

"I decided a long time ago that Hawaii would be my last nest." She paused weighing her words. "I still plan to come back here and stay for weeks at a time, at least twice a year." Another pause as the large clock in the foyer ticked. "Grace, this isn't easy for me either."

Grace recalled Bud using very similar words when he told her that Peter's death had been hard on him too. *You assume that no one else is suffering* came to Grace's mind.

Ceil closed her eyes and then continued, "Grace, I want Bud to have all of you, which is really all you want if you're honest. I've come to think of you and Bud as a sister and brother, siblings I've always longed for."

Grace picked up the crystal swan on the coffee table. It was heavy. "I know you're right, and somehow I'll get through this feeling of having been abandoned, left out and unloved." Grace studied the sculpture. "This is very lovely."

"I want you to have it as a reminder that you'll always be my dearest friend."

Grace started to object, but Ceil stopped her. "Please accept this without a fuss. It will go so well with your painting in the living room."

Grace got up. "I have to go." They hugged and then remained in each other's arms savoring the strong bond of love between them.

Grace left holding the swan next to her heart.

CHAPTER THIRTY-FIVE

After the last student filed out, Angela busied herself with the composition papers her sophomore class had turned in that day. A light knock on the door interrupted her from marking what seemed like the millionth error she had noted in the last hour. Joseph Hensley stood in the doorway, smiling from ear to ear. He was attractive, somewhat boyish and innocent with clear blue eyes and haloing blond hair. He had waved to Angela at the faculty meeting the day before school started, but she'd been too overwhelmed getting ready for her classes to stop and talk. Her old energetic self hadn't yet returned. She was in bed by eight thirty every night, yet by noon the next day she was exhausted. Teaching five classes, along with the preparations and grading, was proving to be more than she had imagined.

She had been trying to build up her strength by walking the four blocks from the Dollard house to school and then back again. At first Angela couldn't find a place to rent, so Regina offered to share their grandfather's home with her. However, both sisters breathed a sigh of relief when Ceil offered her a bedroom at the Dollard home. Regina remembered how particular Angela had been as they were growing up. Angela's room was always perfect while, as their mother said, Regina's looked "like a tornado's just gone through here."

Likewise, Angela appreciated her sister's offer but realized that the noise level there would soon be intolerable. Her nieces were lively and argued almost nonstop. Regina didn't seem to mind. "I think it's best if they learn to solve their own problems."

"But perhaps sometimes you need to help them negotiate," Angela said hesitantly, not wanting to offend or tell her how to raise her children.

"Oh, I do when they ask me," Regina answered self satisfied.

Ceil was a godsend, telling her she could have it rent free; however, Angela wouldn't move in unless she paid something. *You can't give anything to anyone in this damn family,* Ceil thought. "Okay, okay how about being the weekend cook when Lizzie is off?"

"Why hello, Joseph. "

"Hello, there. How does it feel to be back in your old stomping grounds?"

Angela sighed, "I'm still getting my land feet. High school kids have more energy than I remember." Joseph agreed with a friendly smile. He seemed comfortable in his skin.

Regina had told her about the tutoring sessions. "He asked about you every time, until I told him you were a nun. I bet he'll do a somersault when he sees you're teaching with him," Regina had teased her.

Angela remembered he had a crush on her, but at the time she had eyes only for James. She smiled, thankful that she could hardly remember James' face. It was James' adoration of her that she had been in love with. She prayed she had matured some since then.

Joseph took a couple of steps inside and cleared his throat. "I was wondering if you'd like to drive over to

Westerly for dinner. They have a really good steak place there."

Angela wanted to giggle. *I'm actually being asked out for a date. What a grand feeling!* She looked up and smiled, "That sounds wonderful. When did you have in mind?"

Joseph could hardly hide his enthusiasm. "Well, anytime is fine with me."

"I don't know if you've heard that I'm recovering from tuberculosis, which means I'm tired most of the time. Saturday night would be best for me."

"That would be perfect for me too."

As if not to lose the magic of the moment he did an about turn to leave before remembering he'd forgotten the details. He turned back, "What time on Saturday?"

She decided on six. "I'm staying at the Dollard place."

He laughed, "Oh, that's good to know. Not as long a drive." Once again he turned to leave.

"You know the administration has a ruling that faculty are not to fraternize?" Angela paused wanting to bite her tongue. "But I don't suppose they'll know if we go all the way to Westerly," she added quickly. *Still the damn rule follower,* she thought.

Joseph grinned and said, "Let's live dangerously." Angela liked him already.

He fairly skipped down the hallway. At that moment the prospect of losing his job didn't bother him in the least. Angela shoved the remaining papers into her carry bag with more energy than she'd had in almost a year. She was ready for the delicious dinner Lizzie would have waiting, a hot bath and then planning what she'd wear Saturday night. The papers could wait.

When Angela got home she rushed to tell Ceil. As soon as the words were out of her mouth, she remembered she was Saturday's cook. "Ceil, I forgot about preparing dinner that evening."

"Never mind that," Ceil laughed. "Lizzie or Sarah can come." Lizzie and Sarah were now working for Ceil every day after school cleaning the house and preparing the evening meal.

Angela baulked, "I won't hear of it. Those girls are teenagers and need to have the weekends for themselves. I'll manage."

Ceil backed off. "Okay, Okay. But I do want you to take a long nap Saturday afternoon and then spend time making yourself more beautiful than you already are."

Angela's upbringing and the convent training came through on Saturday morning. She got up early and made a big pot of potato and bacon soup and a chicken salad for both the noon and evening meals.

The doorbell rang exactly at six. Ceil ushered Joseph into the living room. He held a single red rose. He introduced himself and looked around the room. "These floors were done by a master craftsman. Same with the doors."

Ceil liked him. He began to explain how difficult it was to make doors like that, when Angela started her regal descent down the stairs. She wore a green sheath dress that accented her hazel eyes. Auburn hair bounced in soft curls just above her shoulders. Watching Joseph watch her, Ceil thought, *Oh yes, he's smitten.* As Angela came to the last step, he gave her the rose. Ceil felt sadness and some jealousy. She wanted someone to look at her like that and give her a red rose.

The evening was a dream. Later on, neither Joseph nor Angela could remember what they had eaten or how long they had sat at the table. They both loved to read and learn about different things, from scientific advances to other cultures to ancient history. Each had a strong desire to travel to far-off places and had recently been reading travel books.

"I would love to teach abroad," Angela said. Joseph looked up with fork in hand and said, "Just today I got information about teaching positions at various army bases in Europe." Neither could speak for a moment.

Neither cared that much about making lots of money or "getting ahead." Angela told him about how she was preparing to take a vow of poverty. They both laughed when he replied, "Well, I don't think I'd want to go that far." Both liked the outdoors…and on and on until no one else was in the restaurant and the waitress began walking by their table with heavy sighs and low moans.

When they parked in front of the Dollard house, Joseph reached over and kissed her. She had no doubt in that moment that she had made the right decision. She wanted to go through life being kissed by a special man, a special man like this.

Joseph pulled back and brushed a curl from her forehead. "I'd love to dance with you. There's a hall over in Lakey that has great bands every Saturday night. Would you like to dance with me next Saturday?"

Without a hesitation she said yes.

ANDY AND SHEILA'S weddings came and went in great style. Tongues wagged when word got around town that Bud and Grace's son, like their daughter, would not have the ceremony in St. John's church. This one would be in Grace's garden under a gazebo Bud had built for the occasion. With the discovery that Sheila was not a Christian many had refused to attend fearing the fires of hell.

"Well I don't give a goddamn if they come or not," Grace blurted out over breakfast. Bud barely avoided spitting oatmeal across the table as he choked with laughter. Regaining his voice, he said, "Gracie, I've never heard such language come out of your sweet mouth."

"Well, I've thought bad words all my life, just never gave my tongue permission to say them."

Bud looked at her with a new admiration. "You can let your tongue go wherever it pleases around me."

"Well, I've been told enough times to stop holding back."

That coil of jealousy tightened slightly around his heart. *Yeah and I know who's been doing the tellin',* he thought. He got up and went to the hat rack.

Grace took the dirty dishes to the sink. "My own sister isn't coming! They don't begin to know what a wonderful person Sheila is." When she turned around Bud was already heading out the back door. Puzzled, she started to go after him to give him the usual morning-goodbye kiss. *It's there between us.* Feeling weak, she sat down at the kitchen table. "I have to tell him," she mumbled, then shook her head. "It can wait till after the weddings."

THE DAY was glorious, teeming with fall colors - golden leaves, crimson chrysanthemums, browning grasses, soft, yellow sun beams. Grace prayed, *"May their marriage be as beautiful, vibrant, and colorful as this day."* She was grateful that the harsh and cruel Father Unterminon had been replaced by the kind and tolerant Father Gilbert. Grace especially appreciated how he explained the ceremony to the Blumbergers.

And she was grateful her son and Sheila were having a Catholic ceremony. A month ago she had called Andy to tell him there was no need to go to the trouble of two weddings. "Are you kidding, Mom? I've got to do this. Remember I was an altar boy."

Grace chided him sweetly. "Not a very devout one. Father Unterminon kicked you out for splashing the wine because you were cranking your head around to look at Cynthia Parker."

Andy laughed. "Okay, okay, please don't bring up my history with other women right here before my marriage. Mom, Sheila and I want to have this ceremony for you." Deeply moved, Grace was about to voice her gratitude when he continued, "And then too, none of my friends from around there will drive all the way to Houston just to see me get hog-tied."

Grace laughed. *He can't be serious for more than a few seconds.* When she hung up, she vowed to never interfere in any way with how they raised their children. *It might be very interesting to have Jewish grandchildren,* she thought. She felt happy to be able to think with tolerance. Life was so much easier.

The yard was filled to capacity with relatives, family friends, Andy's school friends and buddies. Cynthia Parker was there with her husband and new baby. Grace spotted some people from the parish whose curiosity won out over the threat of damnation. Sitting on Peter's bench, Mayphelia spoke up as Andy took his place on the gazebo. "I looks forward every day to see dat boy runnin' the fields barefoot and in overalls comin' over to hep Radio Man." Several people turned to look. Ceil gently shushed her. She wanted to whisper to the turned heads, *"She's not in her right mind yet."*

Ceil had taken Mayphelia to see her new cabin a few hours before the ceremony began. Nearly finished, it reflected all the love, money and careful planning Ceil had put into every detail.

Excited, Ceil opened the car door for Mayphelia, "Here it is, May-May, your new home."

Mayphelia stood erect and looked at it a long time. "What you talkin' 'bout? This ain't my place. Radio Man had ours fixed up better than this."

"May-May, that house burned down. This is the same land. Look, there's the peacock and peahen coming up from their fort and there's your garden."

Ceil noticed a flicker of recognition in her eyes. Relieved, she went on, "Come, let's look inside. I found a wood stove that's almost the same as the one you had before."

Mayphelia balked, "No, I don't wants to see that house. Now you be a good daughter and takes me to my own place."

Ceil controlled her impatience and helped Mayphelia get back in the car. As they pulled away, Ceil was deeply disappointed over the outcome of this visit. She was being forced to deal with an illness of the mind, and she was pleased that she was handling it with love.

BOTH bride and groom were perfectly dressed for the bucolic setting. Sheila wore a simple long cotton dress of pale amber with a beautifully embroidered bodice while Andy wore khakis and a cowboy shirt. In the middle of the ceremony Mayphelia began humming and then softly singing the Negro spiritual, "All God's chillung got wing." Andy paused in the middle of putting the ring on Sheila's finger and turned around. "May-May, you know Sheila and I got wings today." Subdued laughter broke out among the spectators.

Afterwards barbeque, coleslaw, potato salad, red beans and beer were served from long tables set up under the trees in the front yard. When so many of Andy's friends from high school and college showed up, Bud became worried they'd run out of beer. Angela patted her dad's arm. "If that happens, then let them drink tea," she said glibly paraphrasing the words of Maria Antoinette.

For weeks Grace had fretted over whether Andy's choice of food and their yard would be "nice enough" for Sheila's parents. "They are so wealthy," Grace sighed.

"Why should that make any difference?" Ceil scolded.

Grace knew she was right, but it helped when Ruthie took her aside and said, "You have such a lovely place, so peaceful, and wasn't it something to hear cows mooing as they were saying their vows?" She began to walk away, but turned back. "Oh, and your friend's impromptu singing was so perfect. I'll always remember this wedding as well as the wonderful barbeque." Grace's step was lighter through the rest of the evening.

When the fiddlers sat up in the tractor shed, Regina's old tap-dancing space came alive with polkas and two steps and laughter. Regina danced the whole evening, mainly with Angela leading. Heads turned in admiration to see she could still burn-up the floor.

A week later family and friends gathered in Houston at the Warwick Hotel for an extravagant evening totally opposite from the previous one. The bride and groom greeted the guests as they arrived. Sheila was dazzling in a beaded silver gown overlaid with antique lace and Andy couldn't have been more handsome in his all white tuxedo. At the door, the men were given skull caps to wear. Bud had a time getting his to stay on. Finally Grace dug a bobby pin from her purse and secured it.

After welcoming everyone the bride and groom along with their families gathered under a canopy. Various Hebrew texts were read which could be followed in programs given out at the door. Grace was fascinated by the ritual. At the end Andy and Sheila smashed a glass with their feet. *"...which is a reminder that pain will lay ahead,"* Grace read these words and then thought, *I wonder how much shattered glass they will have in their married life*? Everyone was now shouting *Mazel Tov.* Joyous, melodious music erupted. Grace realized that joy and celebration can always follow pain if one can let go and not come to *enjoy the suffering.*

A little later Andy and Sheila, seated in chairs, were lifted above everyone. They held a napkin between them as they were paraded around the room. Bud leaned over and whispered in Grace's ear, "Look at him in that skull cap! If I didn't know better, I'd think he was the Jew and Sheila the Christian." Grace laughed and remembered the old folk tale about the stork dropping babies in the wrong chimneys.

Andy's transformation from a small-town farm boy into a charming cosmopolitan man amazed both his parents, who couldn't help but feel a little awkward in this setting. At one point during the evening, Sheila came over to Grace and Bud and whispered, "I want to go back to the farm wedding. That's more my style." *Yes,* the *stork made a mistake alright,* thought Grace. Sheila was going to be the perfect daughter-in-law for them just as Andy would be the perfect son-in-law for the Blumbergers.

The dinner was lavish. Wine and champagne glasses were filled before they were emptied by tuxedoed waiters who were always by one's side offering more lobster, shrimp, steak, potatoes, asparagus, salads, whatever one's palate desired. An elaborate wedding cake decorated with birds and butterflies reached halfway to the ceiling. Andy told Ceil, "Be sure to take a big slice home to May-May. Tell her that her wedding song inspired us to cover our cake with winged 'chillung.'"

Grace scanned the room, checking on Angela. Two weeks earlier she had collapsed in the classroom and the doctor ordered her to work half-days only for the time being. So now she was teaching morning classes while the retired Mrs. Farley had come back to cover the afternoon ones. "You know Joseph stops by every afternoon after school to check on her," Ceil had told Grace.

Grace was concerned about both her daughters and their new social lives. "It's just too soon for both of them," she said. "Angela's just left religious life and Regina's just been released from a nightmare marriage."

"All the more reason for them to be having a good time," Ceil shot back.

Angela and Regina were together on the other side of the room, both beautiful in their gowns. Tessie was nearby, hopping to the beat, in perfect sync with the music. She had inherited the dancing gene. Angie stood back a couple of feet and kept an eye on David. Every time he went near her mother, she ran and got between them.

A FEW weeks before, Regina had brought David out to the farm to meet her dad. He impressed Grace with a gift basket of acorn squash from his brother's farm. Once settled in the living room David wasted no time. "Mr. Wolansky, I would like your permission to date Regina. I realize she's newly widowed, but still I'd like to come over from San Antonio every two weeks to see her."

Bud and Grace hardly knew how to react to such a courteous request. Grace thought, *He certainly is no Billy Wayne, God rest his soul.* After a pause, Bud said, "Well, I can't see no harm in that."

Angie was quietly working a puzzle at the kitchen table and listening to every word. Later after David had left and Angie was brushing her teeth, she heard her mother ask her grandparents, "Will it be okay with you if I invite David to Andy's weddings?" Before Bud or Grace could respond, Angie was in the room blurting and spitting out toothpaste, "No, I don't want him coming with us."

Regina wanted to grab her up and spank her, but Grace intervened, "You're not ready for that, are you, dear?"

Angie's lip quivered. "Well, come along, let's talk while I put you to bed." Grace took her hand and led her to the bedroom.

Just as the season was changing, so did Angie's attitude. During the farm wedding, she watched her mother dance mostly with her aunt. During breakfast the next morning, she said, "Mama, David can come to the next wedding so you can have a boy to dance with."

However, during the course of the Houston wedding Angie realized she had made a mistake. Seeing David and her mother dance made her stomach hurt and before long she couldn't hold in the tears. She cried and complained until Regina took her up to their room. Seeing David's disappointment, Angela approached him. "I'm no Regina, but I'd love to take a spin with you." David smiled. So far he liked everyone in this family, even little Angie who didn't seem to like him one bit.

Angela had invited Joseph. He paused and took a few breaths before explaining, "I'm sorry, but I've already promised to take my aunt to Fort Worth to see a sick friend. Her friend is dying and well..." Angela was disappointed but admired his sense of commitment. "It's so nice of you to do that." If he had changed these plans for her, she wouldn't have had the same respect for him.

Angela was feeling confident these days. Her figure was back, her hair was back; her health was almost back and she had met a man who seemed about as independent in his thinking as she was. He had made an appearance at the farm wedding, met the family, and left right after the ceremony because he had volunteered to oversee decorating the gym for the fall dance that evening. "I need to get as many Brownie points as I can since I intend to fraternize, a lot," he explained, giving Angela a big wink.

The new doctor in town had also boosted her self esteem by asking her out. "I know I can show you a good time," he assured her. *He reminds me too much of Sister Mary Clare, controlling and always right,* she thought as she politely declined, saying that she could only date Catholics, which was more or less true for her.

IN a corner of the room, Tessie stepped to the music while holding her grandmother's hand. Suddenly Ceil appeared at Grace's side with a fresh glass of champagne. "You ready for a fresher-upper?" she asked.

"Goodness no, I already feel a bit light-headed."

Ceil was striking in a royal blue silk dress with a matching cropped velvet jacket. She was beautiful and Grace knew no matter how much she prayed, an attraction was still there.

Then on the same line of thought, Ceil said, "Grace, you're lovely in that dress even though I thought we were going to have to tranquilize you to get it." Ceil was referring to the shopping day when she, Regina and Angela had practically forced Grace to buy a dress for each wedding.

"Now I'll have three dresses hanging in the closet that I'll hardly ever wear," Grace fretted as she stood in front of the floor length mirror admitting to herself that the cream brocade with long sleeves and scooping neckline did elevate her to elegance.

Regina had sighed with frustration. "Save them for my wedding and Angela's and then when your granddaughters get married, you can wear them again." Grace's frugality was always a source of humor for her children. She wanted to shout, *If your dad and I hadn't been careful with every penny that came in, we'd all be the poorhouse.*

"Thank you," she whispered, realizing that until tonight she'd always felt a little dowdy around Ceil.

Bud interrupted his lively conversation with Sheila's dad to glance over at the two women. Grace saw him and waved. Referring to Bud and Jacob, she said, "Ceil, isn't it strange how God brings people together, people who are so different yet connected in some way."

Ceil thought she was talking about their friendship. She put her arm over Grace's shoulder in a slight hug. Bud's smile quickly changed to a frown. *"They can't keep their hands off one another,"* shot through his head like a bolt of lightning.

Bud had never looked at her like that. "I have to sit down," Grace stammered.

"What's wrong. I'll get you some water." Ceil got her a chair, then hurried off.

Bud was suddenly at her side, his voice full of concern. "You okay? You're as white as a sheet."

Grace tried to brush it away with a slight laugh. "It's just the champagne," she lied.

"Do you want to leave?" Bud asked.

"No, no, I'm okay." She took his hand. "You're always looking out for me, aren't you?"

Ceil came back with a cup of coffee. "Here, drink this. It might help." Bud took the cup from her with a strained "thank you."

Then the music started up again. It made Grace feel joyous and happy in spite of the shattered glass in their marriage. Sheila and Andy appeared in the center of a circle which continued to expand as the music continued. The clapping and stomping of feet reverberated throughout the entire room. Then circles were undulating back and forth in a rhythmic side-step dance.

"Let's join a circle, Bud." She pulled him unto the floor. Everyone was flowing. An elderly woman in a wheelchair glided along within a circle. The mesmerizing music continued to get louder and louder knitting the individuals into one giant organism. Lost in the trance, Grace found peace. She re-dedicated her life to this man moving beside her in surprisingly graceful strides.

CHAPTER THIRTY-SIX

At three thirty in the morning Grace and Bud pulled up to the farm. Ruthie had tried to get them to spend another night at the hotel, but Bud had hired Donny for just one day so he had to get back to his cows. On the ride home, Bud's mind went down one worm hole and then another. *Huggin' like no two women should* kept spinning through his mind like a stuck record. His suspicions weren't helped any by what had happened during the evening, the smiling glances, the warm embraces.

Once he got in bed, Grace moved over to him. All he could do was kiss her quickly on the cheek and then turn to his side away from her. He had to find out what really happened because the cruelty of not hugging or holding her was nearly as painful as the thought of what might have happened between the two women. He heard her sigh and then silence.

The next morning, as usual, Bud rose earlier than Grace, put on the coffee and set up the bread and toaster before heading out for the barn. Grace began planning the evening as soon as she woke up. She would make lemonade just the way Bud liked it with honey and cherries. They would sit on the front porch, look over the flower garden and sip their drinks while she confessed. A tense cord within her began to relax.

She walked through her empty house. She hoped it would be like this for the rest of their lives. There would be visits from the children, of course, but she and Bud had prepared them to have their own lives. Now she was ready to put her focus on Bud and herself and there couldn't be any secrets in their new life. She had to have the bliss that only honesty can bring. Her future would be filled with painting, studying art, her home, gardens and Bud, most especially Bud.

She was aware that Ceil had given her wings to fly to new horizons, but Bud had always provided her with a tether to security, a sense of belonging and peaceful happiness. Even though she now had wings she was still anchored to Bud and their life, and that's how she wanted it. Flying with an anchor.

The phone rang. "Mom," Angela's voice rang through the line. "Just wanted to let you know that we're all home."

"So early?" Grace was stunned.

"Yes, when I got to the room last night, Angie was running a fever and Regina insisted on getting home. David followed us all the way to the San Antonio cut-off."

"How's Angie?"

"She's okay this morning. Regina was really upset because she had wanted to spend the whole evening, maybe even the whole night with David." Angela laughed. "You know I'm teasing."

"I'm sure it crossed their minds," Grace said, remembering when Andy told her just a few weeks ago that he and Sheila had been living together.

"What did you say?" Grace had almost yelled, too shocked to continue.

As usual, Andy joked, "Don't fret. I've gone to confession."

Then in a serious tone, he said, "Mom, I don't want you getting worked-up right before the wedding when ya'll are over here getting dressed. The way you pick up on every little thing, I know you'd be able to tell I've been nested here at this apartment for some time. Besides, you know I can't live with secrets."

"Yes, secrets are as bad to carry around as guilt, maybe worse," she replied.

In that moment Grace accepted that her mothering job was done. Her children were their own persons now. She no longer was responsible for their behavior, their morals or lack thereof. She felt a new freedom, no more responsibilities concerning their spiritual welfare. *They've got to fly on their own now.*

Angela continued, "Mom, wasn't Ceil's wedding gift wonderful? Sheila and Andy didn't even go to bed because their flight left at seven this morning. Two weeks in Hawaii. They'll be staying at her home equipped with a maid, a cook and a yardman."

"I didn't know about that," was all Grace could say. A twinge of anger welled in her. She felt betrayed. Ceil hadn't mentioned anything about this gift.

"Well, Mom I've got to go. Joseph is coming by to take me to Mass. He and his aunt got back late last night. He called first thing this morning. Funny thing, I feel wonderful on just three hours of sleep."

Bud came in the back door. "Gracie, we better hurry if we're going to church for first Mass." Grace noted that he hadn't called her Gracie in a while. *Maybe it is just the guilt that's making me suspicious.*

Grace applied her lipstick. *But never mind that. I'm telling him today. Like Andy, I can't live with secrets.* With that thought she put on her hat and grabbed her purse.

When they got back from church, Grace prepared fried chicken, mashed potatoes, gravy and biscuits. After all of yesterday's fancy food, she was ready for a plain meal. As they were eating, Bud said, "You know days before he died Billy Wayne said somethin' that's been eatin' away at me. I can't shake it, cause I guess I noticed some things myself. Irregular things, you could say."

"What did Billy Wayne say?" Grace's voice was weak. She knew what was coming.

Bud looked directly at her and struggled to push the horrible words out of his mouth. "He said he saw you and Ceil hugging not the way two women should be. I'd heard of people like that. You two got awful close, closer than any women I've seen." He stopped, unable to go on.

Grace put a trembling hand over his and was silent for some time. Could she really do this?

"The first time was after Mrs. Dollard's funeral. I can't explain how, but...." she stopped, not wanting to degrade what had occurred between her and Ceil. "It was...." Once again she paused, swallowed and confessed, "We made love."

She wanted to run and hide, not because she regretted what had happened but because of what this was doing to Bud.

"The only other time was the night in San Antonio...." Bud turned to face the window, but she continued. "This hasn't affected my love for you. If anything I love you more deeply than I ever did." She resisted taking him in her arms. "Before I was like a green bud, tight and unopened, and now I've become a released flower. I wasn't doing anything to you. I was doing something for myself."

Bud bent over with forearms on his knees and eyes glued to the dropped dishtowel by the sink. He had not felt such grief and loss since the days of Grace's breakdown. Then, like now, giant hands were wringing out his lungs. She was the breath of his life, and now he was without oxygen. With a guttural moan, he pulled himself up and weaved to the bedroom. Grace looked at the cold chicken and dried out potatoes. She felt so weak she thought she might not be able to stand up, but she pulled herself up and followed after him.

Bud was putting clothes in his old suitcase. *Before we go to Hawaii, I'm going to get him a beautiful new suitcase* ran though her mind. "Bud...dear, where are you going?"

"I don't know. Probably my uncle's old deer lease. My cousin don't ever use it and it's still in pretty good shape. I can't stay here." He closed the case and walked past her to the back door before turning, "Never in a million years would I have thought it would end like this."

He got in his pickup and drove off. Grace walked out to the gazebo and sat down on the top step. She watched as the pickup was absorbed by the distance, too hollow and dried up inside for tears or anything, besides emptiness. All afternoon she sat and looked down the road. About dusk, an old car turned in at their lane. It was Donny. He waved at her as he got out of the car. "Bud asked me to look after things for a while."

Grace nodded and went back inside the house to her bed. She burrowed under the covers, aching in every fiber of her body, depressed and abandoned.

And there she stayed until Ceil walked into the bedroom, days later. Grace sprang up to sitting. "What are you doing here? It's all your fault. I regret the day you came here, and I would give my life if I had never met you."

"Grace, I sincerely hope you don't mean that. Now get out of bed and go take a bath. You stink. I'll make some tea and we'll talk." Ceil began to leave, then stopped. "But first I'll clean up the kitchen. What a god-awful mess! Has that food been sitting out like that since Sunday?"

"I've lost everything because of you," Grace shouted at her. "And I don't want you giving my children all these things, like honeymoons to Hawaii. You want to take over, don't you?"

Ceil stared at her and was tempted to slap her, but instead she spoke calmly, "Listen, the only reason I'm here is because Bud asked me to look in on you."

"Is he going to come back? Will he forgive me?"

"I don't know." She paused. "Grace, if because of me your marriage has been destroyed, I'll feel greater guilt than anything you've ever experienced or can imagine."

Grace wanted to pull the covers back over her head and maybe even die.

Ceil continued, "When Clem told me that Donny was looking after the farm because Bud was taking a trip, I knew you had told him. I was devastated. Grace, I tried to assure Bud that it was over between us. I mean it when I say I love Bud the same as I love you."

Feeling like she was about to burst into tears again, Ceil turned abruptly and headed for the kitchen.

DONNY had given Ceil enough details to get her to the courthouse in the next county. The young clerk was eager to help the well-dressed, pretty woman find a particular piece of land. Within an hour, Ceil walked out with the ex-act location of the cabin. The captivated clerk even drew a detailed map. As Ceil left the courthouse she thought, *It sure helps to have nice tits even at my age.*

BUD had driven away that Sunday a broken man. When he got to the cabin, he put away the groceries. He was grateful Mr. Carbon kept his store open after Sunday services, even though many in the community criticized him for working on the Sabbath. When Bud got to the cabin he was also grateful to see that his cousin had left an ice box full of beer. He put the block of ice he had bought into the top section and placed several beers around it.

He kept moving around finding things to do, airing out the mattress, sweeping the floors, filling the lanterns with kerosene. He didn't want to think because then he'd have to feel. He wanted to escape. Once the beer was cold, he began to drink. Each time he finished a bottle, he took it out to the target stump, aimed carefully and shattered it with his rifle. He promised himself that the first bottle he missed would be his last. He missed on the seventh, not only because he was drunk but also because it was almost dark. He went back in, dropped down on the cot and passed out.

Around two in the morning an awful clamor rattled him out of sleep. He yelled, and three sets of raccoon night-eyes stared back at him. He'd left the screen door wide open. He whipped them out with a towel, lit a lamp and assessed the food he had left. Staring at the opened bread loaf, scattered crackers and mutilated cereal box, he dropped back down on the cot and cried as he had never cried in his life.

When he awoke the next morning he saw he'd left the lamp burning. "Damn, the next thing you know, I'll burn down the place," he said to the empty room. Then the memory of the previous day came to his consciousness and emptiness consumed his whole being.

After a breakfast of eggs with no bread, he headed out for the river. He would fish today. He could always depend on fishing to clear his mind and help him put things back in order. When Grace had been so sick, he'd often gotten his mother or mother-in-law to stay for a few days while he'd go fishing.

By the end of the first day, he had caught six catfish but hadn't resolved anything or alleviated any sadness or confusion. He cleaned the fish in the yard and dumped the heads and innards in a ditch a long ways from the cabin. On the way back, he stopped to watch a fox roam across a pasture back-dropped by the setting sun. "I bet Gracie would love to paint this," he said out loud to the surroundings. His chest tightened. He realized he loved her more than anyone or anything in the world. He couldn't help himself. He would love her no matter what she did. He had to face the terrible fact that she didn't love him the same. She needed more. He wasn't enough for her.

Again the tears flowed as he fried the fish. He thought about getting another beer, but knew that wouldn't help. Yesterday he had drunk more than he ever had in his life and had solved nothing. Instead he made a pot of coffee, pulled a chair out under the stars, and spent a good part of the night studying the sky and drinking coffee.

Late in the afternoon on the third day, with soap and towel in hand, he headed to the river for a much-needed bath. He shed all his clothes and swam the entire width of the river several times, willing the water to wash away the pain that wouldn't stop. He didn't bother to put on any clothes as he headed back for the cabin.

Halfway there, he saw Ceil's car stirring up dirt down the lane. For a moment he felt so much rage he was afraid of what he might do to her. He ducked behind a sage bush and dressed. Then he decided he'd just stay there. *She's the last person on this earth I want to see.*

He watched her go to the cabin and knock on the door. She turned around and called, "Bud, you around here?" She began walking down the path towards the river, heading towards his hiding place. When she got within six feet of the bush, he stepped out.

Ceil jumped back and cried out, "My God, Bud, you been hiding?" Bud felt like a naughty school boy. They both stared at one another for a long moment.

Softly, Ceil said, "I would like to explain what happened."

"It don't need any explaining. It's all pretty clear. You might as well go back where you came from." Bud stepped out in front of her and headed towards the cabin.

When he got there, he sat down on the only chair in the yard, not bothering to get one for her. She looked down at him. "Grace didn't send me," she began. "In fact, she doesn't know I'm here. When Clem told me you had gone, I knew she had told you about us."

"I really don't want to talk about this." Bud got up and headed for the cabin.

"But Bud, you need to forgive her."

"Forgive her?" he shouted. "You're the one who's responsible."

Ceil responded angrily, "You really think so little of her as to think she has no control over her own actions?"

This hit a nerve. Bud turned and glared at her.

Ceil continued, "It's true that she didn't realize where our friendship was going, whereas I ... did." Ceil fidgeted, feeling a little frightened. But she was determined to have her say. "I would like something to drink."

"Beer or coffee?"

"I was thinking of water but, yes, I would like a beer."

Bud left and came back with a beer as well as a chair. "I forgot. Do you want a glass?"

Ceil was touched. Even in the middle of all his anger, he was a thoughtful, kind man.

"No, no this is fine." She took a sip. "And thank you for the chair."

She looked across the pasture, appreciating the quickly fading Indian summer day, with all its radiant colors. "Bud, what happened had nothing to do with you or the way Grace feels about you. She's told me numerous times she was going to tell you because she loved you too much not to."

"But I'm not enough for her," Bud whispered.

"Is any one person enough for another? For years you were the only close friend she had, you said so yourself. Plus you were her husband. That's not the same as having a woman friend."

Ceil paused, wondering if she should go on. "Bud, one day Grace said something that really hit me. She said it was wonderful that she was growing to love you the way a wife loves a husband. Up to that point she said she felt she had loved you more like a child loves a father, a love she never experienced while growing up. You made her feel safe, protected and valued as a good father makes his child feel."

Bud stood up. "You need to go now, Ceil. I don't want to hear any more. I have to figure this out for myself.

Ceil called after him as he walked towards the cabin. "It won't ever happen again. That sort of love we had has been replaced by the love of a deep friendship. She can't, Bud. She's not made that way."

He walked into the cabin, leaving her standing there staring after him in the twilight.

"It won't ever happen again," she said once again and then began walking towards her car.

"Ceil," Bud called out. She turned.

"Would you mind looking in on Gracie? Appreciate it."

The crickets began their symphony as darkness began to drop over everything including Ceil's heart. She felt as if her grandfather's whip had just lashed her back. Her muscles were mush. She staggered back to the car. She drove the long distance back crying until there were no more tears, and then she cried some more.

Bud lit the lantern and fixed a cup of instant coffee with luke-warm water. He didn't feel like building a fire just to heat water. He dragged one of the chairs onto the tiny stoop, sat down and looked up at the sky. "Dear God, help me to make sense of this and come to some understanding."

The fox he had seen earlier was standing next to the well staring at him. "Can you help me figure it out, pretty thing? I sure wish I had a camera." *Gracie would love such a picture.* He sighed and thought *she's always the first thing on my mind.*

The fox stood still, looking intently at him. "Listen, I'll get you some food if you'll hear my story." Bud left and came back shortly with a flat cookie pan of leftover red bean gravy. He slowly walked halfway to the fox and put it on the ground. "You look like a statue, you're so still."

After a few minutes of staring at the seated unmoving man, the fox flattened itself on his stomach and inched his way to the victuals. He lapped at the food slowly, being polite rather than greedy.

"I was uncomfortable with Ceil being around Grace from the very beginning. But if I'm honest, it wasn't because I thought they'd…you know, but because Gracie didn't seem to need me as much. I guess maybe I have been more like a father to her. I liked taking care of her and I liked that she was dependent on me for most things. I guess in some ways, I treated her like she was my child. But she's changed and I've liked those changes too."

Bud drank his coffee. The fox lay on the ground and listened. The lantern light just inside the cabin cast Bud's shadow over him. "I always said I wanted her to have her own life and not be afraid like she was with her dad, but I sort of wanted her depedin' on me too. I guess, to tell the truth, I wanted to be in charge of her."

The fox suddenly lifted its head, ears cocked, and stared intently through the blackness at a nearby field. Then he got up and left. "I'm not finished," Bud called after him. "Am I gonna' live the rest of my days by myself?"

He heard his words come back at him in the night air. "Hell I can't go on by myself," he shouted.

He went back inside, secured the screen door, put out the lantern and lay on the cot. *I need Gracie and always have every bit as much as she's needed me. I'll find my way through this. I have to.* With those thoughts, he fell asleep and slept until nine-thirty the next morning. He had never in his life slept that late.

AFTER Ceil had scrubbed all the dishes and changed the sheets on Grace's bed, she decided to make some tea. After her bath Grace had slipped out to Peter's bench, making sure to avoid Ceil.

Ceil walked out onto the front porch and called. "Would you like some ice tea and the girls' animal cookies? You haven't baked lately, have you?" She set the food and drinks on the small table.

Grace left the bench and came to the porch. "I'm sorry I talked to you like that. It was awful the things I said. The long bath washed away my meanness along with the stink." She paused and smiled. "You know, no one's ever told me that I stink."

"Well, it's about time someone did." Ceil handed Grace a glass of tea. "I forgive you, even though at the time I wanted to knock the pee waddles out of you."

"The pee waddles? My mother used to say that."

Grace laughed for the first time in days and then Ceil began laughing and soon both were hysterical, releasing the past days of sorrow, regret and anxiety.

"Oh my gosh, the pee waddles is coming out of me. My panties are wet," Grace screamed. Soon a peaceful quiet settled in.

Ceil said, "A good laugh feels as good as a good cry. Maybe even better."

"Ceil, you know under those bed covers I came to realize that, like you said, I'm not made that way."

Ceil cleared her throat. "We'll always be close, sister friends."

The women sat as the afternoon sun baked their resolve. Finally Grace whispered, "I'll always value our friendship as much as I do my marriage."

Grace looked out across the pasture and saw Mayphelia walking through her yard with a bucket. "Ceil, there's Mayphelia. How did she get over there?"

"I dropped her off before coming here. She woke up on Tuesday morning, came downstairs and into the kitchen.

She poured her coffee and said, 'Baby, it's lifted. That tote sack over my head is gone. I remembers everything and I's ready to move into my new beautiful home.'"

Ceil swatted at a pesky fly. "She went on to say that she had been walking in the land of the half-dead, whatever that is, while another part was walking right here and knew what was happening."

"You think she's strong enough, physically?"

"She walked to the store yesterday afternoon and came back carrying two sacks of groceries. So yes, she's back in every way.

They watched Mayphelia pull weeds in her garden.

"And I'll be getting back to Hawaii as soon as Andy and Sheila return."

"Bud asked you to check on me? I hope that means he still cares."

"Grace, I'm sorry for what happened."

"If he doesn't return by tomorrow, I'm going after him."

THE next morning Grace donned her beat-up straw hat and went outside. She had awakened feeling like her world would soon be back in order. *Today is the day I'm going after him,* she thought as she jumped out of bed. She had dreamed that Bud was snuggling next to her. She took that as a sign that he was coming back.

She looked across the field and saw Mayphelia in one of her colorful turbans feeding the peas. They waved at one another. Grace filled the bird feeder. At the sound of a motor, she looked around and saw a pickup turning onto their lane. *It's Bud.* She began walking down the lane, faster and faster.

The pickup came to a stop beside her. "You needin' a ride, pretty lady?" Bud grinned.

My beloved Bud is back. Grace caught her breath. Flirtatiously, she replied, "If you're goin' my way,"

"You better believe I'm goin' your way. I can't go no other way." He opened the passenger door. "Hop in."

She scooted next to him. Gently they held each other a long time, savoring their closeness. After a while, Bud got out his handkerchief, handed it to Grace and wiped his eyes on his shirt sleeve. He drove on to the house.

He stopped and ran around, opened her door and helped her out. Then he took her in his arms and led her in a dance while singing,

"When you look at me with those stars in your eyes,
I could waltz across Texas with you.
Waltz across Texas with you in my arms.
Waltz across Texas with you."

"You remembered our wedding song," Grace said.

"You bet I do," he replied. "The singer in that little beer joint was almost as good as Ernest Tubb."

After a few more turns on the dirt ground, she untangled herself and pulled him towards the back porch. "Come on, I'm ready to remember our wedding night."

Bud laughed. "Why Gracie, we haven't done that in the daytime since before the kids."

"Oh, but now the kids are gone," she said opening the screen door.

They disappeared into the house. The back door closed.

THE END

ABOUT THE AUTHOR

Barbara Frances has plenty of stories and a life spent acquiring them. Growing up Catholic on a small Texas farm, her childhood ambition was to become a nun. In ninth grade she entered a convent boarding school as an aspirant, the first of several steps before taking vows. On graduation, however, she passed up the nun's habit for a college degree in English and Theatre Arts. Her English professor was aghast when she declined a PhD program in order to become an airline stewardess, but Barbara never looked back. "In the Sixties, a stewardess was a glamorous occupation." This career's highlights include an evening on the town with Chuck Berry and "opening the bar" for a planeload of young privates on their way to Vietnam.

Marriage, children, and school teaching distracted her from storytelling, but one summer while recovering from her divorce, she and a friend coauthored a screenplay. "I never had such fun! I come from a family of storytellers. Relatives would come over and after dinner everyone would tell tales. Sometimes they were even true." The next summer Barbara wrote a screenplay solo. Contest recognition, an agent and three optioned scripts followed but then she decided to turn her attention to novels. Her first, *Lottie's Adventure* is aimed at young readers. *Like I Used To Dance* is her second book. She's at work on a third, *Shadow's Way*, a "Southern Gothic tale" about a woman caught in a struggle to keep her beloved plantation home from a vengeful archbishop. Barbara's fans can be thankful she passed up convent life for one of stories and storytelling. She and her husband Bill Benitez live in Austin, Texas.

Barbara welcomes comments or questions about *Like I Used To Dance* at: barbara@likeiusedtodance.com.

If you enjoyed *Like I Used To Dance,* please go to Amazon.com and write a review. Thank you.

www.ingramcontent.com/pod-product-compliance
Lightning Source LLC
Chambersburg PA
CBHW060550310726
48982CB00008B/1080/J

* 9 7 8 1 9 4 4 0 7 1 7 0 7 *